Ms. Money

T L Ashton

"I was rich, and I understood what rich meant. It was never having to think about money. My money could think about me."

—Mae West

Ms. Money

INTRODUCTION

(March—April 2008)

1

The overhead speaker suddenly crackled with the pilot's voice. More bad news. "Sorry folks, we still don't have a gate. We got here early, but ran into a traffic jam."

I wanted to scream. Nothing is worse than endlessly circling an airport. I felt trapped. I grabbed the newspaper from the empty seat next to me, but it was open to the sports page. My impatience won out, and I threw it back down. Instead I thought about the bad news I was bringing to my billionaire boss. *Yes—he deserved it! He couldn't have everything he wanted. After the scheme he had gotten me mixed up in, I just couldn't trust him. But I'm not going to be his hand puppet for much longer. I'm hoping to liberate myself by the end of the year. But if the hint I got about my future in Washington turns out to be true, you're in for a bang up surprise at the end of this book. Let's hope so!*

You probably know that I'm Chief Investment Strategist for Traub Securities, the major nationwide brokerage firm. I'm 'Ms. Money.' If you're an investor, you've seen me on TV. I'm the woman who puts a brokerage house spin on the financial news. I'm surprised no one on this flight has dropped into the empty seat next to me and asked for a stock tip. They'd be disappointed because

I rarely follow individual stocks. My job is about market trends and asset allocation, and I've learned how to do it well. Like most money gurus I can be positive or negative on the market as called for and with absolute sincerity. That's something a woman can do better than a man. I'm not denigrating my sex, don't get me wrong. Women just are better communicators. They know there are two sides to every message—the 'yes' and the 'no.' That's especially true if the people talking are a man and a woman. They say Tiresias was the wisest person in the ancient world because he lived for seven years as a woman and seven years as a man before going blind and becoming a prophet. He would have been dynamite on CFN!

Timing is why even a billionaire with the Midas touch can't get everything he wants. For years now, my boss, Melrose Traub, has wanted to be a Washington player. But because of bad timing he's been repeatedly passed over for the post of Secretary of the Treasury. First Paul O'Neill, the aluminum king, beat him to it, but he turned out to be only a tin man in disguise and got fired. Then John Snow from the oil patch got it, but he was forced out when the sharp-eyed financial blog *StreetWalker* reported that he owed income taxes on $24 million of loan forgiveness. Already a two-time loser, Traub tried again, but his luck continued bad. I pitched him to Josh Bolten, Bush's new Chief of Staff. But I was wasting my words because he came from Goldman Sachs. Bolten told the President he needed a Wall Street insider at Treasury. Snow was out, and Goldman Sachs CEO, Henry 'Hank' Paulson was in.

Now, in March 2008, all signs were pointing to Barack Obama as the next President. Traub saw one more chance. He put on Democratic sheep's clothing and made the right, or rather left, PAC donations and sent me to DC with the message that he still wanted another crack at the job. My mission was to be sure Washington got the word and eventually the money. Now I was flying back from a meeting with a high-ranking member of the California Congressional delegation. Need I say who? Traub Securities was headquartered in Los Angeles at Century City. Big PAC money can make a big difference. But it was tough luck all over again. Traub's money still wasn't getting him anywhere. I was told that if elected Obama was picking Timothy Geithner, current head of the New York Fed. Back in the 1980s, Geithner's father had supervised the Ford Foundation's small-business lending programs in Indonesia, which at the time were being administered by Ann Dunham Soetoro, Obama's mother. Traub didn't have a chance.

As far as I was concerned he was just too ambitious. He never, never stopped wanting, and he always wanted more. But on his terms only. *No money down. He often got his own way. But I was fed up with Traub.* When the chips were down, he couldn't make the commitment I needed as a woman. Yes, he had saved me from the biggest loss of my life. But he had used me badly in the process. I mean like garbage. He made me do something I'll never feel good about. I was disillusioned and tired of his one-way demands. When it came to Treasury Secretary he was already a three-time loser. *Get the message.* And if I was right about the future of the financial markets, he would very soon be needed at the top of his own empire.

I was convinced that Wall Street was on track for big trouble. It was only a matter of time. I was ahead of the herd mentality that governs the financial world. The trouble was I was too far ahead. I had badly underestimated just how long the Bulls could keep the party going—and to what lengths they were willing to go to do it. I was worried about my Street credibility. I had been called 'Chicken Little' till I was sick of hearing it. But I continued to warn investors to stay away from mortgage-backed bonds, mortgage lenders,

Fannie Mae and Freddie Mac, and big-city banks. I knew it was the right advice. But nobody wanted to hear me. My ratings were down. Even the millions of investors who knew me as Ms. Money and watched me weekly on *Smarter Than The Street,* the highest-rated nationwide financial TV show, were calling me a financial Cassandra. On Wall Street I was branded a perma-Bear.

Certainly I wasn't alone when it came to recognizing that the Bull market, after charging back strongly since 9/11, had turned shaky. Gold was sending a warning signal in the form of new highs. Oil had closed over $100 a barrel, threatening economic chaos. But Ms. Money knew the real trouble was the extremely aggressive, greed-driven leverage that had inflated an enormous housing market bubble with Wall Street hot air. The research I had checked and re-checked said that from 2004-07, the top five U.S. investment banks had increased their leverage to a colossal $4 trillion. But that was only the tip of the iceberg about to sink the titanic financial markets.

Let's say you borrow ten dollars and use it to get a loan for a hundred. Then you put the $100 down on a thousand dollar debt and use the thousand to borrow ten thousand! At that point you can get a mortgage on a $300,000 house. Then you use the house as collateral for a million dollar loan that gets you a mansion. Now, fearless speculators convinced that risk had entirely disappeared from the markets, had mortgaged their mansions to buy another, and another, multiplying million dollar debt into the billions, which soon became trillions. I couldn't believe bond-rater Moody's was still boasting "in our view U.S. financial institutions ability to withstand shocks is higher than ever." The truth was that using options on securities, hybrid derivatives based on structured financial paper, and finally synthetic securities grown in hydroponic tanks, Wall Street had multiplied its debt many, many times over. Considering that a robo-signed subprime mortgage could be obtained with nothing down, the leverage was beyond immense. The debt berg that measured $4 trillion above water was an underwater monster $683 trillion huge!

Trying to help TV viewers get a grasp on just how much debt was out there, I wrote that staggering number on screen—$683,000,000,000,000! I repeated that a billion is a thousand times bigger than a million, and a trillion is a thousand times bigger than that. I tried to quantify just how big a bubble Wall Street had blown with a simple PowerPoint:

- A stack of 1 trillion dollar bills would be roughly 68,000 miles high, almost a third of the way to the moon.
- They would go around the earth almost three times given a circumference at the equator of roughly 25,000 miles.
- If laid flat 1 trillion dollar bills would cover almost 4,000 square miles, an area larger than the state of Delaware.
- $683 trillion dollar bills would carpet the entire United States three times over.

The iceberg about to sink the titanic U.S. financial markets was even bigger than the biggest glacier. It was a huge chunk of Antarctica itself.

The cockpit speaker suddenly interrupted my thoughts. *At last.* But it was a false alarm, "We have a gate—but it won't be free for another 20 minutes. We regret the delay."

I snapped open the gleaming silver clasps of my Versace briefcase. Time to go to work. The 'Medusa' bag was crocodile-embossed, and I loved it. I had it since New Orleans, when it was a surprise gift from ex-Senator Matt Shepherd. We had worked together on the President's GSE Review Panel, which reported on the mortgage giants, Fannie Mae and Freddie Mac just over a year ago. Yes, he was an admirer, no, it wasn't working out. In fact it had gone from bad to worse, much like me and the markets. I remembered my last meeting with Shepherd. It was ugly to say the least.

2

My old gal pal, the designer Karen Koren, invited me to join a celebrity party to catch the end of singer Gwen Stefani's *Sweet Escape Tour*. Late in October, I flew from New York to Las Vegas. My closest friend, the fashion model known as Gia, came too. We met at the Palms Casino Resort. I thought the off-the-Strip location was great, and even better, Koren had rented the two-story Sky Villa on the top floor of the Fantasy Tower, paying $35,000 for the night. We would have a ball.

I joined the screaming audience in the Pearl Theater when Stefani sang 'The Sweet Escape' from a jail cell built on the stage. It was a duet with Akon and a six-piece band for back up. The sets were amazing. Stefani jumped and gyrated in front of a screen filled with gigantic video images in shifting colors slashed by black bars. And her costume was fabulous—a black and white striped bustier worn above brilliant red spangled hot pants. She even ran right into the audience to sing 'Cool.' Then the band switched to—'Don't be sore about the stripes, / I meant you no bad-girl pain!' I couldn't get the lines out of my head. *I was thinking of Matt Shepherd.*

Before joining the private party in the Sky Villa, I wandered back through the casino with Gia and another younger model. We were a trio of gowned and jeweled women, each with a $100 chip party favor. How could we not stop at one of the roulette wheels! I smiled privately as the young model placed her chip on red, making a relatively safe two-for-one bet. I saw her fingers were crossed. The three of us focused on the spinning wheel and suddenly the ball was clattering in it. But there was a groan when it landed on black.

The model turned a sad face at the loss, but Gia hugged her, and I handed her my own chip, saying, "Look—there's nothing wrong with playing safe, especially when you need the money. But now I'm giving you 'free money.' Imagine you can always get the same chip for free. So what are you going to do with it?"

"Go for broke!" the girl answered. "What can I lose?"

"Good, let me bet for you." I showed her how to place an inside corner bet.

Without a thought, Gia put her own chip on top of mine. "Double the money—double the fun," she laughed out.

The wheel spun again. There was silence, tension, and then the ball was bouncing in the spinning track. Rattle, rattle, and finally it came to a stop. Gia screamed. We won—with 8-to-1 odds—almost two thousand dollars!

"That's great," I lectured as the croupier slid our pile of chips across the table.

"That's Ms. Money talking. You can always bet on her," Gia added, now happily dividing the chips into three heaps.

"Look, I'm happy we won—don't get me wrong. But there's one problem—risk! You can't believe in the Tooth Fairy! There's no such thing as free money. It's never free—never! It's a big mistake to think it is. When people think money is free, it's just an excuse to make bigger and bigger bets. You get high on risk and it doesn't take long to go broke! Never, never forget—free money is the most dangerous drug of all. You'll overdose every time." *I mean it.*

A hand suddenly pulled my shoulder. I spun around, almost falling into the man. My surprised eyes looked up into Matt Shepherd's face, targeting his blood-shot glare. He must have gone straight downhill since I saw him over a year ago at The Belmont. He looked terrible. He was red faced. He needed a shave, and his dinner jacket was wrinkled and stained.

"Hey! Can Ms. Money spare me a dime?" he challenged hoarsely.

I just stared back at him. Shocked. He had never looked worse.

"I said gimme a chip, bitch—I'm down."

A woman's hand on his shoulder was trying to pull him away. Her dress and makeup said she was a hooker.

"You aren't worth anything." I screamed at him.

"Buy me a drink."

"Get one from your girlfriend."

"You used to be mine," he said, trying to put his arms around me, even as the hooker was pulling him off. A guard was closing in.

"You're just too stupid! You couldn't figure out what I'm worth!" I spit out the words—because I wanted to slap him. But the guard intervened. Shepherd dropped his arms and walked off. Gia pulled me away, but not before I shoved my chips into the hooker's surprised hands, saying angrily, "Tell him it's a campaign contribution." *What am I going to tell you? Of course I know I'm not supposed to ask you a rhetorical question. It's rhetorical because I know you know why I did it! He needed me! And some part of him knew it.*

3

Interminably circling gave the plane's ultra-dry air plenty of time to turn the cabin into Death Valley. Thank god for moisturizer. La Prairie is a must for jet travel. I wished more and more that I had taken Traub's corporate jet. But it was headed back to LA. Instead, I hopped on a 'jumbo' from Reagan National to New York, which was stupid because catching an executive flight to Teterboro in Jersey would have been a snap. I stretched out in my 'travel clothes,' just comfortable, black Armani slacks, a pocket tee shirt and a small zip jacket both from Helmut Lang with black flats and cotton socks. I have dressing space in my offices so I can sneak a change before an important meeting. I buzzed for the first-class attendant, who arrived immediately with bottled water and ice. Did I want a cold compress? No! That was the last thing my Chanel makeup needed. I stared up into her young face, debating whether to tell her that more years ago than I now want to remember, I had worn a similar uniform. But in a much smaller size, and with better hair. Would you believe that I was a flight attendant long before I became Ms. Money?

Just before Christmas, Bradley Lufkin had called from the Treasury. The President was implementing a Financial Emergency

Advisory Committee (PFEAC), chaired by Treasury Secretary Paulson. My name had been put forward. If I accepted, official confirmation would follow in the first week of January. I said 'Yes' immediately, without consulting Traub. Wall Street's Bulls were still partying hard even though signs of the silently spreading financial plague were evident. I felt like I was back in Perpetual Mercy Academy reading Poe's 'The Mask of the Red Death.' The Prince has just entered the Green Room, the third of seven. I wanted to be in place when he got to the Black Room, the last of all. *When the bubble broke and the plague struck being in that room was going to be very important. There was money to be made. I wanted in—not out.*

Now, Paulson had called an abrupt emergency meeting in New York. I gave up my seat on Traub's Los Angeles bound corporate jet, and detoured to a Delta flight to New York that didn't want to land. Ms. Money was going to meet the Secretary of the Treasury, along with the boys, and a lot fewer girls, who make things happen in the financial world. I had last seen Paulson back in December 2006, in an auditorium at the Office of Thrift Supervision in Washington. The occasion was an all-day housing symposium at which he gave the welcoming remarks. Seen from the audience, he looked even bigger than in his press photos. He had the build of a football player, and his big skull reminded me of a bald Tom Sizemore. Below the powerful naked dome of his head, I remembered a smaller face made up of hard, penetrating eyes and tight features that ended with a blunt thrust of jaw. When I was introduced, his stare was absolutely icy.

My friends among the women financial anchors who had blossomed since Ms. Money's debut, were unanimous in their opinion of Paulson. In spite of his being a bird-watcher, Christian Scientist, and Coca-Cola-only drinker, he was considered among the most ruthless men on the Street of Dreams. Later, I learned from Beth Rooney, CEO of Bolt Bank, that the only birds he cared about were hawks. "Listen," Rooney told me, "you know back in 1999 it was Paulson who forced out that sleaze-bag Goldman CEO John Corzine. Corzine is said to have screamed at Paulson, "I didn't know you were such a tough guy."

"If you've got a bazooka, and people know you've got it, you may not have to take it out," Paulson answered back with one of his favorite sayings. But then he added, "So just let me show you how it works," and fired the anti-tank missile that blew Corzine away.

His dedication to Goldman was total. They were one and the same. Paulson was the driving force behind the investment bank's steadily advancing revenues since its IPO. In 2003 revenues were $21 billion, climbing to $25 billion in 2004, $30 billion in 2005, $38 billion in 2006, and now more than $45 billion. His personal net worth numbered in the billions. What I couldn't figure out was why he took the job after Bush Jr picked him as the 74th Secretary of the Treasury. The way I saw it, Paulson, as chief of Goldman, had the most important private sector job in the world. He was at the top, the TOP, and his power and perks were certainly far greater. His salary would drop from $40 million per year plus options to around $183 thousand. *And he certainly didn't look that altruistic.*

Then I learned just how brilliant his move was. Paulson was due to retire and sell his partnership share back to Goldman along with a $500 million portfolio. The sale would be subject to huge taxes. But a very special loophole, created by the government in 1989, allows highest-level cabinet officers and high ranking members of the Federal Reserve to liquidate without paying a dime in taxes. I should be so lucky. Paulson's timing was absolutely perfect. In July of 2006, he sold just over three million shares of Goldman, for about $150 per share—representing a tax free gain of almost $500 million—half a billion dollars. He beat Uncle Sam out of more than $200 million in capital gains taxes. Yes, he could have made a few bucks more if he sold a few months later at the top of the market, but that was nothing compared to what he saved. No wonder he went to work for the government. But I was sure that he had never stopped working for Goldman.

I pulled a report stamped 'Confidential' out of my briefcase. Paulson had circulated New York Fed chief Geithner's proposal to lend $25 billion to Bear Stearns, collateralized by its dwindling cash assets and its sixty-story office tower. I saw immediately that the loan proposal wasn't going anywhere. They say the devil is in the details, but in this case it was the attachment that was the problem. Joined to the proposal was a copy of a widely distributed e-mail from Goldman Sachs research. It spelled out why Goldman no longer had Bear Stearns back. I was shocked when it crossed my desk earlier in the week. Goldman was signaling the risk of backing Bear shares was too great. Forget about the fat fees it was charging for the derivative mortgage paper it had sold Bear in the first place.

Bear Stearns was in deep doo-doo. In real money terms, the investment bank was trying to leverage $395 billion of worthless paper assets with only $11 billion of cash on the books. The Goldman report really meant 'nothing from nobody nowhere.' There wasn't a hand on Wall Street that would lend Bear Stearns a dime. *Had Paulson called for the PFEAC meeting to block Geithner's loan proposal?* I felt sure that my days in the financial media doghouse were over. The housing bubble contagion I saw coming had struck at last. It was March and the debt plague had infected one of Wall Street's major investment banks. But once again my timing was off. As you'll soon see, the boys in charge managed to deny the debt crisis once again. *'Chicken Little' was still Ms. Money's nickname.*

4

Just then I felt the aircraft break from its lazy circling. The jet's speed picked up. *We were going in—finally!* I saw the flight attendant rush to buckle into her landing harness. I remembered once again how much I hated being strapped in when told to 'Prepare to land.' I looked at my watch, closed my briefcase, and then snatched up the newspaper and refolded it to use as a screen to hide behind. I was staring at the front page headline. "Gov on the Hook!"—it blared at me. *OMG.* Eliot Spitzer, the Governor of New York State, had been trapped in a sex scandal. *He resigned!* I live in the San Remo, and I'd seen him walking his dogs in Central Park. Shocked by the sheer stupidity of it all, I read on as the big jet descended. Spitzer was caught patronizing a high-priced prostitution service called Emperors Club VIP. He was involved with a $1,000-an-hour call girl going by the name of Kristen, one of at least seven or eight women he had slept with over a period of six months. His total taxpayer-paid tab came to more than $80,000.

Kristen turned out to be Ashley Alexandra Dupré. She was 22, an aspiring pop recording artist living in Manhattan. *The Post's* photo shoot showed Dupré in provocative poses. The pretty brunette was about 5 feet 4 and petite at what couldn't be much over a 100 pounds.

A baby—but hot all right. I was older, five-inches taller and only ten pounds heavier. *I'm still in shape. Men are just so stupid. They're dummies who believe any woman over thirty isn't worth it.* A grown woman can radiate sexual intensity with a single look, which at least has the benefit of saving a lot of time and trouble. True, my hair is professionally done to keep its original jet black and I've been to Dr B, New York's top plastic surgeon, twice. I've always had a perfect oval face with small-scale sharp features. On TV it shows no trace of ravage, and my deep green eyes are perfect. Dupré looked like her boobs were enlarged. But I didn't wonder when the paper said that Spitzer had done it with his socks still on. *That's what hot means all right.*

   I felt the thump of the landing gear being lowered. I was about to fold up the newspaper when a name caught my eye. The prosecution referred to Spitzer as 'Client Number 9.' Clients one through eight included two British royals, three Japanese billionaires and three Americans, all politicians, and then a name leaped right out of the paper to strike me hard in the heart. I gasped. There it was in print. It was ex-Senator Matthew Shepherd. *It can't be true!* My eyes ran down the list and again came to a stop at Shepherd's name. *No way. The man who had paid for my Versace briefcase was now ruined politically once and for all!*

The New York Fed never fails to impress me. It stands solidly on massive stone-block walls with huge wrought iron gates. Even more impressive is its 200-ton vault, which sits about 100 feet below street-level. It's full of gold. But what makes me smile most of all is the irony of the Fed's address—44 Maiden Lane. When I was Traub's delegate on FLEC, the commission charged with improving U.S. financial literacy and education, I read somewhere that one historian of old Manhattan claimed the street got its name from young lovers who strolled along the brook running down its middle, which was filled in after the War of 1812. That's as bad as being taught to mispronounce Shakespeare's Doll Tearsheet and Mistress Quickly in a way which disguises their real meaning—the way I was taught in my four years at Perpetual Mercy Academy. But 'Tearsheet' is really 'tear sheet,' as in torn, not tears to be cried, and 'Quickly' is 'quick lie,' as in get laid. Take a look in Washington Irving's "Knickerbocker's History" and you will learn that it was prostitutes who hustled their wares along the creek on Maiden Lane, stepping around washer women with piles of dirty bed linens. *Which means the Federal Reserve is a gigantic Mermaid Tavern, dispensing ale in the form of free money to one and all, until the party gets too hot and the cops shut the place down. Paul Volcker was the last cop I could remember.*

There was no time for introductions when I entered the Fed board-room. Paulson was fiddling with a large overhead digital monitor. I eased into a seat next to Beth Rooney, who whispered, "They're setting up a Skype connection."

"Thanks for holding a seat."

"I thought you might be late given the short notice. I only made it about a minute ahead of you."

Paulson appeared to be satisfied with the TV, and turned to the faces at the huge table. "We're taking testimony from Bear Stearns' CEO Alan Schwartz. I'm sure many of you know him. He's in Palm Beach—*on vacation.*" His eyebrows lifted as he spoke. *He didn't sound like a happy camper.*

"Nero fiddled while Rome burned—so what's new," a voice cried out from farther down the huge table.

There was a burst of laughter. Beth Rooney scribbled a name on the pad in front of her and slid it over—'Masterson.' I nodded. Brad Masterson was Fed Chairman Bernanke's 'Mr Fixit.' I met him when the new Fed boss was first sworn in. He was known to be brash, but the work cut out for him that afternoon wasn't going to be easy. Still the tension in the room was a lot less than I thought it would be. I expected more confrontation and certainly no jokes. But doom and gloom were nowhere to be found. Spring time had come early to New York. In spite of my fears, the Fed would fix Bear Stearns, and Wall Street would party on.

I looked up at Schwartz' face thrust forward on the monitor. The resemblance to Richard Gere was a surprise. But I was shocked to see a black eye. Later, I heard the rumor that he'd been in the gym when another Bear executive punched him in the face. But what he said next was even more shocking.

"We're not being made aware of anybody who is not taking our credit as a counterparty," he challenged. "So what's the problem?"

I couldn't believe what I was hearing. Schwartz had been head man at Bear for just a few months, but he had to know why Paulson was confronting him. It was only six months since his old boss had been forced to resign after two Bear Stearns highest-leverage hedge funds failed. Didn't he know his professional obituary was being written under the headline 'Bear Dead of Plague'?

"Are you out of your mind?" Paulson screamed. "Alan, for god sakes! Your balance sheet is leveraged almost 36-to-1!"

"Didn't you see Goldman's e-mail? They don't have your back," Geithner cut in.

"We can live on equity—if we have to," Schwartz fired back. But his full-screen face had started to bob and weave to avoid the verbal battering.

"Merde! You're a deadbeat. Don't you know it?" It was Françoise Zuger from the IMF speaking. I had been invited to her chalet the year before after the annual global get together at Davos. She was the only woman sitting by herself. I was clustered with Beth Rooney and Carol Carson of the Bank Supervisory Board.

"We'll do a buyback," Schwartz insisted.

"You must be in denial." Paulson countered.

"Are you crazy?" Masterson interrupted loudly. "You don't have a dime in your pocket. Didn't they tell you Jimmy has bailed out totally?" It was a reference to former CEO James 'Jimmy' Cayne, who owned more Bear Stearns stock than anyone. The Traub research report, which had been prepared for my eyes only, said Cayne had sold his entire stake, well over 5 million shares, for just under $11 a share. And the stock was still falling, to under $5.00, way, way down from $100 at the start of the year and an all-time high of $172. "Get it straight—this isn't a wake-up call. It's your funeral announcement!" proclaimed the voice of the Fed with a foregone conclusion.

I stared at the tough talking, Masterson, who had worked for Goldman in Japan—after Princeton and Harvard Law. Then he had moved over to the Fed.

"Your only equity is negative," said Paulson.

"So let the government come in," Schwartz replied. "What kind of authority do you have—anyway?" *The weather must be even better in Florida.*

"That's not going to happen while I'm Treasury Secretary." Paulson was firm. A bailout for Bear wasn't in his plans.

"Listen," Masterson blasted Schwartz once more. "I'm going to ask you a simple question. Do you know what a Zombie is?" He answered before the Bear chief could speak. "You're one of the living dead."

Paulson was more diplomatic. "Alan, we're going into executive session—we'll get back to you. Keep the connection open. I won't be long." I watched Schwartz' face break up into digital fragments before Paulson killed it with a click. Turning to the room, he announced, "Take a break—no more than ten minutes."

I turned to Beth Rooney. "I just can't believe they don't know how bad things actually are. Doesn't anyone on the Street have an inkling of what's coming? Tsunami big time."

"Look—you're forgetting that when their hedge funds failed all Standard & Poor's did was drop their rating from double A to single A. That's all. Don't forget our glorious credit raters get paid by the same guys they rate."

"It's worse than that. Even the top-dollar quants don't know what the real risk is. It's based on synthetic derivatives packing mega-leverage. They're so complicated that the credit raters had to rely on the issuers for their risk assessment."

"That's just what Shakespeare meant by being hoisted by your own petard. The boys really outsmarted themselves this time. You're 'spot on' about what's coming. We've started to pull back and tighten up."

At least some one is finally listening.

5

Internal conflict boiled over when Paulson returned. His face wore a look of no mercy. Masterson and JPMorgan Chase CEO Jamie Dimon returned together. Geithner entered last, switching off his mobile as he sat down. Paulson called the meeting to order casually, "Okay Tim—take a shot at it."

"You've seen the plan," said the New York Fed boss. "We're proposing a $25 billion loan—right from home—the New York Fed. That should give them enough time to pull through. This is a liquidity crisis. We need to stand up for them. That will stop this from spreading." He looked around the room for support.

"You New York boys have to stop playing favorites," Masterson said harshly. "Less than a year ago you told my boss, let me read it." He went on to read from a sheaf of papers in his hand, 'Direct exposure of the counterparties to Bear Stearns is very, very small.' Then he looked up at Geithner, "You put us way behind the curve. Then your number two guy, Dudley, told the chief, 'We've done quite a bit of work trying to identify some of the funding questions surrounding Bear Stearns, but so far it looks as though nothing is really imminent.' That turns out to be pure bullshit! So don't even think Fed loan!" *That's Ben Bernanke talking in case you don't know it.*

Geithner ducked into silence. Instead it was SEC chief Chris Cox, who rushed to Bear's defense. "Look this is due to a lack of confidence, not a lack of capital." Then he looked at Paulson— "Your friends at Goldman did them in with that memo. It really screwed the Bear!"

Paulson stared arrows at him. It was Masterson who answered, "There was plenty of talk about a liquidity crisis ever since their hedge funds went under. It's a shame it didn't get as far as Palm Beach. Don't blame Goldman. Wasn't the $3.2 billion it cost Bear to bail out their High-Grade Structured Credit Enhanced Leveraged Funds enough of a warning. Just the name is a joke." Then he pronounced the title word-for-word. "High-Grade, Structured, Credit-Enhanced, Leveraged Funds. In other words 'Hot Air Only.' You reap what you sow."

I heard the death penalty in his final comment. Then Carol Carson butted in from alongside me. "We're opposed to giving them a cent. Our money is to protect depositors not bankers." She was joined by Beth Rooney, who waved her hand to show support.

But it was Masterson, speaking to Geithner, who told them what they were getting. "Look Tim—tell them it's no go. No 28-day loan! We're willing to lend $30 billion to Mr Dimon here against Bear's pile-of-crap assets and Morgan will acquire Bear for 2 bucks a share. That's final!"

I saw the smile on Dimon's face widen. They all knew the Morgan chief couldn't lose with a deal like that. But I could hardly believe the $2 a share offer—that was peanuts. My face must have exposed my thoughts. Dimon was staring at me. I was the only woman who had said nothing. "Over ninety-five percent of Traub clients are out of the stock," I told them.

"The rest are probably short," Cox followed, getting a laugh.

"Traub doesn't recommend short positions to retail clients," I announced in an even tone. "We follow SEC policy." Cox turned away, but Paulson looked directly at me for the first time.

Then Mr Secretary took over speaking like a doctor explaining that the operation really was a success because the patient had died. "They were greedy— the market warned them. You saw the memo Goldman put out. So what did they do?" he asked the room. "They went out an increased their poisonous position, and leveraged it with even more higher-risk mortgage paper. I vote we take them down." We all heard the flushing sound.

Later, Beth Rooney and I talked in the Ladies Room. "Don't forget—that's the same Goldman who created the $1 billion ultra-high-risk collateralized debt obligation (CDO) called 'Timberwolf' for institutional investors." It was full of mortgage backed securities derived from Washington Mutual (WAMU) Adjustable Rate Mortgages (ARMs). Goldman pushed hard to sell it."

Don't tell me," Rooney interrupted, "the Bear ate the Wolf."

"About $300 million worth. But the WAMU paper went into default. Timberwolf is worthless. Totally. And then the third-party insurer who was guaranteeing the CDO went broke."

"So the Bear became a rug! No wonder they call you Ms. Money."

It took two days for Bear Stearns to agree to die poor. Former long-time Chairman and CEO, Alan 'Ace' Greenberg, negotiated a better deal. He wasn't known as Wall Street's 'Long John Silver' for nothing. Greenberg was way more resourceful than Schwartz. Facing a walk off the plank, he got the best he could get. JPMorgan

Chase raised its offer to $10 a share, for a total of $1.2 billion. Masterson, speaking for Fed Chairman Bernanke, immediately defended the revised deal in a memo circulated to the Committee. He argued it would prevent damage to the real economy. Paulson's bazooka had blown up the world's seventh largest investment bank. *Case closed. There's no need to talk about it. This is only target practice!*

I stayed in New York. I wanted to see the new Pope. After two days in Washington, Benedict XVI came to the City on April 17 for a three-day visit. He said Mass before a crowd of nearly 60,000 at Yankee Stadium. An altar was set up on second base. I watched on TV. Even on screen, it was a profound experience. You could feel the faithful as they prayed. To have faith is to believe, and the Pope's followers believed in him. You could feel it. I wanted to be part of it.

I had my PA, Robin, call Mayor Bloomberg's protocol officer. That and my campaign pledge got me added to a very select group of 9/11 victim families and first responders who attended a special Mass at Ground Zero. It was celebrated by the Pope on his very last day in New York. I was first row and surrounded by people still in pain and grief and loss. I knew what that was like. If BJ Hanlon had never gone downtown that morning my life would be different. I knew the Pope couldn't bring him back. I took my daughter Mimi—she was almost a teen. We knelt with the small group receiving the Pope's personal blessing.

The Pope raised his hand to make the sign of the cross. I looked up into the face of Benedict XVI. I couldn't believe what I saw on it. Pure faith washed over me. He was joyous! *Holy with love.* I wanted to understand his joy. His eyes were sparkling beneath a square brow and his heavy lips wore a smile. I saw snowy white hair at the sides of his tall gold miter. I could feel him see into me. He saw who I was. Ms. Money was absolved. The Pope's purity cleansed my guilt. I was Mary Magdalene. He was the Holy Father. My father. My father whose favorite game was to hold me on his knee and ask me what I was worth. "Ice cream," I would say grinning. *Because I was worth something. I was a woman, a woman who could love again. I would save Matt Shepherd.*

PART I:
MICHAEL WORTH

(1960—1982)

6

My father, Michael Worth, wanted to name me Elizabeth, after his own mother. His parents had died in the Los Angeles flood of 1938, when the San Gabriel Mountains dumped tons of water down into the LA basin, washing away more than 5,000 homes. *I would have been a Lizzie or a Beth.* But my mother's movie star worship was totally dedicated to Marilyn Monroe. She wanted to name me after the global sex queen, and I'm sure that some people who claim to know me would call that the right choice. But it was Granny Sharp, my only surviving grandparent, who decided the issue.

Having flown across the country to attend my birth, she wouldn't hear of either proposal. 'Margaret' was the only possible choice for my name. Back in her Brooklyn home, as I would one day see, two cheaply-framed *Daily News* Sunday magazine covers hung right above her bed. She had carefully cut out the colored pages showing her favorites, Princess Margaret and Margaret O'Brien, the child star. The Princess was there because she should have been allowed to marry the divorced war-hero Peter Townsend. Margaret O'Brien won Granny's worship because of her role as Beth, in the 1949 movie version of *Little Women*. The film had made Granny cry even more than *Gone with the Wind*. Hanging between the framed magazine photos was a crucifix with some dried-out palm fastened to Christ with a faded twistee. Could there be any doubt when her own daughter, now Mrs Eileen Worth, nee Sharp, delivered a girl what she would be called? So the two women movie goers prevailed completely. And my mother's choice became my middle name because she was certain the near death of the sex star on the set of *The Misfits* in 1960 triggered the contractions that brought me into the world too early. I was born a preemie, emerging as Margaret Marilyn Worth, or 'Maggie Lynn,' as my father called me.

We were a quiet Los Angeles family. Our neat little ranch house sat next to other just as neat ranch houses on a street in the northern quarter of San Gabriel, just below Huntington Drive and near to San Marino. The house had a swimming pool instead of a backyard, and I remember my father relaxing in it when he was home between trips. He had become a commercial pilot after flying Air Force combat missions in Korea. He was a big man, but still trim, with a square face whose red color I haven't forgotten. Thank god I never inherited it. But I did get his thick, jet-black hair, and his emerald-green eyes. But what I got from my mother, as you'll soon see, was worth even more.

I thank both my parents for much more than my genes. They loved me with a certainty that made childhood a perfect time. I loved them totally. I know it is fashionable for fiction writers and their editors to favor childhood abuse and dysfunctional families. Parents, siblings, relatives, nannies, neighbors, classmates, teachers, ministers—indeed anyone—as portrayed by popular fiction, TV and the movies is ready to pounce on young people to destroy their childhood dream worlds. Hate is now a crime, and yet we hate more than ever—especially and unfortunately ourselves. As my own heroine, I know that I risk losing your attention when I say that

I grew up normal. But that is the truth, the whole truth and not the awful truth that sells books.

My father flew jumbo jets, my mother went shopping, and I took my baby brother to school, holding his hand until he preferred going with his friends. And I don't think the world has changed much. We seem to devalue childhood more than ever, pushing adulthood back in time, literally adulterating the innocence we need to live happily ever after. I want to say categorically that my success, money, fame and men are owing to one thing—my ability to grow up slow. As much as I love reading Candace Bushnell, and watching *Sex and the City*, I was not giving boys blow jobs as a pre-teen. I was in no hurry to get where I've gotten. I assume you know where that is because of my relative celebrity, or why would you be reading this, other than as a tale of how a very successful investor made their money. My fairy tale life is, simply put, no fairy tale. It's just that I love being a woman, being who I am, being my special me.

What was customary populated my past. That was the best part of my idyllic and rather typical development. My father's love and mother's care added up to a quiet upbringing, which meant that ultimately I found it hard to believe in anything else. I continue to find sensational stories and their gruesome headlines shocking. My early years bred a distrust of media sensationalism. I've been on TV, even had my own show, so I know how ordinary rain can become a storm, then super storm, monster storm, cataclysm, hurricane and finally storm of the century, before fizzling out as a daytime shower.

Despite a world that spreads unhappiness by insisting that we should be something other than what we are, I believe that most people are happy being just what they are. That happiness means first finding out who we are, learning to live with that person, and then fulfilling our promise. People have to discover themselves, that's the absolutely first step. When you know who you are you can go on to construct an identity. And as an individual person you can win the prize and share in a relationship—even if it's only with a goldfish. Better a relationship than no relationship. Joy exists to be shared. That's a lot better than running away from ourselves in a futile and contradictory escape that is doomed to fail. I've tried to tell my son and daughter how important this is. I want them to know that the highest-rated darlings worshipped by the media truly don't like being who they are at all. Instead they profit by exploiting their self-hatred. I'm a winner, as you will discover, because I can be just the woman I am.

The first disruption in my otherwise lullaby childhood occurred when I was ten, forming one of my earliest memories. *Is it funny what you remember? I don't think so. That's because I've never forgotten the experience I'm going to share with you.* I've never been so embarrassed, and that must be part of it. My face was burning throughout. But it goes deeper than that because what we remember forever as 'first' is when the puzzle that is us begins. It's the first time we don't know what to do and have no one to help us. After falling down the rabbit hole, Alice, of *Alice in Wonderland*, has to choose 'eat me' or 'drink me.' Having something to remember says autonomy has arrived. That's more than a first dress, and high heels come way later.

My parents could afford private day school for me, and every morning my mother drove us up into Pasadena, near Cal Tech where the school was located. Later, when I was old enough, on California dreamin' days, I could walk home with my friend Daisy Sanchez, the only other girl on our street. We would stroll together, ignoring the swarm of little boys playing driveway basketball games.

Both older and taller, we were smug in our gender superiority. We learned that we could shorten the walk home from school by sneaking into the gardens of the Huntington Library through a back gate that wasn't intended for little girls thin enough to slip through its wide-spaced bars. So we were treated with an immense treasure of flowering beauty, including jade vines and cereus cacti.

But along with my aptly named friend, I got into serious trouble for the first time on the afternoon we were caught with two bouquets of very red roses just as we were attempting to slip out of the Huntington gardens. *They were the most beautiful flowers I have ever seen.* Daisy screamed at me to run. But all I could do was freeze. So we were both caught and made to wait nervously in the guardhouse for an hour until my mother arrived to free us. Two ten-year-old girls in pinafores, we sat frightened as uniformed guards watched over us. Even though I thought I would die, there was no mistreatment. I was more worried about my mother than the guards, and I needed to go to the toilet, and kept squeezing my legs together. Daisy was chewing on the hem of her dress.

The men were like my father. Big. Uniformed. After I gave them my name and address, I rattled on nervously and told them he was a pilot, and that once I had flown all the way to San Francisco in the cockpit. But the bulky grey-suited men standing about in the guardhouse by the gate weren't impressed. I sensed they weren't even listening. Instead they spoke into headsets that echoed with static and barked replies. Daisy whispered in my ear to look at the holstered guns hung on their wide leather belts. But it was their ambivalence that worried me, and because they were men I knew I couldn't bring up going to the Ladies Room. We were two tiny girls who had done something wrong but something outside the guards' purpose—they needed to be told what to do with us. We didn't seem to matter at all, and it was that which frightened me the most.

The pretty child I was expected attention from adults. Now I didn't know what to expect.

But everything changed when my mother arrived. I'm really happy that you'll get to know her. While she was meek with my father, she was what I've heard men call a "tough broad." She stormed into the guardhouse bearing a hostile challenge. They had sent a car for her, which returned with lights blinking and a siren. *Just like an ambulance,* I thought. Her entry brought a sudden change that held my attention. It filled my head with deeper unspoken questions, even to the point where I no longer feared her punishment. Somehow my mother made the guards pay attention. I didn't know how or why. When confronted by Eileen Worth, a tiny blonde woman in a house dress who weighed little more than 105 pounds, their authority seemed to fail them. That was the mystery. It was something in the way she held herself as she gave them a scornful look. And all she said was, "I'll just take these two little girls home right now—where they belong!" I saw her simple words somehow overpower the men, shaming them. It was they who had done something truly stupid, and she let them know she knew it. I realized years later that she was somehow projecting her role as a mother with a capital 'M.' She was a grown woman, invoking centuries of little boy stupidity. She was all instinct. She became an angry Maureen O'Sullivan telling them never to cash their paycheck at the pub before they took it home. After all, Ronald Reagan was Governor of California. He was a real man who didn't go around arresting little girls with a handful of flowers.

One of the guards barely muttered a warning about "trespassing." But her scorn burnt him when she looked at him and said, "Ten-year-olds! Don't forget what you're here for. You're supposed to be watching what matters—isn't that so? There's paintings and the silver to worry about. Not ten-year-olds. These girls just got lost.

If you don't mind. A few flowers don't matter. I'm the mother. I have a little boy at home—you know." And her attitude warned them to be careful or they might find out that they were nothing but little boys inside the uniforms they were wearing. What business did they have arresting two little girls! Badges and guns and all. I could feel the men cringe, even without understanding just what was happening. My mother picked me up and took Daisy's hand and our stay in the guardhouse ended immediately. One guard even reached down to hand me the flowers, which had started to wilt.

My mother walked us both home, and when we got to Daisy's I again felt something else was being communicated that went beyond me. Just listen to my mother's explanation to Daisy's mom: "Well they certainly managed to scare two poor little girls who took some flowers for home."

"I'm sure Daisy didn't understand," my friend's mother replied defensively.

"No," my mother answered back, establishing that the two of us were equally innocent. "But it wasn't really criminal, you know," she insisted. "The two of them should just have left the way they got in. All those men worrying over flowers and scaring two little girls. They could have done with just a talking to. What would they do if they had real thieves to catch? Call the cops, I suppose!" She burst out laughing, "Those museum guards need to have their heads examined. They're supposed to worry about what's valuable. It's a treasure house. A few flowers are hardly worth the trouble."

What I took from her words were a bunch of questions. They were first about my mother's clear belief that taking the flowers was no crime at all. That somehow we were entitled to their natural beauty because we were just ten, by which she meant that we were innocent, that we had no criminal intent, as a defense attorney might argue. She seemed to know why, in a larger sense, we were entitled to the flowers because we were female and the guards were men. I didn't know why that mattered. But I never forgot the experience, which, as you will see later, was to prove only dormant not finished forever. It was all part of a puzzle I failed to solve at the time, and which I would spend much of my life working on.

7

My little brother showed up some four years after me. I became the sister who learned to change his disposable diapers. He was Brian Declyn Worth. My father had his way since Granny Sharp was resolved not to come between a man and his son's name. My mother took a Catholic attitude towards Marilyn Monroe's suicide, meaning she didn't contest my father's insistence that 'Monroe' wasn't a fit name for a boy. But notice that Brian Declyn, nicknamed 'Brindee,' does include a 'lyn'— probably as a reminder of the movie star's passing in August 1962.

The biggest tragedy in my life was that my baby brother never got to be a teenager. He drowned at summer camp near Laguna. He had doubled up on a jet ski driven by an older camper. They were in the ocean, showing off with high speed spinouts and tail stands and porpoise hops. They were doing more than 40 miles an hour, when the powerful jet ski flipped and threw the two of them. The driver died of a broken neck, impact with the machine knocked Brindee out as he was thrown into the ocean. It was so awful. Awful, meaning I felt that part of myself had disappeared! My beautiful blond brother, who had never done anything but smile, was gone forever. The funeral was held in San Gabriel. We had to wait for Granny Sharp to fly from New York. I wore black for the first time. It was the only time I ever saw my father cry. He hugged me, kissed me, and I felt the wetness of tears on his face.

"Be careful," he whispered. "I could never lose you."

"Don't you ever take chances like that," my mother warned, between her sobs.

The trouble was that my brother's death was Act One of a two-part tragedy. Act Two followed in 1975, the most terrible year ever, ever. My father's plane crashed in New York during a landing at JFK. He died in one of the worst air disasters on record. Only 12 people, ten passengers and two flight attendants in the back of the plane survived. More than one hundred others, including my father and his co-pilot were killed. The FAA investigation said it was a micro burst. An unpredictable and brief but violent storm struck the runway. Wind shear slammed the jumbo jet just as it was powering down. There was an alert, but my father must have decided the risk had passed. The powerful wind picked the plane up and just threw it down. Too fast and too early, the big jet struck the elevated runway lights and rolled over and crashed and exploded. He was better off dead. Losing even one passenger would have killed him—I'm certain of that.

The investigation cleared him. But my mother knew why. "He never got over losing Brindee," she sobbed, hugging Granny Sharp at the small funeral in New York. I knew she was right. My father was never the same after my brother died. But then my mother learned a worse reason. We were broke, flat broke. Michael Worth had loaded up on stock in the Bull market of the Sixties. When the Bear market awoke from hibernation in 1973, he lost heavily. He was losing money all through 1974 and was totally wiped out at the start of 1975 only months before the plane crash. My mother found out he had been borrowing money all over. He had even taken out a big second mortgage against their house. It was all gone. We owed everyone. I didn't understand. All I knew was that we never went back to our house in San Gabriel, not to Los Angeles, nor even California, which I loved dearly.

"The money killed him," my mother told me when she thought I would understand. "He was worried about paying it all back. The insurance helped a bit, and we still get worker compensation and survivor benefits, but the house had to go." I thought she was stupid to even think about money. Money wasn't worth anything to me. My dad was dead, Michael Worth, my father, and our mutual man. At night I could hear my mother crying for him. I knew it was him she was crying for because I was doing the same.

The results were massive. Granny Sharp had to take us in. We moved to her house in Brooklyn, New York. Southern California was 3,300 miles away. My mother and I lived in a three-story brownstone on a tree-lined street in the Bay Ridge section. There was no swimming pool. Granny had to stop renting out her top floor, which meant she had a lot less money to live on. That made it easier for her not to get along with my mother and me. She dropped the 'Lynn' that my father and mother always added to my name. I became just plain Maggie from that time on—until a long time later, when I became Ms. Money!

You won't understand why what I've become is about exactly who I am if I don't tell you about high school. That was no easy experience. I had to start my second year in high school in a totally new place on the other side of the continent from California. Brooklyn was another country, and I was an immigrant outsider. To make it worse, Granny Sharp insisted that girls in particular must have a Catholic education. So she and my mother managed to afford Perpetual Mercy Academy, an all-girls parochial high school nearby. I became a 'Pommie'—as the girls were called.

Going to high school with girls I didn't know was horrible. The only friend I made was Annie Trang, my lab partner in chemistry. A Vietnamese refugee, she was the school's only Asian student, which made her as much of an outsider as I was. Plus her first home in America was in San Francisco, and as Californians, we were never even near popularity. But we shared the experience of group puberty. It was Annie who told me the initials PM, in Perpetual Mercy Academy, stood for Pre-Menstrual. We joked over that because all the Pommies were going through puberty at about the same time and must have been stimulated by a massive cloud of mutual pheromones.

We were both good enough swimmers to make JV. But except for swim practice, we were at the age when girls cover up. I wore a raincoat over my navy blue school uniform to disguise the changes that were taking place in my body. Annie was always hidden under a used man's overcoat she had gotten at a vintage store. We started going to movies together on Saturday afternoons—always wearing our respective coats. I loved re-runs of Peter O'Toole's films, and cried through them because the star's voice was my father's.

It was Annie who told me the rumor about the school's mansion on Ocean Road. It was said to have been built originally for the actress Lillian Russell by the financier 'Diamond Jim' Brady. I knew what an actress was, who wouldn't. But I asked Granny what exactly a 'financier' was. "It's a word for big money, you know," she told me. "It means really big. Wealthy. Rich men like that can buy what they want. A woman had to learn a lot to get that house for a gift. No wonder she gave it to the church." So I learned the meaning of the word, but I'm afraid that at the time I missed Granny's point.

The best thing about Perpetual Mercy were my religion classes. They were all about brave nuns and usually set in the time of Henry VIII and Thomas More. *A Man for All Seasons* was shown repeatedly at school assemblies. In junior year, we saw *The Song of Bernadette,* based on the novel by Franz Werfel. Jennifer Jones won the Oscar for Best Actress playing the title role. The film was over 30 years old, but I was only sixteen and loved it. Granny Sharp was more and more bedridden, and I told her all about it. Bernadette's teacher, Sister Vauzous (Gladys Cooper), was awful. She shamed the poor fourteen-year-old girl in front of the class for not having learned her catechism. But later that fateful day in 1858, while collecting firewood outside of Lourdes, Bernadette is distracted by a rising wind and sudden darkness. She enters a cave and sees a beautiful woman standing in brilliant light, holding a pearl rosary. She is stunned, but the vision identifies herself as 'the Immaculate Conception.'

But then the authorities close the cave, and try to have Bernadette declared insane. Soon after, the King's infant son falls ill and the Queen orders the child's nanny to fill a bottle of water from the cave. The baby drinks the water and miraculously recovers. The Queen believes. But the King is not convinced. Finally, the Queen gets him to reopen the grotto; the Bishop launches a religious investigation; and the Church eventually determines that Bernadette did experience a vision of the Virgin Mary.

"The Virgin was played by Linda Darnell," Granny suddenly remembered. "I never believed her because she was the other woman in *Brigham Young*. That was a Mormon movie—she was wrong to play Our Lady!"

But retelling the film to her, I knew it was true. *It just had to be!*

I couldn't wait until we talked about the movie with Sister Albertine. The girls all called her Sister Tina. She was a nun from a religious order known as the School Sisters of the Divine Sepulcher and met weekly with a small group of Perpetual Mercy students, to facilitate the progress of girls who felt a call to religious life. All the girls in the study group were in love with her. But my crush was the real thing. I just sat and stared at her face. Her skin was so white. She looked just like Ingrid Bergman in *The Bells of St. Mary's*, which the school showed every year at Christmas. She had the same light brown hair and Bergman's hawk-wing eyebrows and long lashes and eyes. Her heart-shaped face had the same Swedish pouting lower lip and linear nose. All of her features were framed by skin so white I was sure it glowed. That was real holiness.

I wanted to shine for her. So I asked why Bernadette must suffer painful death by tuberculosis, calling to the Mother of God on her death bed.

"Hearing the word of God we do not suffer—because we are going to Him," Sister Tina answered. Her face just beamed with faith. *She is so beautiful, her faith is beautiful, I just love her.* That was the first night I ever dreamed about becoming a nun. And I added Sister Tina to my daily prayers. Even before Karen Quinlan, the comatose twenty-two-year-old who had drugged herself out at a party, and whom all the Pommies prayed for as instructed.

My prayers were answered in the spring, when Sister Tina told me I was one of five girls chosen for an Easter retreat at Divine Sepulcher of Maryland (DSM), the religious college where she had taken Holy Orders.

We rode down in a bus on the Tuesday after Palm Sunday. Spring had told the pear trees along the Narrows to bloom, and my view of the lower Hudson was framed in white lace. It was a surprise to see the Sisters without their full gowns and habits. *Sister Tina looks great in jeans,* I thought. And a bigger surprise, we were soon joined by Sisters and students from Saint Savior's and Fontbonne Hall, well-known Catholic girl's high schools also located in Brooklyn—fifty students in all. One of the nuns had brought along a guitar, and we sang Joan Baez protest songs. These were followed by 'Amazing Grace,' 'Walk on Water,' and 'Ave Maria,' but soon the long five-hour ride put us to sleep. The iPod had yet to be invented.

Once in Baltimore, we were divided into five groups. The College was closed for ten days, which meant visitors could sleep in the dorms of the students who had gone home for Easter break. Prayer and fasting would be our constant activity—along with religious instruction. A very light supper was followed by evening Mass. A Monsignor from Washington gave us a long sermon, explaining that the retreat was a time for renunciation of the earthly life and a renewed dedication to the life of Christ. There would be a high service led by the Archbishop Wednesday evening. Students interested in attending the college would stay over Thursday to meet with the admission staff and then leave for home after lunch on Good Friday.

"I went here, and I think you should do an interview. With your grades there might be something for a girl considering Holy

Orders." Sister Tina told me with a concerned smile. I agreed because I was in love with her already.

I missed Annie Trang. The one place we weren't together was Religion. I had to share a bed room with a girl named Alice Powers. When we finally got to unpack, I learned she was from Catherine Carlisle, another Brooklyn convent school for girls.

By bedtime I was exhausted and too tired to talk, but Alice, looked at me and said, "Your Sister Tina is some hottie!"

"How do you know?" I snapped back.

"Listen," she said harshly, "Carlisle has real police wardens for Sisters. They don't mind using a ruler on you. A lot of kids are from bad homes. You don't know."

"I'll add you to my prayers," I snapped back at her and pulled up my sheets in a huff.

8

O n our first full day, Sister Tina explained that the theme of the retreat was a celebration of the five nuns who had died in the shipwreck of the steamer *Deutschland*, carrying immigrants to America. Each study group would take the name of an individual nun who had died in the tragedy and pray for the continued salvation of missionary nuns everywhere. Our group was given the name of Sister Henrica Fassbender, who was never found. But there were news reports that she was the drowning Nun who had cried out, "O Christ, Christ, come quickly." In the intense religious environment the tragedy couldn't help but weigh on the minds of the teenagers. One girl burst into tears, when she heard the Nun's final words. But my first thought was—*My father's plane crashed.* I saw Sister Tina's face glow with religious rapture as she spoke, and all I wanted was to tell her I loved her and cry. But another girl asked, "It's so sad— what makes it any good? They all drowned."

"That is what you all must pray for," Sister Tina told them. "Pray to understand how Sister Henrica was saved and rose to eternal life in Heaven. Listen to the Archbishop."

We alternated between prayer and instruction all day. A lean early dinner was followed by evening Mass. Then the Archbishop himself led us in high service. It was formal and solemn, and his mission was to save us from sin. He was in full regalia and attended by altar boys with censors. He did the Mass in perfect Latin. But his long sermon was in English. "One of the greatest and most learned of all Saints, the devout Augustine, he who created the City of God, warns you to be a Christian woman. And why is that? Whether it be as a wife or as a mother, all women must beware of the great Temptress known as Eve." His warning look fell upon us.

"The eminent Saint Ambrose, himself the Archbishop of Milan, tells us that Eve sinned with forethought, and knowingly made her husband a participant in her own wrong doing. We can discern the sex that was liable first to do wrong. The woman is responsible for the man's error. You must pray to understand this."

The girls were fixed on his words. His eyes scanned them slowly. "But you can be truly Christian women. Pray to be such. You must be a Virgin to be as Mary."

Then he went back to scripture. "The illustrious Justin Martyr tells us that Eve was brought forth from the serpent of disobedience and death. But the Virgin Mary, having received faith and its joy, when the angel Gabriel announced to her the most blessed of all tidings, she then answered, 'Be it done according to thy holy word. I am the divine Sepulcher.' Be as pure as Our Lady. You must choose the path away from Eve by letting Mary always guide you. Remember Mary was the only earthly woman to be born free of original sin. She was God's bride and Christ's mother because her Immaculate Conception removed the curse of Eve. Satanic Eve was the cause of man's Fall."

Later, we knelt around Sister Tina and prayed to understand the sermon. I was right next to her—close enough to make me dizzy. I saw the high-necked scapular over her black tunic. Combined with the coif white head cap and black exterior cowl, it framed the young nun's face. *She is just so beautiful,* I felt. I was beyond thought. *Her face is a perfectly unblemished heart.*

On my last night, I was alone. Alice Powers had left, but I stayed over to interview with the Admissions counselor. The retreat was exhausting and my mind was whirling with the thought of Holy Orders. Suddenly, it seemed so right for me. I was crying, and I kneeled against the bed. *Is God real?* I asked. *How will I know? Can a woman truly be as pure as the Virgin Mary? Do I want to be a nun?*

Then I felt a hand gently stroking my hair. *I knew.* I knew and cried even more. I had never felt and have never felt since the sheer emotional beauty I experienced in that moment of joy. Yes, I was just a girl. Only a girl can feel what I felt. But only a woman knows what its worth, knows the absolute value of love so pure. It was Sister Tina's arm hugging me, the most beautiful touch in the world.

Love is holy. This was devotion. And I knew it totally. I was shaking in my white tricot robe. Sister Tina was wearing silky-smooth pink pajamas, and I turned into her arms and my robe opened and my skin exploded as it came in contact with her warmth. I kissed the Sister full on the mouth. My lips locked on the mouth I wanted, and it pressed back heavily. She pulled back for a second, saying, "You are my Virgin." I knew she was crying too. Then we were in bed together. I was naked with Sister Tina. She was on top of me and kissing me passionately, and I opened my mouth and felt her tongue slide gently into it and I pulled hard on it. Soon her kisses worked their way down to my just budding nipples. They were so erect. I felt the moisture on them as Sister Tina licked them. I just had to do the same. I hurriedly pulled open her top and touched her heavier breasts. They were beautiful. I felt their swelling curves and then I kissed them. Her hand touched my cheek, and I could feel something happening inside. I needed to push myself into her. And then I felt her fingers slide into me. There was pain and then an electric wave of pleasure. I bathed her fingers with cream. She was excited, and we kissed tightly. Her mouth went down between my legs, and I felt a tongue pushing aside downy hair to find what it wanted. And I cried with new pleasure.

I slept only briefly because I was living a dream. But when I awoke, it was to guilt. What I had done was wrong. *But it was so totally beautiful. How could it be anything but good?* Sister Tina was standing next to my bed. She bent down to kiss me. Her lips rested tenderly on my mouth. There were tears on both our faces. I sensed immediately that it was more than a simple goodbye. "Why are you going?" I asked.

"I'm flying to Guatemala City. I will work in our school in Livingston. Jesus wants me to teach children there."

Now it was my turn to cry. "You can't leave me."

"You must not cry. God has rewarded me. You gave me his blessing," she said her parting words. "Remember, God understands. If you love someone you will always be the Virgin."

I shut my eyes. I knew that when I opened them next she would be gone. *Maybe it was all a dream.* I remembered the Archbishop had looked right at me when he uttered the name, "Eve."

9

My mother met me when I got off the bus that brought us from Baltimore back to Brooklyn. I told her what I now knew. "I'm going to be a nun. The Order will pay my college tuition." Saying it made it true. But I saw shock on her face.

"Well, I'm not going to be the one who tells your Grandmother."

"I'm sure she'll be thrilled," I answered her one hundred unasked questions.

My admissions interview at Divine Sepulcher of Maryland (DSM) must have been a success. I told the Nun that during the retreat I had experienced a spiritual call. And my grades from Perpetual Mercy were excellent. I wanted to major in Holy Orders, becoming an aspirant, then a postulant and finally a novitiate. Those were the stages before I would enter the Order. I would earn a college degree in education, which would let me teach math in a mission school. But my heart was on its own career path called 'following in Sister Tina's footsteps.' It was sure we would meet again. If I needed further proof, I was granted early admission.

I went to Baltimore when Jean Paul II became Pope and graduated four years later when he was attacked by a crazy Spanish priest at Fatima. Those events bracketed my college years. During that four-year period, along with my classmates seeking Holy Orders, I prayed for the lost souls of Jonestown, the ousted Shah of Iran, Lech Walesa and President Reagan after he was shot. The entire school was devastated by the murder of John Lennon in 1980. The Nuns and Novices treated me warmly. I was part of it, and needed nothing else. I prayed to the Virgin night and day, waiting for a true call to join Christ and the Order—and to see Sister Tina again.

My mother came to Baltimore only twice. I took her to a traditional seafood restaurant down by the inner harbor, where we ate crabs, pounding them with wooden mallets on a table covered with brown paper.

"So are you still going to be a nun?" she asked. It was her only question and entered our conversation continuously in one form or another.

"I want to—I'll probably teach for the Order somewhere."

"What about men? I see you finally gave up that stupid overcoat, and if anybody looks really good around here it's you."

"I may go to Guatemala." I hinted. "Our Order has a mission school there." *Sister Tina was teaching in it.*

"Just remember we only have each other."

"Yes," I told her, "and I'll pray for you!"

I was a Junior before I knew it. But in my third year at DSM, Granny Sharp died. I came home for Christmas break, knowing she was ill. Her one-night funeral was a sad affair—tiny, attended by only a handful of very old women, along with my mom and me. My mother was an only child, and I had never seen my maternal grandfather, who had been killed in WWII. No other Sharp relatives were still alive, and the Worths were a distant few. Granny's neighborhood friends left early because of the cold weather. On TV it said there was snow in Florida. We sat on folding chairs, trying not to stare into the open coffin. The experience raised the ghost of my father. Not surprisingly, my mother was thinking of her own past.

"She's gone to join my daddy," my mother said. "She waited over thirty years. I hope I don't have to wait as long to see yours." I loved that she was thinking about Michael Worth too.

I hugged her tightly. *I can't lose you too.*

I stared at Granny's face. She didn't look real. During my years at Perpetual Mercy, I had come to truly love the old woman, despite her general bitterness. Even when I left for DSM, I still thought of her. Now, staring at death, I somehow knew I would hold Sister Tina again. That was what my body was for. Not this. Then I heard a voice in my head. It was saying something hard to hear. Granny was talking to me, saying, "Kiss me." I stood up and knelt before the coffin. Granny Sharp wanted me to kiss her goodbye, but she didn't seem human. I leaned over and grazed her lips, and the voice in my head said clearly, "Not for nothing, always remember, not for nothing."

I was startled, but then I remembered. It was the only thing she had said when I told her I had enrolled in Holy Orders. She was pleased to hear I was getting free tuition. But it wasn't enough for her. "Remember, just don't give your love to God for nothing!" she had warned. But I was in love with Sister Tina. *And love is free!*

One thing I have to thank Annie Trang for was all the math classes we took together in high school. Being math majors spared us the ridicule of the popular students, who were enrolled in more desirable subjects. At DSM, the nuns saw me as a potential math teacher, which brought a surprise reward at the end of my third year. The Mother Superior called me into her office. "We are so proud of you. Your faith is strong and now our Lord has acknowledged your studies," she said handing me a letter. It was from the National Science Foundation. I was chosen for a six-week Women-in-Math summer program at Cal Tech. I would receive a stipend for travel and living expenses. I called my mother immediately. "I'm going to Cal Tech for the summer. It's wonderful." Cal Tech was in Los Angeles, and Los Angeles was in California. *Jackpot!*

Instead of answering, my mother just cried, before whispering "Of course you can go."

California here I come, my mind sang silently.

I flew out early to San Francisco to spend a week with my old Pommie pal Annie Trang and her family. They were wonderful. Annie was great. She took me shopping in the Haight. We rode the ferry to Sausalito and had lunch at Zack's. I wish now we had gone to college together, and I still miss her. She was the first person outside of my family to die. She was killed in a car accident in the South Bay quake of 1984. I still get sad when I think of us as Pommies.

Soon enough I was back in LA. The trouble was I almost never left the Cal Tech campus. I worked hard hoping to impress Sister Tina on that day in the future when we would meet again. We had six hours of advanced math every day—and homework—and our instruction was geared to Cal Tech's mainframe. I had never seen a computer, and it was awesome. But my math skills put me near the top of the class. The big Cal Tech pool was right by my dorm—and swimming took up the rest of my time. But all I had was a plum-colored, shirred Speedo swimsuit with a racing back. I wished it were two-piece. Some of the other girls were very sexy. I was still a bit of a stick figure, and wished for more curves. But at least my boobs had started to bloom, and were more than buds.

Our group leaders took us on a trip to Disneyland in Anaheim, which reignited my memories of family visits there. We got to see the new Bear Country part of the park, which wasn't there when I went with Brindee. I remembered being on the Skyride with him. He was so bold—lifting both his hands high. But his bravery was probably a sign of what was to come. A sudden flood of memories forced me to confront what was proving a hard question to answer. Why hadn't I run down after class to see my old house in San Gabriel? Cal Tech was close enough. But something kept stopping me. I could walk there and get back in time for dinner in the dorm. But I resisted making the visit. I felt somehow that seeing my old home would mean I hadn't changed a lot. But I had. I was going to be a nun. Perpetual Mercy academy followed by three years at DSM were turning me into one. So I stayed away from San Gabriel and went swimming instead.

But my roommate, a shy girl from Keene, New Hampshire, needed a California gift for her mom. The best thing might have been to get something Mexican on Olvera Street. But instead I retraced with her my memory of a typical trip with my mother to Lake Avenue, by Neiman Marcus. On the way, we passed an In-N-Out hamburger place I remembered because I used to feed taco chips to the sparrows that made a meal stealing tidbits from the restaurant's outdoor tables. They were just so cute. I remembered seeing the boldest of the tiny birds hop around on our table to peck at the chips closest to me. The *dejá vue* put me in a strange mood. We decided to buy shakes. And then I got the surprise of my life. The counter girl serving them was my childhood friend and San Gabriel neighbor Daisy Sanchez!

We recognized each other instantly, even though Daisy had filled out faster. She was wearing denim ultra-short shorts and a tee-shirt that said 'Cherry Garcia.' I saw she was bra-less. She left the counter and hugged me. She told me she was still living on the same street in San Gabriel. If we walked back together I could see where I used to live—and show my old home to my roommate. But the girl from New Hampshire suddenly needed to go. Daisy pointed to the toilets and then jumped into a booth with me. We started talking about school. She was a year behind me, at Pasadena City College, where she got financial aid. But she had to work in the summer. Just then Louise returned from the 'bog' as she called it. She had something crumpled up in her hand. "Look what I found," she told them. It was baby pink lollipop cotton panties. "Somebody must have lost their undies," she said laughing.

But Daisy didn't join in the laughter. "Are you stupid or something?" she said looking at both of us. "I guess you're retarded in Baltimore. Lots of kids leave their little-girl panties here. They want to give their guys a surprise with a thong. They change here—somebody must've forgot these. Give them to me. I'll put them in the back. Some girls' moms keep tabs."

I was amazed by the speech. Daisy may have been a year behind me academically, but her explanation said she was obviously way ahead when it came to boys. We just stared at her. And our amazement turned into a bigger shock when she asked, "Don't you know what thong panties are? Haven't you ever put something sexy on your pussy for a guy? I like it—it makes me hot."

I didn't know what to say. My roommate was practically cringing with embarrassment. But our speechless reaction didn't matter because just at that moment a boy jumped into our booth and draped his arm around my Latino girlfriend. "You off now?" he asked her with a look that made me certain the little-girl panties really belonged to Daisy herself. She should have seen what I and my peers wore underneath at DSM.

"I came to give you a lift," Daisy's boyfriend went on. He was tall, wearing jeans and a black Dead Head tee-shirt. He looked maybe five or six years older than Daisy. There was no question that he was good looking, with a blond cowlick and to-die-for brown eyes. But I didn't like something about his mouth. It was very thin, and much too wide, and when he smiled at us he looked like he was baring his teeth. The rest of his features were small on a longish face. On his muscular arms, I could see a tattoo that said 'I'm Grateful.' Daisy gave him a kiss immediately, and said, "Hey Ralph, let's get out of here. I'm up for a ride." But the smile she gave him said she was up for more than that.

He barely seemed to notice my roommate or me. But he paused for a second after he got out of the booth with her, asking, "Who's this?"

"Just old friends," she told him.

"Maybe not old enough!" he remarked. He was looking right at me when he spoke. "Tell 'em to come to our pool party on Saturday if they want some candy." Then he laughed.

My roommate's face was down into her shake. Daisy just ignored her and spoke directly to me, "Gotta go. See you. Come by if you want Saturday afternoon. You know where it is." Then she let him pull her out of the booth.

10

O n Saturday, just before lunch, I started walking back to my past. My hair was down, long straight and black. I had on jean shorts and my oversize DSM hooded sweatshirt on top of my one and only Speedo. The smog had lifted, exposing a southern California day. It was hot and dry, but everything was bright, bright green and lush. The desert had bloomed. Finally, I stood alone in front of the house I had grown up in. But I was disappointed to find it worn and wan. The white stucco had faded to gray. The red tile roof was dirty and dull. I wondered who lived in the house now because the present was not the past. It should have been, but I was only learning that it never is. Most of the lawn sprinklers weren't working. They would all be on if my father was alive. He was just so absolutely proud of his small patch of green front lawn. I took a long last look and then continued down the very quiet street in my flip flops. I saw a pickup parked right in front of Daisy's place. But other empty driveways said most of the neighboring families were out on Saturday shopping trips.

You probably know what's coming. I surely didn't. Some people always do. They are never clueless. I was still young enough to want to experience life without early warning. I wanted it just as it happened. Whenever I did a jigsaw puzzle with Granny Sharp, she always began by sorting pieces into groups of roughly matching shapes, looking for edge pieces to make the frame. I just didn't see any fun in that approach. I never made the border first. I liked to pick up a brightly colored or oddly shaped piece and then stir the pile of pieces for something just as bright or complex and try to fit it together. So forgive me because I never guessed what was coming as I stepped into the future.

My steps flip flopped up the Sanchez' driveway. Daisy's house looked unchanged except for overgrown landscaping. I couldn't remember a pool in the past. It was probably new. The quiet felt like nobody was home. But I soon heard loud music blaring from the back of the house. My ears tracked the Grateful Dead playing 'Truckin.' I remembered the tattoo on Daisy's boyfriend. A boom box was blasting from the raised deck of an outdoor Jacuzzi—not a real pool. I counted only three people in the tub, which was boiling away with foam. They were screaming to the music. I saw Daisy locked around her boyfriend. She waved me into the hot tub, pointing to the other boy and crying out, "Say hello to Steve." Then she went back to kissing her boyfriend. Steve was taller and bouncing in the water by himself. Wow. He looked perfect, with jet black hair cut short and blue eyes and a great smile.

I got up on the deck, kicked off my flip flops and got out of my shorts and hoodie. I wondered if the steamy water would bleach out my X-back racer. The color was already drab enough. Steve moved to the edge of the tub, reaching out a pair of long arms to help me in. But I just jumped into the hot foam. For a second the heat of the water and the strong bromine fumes made me dizzy. Steve welcomed me with an "Atta girl—glad you came!" greeting. Daisy was glued to her boyfriend. I let myself go almost underwater, soaking the ends of my hair, and then popped up.

Steve had closed the gap between us, and he grabbed my hands, leading me into the dance rhythm as the water whirled around us. Quickly he pulled me in closer, then unexpectedly leaned in and started kissing me on the neck. I didn't know what to do, but he looked so nice. I didn't want to spoil the fun. I felt I could trust him. I thought he was just kidding. But then I felt his chest push right against me. He wanted to kiss me on the mouth. But I pulled back. My lips still belonged to Sister Tina. The Dead were now doing 'Ripple.' It was just at that moment that I froze with the realization that none of them had any clothes on. They were totally nude. And Daisy and her boyfriend were actually doing it. I had never seen anyone do it, but I knew enough to guess right. Daisy was straddling him and bouncing up and down. I stared at her, seeing her hair bobbing above the swirling surface of the tub as her back arched. "Now baby, now," she suddenly yelled.

As I stared at Daisy, Steve passed me a cigarette. It was strong, but I drew on it and then choked on the heavy acrid smoke, letting the cigarette fall into the water. Steve quickly scooped it up, saying "You gotta be careful, little girl. That stuff costs money." Suddenly he moved closer, and before I could step back, he pulled down the straps of my swimsuit, trapping my arms. I felt my nipples press into his wet skin. Then he kissed me again, breathing smoke into my mouth. For a second his embrace excited me, but I was frightened with my arms trapped. Everything was happening way too fast. I was going to scream out that I was going to be a nun. Then Daisy crossed through the hot foamy water with something in her hand, and her boyfriend came around yelling, "We gotta warm up your friend Daisy girl. She needs a drink." Then he threw his arms around my neck and pulled me underwater.

There was no air and I swallowed a mouthful and my eyes burned and they wouldn't let me up. I was drowning and kicked out, but

Daisy pulled the rest of my Speedo off before they let my head up. I gasped and choked, but Daisy quickly slid a bottle into my mouth, almost chipping a tooth, and poured a fiery drink down my throat. "You need some tequila to loosen you up," she cried out, "we're only having fun." She took a swig from the bottle herself. Then she kissed me, and before I could close my lips she sprayed more tequila right into my mouth. Daisy raised her own boobs with her hands and she rubbed them right into mine. And then her boyfriend pulled me underwater before I could barely catch a breath.

I struggled to break free, but he was stronger than me. I wanted to scream, but my throat was raw and the boom box was roaring with 'Johnny B Goode.' I tried to kick free, but the two of them dragged me to the side of the tub. Steve was sitting waiting for me. He lifted me up onto him. I was horrified because I knew what he was going to do. I could feel his stiffness. Daisy grabbed my legs, forcing me onto him. She was screaming right in my face, "Now I'm going to show you something else you little bitch—now you can find out what my father did to me because you got us caught stealing the flowers. And I was practically a baby."

Hearing her, I fought as hard as I could. What I once thought was a joke that would soon end was now bitter revenge. I prayed to Sister Tina. Steve was chanting, "Be good, be good," over and over again. I struggled, but his hands were clamped onto my breasts, holding me, and his nails were digging in. "Just relax and enjoy it girl," he commanded. And suddenly, pain told me he was inside me. Just at that moment, I gathered myself into a coil and broke free. I leaped out of the Jacuzzi using all the strength I had. I was naked, but I quickly grabbed my clothes, leaving my flip flops behind, and crying and gasping and shaking I jumped off the deck and ran back down the driveway. There was no pursuit. I heard them laughing. That was the worst thing. "Hey—there's more tequila," Daisy yelled after me.

"You missed the best part girl," Steve's voice called out. It was followed by more laughter.

I was a complete mess. I got my clothes back on behind some bushes. I had to walk back to Cal Tech barefoot. I threw up twice along the way. My shorts were wet between my legs. I pulled the long hoodie as far down as it would go hoping to hide any visible stains. I got back to the dorm on the strength of my anger. It was self-directed. I told myself that I would never be so powerless again, never. Never.

I cried myself to sleep on four Tylenol's. In a few days the summer program ended, but I sobbed quietly all the way back to New York. My mind alternated between grief and fear and anger. I was crying because I could never go back to California again. That meant my father was truly gone forever. And I was afraid the rape had made me pregnant. As soon as school started in the fall, I went to Mass and prayed, and it was not long before a heavy period erased my fears. But most of all, I hated Daisy and her friends because I knew they were only tools. I was no innocent. I was being punished because of what I had done with Sister Tina. This was a sure sign. I had been raped because I loved Sister more than our Lord. I would never be allowed to marry Christ.

And then, just as I finished my last months at DSM, an even greater tragedy struck. Guatemala was devastated by the worst floods in its history. The area near Livingston, across from Puerto Barrios on the other side of the mouth of the Río Dulce, was totally destroyed. The 'Luba Awanselula,' the Christian school, was washed away. Sister Tina drowned trying to save a boatload of small children. It overturned in the wild and rough, muddy river. Her death was announced during Mass, and I was stunned and sobbed while praying in my pew. Our union had been so brief that there were times I thought it was only a dream, but the angry pounding in my heart and head and body said it was real. This was the final sign that I could never be a nun. God had seen that deep inside I could never give myself to anyone who didn't know what I was truly worth. And I still didn't even know how much that was.

11

My mother called. "I'm going to your graduation? Yes?"

"I'll just take the bus back to New York."

"But I want to see you graduate."

"I'm not becoming a nun. I just told the Sisters. It's better if I leave now." Hearing only shocked silence after my statement, I rushed to fill it. "Just don't come down."

"Well, come home then," my mother finally said. "I bought a condo for us—two bedrooms. It's in a 'white-brick.' You know—an apartment house on the Upper Eastside."

"Mom—I have to go."

So I sent two boxes home and took the bus back to New York. I didn't want to face the other girls in the Holy Orders group. They were graduating as Novitiates. Soon they would be wed to Christ, our Lord. All I earned was a BEd in math. At the time I was sure I got the worst part of the bargain—but Ms. Money never regretted it. Instead of graduation robes, I put on my runners and a light-blue fleece track suit I'd worn to class and got a seat on Trailways. That was the best I could do after four years of religious college. Real women's clothes would have to wait, and what I didn't know about makeup would have filled volumes.

Happily I got a place to myself. But I ran out of luck when we stopped in Philadelphia. As soon as the new passengers boarded, a girl plopped into the space next to me.

"Betcha don't remember me," said my new blonde seat mate.

"Alice!"

We had met only once after the retreat. It was before college— in the summer right after I graduated from Perpetual Mercy. I went with my mother to the Brooklyn Museum for a major Renaissance Painting exhibit. We met Alice Powers by accident.

We practically bumped into her as she stood before a full length Portrait of Eve. It was by the 15th-century Brussels painter Hans Memling, who shows her nude and standing with a golden apple in her outstretched hand. Characteristically, my mother spoke first, just as a wave of passing viewers pushed us into Alice. "Just imagine giving away Paradise for an apple! That's as bad as selling Manhattan Island for $24!" she whispered loudly to me.

Alice turned around laughing, and we immediately recognized each other. She gave me a hug, and I introduced her to my mother.

"I was fascinated by her hair—a hip-length perm. Maybe I should try it," Alice said at the time.

But it was Eve's face that attracted me. It was really like my own. The shape was almost an exact match. It wears a subtle smile as it contemplates the apple held delicately between her thumb and forefinger. The painting has a northern Renaissance look, not as real as Italian faces I saw elsewhere in the exhibition. After walls covered with traditional portraits of the Virgin, I found Memling's "Eve" fascinating. The apple seems to mirror her slight breasts. Both are untouched—perfect in their purity. They signify Eve's innocence. She doesn't know right from wrong. The apple seems to puzzle her. How could enjoying it be sinful? I bought a postcard of the painting that I tacked up in my dorm room at Divine Sepulcher of Maryland. But it didn't survive my college years. Nor had I seen Alice Powers since.

She had the same very feline face with cat's eyes. I couldn't remember where she had gone to school, but I remembered it was in Philadelphia. I wondered if she had just graduated. "How's school?" I asked.

"I quit."

"What happened?"

"Look—you don't even know where I went!" But then Alice added, "Hey!—I'm sorry. I went to Moore in Philadelphia. It's women only. It's an art and design school."

"Were you into fashion?"

"No way! The computer is going to be everything. I wanted to do computer assisted design—CAD—especially for advertising. But they don't get it yet. I should have gone out to San Francisco. So I'm not going back. They're just too stupid here. Philly is a dump anyway. I'm doing some modeling in New York now. Excuse me I have to go," Alice concluded. She jumped up from her seat and ran to the back of the bus. She returned a few minutes later.

"Sorry, buses make me sick. And I needed to throw up anyway. Too much food isn't good on the runway. You know? When I'm dressed for the photographers." Her above-the-knee boots of black suede were pressed against my legs. "I can make a thousand a day!"

For a second, I thought the reference to a runway meant she was a flight attendant. But then I realized she was talking about fashion modeling. My second mistake was not recognizing bulimia when I saw it. But the 1980s were just starting, and the media need for women who looked like painted skeletons was only in first gear. Then I blurted out the truth. "I graduated—but I'm not completing Holy Orders."

"What about that little hottie Sister gal-pal of yours?"

I bristled, but told her, "She went to Guatemala to teach for the Order."

"She was really something. I guess you went to Baltimore because of her. After the retreat, I left something in the room. I had to come back for it real late. I saw the two of you in bed."

I went rigid in the bus seat. But I couldn't escape. "It wasn't that way," I stammered back. Then I cried. "I loved her. She's dead. There was a flood—in Guatemala."

"Okay, okay, I'm sorry. Just don't get upset with me. In case you haven't figured it out yet—I like girls too." And then she brought her face right around to me and said laughing. "I'd kiss you right now except I know it would make you pee in your pants."

I cringed. I felt like I didn't know anything. But Alice just lowered her seat as far back as she could, turned her face into the head rest and soon fell asleep. I hid in my book. I was reading *Clan of the Cave Bear*. I was still into historical fiction, and Jean Auel's novels were as far back in the past as you could go. When we parted at Port Authority in New York, Alice borrowed my pen and scribbled her phone number into the book, saying, "Call me baby. I really want to see you. Sorry about your friend."

All I could think of was how strange our chance meeting had been. The bus had made only one stop between Baltimore and New York. Alice was almost the only new passenger. It was a chance meeting for sure. I hadn't learned yet that when fate moves the pieces they never just fall where they may.

My mother wanted me to meet her by Columbus Circle. "I want you to see a place I'm selling. Then we can have lunch at Maurice in the Hotel Parker Meridien. It's the best restaurant in town."

"I'll come, but save the lunch money."

"Don't worry. Things have changed for me. You'll see. That's just why I want you to look at this place. If you're not going into the Convent for life—you need to see how the other half lives. Don't ever be cheap. This condo is staged. That means it's been furnished by a designer to give it sex appeal. The asking price is five-million. It's on the thirtieth floor. Central Park West. You can see the river, Central Park and Lincoln Center. You really have to see it. I'm showing it at lunch time—we can eat after."

But even with taking the bus from Baltimore, I was still early. I walked uptown, surprised by the summer fashion in the shop windows.

The clothes were beautiful. Alice was modeling? New York was so different. And now I lived here. Apartment towers were rising everywhere. My eyes followed a giant crane to its top, but I could hardly keep track of the stories. Over sixty. Outside the building my mother had sent me to, I paused and checked the address. My mom the real estate agent! I went into the sales office, but it was empty. Lunch time. My mother was on the thirtieth floor. I decided to wait outside the apartment. But when the jet-speed elevator that took my breath away stopped, I was in the foyer of the apartment itself.

I was drawn to the gigantic floor-to-ceiling window overlooking Central Park. The view was magnificent. You could actually see the shape of the park framed by its bordering buildings. But there was no sign of my mother. I worried, wondering. *Was she looking for me by the Columbus monument?*

I felt like Goldilocks walking around the three Bears' house. The furniture was ultra-modern. I had never seen anything so beautiful. A fabulous painting of jet black gigantic jagged vertical strokes hung over what had to be a designer sofa in white leather. I had seen a painting like it in Baltimore, a Robert Motherwell. It had to be worth more than a million. My steps were soundless on the deep wall-to-wall carpeting. I decided to peek into a small bedroom. One after another they were empty. But then I looked into the huge master bedroom. And right in the King-size bed I saw my mother. She was with a man! I wanted to scream.

Her black skirt was pushed up around her waist. She was kneeling on a huge bed. She was kneeling on top of a man. His pants were down. They were having sex! My mind said it couldn't be. Not my mother. But my eyes said it was. And my cheeks turned redder than anything.

My mother still didn't know I was in the room. But the man on his back was looking right at me as I stood frozen, reliving the primal scene. I felt his eyes map me with a single look. He had steely gray hair and florid skin and a hawk-like face. His voice was loud and hoarse when he said, "Look honey, why don't you drop your pants too. I'll bet your sweet little box would love a horsey ride."

What a creep! And if it was bad enough to catch my mother in bed with a man, believe me watching her go through the mental equivalent of a heart attack was even worse. For a second I thought she would die. She whipped her head around and saw me standing totally paralyzed. The look on her face was pure shock. I tried to return it with a look that said I knew about these things. It must have failed. In a second she was off the man and pulling her clothes together. She was fast. The man hadn't moved—but then my mother slapped him hard right on the face.

"That's for hitting on my daughter you little shite!" she screamed at him. And then she slapped him hard again on the other cheek, saying, "And that's for even thinking I would pimp her to a greasy slob like you!"

"You're fired!" the man screamed back.

But we had already fled. Thank god the elevator was still waiting where I had left it.

12

My mother was in tears. "I'm sorry about that," she sobbed out. "Really sorry."

"Who was he?" I asked, my mind still reeling. I felt like throwing up. "A buyer?"

"No, he's the listing broker. I had to do sex with him to get a piece of the change. I could have gotten a quarter percent on $5 million." She was already going through her bag for repair make-up. "If you don't give him what he wants—you don't get the hot properties!"

"I didn't mean to get here early." I apologized, but part of me was actually glad. It was the first time in my life I had seen my mother as a woman!

"Don't be sorry. It means nothing. Or maybe it does. I'm sorry too. But in real estate it's either 'the nooky road to the top or the rocky road to nowhere.' That's what they say. Let it be a lesson. I've changed a lot since daddy died. A woman has to use what she has to make it in a man's world. We have to pay more for every little thing. Wait 'til you have to get your hair done in New York."

"I shouldn't have walked in."

"No—if you learn this then you'll know something they don't teach you in school. They say the only reason man could walk upright was so that he would have his hands free to play with himself."

Could this be my mother?

"Don't worry. This won't set me back. I'm developing my own listings now. While you've been studying to be a nun, I've become a very good broker. It makes me happy. The important thing is I'm making good money. I sat around with your grandmother for way too long. You heard about that woman the other day—she's training to be the first woman in space. And I'm into space too—only it's living space."

My mother stepped into the street to hail a cab for us. A driver saw her signal immediately. "We can skip lunch. There's food in the apartment. I want you to see your new home."

My eyes just couldn't believe the towering buildings, as the cab bounced uptown. "How far is it?"

"We're close now. What about school?"

"I've graduated. But I won't be a Novitiate. I told them."

"I'm glad because I'm out of the convent too. I'm through mourning for your brother and your father and taking care of my mother. It's my turn to be me. I'm not some little Southern California homemaker, or some Brooklyn housekeeper. I got my real estate license, and the important thing is I'm good at it. With these prices even after everybody's cut I can still make three percent. So turning on the sex appeal when I need to doesn't bother me. Winner takes all! I could even get married again."

"Mom—you belong to me," I said, hugging her in the cab.

"No! You belong to you."

As we entered the lobby, I couldn't help but notice a huge portrait hanging near the elevator. "Whose picture is that?"

"That's Leona Helmsley. They hang in all her buildings. She's the biggest of the big in real estate. They call her the 'Queen of Mean.'"

"What did she do?"

"She screwed a lot of rental tenants out of a lot of money by forcing them to buy condos. They thought it was 'own it or leave it.'"

I stared at the face in the portrait. The woman's eyes were hard. The cheeks were drawn in. A lean look.

"But she got lucky the third time around," my mother continued. "She married a very old, very rich man. She started sleeping with him when he was still married." She explained that Leona's husband was the real estate magnate Harry Helmsley, who was responsible for hanging her portrait across his empire. "She knew enough by then not to waste what god gave her on a poor jerk."

I was shocked by the sudden bitterness in her voice. *Was she talking about my father?* "She only made one mistake. She told her maid that 'only little people pay taxes.' The IRS didn't like that."

"What happened?"

"It's still in the courts. But my life now is all about money. It just makes me feel good. I'm worth it. It's like I've been reborn.

And I've got a nice man to show you. We reconnected on the cruise I took."

Only a week later, she introduced me to Brian Connelly. (Pay attention to him because he lasts right until the end of my story. He's my gold standard—someone I could always count on.) The occasion was a surprise Sunday brunch at the legendary Luchow's—supposedly to celebrate my graduation. But I knew my mother was anxious for my approval.

The German steak house's name confused me into expecting Chinese food. And I was awkward even in medium heels and a white dotted Laura Ashley preppy dress, both bought with my mother. I still hadn't attempted makeup. My mother was wearing a black Lilly Pulitzer suit. We arrived early and were led through a maze of rooms filled with Tiffany stained glass, potted plants, darkly gleaming wood-work and waiters in black aprons. Shiny brass plaques announced chamber after chamber. I saw one labeled for Lillian Russell and thought of my Pommie days. Finally we were seated in a mirrored conservatory where mounted stuffed animal heads stared down at us.

"Now when you meet him, don't be upset with me," my mother suddenly pleaded. "This wasn't just a shipboard romance. His wife is dead, and I'm marrying him. Now you know."

"Oh, Mom!"

"Your dad's been dead for over seven years. I loved him even though your Grandmother called him 'a glorified bus driver.' She knew about Irish men. If they're smart they're politicians who drink, if not they drink and haul trash. Drinking's their job. That's what she told me. Your Dad was a huge improvement—but if I'd known he was gambling in the stock market I would have strangled him. He cost us more money than I thought I'd ever see again."

"Can't we talk about something else?"

"I still love him," she said. I saw tears forming in her eyes. "It just hasn't been easy," she went on. "At least he never tried to dump me for a newer model, one of those smart looking flight girls."

"If you keep talking like this I will go into a convent after all." I spoke harshly.

But just at that moment, one of the mounted animal heads seemed to fall into the seat next to me. Only it was a man instead.

"Brian Connelly," he said in a hoarse baritone, as he held out his hand. I grabbed it like a person about to fall. I was surprised, and had absolutely no idea what to say. He was smiling. And his skin was as red as my father's, the man he would be replacing in my life.

"Pleased to meet you," my mother filled in.

Connelly poured some white wine that had arrived with him. He was older than I expected. But he was the same age as my father. He only looked older because my father's permanent image had been engraved in memory at the time of his death. Connelly's red face hid behind a big silver mustache, bushy silver brows and a full head of gray hair. He was shorter than my father, but still taller than my petite mother. His hazel eyes twinkled at me, and I couldn't stop myself from liking him. And he had been a friend of Michael Worth. We could speak openly—there would be no need for pretense.

"Did you know my Dad well?" I just had to ask him.

"Flew missions with him in Korea, but I quit Eastern to go with Delta. I wish he had too." Then he got to the point. "I don't think he intended for your mother to die a widow. I hope you're happy about this."

I was totally disarmed by the speech. His logic was perfect. And I didn't think my suddenly changed mother should stay single.

But Connelly was pulling something out of his vest pocket. He was smiling. "Well," he took charge, "there's good news too. Your mother got everything she could, but there was one thing she didn't know about. I got this from the pilot's union. You're totally entitled to it." He handed me an envelope. "It goes with graduation."

I didn't know what to expect. It had to be some sort of graduation present, hopefully a check. But inside the envelope was a letter on the stationery of the Airline Pilots Union and a certificate with a raised seal from someplace called The Travel Academy. They were giving me a free one semester Flight Attendant training course starting in September. I knew it was from my father. This was what he wanted for me. Connelly was his agent, but I hugged him warmly. He was embarrassed. I kissed my mother.

"That will help you get a good job if you want to fly. These days the airlines only take attendants with degrees plus extra training. I didn't know it was a union benefit. You were entitled to it."

"It's perfect. I want to travel!" And then I burst into tears, sobbing and gasping. They just sat and stared at me.

"I'm sorry. I didn't know you wanted to be a nun so much," my mother looked at me.

But I just shook my head and continued to cry. Finally I dug out the crumpled letter in my handbag and handed it to her.

"My God! That's like $100,000!" she gasped.

"I'll pay it back. I'll work and pay it back. It's my fault. I couldn't go into the convent. I didn't want to join their stupid Order. Now I have to pay them for my last two years before they will officially give me a degree. I'm done. I passed all the courses. But I need to pay the bill to get my degree." Connelly was reading the letter and interrupted as I calmed down. "Well I think we can find a way to borrow this. You can make payments. Over a real long time."

And hearing him, my mother cheered up. "Well you got two years of school out of them—that's something. I can help with some of it too."

"And I'll back you at the bank," said Connelly. "Now let's eat."

And suddenly I knew exactly what I was going to do. It was simple. I would move in with Alice Powers, and ask her about getting a modeling job. I would pay back as much as I could on the loan. And after the summer I would leave for Minneapolis, finish the Flight Attendant training program, get hired and fly. *Just what my father wanted!*

13

Maggie and Alice were a striking pair—like a sleek jet-black Bombay short hair and a furry white Angora. They were each 22, about 5-9 in height, completely flat at the tummy and without much of a behind and narrow hips. Alice's larger bones and fuller breasts, radiated a tomboy's sexual attraction. Maggie's was more the sex appeal of a ballerina. The two of them could hardly have a drink together before a man interrupted. But to go any further he would have to pay in cash because what Alice meant by 'modeling' turned out to be dancing at a topless club called the Platinum Bikini Bar, known to its clientele as the 'Push Button Box,' after its initials, or simply 'The Box.'

"Look, I'm funding a startup." Alice told her. "So what if I'm showing my boobs. It's for over $1,000 a week. But just 'til September. I'm going to have $30K in the bank by then. I can get another $3,000 for selling my eggs to a fertility clinic! Altogether maybe $50K with borrowing on cards. Then I'll go after more venture money in San Francisco. Haven't you heard about Silicon Valley?"

I shook my head, and she must have seen the blank expression on my face.

"You know what *Time* put on its cover this year? Not a person—a computer! One day everyone's going to have a website—you'll see."

I didn't know then how smart Alice really was. She was on to the high-tech trend years ahead of everyone. (Today she owns an art gallery in San Francisco—where Eric Zimmerman, the neon artist, just had a show. Her husband is an adjunct professor of programming at Stanford. Neither of them have to work. They're both what Silicon Valley labels 'Cisco millionaires.' I'm really thankful she's stayed a friend for life.)

Alice pushed me into a job at The Box and helped me overcome my worst fears. She promised the tips would be big, and I wanted to wipe out my debt to DSM. She introduced me to the manager, and after his slimy eyes slid all over my body, it only took a minute for him to make me a cigarette girl. Alice took me to a new store called Victoria's Secret for a uniform. I paraded around The Box in a white ultra-mini bikini swimsuit and a black sheer shirt whose tails just covered my nearly bare bottom, with a tray of cigarettes and cigars suspended from my neck. And Alice was right. The tips were big.

As my first night on the job progressed the music got louder, the room darker, the smoke thicker, and the men drunker and more aggressive. They spent their time trying to grab as much flesh as possible from the lap dancers who straddled and bounced on them. The entire club was a hot swirl of nearly-naked women coated with oils and makeup who let themselves be groped more and more as the bills got larger. I worked for tips only, but even after splitting them with the club, I was taking home almost $200 a night from men who paid $5 for a pack of cigarettes and gave me a ten or a twenty. Then they'd tell me to keep the change because the Eighties financial boom, which I knew absolutely nothing about, was accelerating daily.

I had to light what they smoked, which gave them a chance to grab and squeeze my behind. But the groping stopped there, and I quickly moved on to the next customer. Strangely, my almost total innocence protected me. It seemed to drive most of the smokers back to the stage show in a rush, and I was less horrified than I thought. I had never told a soul about what happened to me in the hot tub in Los Angeles—not even Alice. That experience was all I knew about men, and I hadn't yet learned that The Box patrons were no different. I wanted their money. If they wanted to rub my fanny so what. I was using them as much as they used me.

I was stunned the first time I saw Alice dance. In a sleek electric blue satin gown, she went on stage to the left. This was what we called the 'next-up position,' where she just moved rhythmically, caressing herself. There were always three girls on stage at the same time. The dancer in the center was stripping just at the edge of the stage, bumping and grinding with total sexual energy to the music of the Commodores' 'Too Hot Ta Trot.' Men shouted coarsely from the audience, reaching up to shove money into the girl's G-string. When the music switched, the almost completely bare center girl replaced the pole dancer on the right, swinging and flexing to show every aspect of her nakedness.

Alice moved to center stage, stripping to 'Twisted Nerve' from the Damned's *Black Album.* Even the usual raucous din quieted. The man buying a pack of Marlboro's just threw a ten at me and went back to the mosh pit, where they were already throwing money at her. I was mesmerized. Alice was really hot—hotter than anything. Her stripping released blistering heat that burned her entire audience as her blue dress slid down. She kept right on moving to the beat, except to drop lower so a man could stuff a wad of bills into the top of her G-string. Then her bra came off. *Can I ever do that?*

We got back to our apartment on Stanton Street about 3am. Alice just dumped her clothes on the floor and headed for the shower. My neck was sore from carrying the cigarette tray, and I went into the shower right behind her. Alice was surprised, but said nothing. The water was super-hot, and I soaped a sponge and started to rub off Alice's body paint, along with her special mix of body oils whose heavy musk excited her lap dance clients. My mind saw Alice on stage pulling off her gown and dancing completely free with almost nothing on. Suddenly I wanted her. She was just too beautiful for her coarse admirers. I pulled her around to wash between her boobs, lifting them, feeling her nipples stiffen. Suddenly I felt Alice's hand between my legs, soaping my tiny pubic patch. Then Alice's wet arms went around me, and she said excitedly, "If you're going to dance, I have to shave you."

"Not now," I said and kissed her.

"No—now!" Alice insisted. She grabbed shaving cream and a razor and on her knees sprayed soap onto my dark triangle, and then slowly began to shave me. I had never felt so hot and cold at once. The menthol in the shaving cream excited me. The razor slid across my most erogenous zone, stroke by stroke. And when Alice finished, she started to kiss its bare lips. We were both quaking, as Alice's tongue darted into my throbbing cache.

Alice was making five times what I brought home in tips. I needed to move up from cigarette girl to dancer. But the manager didn't agree. "Not so fast. We need to see how much you make as a lap dancer first!"

So I joined the 'Pussy-Posse,' meaning the cocktail waitresses who also worked as lap dancers. The tips were bigger. But Alice laughed, saying "You'll get a raise all right." Then she showed me what to expect, making me sit on her lap, twisting and thrusting to the beat of 'Sister,' Prince's red-hot hit, while she jabbed a stiff carrot between my legs. "Remember the idea is to excite them so they want more. Then you'll get better money. But if they come in their pants they always tip less."

The first night I thought I wouldn't be able to do it. The shame of the hot tub attack came back. But it was followed by anger. Anger wanted me to take advantage of men who thought they could buy me. I was topless now in The Box, wearing just a silky chemise that was split down the middle. My first lap dance was inconsequential because the man was even more frightened of me than I was of him. I twisted on his lap to the rhythm of Aretha Franklin singing, 'You make me feel like a natural woman.' He was too scared even to get hard, and he kept his hands off me. Eventually he sent me to get him a drink and tipped me twenty dollars. It was an easy start that soon got worse. Paunchy men smelling of booze and cigars put their hands on my sides and tried to slide them up to under my breasts, lifting their lap to the beat of the music. Some of them were hard. The worse ones dug their chins into my shoulder and tried to put their lips on my neck. I even tipped a drink over on one of them.

But I soon learned how to handle even the creepiest—and still get a bigger tip. It was ugly, but I was in control. Detached—something convent school had taught me applied. None of it was real. They just couldn't buy me because I was worth more than they were. So all they got for their money was a fiction. And then I saw that it wasn't any different from the Church. Being the Bride of Christ was the same sexual fiction from an opposite perspective. All I was peddling was the illusion of sex. When they talked dirty in my ear, I told them they were too cheap. That way I got even more out of them. I brought home $500 by my third night. The girls at The Box called lap dancing "crochet"—it was their joke word pronounced 'crotch-shay.' Very soon, I was knitting with the big tippers only.

Alice wanted me to go on stage as a dancer. "It's where you make the most!" But I was afraid. We were in bed. She kissed me. I started to cry. Instead of asking me about it, she just held me tighter. She kissed the tears on my face. So I told her. I made my full confession. She already knew about Sister Tina. Now I told her what happened in the hot tub. "That's so terrible," she whispered in my ear. She was crying too. And then she told me, "At Carlisle it wasn't all Nuns. There were Brothers too. One of them wanted me. He just looked so good, and I let him do it to me. At the school. But I got pregnant, and he made me get an abortion. He knew where to go. They know in the church. But you know I still like men. And I love you too."

So I went on stage. It was actually a lot easier. At the front of the platform the glare was so intense I couldn't see the faces. The money was a lot more. I loved the new wave punk-style rock and roll, and I stripped for the first time to 'Uptown,' from Prince's *Dirty Mind* album. In spite of thunder-loud music and smoky air, my feeling of being in control extended to the men I knew were behind the dazzling lights. I made them respond to whatever moves my body made, twisting seductively at the front of the stage, while disconnected hands stuffed money into my G-string. They reached out to paste spit-soaked bills on my skin. It was ugly, but once again all they were getting was a mirage.

But there was something else. I could feel the hostility within their desire. I knew they wanted to shame me. To brand me a whore if they could. Now I really was back in Los Angeles. They wanted to rape me and call it my fault. But my dance was seduction that never gave them what they wanted—even though they paid for it. And I soon realized that it didn't matter. I saw that it wasn't sex that drove the men trying to buy me—it was greed. Their insatiable desire was intended to keep another man from having me. I saw that the money they spit on and then pasted on my skin was intended as a brand signifying possession. But it granted only the illusion of ownership. That was when I took my very first giant step to becoming Ms. Money. I realized that sex and money were the same. Money is a medium of exchange, and sex is no different. Sex is money because sex is the ultimate medium of exchange. And there wasn't enough money in the world to buy me because I couldn't be bought. No one would ever own what I was, who I am, me. Period. Even though, one night the string bag tied to my arm had more than two thousand dollars in it, and I wished every cent of it was mine.

14

Alice was worried. "I never did this for more than six weeks in a row before changing towns and clubs," she told me.

"What happened?"

"You can't trust the guys running the club. They put rats out on the floor who tell you they will get money out for you. And they have guys that slip you marked bills that show up under ultraviolet light. They expect to see them back in your bag. Polly got in big trouble. Didn't you hear?"

I shook my head.

"She got caught trying to smuggle out a 'Billie'! That's a $500 dollar bill—with the face of William McKinley. They locked her in the back room with a heavy hitter client. Nobody's seen her since last night. We need an exit strategy."

"You're right. One guy has been watching me. I can feel his eyes. He stands in the back, always. He's tall. He comes with a bunch of Japanese. Very well-dressed. But strange."

"That doesn't sound too good."

"I wanted to see the Judas Priest concert—it's next month."

Suddenly Alice swore. Ouch. She was ironing a blouse as she talked. But the lights went out. She had blown another fuse.

"We can't wait that long," she said. "No! I got it. We have to blow the fuse there—at The Box! What we need is a distraction—a big distraction. If we can get out in the panic, we can take all our money for the night."

"You mean kill the lights?"

"And set off the fire alarm."

Our plan was simple. Plunge the jam packed strip club into total darkness, pull the fire alarm, start the dancers screaming and turn the crowd into a panicky mob bent on escaping. Then open the massive sliding fire door at the back of the stage and escape into the alley behind it.

"We just need someone to drive us away."

"I know just the man." And I did because I knew Brian Connelly would help us. He was coming for dinner at my mother's, and I knew she wanted me there too. I would bring Alice.

"You can't tell my mother" was the first thing I said to him.

"No can do. Besides we're going to need her too. Do you think you're going back to your place?"

"What do you mean?" Alice interrupted.

It turned out Connelly was way ahead of us.

So we brought my mother into our plans. She almost choked on her food after we explained.

"Look, the money can wait. Just disappear" was her counsel.

"But they rob us every night. We have to pay them half of our tips. What we're taking really belongs to us!" I defended the plan.

"Then screw the bastards!" my mother shocked all three of us. But Connelly winked at me and Alice. My mother wrote down an address and fished out some keys, giving them to him. "The model apartment is empty. You can change there."

"After you change I'll take you to Newark. You'll be safer flying from there. There's a daily 6am flight to Chicago. Switch planes and head for your final destination."

We both kissed him on the cheek, setting off a bright red blush.

Later that night, in bed, I pressed Alice for the rest of the plan. "You didn't say how the fuse gets blown."

"How do you think? I'm going to make the drummer's day. He's mad to fuck me. We get him to cross some wires—and we're out of there!" All the dancers knew that a massive tangle of cables snaked around the stage to an electric panel right near the fire door. They had to concentrate to avoid tripping on them.

Alice had just finished working on a new routine. She was stripping to Sheena Easton's Grammy winner, 'For Your Eyes Only.' She was a smoldering hot James Bond with a man's hat and tie on. On Thursday she asked the drummer to ride home with us. We took him up to our tiny apartment, put on Duran Duran's 'Planet Earth,' and Alice started dancing with him. I made drinks from a bottle of cheap vodka. He pulled out what looked like a plastic prescription vial. It was coke. We did three lines. Alice was kissing him. He fell into bed with her, and I helped pull off his jeans. Alice slipped a condom onto him, and then he was inside her pumping and moaning until he came.

Then Alice changed the rubber and looked at me. I knew exactly what I had to do—in spite of memories of my hot tub experience in San Gabriel. The speed-up from the drug helped. I excited him with my hand and then rode him from the top. It was over quickly, but not before I had my first orgasm with a man. *Better than I expected!*

In the morning we told him what we wanted.

"No problem," he said. "I already blew it once by accident—all I got to do is max the amplifiers. But if anybody finds out we won't be swimming when they pull us out of the river?"

Alice kissed him and told him to meet them back at the apartment and they would split everything three ways.

"Only if we get to do this again." He was looking right at me when he spoke.

"Okay," we answered simultaneously.

"Shit. If we do this right they won't know what hit them."

We giggled back stupidly. The dumber he thought us the better.

I wasn't nervous at all. Even when the slime bag manager told me he wanted to talk with me after closing. Perfect. I whispered the news to Alice, who gave me an 'I told you so' smile. It was the right night—and now it was the right time.

What made it even better was the money. I was getting $100 for a lap dance—all night long. And I scooped up a pile of bills every time I went on stage. After I stripped for the last time, I stuffed a wad of money from my G-string into the mesh bag tied to my arm. I could tell it was a lot. Then I moved to the pole as Alice shifted to center stage. Then the new James Bond theme erupted, and she began to dance super seductively. The music was hitting crescendo after crescendo. I had never heard it so loud. The Box was shaking. And then one of the giant amplifiers exploded with sparks and hissing. The lights went out. I screamed "fire" for real because there was a sudden smell of burning electricity.

It was pitch black. I heard Alice screaming too. Someone else pulled the fire alarm. Loud hooting replaced the music. Screams from the dancers signaled real fright. I ran towards the fire door, suddenly finding Alice's hand in mine. Shit! We couldn't get the massive metal door to slide open. It was jammed stiff in its track. People were climbing onto the stage. It was very close. But someone pushed me aside. I could just make out a man. It was the guy whose eyes hadn't left me all night. The stalker. He threw his shoulder against the door and it slid open with a bang. I felt the fresh air. We were in the back alley. Connelly was waiting for us. We jumped into his limo and pulled away.

Hours later two flight attendants wearing the uniforms of bankrupt Coral Airlines checked in at the Airwest gate. No one gave them a second thought. They boarded a jet for Chicago. The plane took off, carrying Alice and Maggie and the money they had kept.

PART II: BJ HANLON

(1983-1996)

15

In a few minutes you'll be meeting BJ Hanlon, the next man I loved. He is very special, and the father of my beautiful, wonderful and totally exceptional boy, Jason. Since you already know that names matter a lot to me, I hope you can see why Jason is BJ's son literally. I want to be sure to introduce his father in a way that shows his importance to my story. Without him I would never have been renamed Ms. Money. If I hadn't made that transition I'd never be happy, wealthy and wise. And I know you're reading this story to find out how a woman can do that. That's just so important because a lot of women can't. They are programmed for self-defeat, and if there's anything I do not want it's for you to lose to yourself. That would be even worse than losing to a man.

Maggie Worth studied airport codes, airplane configurations, safety procedures, firefighting rules, security plans, passenger health policy, gate agent manuals and FAA regulations. By the end of the day I was exhausted, but by the end of the year I was certified as a flight attendant. United hired me immediately. The airline was the first carrier to operate the new Boeing 767 jet, and was staffing up for expansion in the trans-Pacific market. I moved in with three other San Francisco-based flight attendants sharing a flat in 'Dogpatch,' whose sole advantage was its access to the airport freeway. We were four women in three bedrooms because one of us was always in the air. I was on the 20-hour run from San Francisco to Tokyo and back and felt I really lived on the airplane.

I quickly learned to cadge sleep whenever I could. But one night, on course from Tokyo Narita to SFX, the big jet flew into rough weather. The plane shook, and for a second I thought of my father. But I was too busy to be scared. Crossing the Pacific in a 'heavy' configured for 300 seats is a serious matter. The crew were as intense as the passengers were upset. The sickly smell of vomit filled the cabin. I was tired, but I had to stand and coax a Japanese woman out of the lavatory, while other impatient passengers backed up in the aisle. Finally, the pilot lifted us out of the turbulence, and the cabin settled down. The passengers slept. I tried to nap in an empty row at the back of the plane, but a charge of adrenaline kept me awake. Instead of a nap, I stared at the movie flickering on the cabin monitors.

It was Barbara Stanwyck in the role of Lily Powers. She's a waitress during Prohibition, in her father's Pennsylvania mill-town speakeasy. He uses her to attract a rough crowd of steel-worker customers. *We know how that works.* Her only friend is a grandfatherly shoemaker, a German immigrant, who shows Lily a marked passage from Nietzsche. It's about power, and so he tells Powers, "Go to the city and learn how to use men to get what you want."

When an explosion destroys the bar, Lily hops a freight to New York City, trading sex with a Railroad Dick for a pile of straw and a ride. Walking the streets to find a job, she passes a towering sky-scraper. The camera pans to its nameplate—Gotham Trust. She rushes inside and encounters a personnel man who asks, "Have you had any experience?"

"Plenty!" she replies and pulls him into an empty office.

This is her first encounter as she sleeps her way to the top. Stage by stage and man by man she moves up—always more glamorous and always in a more important position. The camera work was incredible. As Lily rises, the camera repeatedly pans up the skyscraper's art deco façade, always working its way towards the building's top, while the orchestra plays the 'St Louis Blues.'

Her next man, John Wayne in a bit part, recommends her for promotion to her next partner, Douglass Dumbrille, which brings Lily into the executive suite. Once there, she ensnares Ned Stevens (Donald Cook), a rising young executive engaged to Ann Carter (Margaret Lindsay), literally the boss's daughter. Lily pulls off a brilliant scheme, which has her locked in an embrace with Stevens just as Ann walks in on the two of them. But bank president JR Carter confronts Lily, demanding that she give up Ned. She turns on her charms, and the older man installs her in a luxury Park Avenue apartment. Ned is still madly in love with her, and tracks her to the love nest where she is in bed with Carter. He shoots his potential father-in-law, then himself. *Why don't they make movies as good as this?*

Lily attempts to blackmail the bank for $15,000 in return for keeping her love letters out of the newspapers. But Courtland Trenholm (George Brent) calls her bluff. The playboy grandson of Gotham Trust's founder, he has been elected the bank's new President. She claims she is nothing more than 'a victim of powerful men.' Trenholm, softening during their meeting, gives her a job in the bank's Paris office, thinking she will soon quit. But when he goes to Paris, he is surprised to find Lily still working for the bank and a success. He marries her, but the bank fails, and he is indicted.

He begs Lily to return the million-dollar diamonds he gave her. Lily says 'No.' Trenholm shoots himself. *End it right there,* I thought. But I forgot about *Hollywood.* As the ambulance sirens its way to the hospital, Trenholm opens his eyes. He smiles at Lily, who is sobbing with recrimination. He still loves her! And the EMT tells Lily he will live. There go the jewels!

Soaring at 500 miles per hour, almost thirty-five thousand feet above the Pacific, dead tired and buckled into a seat in a dark cabin, I knew I was meant to see the film. My mother would have loved it, to say nothing of Granny Sharp. Lily used what she had to get what she wanted. *Just what was wrong with that?* What had my mother called it, 'the nooky road to the top'? My stew roommates had revised that to 'the high altitude pussy flight path.' In spite of the airline's zero-tolerance sexual harassment policy, some of the best flights went to women attendants who traded favors with the pilots. Some women do and some women don't. Is it wrong for a woman to choose money over love? *Why is it that only the prostitute gets arrested?*

16

My drifting into dreamland at 35,000 feet was interrupted by a hand on my shoulder—a heavy hand, a man's hand. *Had I overslept?* Then I thought a passenger on his way to the lav had missed grabbing the seat back to steady himself. I looked up, and my mind responded automatically. *He wasn't main cabin. He must have walked aft from first-class? Was the first-class lav tied up?* Then the hand shook me gently, demanding my attention, and a big body dropped into the empty seat next to me. I got the shock of my life. I knew his face! *What was HE doing here?*

I recognized the high dome of the forehead I had last seen at The Box. *Could it be?* I reached up and quickly snapped the reading light on, and in the flash, before I snapped it back off, I saw the features collected in the bottom half of his large oval face that said exactly who he was. It was the face that belonged to the man who stared hard at me night after night but always kept his distance. And now I was sure he was the same man who had thrown himself at the jammed fire door. Without him Alice and I would have been caught. *Why had he done it?*

"I'm sorry, sir. I was asleep. I'm on break." I stalled. "Is there something you need?" I faked another question, trying to slow down my heart. I had to find out if this was about our escape from the strip club. But then my fears ignited my anger. It was the movie all over again. The best thing would be to pretend I'd never even seen him. I was a flight attendant now.

His lips parted to show a perfect set of gleaming white teeth. "I think the door on the First Class lav must be jammed. I came back here. The last time we met, you were having trouble with a door, do you remember?"

My mind was set on denial. He had mistaken me for someone else. I was the wrong girl. No one would recognize me in my uniform. I was a certified flight attendant, and anyone threatening a crew member would be in for it. *But he had helped us.* Just at the critical moment—when we needed help most of all. We would never have gotten the heavy metal door open without him. *What does he want now? Maybe it's all right.* One thing for sure, I won't be able to talk with him alone for long.

"I saw two people go into the First Class lav," he went on. "They haven't come out. It sounds like they're pulling off their clothes, you know, trying to get into the Mile High Club."

He spoke in low tones. But he had a funny smile. He was telling me that he knew who I was. The Mile High Club was about having sex in flight. On one trip, I had caught a couple under a blanket and alerted the Crew Chief. It was true that the larger First Class lavs were sometimes used for the same purpose. Okay. I played it straight. "Are you making a formal complaint? Just put your call signal on. I'm not assigned to First Class." But then my temper spilled over, "Look, just tell me what you want! We can't go on whispering here all night. I'll get in trouble."

"What do you think I want? I didn't come back here to find an empty toilet." He was calm.

"I don't know," I snapped back. "I wish you'd tell me." I was whispering harshly. "Okay. I know you got the fire door open. But I don't want anything to do with the part of the past you saw me in."

"Look, I fly a lot, but I don't do it to hit on flight attendants. I need you to listen—that's all."

"You could've talked to me at the club? Didn't you see enough of me then?"

"Hey! I never bought a lap dance did I? The dancing was your choice. I was just there chaperoning Japanese clients." And then his voice pitched itself for sincerity as he said, "Just have dinner with me—that's all I want. So we can talk. This is business only. Strictly no bullshit."

I couldn't believe it. *He wanted a date?* My anger changed to interest. *A date for business?* Plus I owed him. But before accepting, I added a condition, "Not at your place!"

"Look, I'm not a stalker. I'll send a car. You'll like the restaurant. Just be ready tomorrow at eight. I'm making you a career offer—nothing more."

"Strictly business?"

"Strictly," he said, and for the first time he smiled. He took out a polished, monogrammed, silver case and handed me his business card. He was Boyd J. Hanlon, III, Managing Director, Ledbetter Capital, with an address at Rockefeller Center. "People call me BJ."

"Why should I trust you?" *What does he want with me?*

"That's for you to decide. I knew what you were doing when I helped you. It was more than a fire alarm. Hey—I'm on your side. I'll send a car. Just give me your address. If you change your mind just tell the driver you don't want to come."

His voiced convinced me because it said the choice was mine. *What could I lose?*

He must have seen another attendant approaching because he quickly got out of the seat, adding, "Let me know before we land."

"No. I'm not in first class. No. I'll do it." I whispered my address because I knew all along that I would. *We would never have gotten out of The Box without him.* But I saw the head Flight Attendant approaching, and added a louder, "Certainly, Sir," speaking to his back as he slipped past me.

"What did he want?" the older woman asked me.

"He said the door was stuck on the lav in First."

"He came all the way back here—do you know him?"

"Never seen him," I lied.

"Well you will if you stay on this run. Sometimes he's on board twice a month." Then she asked, "Did you see the movie?"

"It was weird," I answered and closed my eyes.

17

The restaurant turned out to be one of San Francisco's oldest, the Tadich Grill in the financial district. He was waiting for me at the bar. I liked the pose of his tall body and powerful shoulders and narrow waist. His almost bullet head had become familiar, and I knew his face with its too wide mouth, the long nose and the very bright blue eyes. But he was old. Nearer to forty than thirty. This was no kids' game I was playing, even if he did feel safe.

He had on a navy blue blazer—the gold buttons were very bright even in the dim light of the restaurant. I was glad I had bet on glam by borrowing a dress from one of my roommates. It was midnight blue jersey with a high neck. The length was almost perfect, just a bit too big. I wished it was tighter, even after I pulled it in. Naturally I was in heels and pantyhose. I had styled my long jet-black hair myself. The only thing else I put on were the pearls I inherited from Granny Sharp. I hardly ever wore them, but I put them on more as a good luck charm than for looks.

Almost immediately a waiter took us to a very private space in the back of the restaurant. The individual tables were enclosed by tall mahogany booths that gleamed darkly. Stained glass inserts reflected dim lighting. "A good place to talk," he said.

"And not to be seen," I countered. *Was he married? Is that what this is all about?* I wondered.

"Always a good idea when you're talking about money."

"I'm not for sale," I answered flatly.

"But you do know how to sell yourself," he countered, looking straight into my eyes.

I probed his face. But he was hard to read. So I asked him straight out, "Okay—just tell me. Why me?" It was really the only question that mattered. I had thought it over, and even if he was honest, it came to just that. I was forced to wait for his answer by a waiter in a jacket and long white apron.

"Fish or steak?" Hanlon looked at me.

"Fish."

"Have you tried abalone? It's fabulous here."

I shook my head no. I wasn't going to tell him I didn't know what he was talking about. But at least he was trying to please. His voice was softer when he spoke again.

"Pablo," he addressed the waiter, "abalone first then steelhead and we'll drink Montrachet."

"Because I need a partner." He made me wait for his answer.

"But why me?" I couldn't figure out why a man who command-ed so much respect in a restaurant and flew to Japan every month would need me.

"Look—just amuse me," he said. "I want to play a game. What amount comes after $1,000 by tens?"

"First $10,000, then $100,000."

"So what's next?"

"A million," I answered.

"And a thousand million?"

"Okay—so a thousand million is a billion!" I smiled, seeing the boyish look that crept over his face.

"One billion! That's an addictive number. I'm hooked on it. I need OPM!"

"I don't do drugs."

"O-P-M," he spelled it out for me. "It stands for Other People's Money. That's what I'm addicted to."

The waiter came back with the abalone, hot and gleaming white in butter and wine. I watched as he sampled it.

"This is fantastic," I said after trying my portion. He refilled my glass. I saw he was pleased. I took it as a good sign, even if his direction was still lost on me. I was hungrier than I thought, but I forced myself to take very small bites.

"It's really the best thing to eat in San Francisco," he said. "And this is the best place for it."

I said nothing, and continued eating.

"Ledbetter, that's my company, is an asset manager. Right now we've got $500 million in assets under management. Our investors are rich. We invest their money for them. We're judged by our return on assets—that's ROA. Typically we take old East Coast money and invest it out here and in Asia. You've heard of Silicon Valley. Our investors give us discretion. We can buy stocks, bonds, options—or we can use it as venture capital and invest in a high-tech start-up. You probably don't know what an IPO is, an Initial Public Offering, that's where we can make a ton when a private company we've invested in sells shares to the public for the first time. They can go for over fifty times the offering price once they hit the market."

I took it all in, but it still didn't tell me what I wanted to know. *Was he after money or me?* He was good, I realized that. Very, very smart, and great with words. No wonder millionaires were giving him money. At least Alice had told me about Silicon Valley, which was fast becoming the home of all the big tech companies.

The fish came just as he finished. He had ordered a perfect dinner. It was like salmon, only tastier and lighter in color. *'Steelhead,'* he called it. But he still wasn't telling me what I wanted to know most of all.

"The point is like all addicts I want more. It's easier to hit a home run with a big bat. The bigger the assets under management, AUM is what it's called, the more I can make. The thing is I think you can help me make a lot more. That's what I mean by partner.

Once you learn the ropes, you'll be getting rich people to invest with us. You'll help back me up when I go asset gathering."

"I majored in math and religion. Not business. It sounds like you want a Judy for a Punch and Judy show?" *The woman puppet is the one who gets beaten up.*

"Listen, Maggie" he said. It was the first time he had used my name, and we both knew it. "One night I was at The Box. I was with a very smart man. Not one of my Asian clients. He's made a lot of money for me. He saw you perform, and he said I ought to hire you. I thought he was joking."

"'She's just what you need' was what he said. 'I'll bet she knows all there is to know about men and money.' I still thought he was making it up. But then he said, 'Anyone who can stand up and take off their clothes while men stuff money in their underwear is worth giving a try. That's if they have the brains—especially since you haven't found the right person yet.'"

"So I'm following a hunch that he's right."

"I'm old enough to have seen *My Fair Lady*."

"This isn't like that—I'm no Henry Higgins playing games with Eliza Doolittle. I can sell like hell. But Ledbetter needs someone who can front in a new kind of media environment. That's what's changing. It's the web—it's transforming the financial markets— changing the way people view investing. And I want a woman, they can communicate better. I want you for a job I'm practically invent- ing. It's part investment mouthpiece and part market seer and part TV commentator—and being able to strip on stage for money may be just what's needed. I know with the right person I'll get to over a billion. That's who I'm looking for."

"So why not just buy somebody?"

"It didn't work. I need someone who thinks the way I do. I've seen you, and I'm thinking that's you. Not in the same words. But I have this sixth sense feeling about who can do this job. It's better if we start with someone who doesn't know too much."

"When do you get to the part about who I have to sleep with?"

"That's beneath you—and me!" he snapped. "I think you've learned something about money and sex from The Box. But you've got to think beyond money for sex."

"Sorry—I had to ask." I took another drink of wine. It was truly excellent. *That's what money does for you.* But I decided to keep my thoughts about money and men to myself. I had the feeling that when he said brains he meant body. I just didn't know. "You sound like what you want is a shill in a casino."

"It's more than that. But the stock market *is* the biggest casino of all. And the house always wins. It has insider info. I think with the right person I can improve the odds. You'll be gathering information too, after you've learned exactly how we operate." *Kiss the rich, take their money and pump them too. This better be worth it.*

"And you want to be the biggest gambler of all?" I hedged because I had come to the next big question. *Could I really do what he wanted?*

"There's a difference. Gamblers take risks—we don't. We never play games we can't win. It's a rule. You have to understand that."

"How?"

"You'll have to work very hard. All we can give you is six months—you've got to be up to speed by then." He wanted me to start as an intern in New York. My pay would be $10,000 per month with an expense account. "You've got to learn how the investment business works, and you need to pass a license exam. And I need you to be operational by Thanksgiving."

"What is operational?"

"When you know enough. Trust me. We'll know by then if it's workable."

I was surprised—and strangely not surprised. He made sense up to a point. But he had never exactly pinpointed why he had chosen me. So the offer didn't surprise me because I was sure he was holding something back. Exactly what he wanted from me I still didn't know. *My version or his?* But I didn't see how I could lose by going along with the pitch. Mentally, I reserved the right to stop playing his game whenever I wanted to. But I wasn't going to pass on the offer. Not given the money—ten thousand a month and expenses. That was four times what I was making.

"What about my job?"

"I bet you find it boring already."

He was closer to the truth than I wanted to admit. I was already having second thoughts about being a flight attendant—now that the glamour had worn off. And I hated the fear that washed over me during landings. They always made me sick. "How much time do I get? Is this take it or leave it?"

"Go back to New York—visit our offices if you want. I need a yes in a week. Your advance has been drawn. He handed me a check for $10,000. It was made out to me.

"You were certain I'd take this?"

"I'm even more certain now that we've talked."

18

The first thing Frank Agrigento asked me was, "Did BJ send you?" He seemed annoyed. Afraid to speak, I nodded yes. Then he barked a new question. "Where did you go to school?" When I told him, he broke into a smile. "I'm a big believer in Catholic education. Now we know you can at least count beyond two. So I'm putting you in charge of my travel. Be sure I get all the air miles I'm supposed to. Always upgrade me to First Class."

"I was a flight attendant too," I stammered out.

For the first time he smiled at me. "That's a plus! I'll expect the biggest seats and the shortest flights from now on."

I blushed while his personal secretary and two research assistants all laughed.

BJ Hanlon and Agrigento were good friends, and I suspected the original idea to give me a try out came from him. He was Chief Investment Strategist for Pillar Securities. A very, very busy 24-7

man, he spent all day on the phone, talking to important brokers, research analysts, fund managers and the financial media, including radio plugs and television interviews. He broadcast twice a day on the firm's internal radio system, called 'the hoot,' analyzing the market's trend and tipping hot stocks. He made client presentations for the biggest of Pillar's investors. His two juniors turned his ideas into research reports, and his secretary got them posted fast. He had one of the first, just out, Bloomberg machines, and my first job was to get up to speed on it and pass hot news on to him. And when he wasn't doing anything else his eyes were fixed on a huge, wall-size screen pulsing with multi-color technical charts of individual stocks and the financial market indexes all in real time. It was more technology than I'd ever seen in my life.

Agrigento was fifty-five, trim and fit and just above average in height. His hair was jet black, thick and wavy and framed a Roman face with a year round tan. *His brown eyes were just huge.* His pure tenor voice added a ring to his words, but his thoughts were even more impressive. He seemed to know in advance everything that was happening in the market. I soon saw why BJ had made me his intern. Even being nothing more than his gofer gave me a bird's eye view of the business. Research analysts pinpoint stocks that can reward investors, brokers hawk those stocks to their clients earning a commission, and they buy them from screaming traders who also make a profit on the sale.

Every time I came back with a sandwich for Agrigento, he would quiz me. "By now you need to tell me what this business is about," he ordered.

And I knew the answer because I had heard him scream it at one of his assistants. "It's about information."

He seemed surprised that I had hit the nail on the head. I saw it in his big brown eyes, whose color reminded me of a leather flight jacket my father used to wear.

"Why?"

"Because the markets allocate resources based on information so if we know the right information we can guess where money will be allocated," I parroted.

"Analyst, trader broker—there's no candlestick maker." Agrigento told me.

"But they're 'all the King's men'—aren't they?" I asked.

"If you mean they all make money for the house, you're right. But investors get stocks, and stocks are magical. That's what I like most of all." He explained that companies have to grow to survive, and growth takes money. So they go public, issue shares, and shareholders get dividends. As stock prices rise investors can sell and make a capital gain. And the company can keep issuing shares to power new growth.

"But if they issue more shares doesn't that lower the value of the existing shares?" That was my math background talking.

"You're talking about dilution, and that's where the magic comes in. As long as a company keeps growing and making more profits and raising dividends—then the increased investor demand for its shares will lift share prices. So there will be no dilution."

"Where does that leave me? Am I being trained to be a stock pimp?"

"More like a model—pushing designer clothes for rich women."

"Usually they can't fit into them," I argued.

"Make them think they can," he said laughing. "Tell them to think long term. Investors who buy and hold solid stocks come out ahead."

Months later I passed my license exams. I saw that Agrigento was proud of me. He was a natural teacher. Somehow the crazy scheme was working because I was beginning to understand the markets.

"If you get too smart, I'll lose you to BJ," he complained. But then he surprised me. For the first time he was taking me to a client dinner event in Westport.

I was excited. But then I thought, *please don't make a move on me.* If he was worried about me going to BJ, what else was he thinking?

It was after five when our limo glided up the Merritt Parkway. But instead of rehearsing his talk as we drove through the early darkness, he asked me if I could guess what he had really wanted to be in life.

"A fashion designer, like Armani," I'm sure.

"Close—but I wanted to sing opera—as a tenor."

"That was my second guess. You have a great voice," I complimented him.

He told me that his family had moved to New York to try and get him into the High School for Music and Art. His voice classes were in the afternoon, and he supported himself by delivering breakfast orders to the Stock Exchange. His rounds brought him into actual trading rooms. He was mesmerized by the noise and the screens flashing in banks hung on the trading posts. A free bagel and coffee, helped him become friends with a young trader. They started making bets on stocks based on the chart patterns glowing on old CRT monitors. First with pretend money, and then with the trader's credit line. They quickly made a killing, and the next thing he knew he was tapped as an apprentice trader. But screaming on the trading floor killed his voice. His opera dreams died.

"But you can still listen to opera." Trying to console him, I kissed his forehead.

"It's not the same. I'll take you to the Met sometime." He didn't react to the kiss.

"Anything but *Don Giovanni*," I told him, which got me a laugh.

"Just pay attention to what I say tonight. I'm not just singing for my supper."

19

The hotel ballroom in Westport was jammed. Agrigento would be introduced by ex-*Barron's* financial journalist Rudy Kaiser. He was now the host of *Smarter Than The Street*, a business-news-only show, which premiered on Peoples National Radio in 1970. Fourteen years later it was the leader among a small but growing number of money shows on TV. As the show's host, Kaiser was called the 'Dean,' and Agrigento was one of the 'Profs,' who participated in round-robin stock market talk. Pillar was paying Kaiser to help attract its wealthiest Connecticut clients to Agrigento's new stock market forecast.

It was a gala. I'd never seen so much free food, and drink. Pillar had shelled out plenty for the event. First for the catering, then for state of the art electronics, and most of all for Kaiser. A corps of brokers, men and women, filled the ballroom with their finery. They all had big-money clients in tow. Two junior brokers, both blondes in evening dresses practically attacked Agrigento. I kept to the sidelines, looking for BJ Hanlon. But he was nowhere in evidence. Then Kaiser called the audience to attention.

In his rumpled black suit, he looked shorter than on TV. But his face was larger. The skin hung loose on it, descending from a mottled bald patch into a big bent nose full of hair. Otherwise, he had almost no eyebrows and lashes, but his purple-hued eyes were even beadier than those that had raked me over at The Box.

He introduced Agrigento with a Brit accent anyone could recognize as phony. "It's taken ten years for the Dow to get back over 1000. What most investors never understand is that the market's long-term trend always reasserts itself. There are long flat periods too—usually following a bear market. But the most important thing is to know the direction of the long term trend and never forget it. You must always be on the right side of the long-term trend. Frank Agrigento told me that years ago, and now he's got some important news for investors."

Agrigento stood to the applause. Everyone wanted to hear his market message "Let's review the historic charts," he began, and the screen behind glowed with the Dow index. I was amazed by the green laser pen he used to trace the trend as he spoke. He explained that stock prices were flat from 1900 through the end of the World War I. But in the 'Roaring Twenties,' the Dow almost tripled. Here he was interrupted by a blast of ragtime music, which made the audience laugh, as he jazzed the pointer's green beam.

"But I don't have to tell you what came next," he went on. Stocks fell sharply in the Crash of 1929. They were flat in the 'Tired Thirties,' from the Great Depression through WWII. But from its postwar low of about 150, the Dow soared almost four times higher during the Eisenhower years and into the Sixties. Again there was a blast of music—this time Elvis with 'You ain't nothing but a hound dog.' The laughter subsided quickly, and he went on. "That uptrend—not a rally but a real Bull market—was followed once more by a Bear market and a flat period when stocks oscillated but really went nowhere. You can't ignore that it's taken almost 15 years for the Dow to get back to where it was in May of 1966." His laser beam followed the chart line. "You can see three major attempts to break out above 1000. That kind of base building means greater up thrust. So where are we going now?" he asked.

The entire room went silent, hanging on his answer. The tense crowd of investors and brokers wanted to know if they were going to be rich or not? The chart on the screen suddenly changed, and the trendline moved up sharply. The music blared again—I knew the song immediately. It was Michael Jackson doing 'Thriller.' I had seen the video. Then Agrigento grabbed the microphone and screamed out, "Dow 10,000! I'm calling for a 20-year Bull market boom. Dow 10,000—starting now!"

The audience reacted with applause, whistles and cheers. I saw the young blonde broker stand and do a Twist. But the fanfare died down quickly. The audience wanted to know more. One of the older Pillar brokers stood up, and spoke into the pause, "Frank, do you really think this Bear's going into hibernation?"

Before Agrigento could answer one of the investors jumped right in. "Look! We've lost a lot of bucks on bullshit like this. You're plain crazy! I'm not putting another cent into this circus. The rally's already over."

But Agrigento held his ground. "I'm calling for Dow 10,000! It may take ten years. But that's where this trend is headed." This time there were a few boo's mixed in with the cheers. But he spoke back calmly.

"Three things are going to create a virtuous circle that spirals higher and higher. People, politics and productivity. They're my three drivers, and they're going to make this market break through and rocket higher."

Again I felt hushed anticipation fill the ballroom. The audience was beginning to believe Agrigento could be right. Big money was on everyone's mind.

A new series of charts flashed on the screen, which he went on to explain. First, the mammoth baby boomer generation would buy stocks for their retirement. When they bought houses, house prices had soared. Stocks would follow suit. The next people issue was an unprecedented global expansion that would sell millions of dishwashers to an emerging Third World middle class. And lastly under this heading, the world was at peace. War wastes resources. Stocks would gain now that the nightmare of Vietnam was over.

Then there were the Political drivers—including pro-growth supply-side Reaganomics and lower taxes overall. Deregulation was good for business and even better for mergers and acquisitions— M&A. And best of all, with Alan Greenspan replacing tight-money Paul Volker as Fed chief, the central bank will be a lot more accommodating.

Productivity was the last of his Three P's. "High technology in the form of the Personal Computer and the Internet will drive an information revolution." The Web would change how everything was bought and sold. New profit opportunities would drive the economy. Then he wound up with a sure winner. "This Bull will charge right to the end of the century," he said smiling. The applause was wild. People were actually cheering.

New questioning hands shot up. But Rudy Kaiser stood and interrupted. "No more questions—please! Your Pillar broker has a copy of Frank's report earmarked just for attendees."

Slick, I thought. But then I saw Rudy Kaiser and a Pillar broker and three women, including the young blonde, leave in a pack. Frank Agrigento went with them. *So how do I get home?*

I stood and gawked. But I was more surprised than hurt. Agrigento had always treated me like a child. I had even encouraged him to play father. *What right did I have to be jealous?*

But then the voice of the man who I had hoped would be there said, "Off to Raoul's." It was BJ Hanlon.

I knew he was talking about a hangout in Greenwich Village. "For an all-night party?"

"Not for you," he answered. "This will get you back." He handed me a pass for a limo.

"Do you think he's right? About the market?" *Might as well play the role?*

"They need to learn to think outside the box. This is going to be a once-in-a-century Bull market. Frank knows how to read the charts," he emphasized. "It will last longer and go higher than anyone is thinking now!"

And you and me?

20

In Street talk he was 'spot on.' The Bull market lasted for more than 20 years. Investors lived in a constant state of excitement as the Dow topped one new high after another. Nobody would have believed it then, but the Dow stunned investors by peaking over 10,000! My life was transformed. The great end-of-century Bull market was a source of optimism that helped me bet on myself. When things kept turning out right, I increased the stakes, and I won even more. Boom times are better for girls. When the prizes are worth more, men are just more competitive. So hemlines rise, and the boys wearing wide ties are more excited by them. That means women can aim for greater freedom. Time does tell—and to be a winner a woman has to know what it's saying.

Women are too prone to get involved in the short run. Fashion trends school us into short-run behavior. In Frank Agrigento's terms, we don't climb on the long run trend and ride through its minor downturns or setbacks. Women get wiped out too easily because we don't trust the long run enough. But 'buy the dips' is the rallying cry of a Bull market. The trouble is women live in our bodies, and our bodies know that our genetic horizon is a lot shorter. Most ovaries I know don't pump out healthy eggs after forty. But our fertility is a strength not a limitation. A man may be able to fertilize a thousand eggs, but that only means his biological value is worth a lot less. How many children can a women reasonably be expected to give birth to—and more women are having one child only. If they stop there what happens? Value is about scarcity. I'm happy with two children—and even when I was in Holy Orders, I somehow never doubted that I would be a mother one day. It was just something that would happen. There was Granny Sharp and my mother and me, and I wouldn't even be if my mother hadn't been and her mother and her mother. Even Madame Curie had kids.

The phones, faxes, and electronic mail went wild the next morning, as investors reacted to the promise of new wealth. This was a new Gold Rush. Agrigento had been right before, when it came to calling the '70s Bear market. Investors trusted his new call, and the positive Wall Street reaction was overwhelming. The Dow shot 250 points higher on surging volume.

Agrigento was all smiles, when he went on Pillar's hoot, once again telling over a thousand brokers why he was right. His secretary raised the print run on his report by another 50,000 copies. Then it was the media's turn—the networks were demanding interviews, *Barron's* wanted a feature. I was busy scheduling a round-the-world speaking trip that would take him from New York to Miami to Dallas to Los Angeles—then Tokyo, Hong Kong, Singapore, Zurich, London and back to New York. "And don't forget Abu Dhabi," he screamed at me.

"What about *Smarter Than The Street?*" I asked.

"Cancel it! Tell Kaiser I'll do the one after."

The minute I heard him the idea just bubbled up in my mind. And thirty minutes later, when the studio called back, I didn't re-press it. *Just do it!* Rudy Kaiser was on the line. "Listen sweetie," he said, "he told me you're his assistant, right? If he can't come to the studio—you fill in for him. Get him to coach you." *See it was his idea—not mine really.*

"Look, Dow 10,000 is the call of a lifetime. I'll even buy you din-ner," Kaiser added

"You don't have to do that."

"No. The studio is booking a room for you. You're going to stay over," said Kaiser. "We have to talk." *Was that a smile I saw on my mother's face?*

So in my most breathy voice, I told him, "I'm coming." I smiled, knowing it was what he most wanted to hear. It didn't matter because he was just chump change when it came to a man like Agrigento. *And BJ Hanlon would finally learn what his financial Eliza Doolittle was really worth! It was a big risk—and I was taking it.*

But there was a problem. I grabbed one of the first copies of Agrigento's report and read it over and over again, until I memo-rized it completely. Still, I didn't understand exactly how the high tech part worked. I didn't want to risk asking an analyst at Pillar to explain it. So I called Alice Powers in California. The last time we had dinner together was just after I had settled in San Francisco. By then Alice was working at a high-tech start-up called Cisco.

"I'm designing routers now," she told me when I called.

"What's a router?"

"It links up networks—never mind," Alice answered. "What do you want to find out about?"

"Compression and convergence."

"Okay," Alice told me. "Take notes. Compression is really all about Moore's law." Hearing my dead silence, she explained. "Moore's law says the number of transistors on a chip is doubling every 18 months. Eventually we could get to more than 10 billion transistors. It's named after the guy who invented the semiconductor—you know an IC—integrated circuit. That's what a chip is. It's what a computer depends on. Try to see it this way. There are about 100 billion neurons in the brain. That means one-tenth of a human brain could be put on a chip smaller than a penny. A chip like that could do anything—billions of calculations based on trillions of information bytes. The next twenty years are going to see an information revolution that will totally change life as we know it—totally."

I scribbled furiously. "What about convergence?"

"That's putting it all into a single package. The future is closer than anyone thinks. You'll be able to buy a handheld device that fits in a bag and lets you make phone calls, send mail, take pictures, watch TV, read books and surf the web all for a hundred dollars."

"That's incredible isn't it?" I spoke and thought at once. Maybe I could work it into a title for the whole pitch. I still needed to work on that.

"It's what your man is counting on for his market revolution. I'm sure! Just imagine a world where in seconds you can know what something costs in all the stores that sell it, buy it for the best price, and have it shipped for free. So why do you need to know all this?"

"I'm going on TV." I gave her the details. "I still need a real good headline for it."

"Just use his. I'll keep my fingers crossed. But be sure to do everything I would do!"

I laughed and said goodbye. You know what I was thinking don't you? *I love her.*

Smarter Than The Street was broadcast nationwide at seven on Friday, but it was taped at four, right after the close of the market—in a studio outside of Washington, near to where Rudy Kaiser lived. So I dipped into Agrigento's air miles and upgraded myself to a first class seat on the 2pm US Air shuttle out of La Guardia. But only after I went to Max Mara and bought a gorgeous bright red business suit, and had my hair done in a back-set cut that made me look like Linda Evans playing Krystle Carrington on *Dynasty.* I spent more than I ever had, but it was worth it because I felt less of a nervous wreck about being on camera.

My seat put me next to an older Black woman carrying a mesh case with a cat in it. The flight attendant soon appeared to ask if I was comfortable. But the woman interrupted in a friendly tone, "If you're allergic, I'll change seats." Her voice somehow relaxed my nerves, and I assured the uniformed girl I was fine.

"I just couldn't leave her behind. So I hope you don't mind," the woman went on. "She belongs to my daughter. This is her cat BJ, and I think she needs her back after what happened. I was just taking care of her." Hearing Hanlon's nickname made me ask, "What happened to her?"

"She was Miss America, but then they took it away. It makes me so angry. And I know she's just so sad about it."

I realized she was talking about Vanessa Williams, Miss America for 1984. She was forced to give up her title. I had seen a news clip about her being the first Black to be crowned Miss America, back in September. She was ordered to resign because she had posed nude in *Penthouse*. It was outrageous. What about me dancing in The Box. *Why can't women make money out of being a woman?*

I squeezed the woman's hand to commiserate, telling her, "I'm going on TV tonight!"

"Well your hair is absolutely perfect. I remember when Vanessa was on TV. They'll be putting the makeup on you."

"It's not live. They're taping it."

"Don't you be nervous. Just like I told Vanessa, when she was on. You can't be too tense, honey. You gotta' relax. That's the thing you need to know most of all. Don't be gettin' all worked up. Speak slow. If you rush, everything gets mashed together. And don't forget to smile. You're real pretty—you know. So wow them with a big smile. A lotta' teeth. That's the best advice. Relax, talk slow and smile. Now here's the thing to remember. I'm givin' you this joke to think about. What do you call a cat that drinks vinegar?"

I shook my head to say 'no.'

But the woman rushed on, saying, "A sour pussy!"

I laughed at the words. *Was I worried? Back at The Box I was taking my clothes off to make money!*

"So be a cool cat instead. Don't forget, like I told Vanessa. If anything goes wrong you still got nine lives to live!" *My god that's perfect!*

I had memorized every word of Agrigento's report, but I didn't want to sound like a robot recording. I could stick with 'Dow 10,000,' but when I heard the woman's last words I immediately knew they were perfect. My last doubts evaporated. I scribbled furiously as the limo took me from the airport to the studio. *The Bull has nine lives! What could be better?*

21

The atmosphere in the TV studio was high tension generated by spot lights, mammoth TV cameras, teleprompters, computer monitors, and here too a Bloomberg console. I was taken immediately into makeup. Next Rudy Kaiser pounced and introduced the other panelists, John Jacobs, Chief of Research at Salomon Brothers. I'd heard Agrigento once call him by his Wall Street nickname, 'Jack the Giant Killer.' The other was Lazlo Lugosi, the big brain at a private firm managing more than $4 billion and another Bull slayer. Even though my time on the Street was short, I realized it was a trap! Kaiser, had orchestrated an attack on Agrigento's Dow 10,000 market call. He knew what he was doing when he lured me onto the panel. His plan was to throw me in front of two hungry Bears, and discredit Agrigento!

Once Kaiser had recapped the markets for the week, and following a commercial break when none of the three men spoke to me, it was 'air time,' signaled by a flashing red warning light. Kaiser called on Salomon's Joseph, who launched a tirade explaining why the Bear market would soon be back. "It's overdue," he told the camera, turning his head towards me with a piteous look for the TV audience. "Nothing can prevent its return!"

Then Lugosi began to scream at me, "This Bear isn't even on its last leg!" Kaiser liked that one. He interrupted to tell the viewers that market trends typically have three phases or legs. But Jacobs cut him short and said gruffly while waving a finger at me, "There's not enough oomph in the economy." Then Kaiser tried to finish me off by asking straight out, "Listen little Ms. Money—do you really believe in Dow 10,000?"

I was ready for him, and jumped in front of my lectern. I posed for the camera, and saw it move in. Then I spoke right into it, mustering every shred of confidence I had. "This Bull has nine lives!" I challenged. Then I screamed, "Make no mistake! This is a twenty-year call. By 2000 the Dow will be over 10,000!"

"Prove it—you can't prove it," Lazlo Lugosi screamed back at me. Rudy Kaiser was waving at me to get back behind my podium. But that didn't stop the cameramen from going for a full body shot, and I was perfectly posed to tighten my skirt.

"The Bull has nine lives!" I screamed again. "You wanna know why?" And I answered immediately, arguing sound bite-by-sound bite, from "Peace means plenty," to "Boomers need stocks for retirement," and then on to Reaganomics, a favorable new Fed, and ending with the high tech revolution. I thought Kaiser would cut me off. But the camera stayed with me, and I conquered almost five full minutes of air time before the camera winked off. It was time for the show's final segment, a look ahead at the coming week's economic data and earnings releases by Kaiser's female co-host, Sue McCann, who appeared in a suit topped with a scarf that had to be Hermes.

I grabbed my bag, waved to the panelists, and hurried off as though I was headed back to the airport. But as I expected, Rudy Kaiser quickly cut off my retreat. "Hey—Ms. Money—we need to talk. You were good, damn good!" It was the second time he had called me by the name that would become mine, but I didn't know I had been baptized.

"I need to make the last plane." I knew I wasn't getting away with it, but I wanted him to think I was afraid of the 'Big Bad Wolf.' That way he'd be a lot easier to handle—even though I had no fixed plan.

"Listen" he said, stopping me with a hand on my shoulder. "I want you back on the show. Do you understand? We're going to dinner after I get this makeup off. The studio has a room for you at the Mayflower. The car will take you there. You can meet me in the lobby."

He wants me back on the show. Those were magic words. They would give BJ Hanlon something to think about. What had he called me? 'Ms. Money!' It's perfect.

But my thoughts changed after a quick shower. The jitters struck as I dressed. My eyes stared at the huge king-size bed. But I managed to put my Max Mara suit into its garment bag, and I pulled on a deep purple jersey dress with a square neck that was center slit to below the bra. There was just enough exposure to signal availability, and the clinging fit was right. It was Halston and cost me a fortune, even on sale. But I was still nervous. I had no real plan for dealing with Kaiser's advances. Did I want to spend the night in bed with an old letch just to get on TV? Was I truly ready for that? What if he blabbed? I switched my pearls for a silver necklace, but the clasp was frustrating. Just then the room phone buzzed. Rudy Kaiser was waiting for me in the lobby. *The fun never ends.*

Taller than Kaiser, I bent down to receive the peck on the cheek he gave me. Then I told him, "I'm totally hungry—I want to go to the Ebbitt Grill. I hear it's fantastic. Frank Agrigento said to go there if I was staying over."

Kaiser looked like he was going to faint. "Do you think I work for Goldman?" he asked. "This is public TV."

I made a face, and gave him a line from my lap dancing days, "You don't want me to think you're a cheap date do you? You said I was worth it—and now you're having dinner with Ms. Money." My new name sounded great, but I felt like I was in the oldest profession.

The Old Ebbitt Grill turned out to be very new, having just been rebuilt around the corner at 15th Street. We walked, to save Kaiser a cab. I was in heels that let me bump into him, as we skirted Lafayette Park, cutting behind the White House. It gave him a chance to steady me, which he loved. "It's so close to my hotel," I added, knowing what he intended for after dinner dessert.

We got a booth in Grant's bar, all shining richly with gaslight and mahogany, and where a gilt-framed portrait of the General rules. "It's been a long day," I told him as I slid into the seat and then leaned into him.

"You'll get used to the pace when you're a regular guest on my show." But then he suddenly moved away from me, saying, "Excuse me. I need to visit the little boy's room."

"Send over a drink, from the bar," I called after him. "Champagne, please." He stiffened as he walked off. Rudy Kaiser was a cheapie all right.

From my seat I could just trace a pathway leading from a modern atrium into candle-lit dining rooms. Closer by, a life-size painting in a massive gilt antique frame exposed a nude water nymph reclining on the edge of a lotus pond. It looked Victorian—sex mixed with ancient myth. As I stared into her face, I was shocked to find the woman in the painting speaking to me. I could hear her voice in my mind, saying "Look at me! I'm beautiful and I'm alive in this painting. So what if I'm naked—as long as I look great. Now who do you see over there? That's the great Ulysses S Grant? Just another dead soldier. At least I got immortality for taking my clothes off and shaving my legs."

I spoke back to the Nymph, mentally telling her, "I've done that—but I've never been painted."

"That's right kid," from further away Grant's portrait called out to me hoarsely. "Don't listen to that floozy. Every time someone pulls out a fifty they get to see my face. That's what money can do for you."

"The General tells all," the Nymph replied sarcastically. "What does he know about being a woman? Just don't forget you're here with an old letch with hanging skin and droopy balls. Show him how lucky he is to be out with a woman—a beautiful, young woman. You look like a goddess. Just remember what you are."

"But I want to be a real goddess?"

"Make a lot of money—it's the same thing," Grant broke in.

"You have to be immortalized," said the Nymph. "But Ulysses has a point. Become a star—get on TV—and make money. People will worship you because of the money."

"But I have to fuck him to get on TV."

"No you don't. He's already afraid of you. He went to the men's room to try and rub himself stiff. Scare him. Give him a blow job. Even in my day it was the woman's way out. That way you won't have to get sweaty. Besides he knows he can't come twice in one night. Believe me I've seen him operate in here before! He's cheap—you're worth a lot more. Every woman is."

"You mean be like Eve!"

"Exactly!" Grant interrupted again. "She was a take charge girl!"

"Right," said the Nymph. "And she knew the one thing every woman has to know."

"What?"

"You can live without a man, but they wouldn't even exist without you! Remember that and you'll get everything you want."

The portrait of Grant just winked at me.

22

To make him think I was annoyed, I greeted Kaiser's return, saying loudly and petulantly, "My drink hasn't come yet." He waved at the head waiter, and finally a white-jacketed server found our table. I sipped the champagne while he toyed with a martini. "I like the bubbles on my tongue."

He put his hand on my back. "Very, very good—you're a natural on TV. I definitely want you," he said. Then quickly added, "For the show."

"From now on I'm Ms. Money. You baptized me." I could almost hear the phones ringing as viewers called in.

"It just popped out."

"Do you have any other surprises?" I turned towards him holding my drink in the air, forcing his hand to slide closer to my breast.

And suddenly the man who would just love to get me drunk enough for date rape, almost had a fit. He started a sentence, but he couldn't finish, his eyes widened, but with fear not lust. I interrupted his stammer, and gave him the excuse he needed. "We just need some food. You're hungry."

"Maybe something from the bar menu."

"I'm getting a T-bone." I couldn't resist tweaking him one more time.

And when the waiter returned I asked for the steak. "Please make it very rare." And staring into Kaiser's beady purple eyes, I added "I'm so hungry. I could eat raw meat tonight."

He got excited again, flushed, but then cringed. "That's a hundred dollar entrée!"

We were soon served. He had ordered a Caesar salad with chicken. I picked up the massive steak knife, cut a slice of rare meat, and slowly lifted it into my mouth. I saw his eyes follow my fork. "This is delicious. It's like butter!"

For a second, he looked like he might have a heart attack. I quickly changed the subject. "What do you really think of Frank Agrigento's call?"

His eyes were full on my mouth as I chewed on the meat. But suddenly he was all business, "I think he's right about the Fed and the economy. Plus your line about the Bull having nine lives—that was brilliant."

I slid on the banquette till I was right up against him. "The name you gave me was brilliant too. I really like it—'Ms. Money.' It's hot. And you said it just popped out. Was it like this?"

Under the table, I slid my hand onto him. For a second I thought he would choke on his food. Then I felt him stiffen slightly, as I found his zipper and pulled it down. I worked my hand through his clothes until I managed to free him altogether, saying "I hope this Bull lasts!"

"The Presidential race, I mean politics, could make a difference." His eyes were rolling as I massaged him. "You know Reagan was shot right around here?"

"Around here?" I asked and squeezed his flaccid penis. Then I looked right at him, saying "I think I lost my earring." I lowered my head beneath the table as though I was scanning the floor. I let my lips brush him under the table—better an aggressor than a victim.

He really didn't know what to do because I had completely reversed roles on him. "I meant it was at … the Washington Hilton," he just managed to get the words out.

I kissed him again under the table, and then I raised my head, saying, "I couldn't find it. I should have worn studs. But I would really like to be on your show again. Should I keep looking?"

He just nodded his head nervously.

I ducked under the table and took him in my mouth until he spasmed into a soft ejaculation. "Oh!" I cried out when he came. "You must have spilled your drink. I'll never find that earring now."

"You'll be on the show, on the show," he repeated himself. He grabbed his napkin to wipe himself with and then ate quickly. "I'm just stressed out tonight. I'm going to eat and run. I live in Alexandria. Take a cab back to the hotel."

"I'm sorry you're in a rush."

"Don't worry! You'll be on the show. Ms. Money, yeah, I like that" was his goodbye.

There was still time to brush my teeth and catch the late flight to New York. The stress had exhausted me. All I needed was a blanket to crawl under from the flight attendant. But instead Sue McCann claimed the first-class seat next to me. She was still wearing the elegant Hermes scarf that I had seen in the studio. I realized she wasn't much older than I was.

"Frank always goes back to Hartford. He takes the back way to Chappaqua. It's faster. So I usually fly back to New York alone. It's great you could make the plane—I thought you were in the Mayflower?"

I was tired and misunderstood her. "I'm no Mayflower blue blood. My mother was a transplant, Brooklyn to LA, and my dad's family came from Ireland."

"Don't worry. My dad was a shoe salesman and mom kept house. I meant the Mayflower hotel. He never stops trying to turn it into his personal bordello. It doesn't matter when it comes to men exploiting a woman who's trying to make it. They all think we work for an escort service. Did you ever hear about Cachet? You know—at the New York Mayflower. It's run by a woman some girls call the Mayflower Madame!"

I had heard the rumors about a socialite who was running an escort service from a dancer at The Box. Supposedly she introduced trust-fund girls who wanted extra money for cocaine and other treats to the world of high-class prostitution. But I said nothing more than, "I guess I know how to play 'poke-her' a lot better than he does. I just dealt myself a winning hand."

"I know exactly what you mean," my companion said smiling. "Well if it makes any difference to you, in the words of Huckleberry Finn, 'I've been there before.' Now I never stay for dinner with him. He puts the 'pound of flesh' routine on every woman guest."

"More like three ounces."

McCann laughed and said surprised, "Ms. Money—that's what he called you. Well you really are a California girl! I'm from Brentwood. I went to Cal State Northridge," she said, handing me her business card.

"I grew up in San Gabriel," I said, studying the card and wishing I had one to exchange. "I've seen you on FNN."

"I was a business news intern at KNXT TV in Los Angeles. We must be the only women who are more interested in stocks than in clothes. You were great on the show. You have it. You were just as credible as Frank is. And you fought off the Bears too. I'm going to interview you next week—on my show. And I'll introduce you as Ms. Money."

I was thrilled. The offer was fantastic, and even more important, I had found my first woman pal in the business. "Frank is one of your big fans," I told her, hoping to return the favor.

"He helped me get on this show. You're lucky to be working for him. How'd you pull that off?"

"Thank God I didn't have to pull off anything. Not with Frank."

"I know what you mean. Some guys just understand. What's that song? 'It's hard to be a woman?' I got my break from Rod Buchser—he was the guy who invented FNN—a sweetie."

"Frank is great, but I'm not staying with him at Pillar. This is my internship. I needed to learn the business. I'm going to Ledbetter with BJ Hanlon."

"Wow! Hanlon—you're really lucky."

"He met me when I was a stew for United."

"He's one of the brightest minds on Wall Street. Could work wherever he wants. It's such a sad story."

"Why?" I was immediately interested.

"Didn't you know?" And when I shook my head, she went on. "His daughter died and his wife went nuts. I mean she's in McLean's, I think, or someplace like it. You know a luxury mental health spa that you can't leave."

"Tell me what happened—please?" I asked anxiously as my mind reeled.

"His wife was driving their kid to school. It was in Alpine—in New Jersey. That's about 15 miles out of the City. It's ultra-rich big time. They were smashed by a tractor-trailer. The car exploded. They tried to save the daughter, but she died in the hospital. I heard his wife just caved in with grief. Not just in pieces—she stopped functioning altogether. It happened about the same time as Harry Chapin and almost the same way."

23

Now you know how I got the name Ms. Money. But that was only the first step in my transformation. My conversion was a lot more complicated—as you'll see! Science says it takes time and pressure to turn a chunk of coal into a diamond. But to my way of thinking it was Elizabeth Taylor who defined the problem, when she said "Big girls need big diamonds." She should know because her diamonds ultimately brought $150 million when they were auctioned after she died. And that didn't include the 70-carat stone Robert Burton gave her in Botswana as a wedding present. Still, I think you'll know when I become Ms. Money for real. I won't have to kiss before I tell.

My TV title caught on. Sue McCann helped by interviewing me on FNN the following week, calling me 'Ms. Money, a market analyst at Ledbetter.' Then *Crain's*, the New York City business daily, asked for an interview, which put my Street name in print. Next, Ted Turner's three-year old startup, CNN, called—someone named Burt Reinhardt wanted to screen me for a financial news anchor job. But I insisted that they interview Ms. Money on TV, and I got it because I was media hot.

My return to Pillar Securities was brief. When I came back from Washington, there were flowers piled on my desk. A bunch of giant pink roses from Rudy Kaiser with a note reading, "To my star—see you soon." And a bigger bouquet of the reddest roses ever enclosed a card from "Your favorite tenor, Frank Agrigento." And my phone was blinking. The first message was from BJ Hanlon. He wanted to see me for lunch at La Reserve, the new French restaurant in Rockefeller Center.

I waited for him at a table that the maître d', who introduced him-self as Jean-Louis, ushered me to. Hanlon appeared five minutes lat-er. During that time my brain continued to spin with the thoughts that had started when the words left Sue McCann's lips. 'Daughter dead, wife crazy.' I didn't know that Harry Chapin had died—even though the Pommies all cried over 'Taxi' when it came out in 1972. *Wife crazy, daughter dead.*

Hanlon looked truly elegant, wearing a perfect navy suit with a wide chalk stripe and a bright golden-yellow silk tie. *He is so big.* I felt his pale grey eyes lock on mine immediately. They said he had made me wait because he was angry. It didn't matter. I studied his face, looking for traces of the grief he must live with. But his expres-sion refused to unlock.

Seeing my stare, he said, "I dressed for you."

"More likely for the chef." I meant it as a joke, but it came out snappish. I saw his eyes widen.

"Actually, Chris, the Chef, is excellent. This place just opened. The Rothschild's are backers. I mean the wine people—Chateau

Mouton Rothschild." But taking in my expression, he added, "Did you have a tough night on TV?"

"Quite the contrary," I answered.

"I thought you could deal with Mr Kaiser."

"It's not Kaiser who's hard to deal with." I spoke my mind.

"You'll be working at Ledbetter from now on—with Paul Stringfellow. He's a quant—a technical analyst."

"I still don't know." I was shocked by my sudden answer. He just wasn't saying what I wanted to hear. Even a compliment on how good I looked on TV would be something. He was still treating me like a prodigy—his prodigy—not a person.

"What don't you know?" he asked surprised. "I'm paying you $150,000 a year—plus bonus. That's more than any of the networks will pay you. And the job's more interesting than being a TV mouthpiece only."

"It's not the job. This isn't about money." I wanted him to know.

He didn't reply because Jean-Louis was serving salmon and spinach in puff pastry from a cart. "We're having the tranche," he said smiling.

I stared at him. My face was burning, but actually I was calm. *How could he not tell me?* I sipped on my wine. *He always picks the best wine, but he doesn't know that much about people.*

"That's a joke," he said. "'Tranche' means cart—the special of the day."

I looked at the food.

"Okay, just try and tell me."

"I don't want to feel like I'm a puppet. I want to know what's going on. I don't feel like you're telling me anything. I need you to stop testing me—that's all." I watched the expression forming on his face.

"Okay," he said. "I deserve that one. I'm sorry you feel I'm high-handed. You certainly couldn't think I would let you go on national TV if I didn't think you were ready—but you're right, it was a test."

He had known all along! *How stupid did they think I was?*

"Kaiser called Frank privately, and Frank called me. He thought you could do it. He was dead right as usual. You came through like a champ. That's good isn't it?"

My anger just popped. "Champ or chump?"

"I just didn't want you to self-destruct," he snapped back. "You know you have more to learn. You've transitioned from the sell side to the buy side. It's not the same."

I softened. "I know you bet on me. But I still don't really know why. The most important thing is—I still need to trust myself. That can't happen unless I know you trust me too." *I know about your wife and your daughter. Let me help you.*

I saw the mental struggle on his face. "What I trust most of all is what I think, and my mind says you're right for the job. I didn't want some prep school feminazi—even with connections. So I went with what my brain told me. So far it's been one hundred percent."

"Okay. But don't mind it if I call you Professor Higgins." I capitulated. He had said a lot, and I could see he wasn't ready to say anything more. I let my face say I was sorry—even if only temporarily.

"Paul Stringfellow will teach you about portfolio management. You need to bond with the BDO ladies, our Business Development Officers. You'll back them up in meetings with key clients. As soon as you're up to speed, you can start partnering with me on my harvesting trips. That will show you what's special about what we do."

Reacting to the added respect in his voice, I laughed and said. "Is he as good looking as Rex Harrison?"

24

Stringfellow was only a few years older than I was, but a bit stooped, and thin with a square face. His light brown hair was combed forward, straggling over his forehead. He had the palest blue eyes I'd ever seen, with almost no lashes. They were covered by light brown brows. His nose was pointed and thrust out over his small mouth with its small teeth. His clothes never matched, and I often thought about taking him shopping. Hanlon treated him like a son.

At first I thought he might be gay, but I soon realized he was just totally sexless. He was pure 'quant,' in Wall Street terms. A man obsessed with numbers. One day I saw him jot something down on a pad and show it to his assistant, who laughed loudly. When I asked her later, she told me, "It was a joke about stochastic functions—if you can imagine one."

Stringfellow spelled out what my shift to the buy side meant. "On the sell side it's just retail—brokers pitching stocks at small investors. The buy side constructs carefully researched investment portfolios for wealthy investors and institutions and pension funds. We have discretion—we decide what to buy." He went on to explain that Ledbetter's portfolios were mathematically modeled to match the risk profiles of ultra-rich individual clients. He called them HENS, an acronym for High-Net-Worth Investors. Speaking with his literally squeaky voice, he told me he ran Ledbetter's 'henhouse,' and then broke out in his characteristic chirpy giggle.

"The real rich hate to lose money. So preservation of capital is rule one." Then he giggled again, "That's why we never put all a HEN'S eggs in one basket. Diversification is the key risk control factor."

"What's so hard about that?" I asked. "Anyone knows it."

"Not as simple as you think," he told me. "Some baskets are less safe than you expect, and, even more important, some look different but are the same when it comes to risk. Tell me something you think is safe."

"What's the risk of cash?" I answered.

He squeaked out another giggle. "It could burn up if the mattress you're sticking it under catches fire. But the real risk is the alternative cost. U.S. treasuries are safe as cash and they earn interest. And there's another risk— inflation—it destroys purchasing power while you sit on your cash. Now tell me, which is safer a bond or a common stock?"

"Obviously, a bond. You get your principle back when it matures."

"Not so fast. If a risky company goes broke, its junk bonds are likely to turn out worthless. You'd be better off with a blue-chip stock. Every asset class has unique risk factors that vary with the state of the economy. Even gold isn't guaranteed—you can't eat it. Just remember Profile, Portfolio, and Performance. If we get those right we can let the investment function on automatic pilot, and keep our HENS happy." He giggled again, but by then I had begun to warm to his goofy qualities. He was a natural teacher.

I went with Stringfellow to watch BJ Hanlon in action at a dinner presentation to a group of HENS with reported individual net worth greater than ten million dollars.

I wanted to be elegant, and raided designer resale for a deep blue Jovani gown, simply cut with mesh sleeves that formed a shawl which knotted over a bodice of dull satin. Stringfellow, with me in tow, mixed with the investors over drinks in a private dining room at the Sign of the Dove. "They lay very big eggs," he told me with his usual nervous laugh. He wore a dinner jacket for the event, managing somehow to make it look less than formal.

I was happy to see that Hanlon gave me a longer look than usual when I arrived. It was a room full of genuine glamor, sparkling jewels, gorgeous gowns and luxury salon styled hair. A stained glass skylight poured starlight into the candle lit room with its brick arches and gleaming silver and bright pink table clothes, each covered with pale pink roses.

Hanlon's presentation was impressive. It was accompanied by a digital slide show projected on a giant-size LCD screen—one of the very first. The intent was to show that Ledbetter was in the forefront of high tech. But then the music came on—Michel Legrand's jazzy theme for the 1983 James Bond film, *Never Say Never Again*. As an attention getter, Hanlon told them the film had grossed $160 million at the box office, explaining that the huge take was owing to the return of Sean Connery in the Bond role.

"Twelve years ago Mr Connery swore he would never do another Bond film. So what made him change his mind?" Hanlon asked. The LCD lit up with the answer spelled out under a silhouette of 007 pulling out empty pockets:

HE LOST MONEY!

The laughter was collective. Then as the music tapered off, a three-slide build first asked the assembled millionaires:

WHAT DO THE WEALTHY WANT MOST OF ALL?
TO STAY RICH—
PRESERVATION OF CAPITAL COMES FIRST!

I looked around the room to gauge the impact. The forks were paused and glasses set down. With a single truth Hanlon already had their complete attention. He went on to tell them that when an investor falls behind they have to run twice as fast to catch up. When you lose money you have to double your return to make anything—and doubling return is nearly impossible!

The slide show followed his lead, by showing James Bond slowly sinking into a pool of quicksand until only his revolver was sticking out. The audience reacted with more laughter.

Then Hanlon put up contrasting photos of Scott Fitzgerald and Ernest Hemingway. The animation was fantastic—making it look like the two novelists were actually speaking to each other.

Fitzgerald: THE RICH ARE DIFFERENT FROM YOU AND ME
Hemingway: YES, THEY HAVE MORE MONEY!
Ledbetter: BECAUSE THEY'RE SMARTER

And Hanlon gave the voice over, adding, "The real difference isn't money—it's brains."

Flattery will get you anywhere. He knows them cold.

Then a new animated slide showed Bond training his gun on a photo of a man above the caption:

WORLD'S WISEST INVESTOR

Hanlon asked if anyone could identify the man in the picture. When no one could, he told them it was a photo of Charles Ponzi. I watched as the group leaned in for a closer look as he explained that pyramid schemes like Ponzi's continue to rob investors year after year. Every new Ponzi pays off early investors with the money from the newest recruits. That goes on until the inverted pyramid collapses and most investors are left holding an empty bag. Here Hanlon pulled one of the restaurant's decor balloons down from the ceiling and stuck a pin in it. The loud pop was followed by silence, and then Hanlon projected another slide sequence:

WHAT MAKES THE RICH SO SMART?
THEY KNOW YOU CAN'T BEAT THE MARKET—
BUT YOU CAN JOIN IT!

He explained that Ledbetter's goal was to match the return provided by the market as measured by its most basic index, the Standard & Poor's 500. More than 85% of money managers never achieve that goal. Trying too hard to maximize results always leads to losses. And the illustration showed Bond in silhouette with his head on a chopping block, the executioner swings his axe and Bond's head rolls off—but his mouth moves and a caption added:

BULLS GET RICH—BEARS GET RICH—
GAMBLERS DIE POOR

Once again the audience roared with laughter. Some of them were applauding. Then a new Bond slide appeared on the giant LCD monitor. It showed Bond tied to the rails, and the roar of train said it was approaching. The caption proclaimed:

DON'T BE RUN OVER BY TAXES

Hanlon explained that taxes on investment gains make winning even harder. There was new applause when he told them investors must minimize taxes by targeting tax-favored investments and using loss harvesting to neutralize gains. A slide then showed Connery pulling the trigger at a target as a flag unfurls from the gun barrel that reads:

LEDBETTER TOLD ME NOT TO TAKE RISKS
BECAUSE
NOT LOSING IS WINNING!

And the music took over as the final slide showed Connery in a dinner jacket hanging upside down over a shark-filled pool, with a giant shark leaping up at him. It was greeted by thunderous handclapping.

The lights brightened, and Hanlon told them he had one surprise for them. Even I gasped. Out of nowhere, Leontyne Price stood up to sing for the group. She hugged Hanlon, and the celebrity endorsement immediately brought a hush to the audience. But instead of her trademark aria, 'O patria mia' from Aida, the opera star sang 'All Time High,' the theme song made famous by Rita Coolidge, from the newest James Bond film, Octopussy. More applause, mine included.

Waiters rushed in to fill champagne glasses, as Hanlon went round from table to table, mixing with potential clients.

"Now you've seen the best there is," said Stringfellow. "Did you get it?"

I had my answer ready. "It's brilliant. Playing safe is smarter."

"It makes the money manager's life a lot easier too," an older man in black tie, with a full head of wispy grey hair and steel-rim glasses, interrupted. "Are you Ms. Money? I'm Fred Fabricant from Gotham Trust. I just came for the music."

Fabricant smiled at her. He was every inch the banker, and numbered among the *Forbes* 400 list of the world's richest men. "I think I've seen you on TV," he continued. His thin lips were curved with the anticipation of seeing more.

"When it comes to singing for my supper, I'm nowhere as good as Leontyne Price," I replied, laughing. "All I sing about is the market." And then I spoke to Stringfellow, "I only hope I make as much sense as BJ. His credibility is off the scale."

"I thought so too," said Fabricant. "It takes nerve to tell the rich not to be greedy. But it's the best advice possible."

"What matters most is protecting our clients." Stringfellow cut in.

"When it comes to that, we're the best in the business." Hanlon had joined us. "I told you that the last time you tried to buy me out, Fred," he continued.

File that away.

"I wish our new acquisition Bronson Bell would follow your rules. We paid enough for them," Fabricant spoke with a sour look on his face.

"Then you should have paid up and bought us instead," said Hanlon. "Not down."

Ducking Hanlon's verbal rebuke, Fabricant turned to me, saying, "You must stop by the next time you're free. We can have lunch."

"My policy is no free lunch—unless BJ approves." I answered, looking at Hanlon.

"Ms. Money and I have a trip scheduled for Silicon Valley," Hanlon said smiling. "But right now I think it's time for our market canary to fly back to her cage."

"Bluebird," I replied to both men, partially twirling my gown.

"Yes, 'To the Bluebird of Happiness,'" said Fabricant raising his glass. "It was a big hit when it came out in 1934. But I hope BJ means your nest—not a cage."

"That was right at the bottom of the Great Depression," said Stringfellow.

"Spare me the history," I said. "And remember the eggs in Ms. Money's nest have to be golden!"

25

Mrs Eileen Worth became Mrs Brian Connelly at a Christmas wedding. The party gathered at the small First Congregationalist Church on Sound Beach Avenue in the heart of Old Greenwich, close to the bride's new home. It was the second marriage for the successful realtor, whose first husband was killed in a plane crash at JFK in 1975. Capt Connelly is USAF, retired. The couple left for a wedding trip to Fort Lauderdale, Florida.

Just before leaving for the airport, my mother whispered in my ear, "He's only a two-dollar bettor."

My mother wanted to remarry, and she got what she wanted. She was not one to believe in an empty bed. I was happy for her. Her real estate pals joined Connelly's ex-pilot cronies at a small reception in the church basement. I smiled watching them eye each other, the women with cake plates in their hands and the men holding a glass of scotch. My new friend, financial anchor Sue McCann, accepted my one personal invitation—a sign of our growing closeness.

Ms. Money's status as an investment strategist grew with greater press coverage and more TV appearances. My now dedicated Personal Assistant, Robin, soon had to hire her own junior just to keep up with my schedule. Between the two of them, they managed to keep me on track. Stringfellow prepped me constantly, supporting my growing confidence. I had my own staff writer and a data guy for charts. I bought a tanning bed, and began meeting weekly with my personal stylist. I took over my mother's empty New York apartment. But I was only there for a few hours sleep a night.

Ms. Money became Ledbetter's 'Talking Head'—after the name of David Byrne's rock group. Talking was my job: talk to prospects, talk to clients, talk to the salesforce, talk to the media, print, radio, TV and streaming video. Wearing a headset, I sat in an ergonomically correct, $1,000 Herman Miller Aeron chair, facing a battery of computer monitors showing the financial news, an LED display of real-time stock quotes and the Internet. When my mouth was shut my eyes scanned economic research, financial statements, annual reports and the financial dailies. When I finished reading, it was my ears' turn. They listened to mutual fund managers, industry experts and financial consultants. And needless to say, I became a regular on *Smarter Than The Street*.

The LBO boom, meaning Leveraged Buyout, was the rocket fuel that sent stocks soaring throughout the Eighties. You had to live it. Day after day the markets went higher and higher. Billionaire ex-U.S. Secretary of the Treasury William Simon and an investor group acquired Gibson Greetings for $80 million. They put only a million down for the cash-rich card maker. Just 16 months later, they took the company public in an IPO. Investors bought and bought, and the offering brought in a whopping $290 million! Simon walked away approximately $66 million richer. That was the spark which ignited more than 2,000 similar deals in the Eighties alone.

Then Michael Milken made it even easier for takeover raiders to find bucks to put down on a deal. Milken virtually invented the junk bond for investors to buy and then opened the money spigot wide. Need $75 million to buy Revlon? It's yours.

Hanlon was soon invited to Drexel Burnham's 'predator's ball.' By now, taking me with him was a foregone conclusion. On the plane to California, I asked what he thought about Milken.

"He's just too aggressive. Remember what happens to the great white shark in *Jaws*. In the end, it implodes."

"But we're into takeovers too," I argued. "Our clients love the IPO's you bring in."

"There's a big difference. We steer clear of these junk-bond deals." He went on to explain why. "Any money manager who can rack up eight percent returns is doing a great job. Over 85 percent of them can't. A lot are losing money even in this Bull market."

"Thanks to you—our clients are getting 12%!" I responded. *It was the truth—as a money manager his record was golden. But I wasn't getting what I wanted from him—was I?*

"So when somebody tells you they're making 20% consistently?"

"They're lying."

"Or they're getting insider information."

"But that's illegal."

"Not the way Milken does it. Look, say you know a company is going to be bought—you load up on the shares. But that's a violation. The reason why Milken is a genius is quite simple. He saw that you can load up on a company's shares and then turn it into a takeover target by using junk bonds to finance a raid."

"You mean he creates his own insider information. Isn't it still illegal?"

"Not the way he does it."

"It sounds like he marries a wife before she divorces her husband." *Will he ever get the message? No matter how close we had become, he wouldn't open up about his personal life. It was insider information that he just wouldn't share!*

It was the most extravagant party I had ever seen. The Beverley Hills setting, the clothes, the entertainment—way beyond lavish. I was drinking Dom Perignon Brut Rosé Reserve at $2,000 a bottle while nibbling on new potato discs covered with melted leeks and black truffle tapenade. Caviar by the ton. I was briefly introduced to King Milken himself. He cut an unimpressive figure. I sensed he had no use for the gala. He was money through and through. You could see it. Hanlon made sure we moved on quickly.

"I want to see Bungalow Eight—we can't miss that! We can sniff white powder with the models?"

"We'll go to Chasen's instead."

"If we go to the Bungalow we can find out some insider information."

"You know better!" He wasn't being teased. "We employ the richest sales people possible—that's so they can prospect their friends. Many of our clients own companies. The more we get into bed with a client the more we learn. So whenever you hear something you think I should know be sure you tell me. Okay."

My shock must have shown because he added quickly, "Don't get me wrong. I'm not telling you or the girls to round heel it for insider information. But gossip is often a clue."

"Round heel?" I asked.

"You know—tip over—on your back."

"Oh!" I said with all the pretended innocence I could muster. I turned my face to the limo's window because I didn't want Hanlon to see what was written there. Ms. Money was becoming richer all the time because she had already been in bed with some of Ledbetter's wealthiest clients.

26

*F*orbes published its first list of the '400 Richest Americans' in 1982—not long after the birth of the great 20-year Bull market. The list was easy to get on because it took as little as $75 million, and there were only 13 billionaires, mostly from the oil patch. Twenty-three of those listed were Ledbetter clients, exposing me to some of the richest men and women in the country. Ms. Money met the wealthiest of the wealthy—aka the 'super rich'— and Maggie Worth was not immune to them. In Florida, at one of her twenty-three mansions worldwide, I met Rosemarie Kanzler, who told me in a nearly eighty-year-old whisper, "I always knew what I wanted. Then I figured out a way to get it." *The best advice is the simplest—isn't it?*

I dined with Charlotte Ford, Christy Walton, the oil-rich Duncan daughters and the Bass brothers. I saw my first privately owned Picasso in one of seven estates owned by Chryss Goulandris, who numbers among the world's richest women. I stayed in some of the country's most exclusive hotels, including the Hay-Adams in Washington and the Ritz-Carlton in Chicago. I was invited to estate homes whose scale and luxury I had never even imagined. I visited the magnificent Rennert mansion in Sagaponack, the

30-room Palm Beach estate of a Mexican billionaire, a Tulsa house designed by Frank Lloyd Wright, Annie George's 'Llenroc,' and Aaron Spelling's huge, 'The Manor,' Los Angeles' most opulent palatial home.

My perfectly styled jet black hair, a beautifully made up face, and the right clothes helped me enter the world of the ultra-rich. Soon enough Ms. Money wanted to live in it. I wore Cardin suits to client meeting, and Italian designer gowns for society functions. A Fifth Ave jeweler was happy to lend me diamonds for display at wealthy social functions. They were gorgeous. As soon as I clasped them around my neck, I wanted them to stay on my skin forever. TV makeup people were constantly telling me how good I looked. The eyes of powerful men signaled that their women-scan radar was still targeting me. Nor was Ms. Money unaffected by their attraction.

The complete confidence these men radiated had a magnetic effect on me. Lips-sealed discretion was the rule of my one-time-only liaisons. I told Hanlon nothing about them. Absolute trust was required of both parties. These were not stupid men demanding a pound of flesh. By definition, the union was without shame or guilt. Each brief affair sealed a decision to trust me with their money. Yes. But the nature of the exchange went way beyond simple barter. I had learned that just like money, sex was a medium of exchange. But for money to work it has to be believed in. Once gold coins solved that problem because of their intrinsic worth. Then paper money linked to a gold standard. Then came currency backed by a government promise only. Money whose value depends only on belief in the backer is subject to sudden devaluation if people lose faith in it. If sex is the ultimate medium of exchange, the partners must also share mutual respect—purity. I found sex with the ultra-rich exceptionally stimulating. They reached deep into me and brought fiery satisfaction. And I was left undiminished and never debased. Instead, I found myself renewed. The absolutely most important part of these unions was that Ms. Money's innocence was perpetually restored. It was renewed in the course of each liaison.

My transformation progressed as Ms. Money became rich herself. I owe that to the great Bull market. Being faithful to its essential theme—'Be long or be wrong'—was what mattered most of all. My Ledbetter account crossed the half-a-million line when the Dow surpassed the 2000 mark on January 8th of 1987. When it surpassed 2500 by July of the same year, for a never seen before gain, I was closer to one million. But Michael Jackson's album *The Bad* was released on August 31, 1987. It proved to be an omen. I was humming his 'Dirty Diana,' when a few weeks later my direct line buzzed. Sue McCann was worried. She asked if I heard that Elaine Garzarelli of Shearson Lehman was predicting a serious market crash. Before I could answer, another talking head on my Bloomberg monitor pulled a trans-species switch from Bull to Bear and blared out, "This is going to make '29 look like a kiddies' party!" Before I even hung up stocks were cratering on my monitor. The Crash of '87 had begun.

Between October 14 and October 19, 1987, the major market indexes dropped more than 30 percent, spilling investor blood. On a newly named Black Monday, October 19th, I watched riveted as the Dow plummeted 508 points, losing almost a quarter of its total value. This was the greatest Dow drop Wall Street had ever suffered on a single day. Ms. Money went into shock, staring at her computer screen, where tumbling numbers appeared as a bright red blur. My phone was soon ringing continuously. The market rebounded, but by the end of a week of gyrations, the Dow was still down a record 296 points.

I ran into Stringfellow's office—*was I going to lose it all?* Hanlon was already there asking, "What's going on?"

"I thought the risk parameters had decayed. The market was overheating. Prices were too far ahead of expected corporate earnings," Stringfellow stammered. My heart fibrillated. But then he added, "So I hedged bigtime. Our people are intact. We even made some money on the short side." I hugged him.

"But what caused it?" Hanlon asked.

"It was the LBO madness." Investors betting on more and more leveraged buyouts just ballooned stocks way too high. The trigger for the Crash was Congress. A bill eliminating tax deductibility for interest on debt used for corporate takeovers passed the House Ways & Means Committee on the 15th.

"I told you they would go after Milken," Hanlon said.

"But there's more," Stringfellow went on. "That was what pulled the trigger. But the bullets came from the computer. I mean the big ones. The Crays."

"How did that work?" I asked.

"High-speed, large-program trading caused share prices to cascade. As trading speeded up, stock prices fell lower and lower, and more and more sell programs kicked in as sell-side stop-loss orders were triggered. Finally, the programs were selling stocks blindly. It was a downwards spiral. As the big mutual funds dumped stocks to raise cash for redemptions by fearful clients, the futures market in Chicago went even lower than the stock exchange in New York. Professional traders bought futures in Chicago and sold shares in

New York." In Stringfellow's words, "They wiped out the guys on the other side of the trade. A lot of jerks who were writing naked—uncovered—were slaughtered."

"So is it a crash—or just a high-speed correction?" Hanlon got to the point.

"Clearly the latter," Stringfellow answered like an academic. "This isn't 1929."

Hearing him, Ms. Money attacked the market breach like a woman scorned. She screamed, "Correction not crash" until she was hoarse in the throat. "The Bull is still in charge," she proclaimed on *Smarter Than The Street,* telling investors that chaos creates opportunity. "Buy the dips."

Only six months after the crash, the Commerce Department reported that GNP was growing at a healthy 4.8 percent rate during 1987's last quarter. I was summoned to Washington by Marlin Fitzwater. Ms. Money stood behind the President and smiled when he quipped that the stock market had predicted nine out of the last six recessions. Finally, even Hanlon was impressed, and sent me a pair of diamond studs.

But the huge LBO wave finally ended. In 1989, Jerome Kohlberg and cousins Henry Kravis and George Roberts (KKR) launched the biggest takeover ever. They raised $31 billion to buy out RJR Nabisco. But the raiders were forced to offer more and more as the battle waged on. To win the hostile takeover, KKR eventually had to bid a super-exorbitant $109 per share. That was way too high. In 1990, trying to keep their acquisition solvent, the raiders had to put in $1.7 billion of new equity. Drexel went bankrupt, and Milken went to jail.

Ms. Money was now worth over a million dollars. I had lost nothing, which I confused with having nothing to lose. Risk became a necessary evil. I began to make bigger and bigger bets with my personal account. After all, I had the money, and I wanted more. And, in my way, I was as good as Stringfellow and a match for BJ Hanlon. When all was said and done, I was fast becoming Ms. Money full term.

27

One thing I would never give up is Seiji, my stylist at Michael Gordon's Bumble and Bumble salon. She knows my hair better than anyone. "What's a 'lift out?'" the Asian woman asked me one morning. "One of my other clients was talking about it, and I didn't know. Does it have anything to do with hair?"

"Maybe a face lift," I answered. But I knew better. It was Street talk for one firm buying an entire team of money managers or research analysts away from a competitor. But I played dumb. It's the best strategy when you want to know something from somebody, and suddenly I got the feeling this was something I wanted to know.

"From up here you should see the scars I see," the hair dresser replied. "Plenty of staple tracks in the scalp."

"Why did you want to know about a lift out?"

"I thought it was something new. Mrs What's-her-name—let me think. Metallic tints, copper, brass, gold, got it. Mrs Bronson was talking about 'a lift out' with a woman getting her roots reworked. I was worried it was a new style."

"I think it's got to be plastic surgery," I insisted. "Maybe it's a boob lift." But I knew better. I had heard the name Bronson before, when Fred Fabricant was whining about Gotham Trust's acquisition of the growth stock money manager Bronson Bell. *That's it—the lift out means Bronson Bell is taking a walk. Gotham would take a hit. I had stumbled on some high level insider information. But the real question was how could I make money off it, and impress BJ Hanlon once and for all?*

I rushed from the hairdresser to meet Georgiana 'Georgie' Dyer, one of Ledbetter's top saleswomen. Labeled BDO's for short, Hanlon's sales force of Business Development Officers differed radically from traditional stockbrokers. Many were rich enough to be Ledbetter clients themselves, and they weren't reluctant to display their status. In the winter, the only mink coats they wore were Black Glama, and they sparkled with earrings, bracelets and wedding rings that were never less than flawless five-carat brilliants. Hanlon paid the highest sales commissions in the business to salesladies whose clients were often their look-a-like best friends.

Ms. Money's pitch had helped Georgie Dyer win the multi-million dollar Park East Synagogue endowment. At the time, she introduced me to the Temple's treasurer saying, "Rosie Goodman and I went to summer camp together." *That's how it is.* Now we were in a limo headed for Sands Point, where I was going to pitch the Land Trust account. "The name has nothing to do with sand—you know—beach," Georgie explained as we crawled in traffic on the Expressway. "It's from Joshua Sands, one of the richest men before the Civil War. He was Collector of the Port of New York. Half of what he took in as duty went into his own pocket."

I responded with an "Oh!" But my mind was focused on the insider information now in my possession. *How could I use it?*

Georgie went on to tell me that the exclusive enclave on Long Island's north shore was once the sole domain of the Vanderbilts, the Belmonts and the Harrimans. Then the Guggenheims built an estate called *Falaise*—named after the famous chateau in Normandy. Around 1900, railroad tycoon Jay Gould's son bought in and put up a replica of Ireland's Kilkenny Castle. "It's now called Castle Gould. But the estates all fell apart. They were subdivided by the end of the War," Georgiana concluded her brief history. "That's how my husband's family got in. We have a summer place here. But the Trust owns the open space that's left. None of it's for sale."

"That must take a pile?"

"Gotham has the account. It's worth over $50 million. The Trust pays the taxes on the empty land. And it buys whatever comes up for sale. That's the only way to stop any more subdivision. You need ten million to buy in now. And you have to be Old Money—this is the gold coast of the North Shore. It's not the Hamptons. Did you hear what Milken's pet corporate raiders did out there? They say Weinberg and Seltzer, part of the gang that put Revlon in play, hired four models to play doubles tennis. You won't believe this— in their sneakers only. Naked women's tennis! Can you imagine?"

"That's so crass!" *But I had no trouble imagining it.*

"The Trust is losing money. They're not happy campers. But you'll be up against Fred Fabricant. He lives out here too. They got the account when he was appointed to the Board, but he's off now. He's actually pretty close to me. He's got three acres of waterfront— but all I have is a dock."

"I'll do my best." *So Fabricant will be here tonight!*

"They haven't done well—ever since they bought Bronson Bell. It's a culture clash. Gotham doesn't understand high tech like BJ. Fabricant tried to tell Ned Bronson how to buy stocks. Now their returns look like dirt. We've got a chance. I'm counting on Ms. Money—you're my secret weapon!"

I know an even bigger secret, my mind shouted, but I held my tongue. I wasn't wrong. Bronson Bell is walking out on Gotham. What's Gotham going to do about that? This was my chance to talk with Fabricant. It's perfect.

"I'm not going back to the city. So you're invited to stay with us. Don't say 'No.' Please! You can stay the whole weekend if you want. There's a ton of left-behind clothes to pick through if you need anything."

"Only if it's nice—it would be fun to read in the sun."

"Did you know this is where Scott Fitzgerald got the inspiration for *Gatsby?*"

"I loved it." *Absolutely.*

"They say Beacon Towers—Alva Belmont built it after she re-married—is the model for Gatsby's mansion. Fitzgerald came out here a lot. Sands Point is the model for East Egg. Nearer in, Kings Point is West Egg."

I remembered when I first read it as a Pommie. Every woman wants to be Daisy. She is so beautiful. And Gatsby has money—it's New Money—a ton of it. He loves her—and she goes back to him. But I don't have to tell you what happens after that. *BJ Hanlon must be the only person who wouldn't understand.*

"BJ has a permanent invitation too."

"Is he coming?"

"I never know now. They used to be here a lot. I'm sure you've heard the story. His daughter loved it out here. She was just like one of our own. And you look so much like her. The same green eyes! And your hair's the same exactly—so black. She was tall too. It's much too sad."

I was stunned. Because she was right—and wrong. I knew about the tragedy from Sue McCann. But Georgie's words still gave me a shock. It was the first time I'd heard his daughter and I were look-a-likes. *But his daughter is dead. And I look just like her. Ms. Money must be his daughter!*

28

I knew my pitch by heart. Following Georgie's introduction, I gave the Land Trust's board a Ms. Money pose that let them know what I was worth—beauty, brains and a big bank account. Then I rolled into my opening joke, "The appetizers tonight, I'm sure you'll all agree with me, were exceptional. So the first thing I'm going to tell you about the market is very simple. Just buy the dips!"

The joke immediately put the audience on my side. Then Ms. Money completely captured them by asking for a show of hands from investors who had lost money in the Crash of 87. And seeing them all lift their arms—I slowly raised my own. Once again they laughed, but then I told them, "Now drop your hands if you're back already!" No hands dropped. They were all still losers. I waited, and then lowered my own hand. I had them right there. *I was good!*

I explained that Ledbetter's losses were small—and our hedging techniques had more than made up for them. I pointed out that diversification depended on making sure the different baskets holding an investors eggs were actually different. Then I screened numbers demonstrating that with nothing to make up—Ledbetter's house portfolio had risen further into the black. "Are you back yet?" I asked. There was nothing left but my three-slide finale:

LOW RISK MEANS FASTER RECOVERY
GROWTH STOCK SMARTS
TIME FOR A CHANGE

Applause followed the pitch. Georgie gave me a squeeze when I sat down.

Now it was Fabricant's turn. His ultra-thin stick figure clutched nervously at the table top lectern. His not-quite-navy suit was wrinkled. He looked eighty, with his mop of purple white hair, and almost wizened ultra-pale face. He put on silver-rimmed glasses, and his colorless thin lips began to read from his notes. Then he took off his glasses and gave the group an icy stare, as if daring them to challenge him.

"He's Swiss," Georgie whispered in my ear. "You figure it? They're the world's most successful bankers, but also the best jewel thieves."

He began with the current investment house mantra, "We wanted the 'first-mover advantage.' So we got big fast." *Just like a man!*

He explained that under third-generation heir, Bostwick 'the Boss' Morey, Gotham had gone public and then used newly issued shares to buy Bronson Bell. "You must have heard of them," Fabricant said, waving his glasses at the group. "They're focused totally on growth stock investing. They know how to surf the high-tech wave. They've earned an average of 27% per year for their clients!"

"In your famous model portfolio, Fred," one board member interrupted loudly. "Not in ours." Even I was surprised by the bitterness of the comment.

But Fabricant ignored it. "We even rewired the building because they had so many PCs."

Then another board member immediately challenged him, saying loudly, "Maybe you moved too fast! We're down by more than thirty percent."

This time Fabricant took on the challenge. "Gotham has been in business as far back as the nation's founding fathers. I'm a Sands Point resident, and I'm telling you Bronson Bell means a bright future for Gotham and your investment."

How could he lie so smoothly—maybe there is no lift out?

And then Georgiana Dyer stood up, and in her best little girl voice asked Fabricant, "Is this where you're going to hand out toasters?" The audience burst into laughter, but she went on. "I live out here too. What I hear is that your new California free-wheelers are having trouble getting used to Gotham's New York couch potatoes. Is that why your bag's empty? I expected at least a free toaster, maybe even a coffee-maker."

"I'm not ashamed to admit it." Fabricant overrode the laughter haughtily. "The '87 Crash couldn't have come at a worse time. Gotham reacted one way and Bronson Bell the other. But we've got that fixed now. I assure you." He glared at her—and left the speaker's podium stiffly.

Just at that moment my plan crystalized. *Empty bag! That was it. Bronson Bell was about to take a walk quotrons and all. I was sure of it. Gotham would be left holding an empty bag. Only it didn't have to be empty! Ledbetter could be in it. I would make a ton of money if Gotham bought it. And BJ Hanlon would finally find out what I was really worth.*

29

Georgie got up to leave as the Board regrouped for its executive session.

It was a beautiful early summer night, with almost no chill, owing to the soft air from Long Island sound. But I looked back and saw that Fabricant was still schmoozing

"I'm tired, but please stay the night," the saleswoman misinterpreted my wavering. "We can walk back—it's not far."

"No—I'm going to stay," I told her. "But I need to go back in." I made it sound as if I had to go to the toilet. "I'll catch up with you."

"No need to hurry—the more you schmooze the better," she told me. "This is the only road. You can walk it in less than ten minutes. I'll leave the light on. Our name is on the box. If you go one house more you'll end up at the water."

Turning back, I ran right into Fabricant making his last goodbye. I felt his eyes give me an MRI look. But then they challenged me—as if to ask why I was still on his turf. His pale lips said, "I didn't know Georgiana was bringing Ms. Money along—Ledbetter's

Wonder Woman! It looks like you've pulled off another customer snatch tonight."

"That's how my Golden Lasso works Fred. It's one of my super-hero weapons."

"Yeah," he said sneering. "You rope 'em and Hanlon dopes 'em."

"BJ's no dope. He has more brains than you'll ever have."

"I know that!" he snapped. "We've been trying to buy him for years. We'd buy you too—just to get him."

My brain buzzed. *Does he want me to help him buy Ledbetter?*

I needed the right approach. As long I kept my insider info se-cret, I could stop anytime I wanted. "I'm sorry—I was just doing my job. I didn't know you were that interested." I stepped closer to him. "Maybe I can help." It wasn't a question. At Perpetual Mercy I had watched Sarah Churchill as Florence Nightingale three times.

"Look—I brought my boat over. I'm just on the other side of Georgiana—around the point. Why don't you go back with me? I'll drop you by her dock."

"Good. It won't take long?"

"Only a few minutes, it's calm."

I let him lead me to the adjacent pier. My heels clacked on the wooden deck. He jumped down into a small white craft, but I turned my back to him and used the ladder. He stood behind, reaching up, and his hands slid under my white linen jacket. Holding me just below the breasts, he guided me into the small boat.

I turned towards him, but just as he began an attempted kiss, I dropped onto the stern seat. He stood facing me, with his back to a standing center console housing the controls. "No wonder they call you *Fast Freddy.*"

"We could certainly use you at Gotham—independent of BJ." *He's trying to buy me! Boy—he's got a big surprise coming!*

The boat tipped for a second, its fenders rubbing the dock, as he moved closer to me. I grabbed his arm for support. "I do want to help."

"We can pay up for talent."

"That depends on how big you are—I'll have to see." I pulled down his zipper, and slipped my hand into his pants. I felt his boney fingers clutch at my breast.

"What's this?" I asked with a smile, freeing his stiffness. I was surprised to find he was uncircumcised. I played with his foreskin, and he drew in a breath. "Looks like there's something wrong here," I continued. "I better examine it closely." I bent down, sliding the skin flap back, and taking him with my lips.

"I was born in Switzerland," he gasped.

I bent down again, smearing lipstick onto him. "No—there's something definitely wrong here. It's telling me Bronson Bell is walking out on you." *Perfect. Point to Ms. Money!*

His prick collapsed immediately. "How the hell did you find out about that?" He whispered harshly.

"I'm Ms. Money—remember."

He sunk back down on the stern seat. "We were totally stupid," he sighed. "Never made an acquisition before—our lawyers didn't lock them in for three years with a retention clause. We didn't even put a non-compete in their contract. Come Monday Ned Bronson will walk out on us with all his clients and more than a few of ours too." *There's nothing more self-pitying than a banker who's been outsmarted and lost a ton of money.*

I kept playing Nursie with him, "There may be a way to fix it."

"I just signed off on the press release. They cost us $150 million," he groaned.

"What you need is a better story," I spoke aggressively.

"What are you saying?"

"If your wife runs off—what the media needs to hear is that a movie star has just proposed to you. That's what people will pay attention to. They don't care about your wife! You've got to pay up big time and buy Ledbetter, BJ, me—right now!"

Suddenly a man's deep voice boomed out, "Pay attention Fred! It's a brilliant idea!" BJ Hanlon was standing on the dock. "Just be sure you listen to Ms. Money!" The voice told me he was angry, very angry. The boat lurched as he let himself down into it. I hoped it was dark enough to cover my smeared lipstick.

"Here's the doctor right on time," I said, covering my surprise.

"Is Ledbetter interested?" Fabricant asked.

"Have you ever been to bed with a movie star?" I asked.

"Think about it Fred—what's that worth? For the right price we're willing to execute and give you retention plus a non-compete. All we want is operational autonomy. I'm sure you've learned your lesson."

"What's it going to cost?" Fabricant's tone said he was hooked.

"Three hundred!"

"You want more than a Cluckman?" Fabricant blurted back. "That's huge!" It was a reference to the recent buyout of the wildly success-ful investment bank formed by Sam Cluckman. The former head of mergers & acquisitions at Merrill Lynch had just sold himself and his four-year-old firm to giant Coronado City Bank for $250 million, the highest price tag ever for a financial boutique. Wall Street traders had jokingly started calling $250 million a Cluckman Unit.

"We're bigger than Bronson Bell, with a third more AUM. Our accounts alone are worth it—not to mention Ms. Money here." Hanlon practically snarled my name as he answered.

Fabricant wasn't stupid. He showed his wisdom by replying, "Okay! I'll settle for a gentleman's agreement. Your terms—you sign tomorrow. We'll put out a new press release."

"Done deal," Hanlon replied as he pulled himself up onto the dock. I felt the tension in his frame. He was still angry.

"Will I get the movie star too?" Fabricant asked me.

"You don't get the star because you're not the leading man," I told him.

"I'm really getting screwed," he hissed.

"That's because we've already got you by the balls," I snapped as I grabbed Hanlon's extended hand and climbed back onto the dock.

"We'll walk back to Georgiana's." Hanlon spoke loudly to Fabricant and myself as well. "I don't want little Ms. Money to get sea sick and fall overboard with all your cash in her pocket."

30

Given sixty days of regulatory review, Ledbetter would join Gotham Trust as an independent subsidiary. We would move to new quarters, but nothing else would change. Ledbetter would maintain its own research staff and sales team. Hanlon would retain his title as President of Ledbetter, but would also became a senior executive vice president of Gotham on par with Fabricant. Ledbetter clients who maintained their accounts for a year post-merger would receive a special dividend. Hanlon would bank triple-digit millions, and my take would be in double digits. It was a pretty picture, but I knew Hanlon was furious with me.

He was so angry his hand was shaking as he pulled me away from Fabricant into the Long Island night. I could feel the rage in his stiff walk. As soon as we were in the open, he exploded. "When were you going to tell me that you had sold my company—after you finished sucking his dick?"

"You sold it—not me," I screamed back.

"But I didn't give him a blow job to find out Bronson Bell was taking a walk. I never told you to go after insider info by pulling down your pants."

"That's not how I found out! You're not smart enough to know how I figured that out. But it doesn't matter anyway. You don't really give a shit about me. I can fuck whoever I want."

Suddenly I charged right at him. I was just as furious, maybe even more. I beat on him with my fists, cursing him. I was so mad that my words shot out in a red hot broken stream. "Never—dare—damn you—shit—stupid— bastard—blame—no good—stupid—puppet."

He grabbed my wrists, but I kicked out at him, striking his shins. When he winced, I broke one hand free and slapped him in the face. "You're so stupid!" I yelled at the man I wanted to love—the man who wasn't strong enough to love me. "I need you! Don't you know I need you?" I cried out so angry that I was sobbing. "I can fuck anyone—but I need you. If you don't want me then it doesn't matter. But I'm not some puppet you made to play with."

"You know I want you—always. But I'm still married." The words just emptied out of him.

"I don't care." My answer was spontaneous. "You don't understand."

"My wife's in Austen Riggs—it's a mental home in Stockbridge. She can't be released." His voice quavered. I heard him unlocking.

"Our daughter died—the pain is unbelievable. It never ends—never—never. My wife tried to kill herself. The last time was close. She's not the same. She can't be. You know the last thing my daughter said—'Don't stop loving mom.' I kissed her, but she was dead. What good is loving anybody? My daughter is dead and my wife is suicidal."

"You've got to let me help you. I need you!"

"You know why I make so much money? It's because I don't want any. That's why I'm good at it."

"No—it's because we are money. We're worth it! You and me. We're worth it because we want each other. You know it. I know you know."

"I should have died too!" he spoke harshly.

"Not the way I feel. You're worth too much to me. That's what matters. I matter—you matter. That's all." I grabbed him and pulled him down. It was the only way to make him understand. My emotions surged in an explosion of passion. We rolled onto the grass. His skin was electric, and I pressed my breasts into him, clinging hotly to his body.

Suddenly he responded. He wanted to, and now he did. He pressed himself over me. I was wetter and wetter and hotter and hotter as I opened to him. He slid into me firm and enlarged. I felt a layer of tissue emerge that met him just as he streamed into me. And the message of his hands on my face as his lips clutched my mouth, was that he wanted me. He went deeper and deeper because he really wanted me. We united in a climax of inseparable union. Finally, gasping for breath, I lay under him. I had told him what I wanted him to know, and now I was sure he knew it.

31

The Berlin Wall came down on November 9, 1989—and stocks skipped rope right over it. The market went up and up and then even higher. The Dow reached an intraday high above 3000 for the first time on Friday, July 13, 1990. I had no fear of the date. Instead Ms. Money announced "the decade of equities"—and what a decade it was to be! In the next ten years over 250 stocks rose 1,000%—or more! I capitalized on the 1994 Sara Lee "Hello Boys" campaign, featuring a close-up of Czech model Eva Herzigová with her ample cleavage displayed in a very sexy black brassiere. On *Smarter Than The Street*, Ms. Money told her TV audience that "the Market is wearing the Wonderbra!" Her words went nationwide, when the media latched on to the comment—making her an overnight national financial celebrity.

Ms. Money was interviewed by Paula Zahn of CBS and Melissa Lee from Bloomberg. She lunched with Wall Street guru's, meeting men like Morgan Stanley's perma-bull Barton Biggs—sexy for and older guy, and ancient perma-bear Joe Granville—nice without spice. She met Alan Abelson of *Barron's*, Eliot-Wave theorist Robert Prechter, financial guru Gary Schilling, strategist Bill Meehan of Cantor Fitzgerald, the little known but brilliant Ned Davis and Swiss genius Felix Zulauf. Her woman friends included Abby Jo Cohen, who left the Fed to join Goldman Sachs as a vice president and co-chair of the Investment Policy Committee, and Suze Orman, who left her post as vice-president of investments at Prudential Bache Securities in 1987 to found the Suze Orman Financial Group.

Ms. Money's work focused increasingly on institutional clients—big pension funds, large endowments and deep-pocket charitable foundations. She spent more and more time with consultants advising these institutions and investment committees. Her professional pitch focused on growth stock alpha, meaning the additional return generated in the context of its beta, or volatility. Performance calculations were explicit, with comparison to the universe of growth managers and the Barra Growth Index. She was frequently asked about inherent risk in terms of the Sharpe ratio, another major risk criteria. And her answers were repeated in *The Financial Times*—giving her 'traction' as the media called it.

Stocks continued to soar because the Internet IPO mania more than made up for waning LBO fever. She and Hanlon flew out to the giant-size Comdex trade show to hear Microsoft co-founder Bill Gates give a keynote address. Gates was convinced that Moore's Law was still driving the chip revolution, which meant the Internet would continue to change society more than anyone could guess. Ms. Money took one look at the Yahoo neon sign flickering over San Francisco's on-ramp to the Bay Bridge, and told investors it was the signal to "Bet the net!" Once again she was 'spot on!' Netscape went public in August 1995. The stock was set to be offered at $14 per share. Then a last-minute decision doubled the initial offering price to $28 per share. But on the first day of trading, the shares soared to $75, a record for a first-day gain, lifting the browser company's market value to $2.9 billion. Netscape revenues went on to double every quarter in 1995, which put its founder, web poster-boy, Marc Andreessen, on the cover of *Time Magazine*—barefoot! *Hey! He's younger than I am.*

I arranged to meet Alice Powers at Comdex in Las Vegas. We were all booked into the Venetian. She was already one of the new breed of what Silicon Valley had labeled, 'Cisco Millionaires.' Alice and her husband were among the networking company's earliest employees, holding some of the first shares ever issued! The stock just wouldn't stop doubling and splitting and then doubling again and then splitting again as the web became a household word. A $1,000 initial investment made when Internet leader Cisco went public was worth almost $70,000 by 1990. By the end of the decade, the same investment was worth an amazing $1 million!

Everywhere, high technology was turning science fiction into reality. The stocks of big tech companies split and split again and then again, and amazingly their share prices spiraled higher and higher. I was worth more and more. Wall Streeters bought second homes in Silicon Valley. On February 23, 1995, the Dow gained 30 points to close at 4003—its first ever close above 4000. And, on November 21st of the same year, the Dow gained 40 points to close at 5023 its first close above 5000. That made 1995 the first year ever when the Dow surpassed two one-thousand-point marks. I was nearly a million dollars richer. TV viewers took a break from screens showing the climbing Dow, to watch police chase OJ Simpson's white Bronco. But all eyes quickly switched back to watch stocks go even higher.

At Comdex, we all met for drinks after a day at the show. Alice and I stood at the hotel bar, in the midst of a crowd of cool, young Gen-X hipsters. The men were already plotting strategies to flip their Internet startups, fast becoming established dot-coms, and cash out as millionaires. We followed along to a cocktail party, where one of the crowd made a pass at Alice. Another came right up to me, asking if I was free for dinner at Guy Savoy. I could guess what he wanted to eat, but he looked to be barely twenty. I let him pull me into a dance, but I started to giggle. Then BJ Hanlon arrived after a few minutes. Alice was laughing so hard, she could only point at me. Hanlon immediately cut in and pulled me away. But I just couldn't stop giggling.

We were partners in every sense. The millions we made on Ledbetter's acquisition by Gotham Trust went into two adjacent apartments on the 17th floor of the San Remo, the art deco twin towers dominating Central Park West. I had the view of Central Park. Hanlon faced south towards Columbus Circle. Somewhere far above us, Bono lived in the penthouse he bought from Steve Jobs for $15 million. We paid $7 million together for 14 rooms, with separate entrances. But I had the interiors connected before moving in. We lived as a couple, and I wanted nothing to come between us. I was sure Ms. Money would find a way to prevent any intrusion.

32

But my mom died, and I still miss her. On March 10, 1990, Evelyn Sharp Worth, Mrs Connelly, the realtor, was found slumped over the wheel of her BMW in the parking lot of a McDonald's off Interstate 95. She was en route to an estate home in Westport, whose sellers had promised her an exclusive listing.

Like many women, myself included, my mother had an obsessive fear of breast cancer. She never missed a mammogram. Instead, she died of a heart attack. Given her low blood pressure and small size— she had nothing in her closet over a size 8 petite—no one expected it. But I should have because she was always two women, the one who mothered me and the one who had risen to the challenge of a new world. We were two explorers measuring our personal progress by the size of our bank accounts. She by necessity, and me through temptation. Only she understood what my transformation really meant. Ultimately she was the one who taught me that after I had made a million, the next million was always easier to make.

Connelly was devastated. I opted for a small ceremony and a closed coffin. I stared hard at the beautiful darkly gleaming walnut box resting peacefully in the funeral chapel, but suddenly I wished it were open. Not because I wanted to kiss her one last time, but just to tell her the secret I had been keeping. It would have made her happy.

So I told Hanlon. We were in bed watching Ed O'Neill playing Al Bundy in an episode of the new sitcom series *Married With Children*. I was exhausted, too tired to make love, and just nestled against him. I started to drift off. But I hit 'volume' instead of 'end' on the remote, and the show's famous theme song, 'Love and Marriage,' sung by Frank Sinatra, suddenly blared out from the flat-screen TV. I jumped and Hanlon put his arm around me, and I looked up and said completely without hesitation, "I'm pregnant."

His reaction surprised me. He just kissed me and he kept on kissing me. He leaned over and kissed my forehead, my eyes, my nose and then his lips pressed harder on my mouth. He pushed my breasts together and kissed each nipple slowly, tracing the aureole with his tongue. Then he went under the sheets and kissed me, and finally pulled me against him tightly, just rocking me until I slept.

The morning after my revelation, he asked, "So what's the plan?"

"The plan is nothing changes," I answered. Like most men he wanted to make a baby. *After that you know what!* Still I worried that grief over his daughter would flare up when he learned he had. "So don't say anything."

"What do you mean?" he asked. He was still groggy.

"Don't say anything—it's just the two of us."

"But the baby...."

"The baby isn't going to make a difference. And for your information it's not a baby—it's a boy. His name is Jason." *For BJ's son.*

"Doesn't Jason need a father?"

"Of course he does. But we can go on just the way we are."

"So?"

"You're smart enough to know the answer."

"I see."

And he did—eventually. Because I had a plan—didn't I. Can you guess what I did? Because if you do I think you will really like the rest of my story. The answer is staring you in the face. Act like Ms. Money. She was learning to think with her heart.

Two months later, Margaret Marilyn Worth, aka Ms. Money, married Paul Stringfellow. Brian Connelly gave the bride away—still wearing a mourning armband for my mother. BJ Hanlon was the best man. The civil service held in New York was simple, with only 20 guests, including Elspeth Stringfellow, the groom's 86-year-old mother, who flew up from Atlanta. Meeting my mother-in-law for the first time, I could see why my husband preferred numbers to people. She simply and totally refused to admit that her son was older than ten. He was her perpetual child—hers and only hers. As far as I was concerned that made him a perfect proxy father. I was right, and he soon became mine.

After my mother died, I purchased a 14-room house on a double-size lot in Greenwich, down by the water near, Byram Beach.

Two months before my wedding, I took Stringfellow to dinner at Aldario's, the Italian restaurant, where I fed him his first Martini. I practically had to carry him back to the house. It wasn't hard to get him into bed because he fell asleep as soon as I kicked the door closed. It was obvious that he had never had sex with anyone ever, but I pulled his clothes off and slept next to him naked. In the morning I told him, "We're having a baby."

"It will make my mom happy," he answered. He signed my multi-page pre-nup without reading it.

This is not to say I didn't respect Stringfellow. I came to love him more than I thought I could, much more, because he proved to be the most loving father ever. In his way, he was the most completely natural person I ever knew. Unlike so many people who are nothing more than 'creatures of desire,' he was a true 'creature of instinct.' I had hoped that his shortcomings would prove nothing more than minor imperfections in a diamond, the kind that can disappear if you look at it from a different angle. Thankfully, I was right. He was the perfect answer. Sometimes the right answer is staring you in the face. You just have to see it, to know it's right. But some women are blind to it. They can't see it—not because they don't want to—but they don't know how to. They just haven't learned how. Ms. Money wasn't one of them. *I never sympathized with Blanche DuBois in* A Streetcar Named Desire. *Stella was more my type.*

The wedding guests were invited to a luxury lunch held at Wild Blue, the private dining room of Windows on the World, on the 107th floor of the North Tower of the World Trade Center. Looking out through the full length windows, you could see outlined the southern tip of Manhattan, where the Hudson and East River meet, and towards the ocean, Ellis Island and Staten Island. The small party included Sue McCann and her husband, and a surprise appearance by Frank Agrigento, who looked older to me.

Vera Wang attended. I was hugely thankful for the gown she had created for me, which totally concealed any trace of my pregnancy. I had become friends with her following an accidental meeting in a TV studio. She had left *Vogue* a year earlier, after being turned down as editor-in-chief—she was literally pushed out to make room for Anna Wintour. At the time, I offered to help find finance for her bridal salon, which opened in the Hotel Carlyle. BJ thought it was a perfect investment opportunity, and we attended Wang's wedding in 1989, and the designer reciprocated.

Alice flew to New York from San Francisco, where her gallery was holding a show for the Fascinations Group of earth metal artists. I was hoping my wedding present would come from them. While BJ and I listened, she complained that the dot.com bubble was making life in Silicon Valley miserable. It took three hours to drive from Market Street to San Jose, even on the faster Route 101. That was during non-commute hours—rush hour was impossible. "And the wait for a table at French Laundry is so long you might as well fly to Paris for dinner," she complained. But then she broke into a smile, and added, "So I did."

Later, I whispered that I was already pregnant, and Alice hugged me hard. It was the kind of hug that told me how important our friendship was.

Jason was slow to leave the womb. He was born a Virgo on September 18, 1990. In the hospital, I crooned 'Sweet Child o' Mine' over him—my favorite by Guns N' Roses. He was beautiful, wonderful, mine. My heart beat hard, saying it was so full. I added bedrooms, a nursery, nanny quarters, and a game room to the house in Greenwich. Brian Connelly, still in mourning, did as I told him and moved in. And he summoned a distant Irish cousin, a pretty girl with red hair called Moira, to be Jason's nurse and nanny. She's been the best ever. Stringfellow sold his condo in Cos Cob and moved in a month later. Together they were Jason's immediate family. I insisted on continuing to live with BJ Hanlon in the San Remo. But we spent as much weekend down-time as possible in Greenwich.

Money poured out, but it poured in even faster—year after year. My salary was huge, my bonus went over seven figures, and that doesn't include incentive options. The Bull market born just after 1980 proved to be the strongest of the century. It charged onwards for some twenty years. Truly unbelievable. From a Dow low of close to 775, the trend lifted the market more than 1,400%! Stocks gained an unimaginable 11,000 Dow points. Wall Streeters ran with the bulls. My bank balance went into outer space. 'Houston—we have lift off!' Ms. Money was at the top, living above the clouds. I truly had it all—including a trust that I paid a European adviser and an authorized Liechtenstein attorney to establish in Vaduz, whose sole beneficiary was my son Jason.

PART III: MEL TRAUB

(1997—2003)

33

Jason turned five, and for Christmas, Brian Connelly, now a totally devoted grandfather, brought home one of the first copies of *Toy Story*. We gathered in the TV room in Greenwich to watch the amazing computer animation. It was Pixar's first full-length high-tech feature, and helped Steve Jobs, then the company's nervous majority holder, make millions. He made even more on the subsequent Disney buyout, which I'm thankful to say put big money into Ms. Money's account as well. Stringfellow had spotted Pixar when years ago it mistakenly went into computers, and BJ had worked on financing its spinoff by Lucasfilm in 1986. Jason insisted on watching Buzz Lightyear again on New Year's Day, 1996, which also found us united in Greenwich as a family. I watched all my four men as the film captured their attention—none more so than Jason. I went to the kitchen to check on dinner and returned to find the three grownups singing "You Got a Friend in Me," to Jason. They were happy for different reasons, but each of them loved him. I was happy for him most of all. He was my boy.

Now, a week later, Connelly was calling on my very private office line with a warning, "There's a blizzard coming. Don't stay too late. Get hold of BJ and I'll drive down and get you."

The next thing I knew, Stringfellow walked into my office. "I'm leaving early. Metro North is good enough—I want to get something at Grand Central. If you get back early, we can build a snowman with Jason." He was the complete father because there was so much little boy in him.

I nodded my agreement at his retreating back. But I continued to stare out the window, looking over New York's canyons, just as a trace of snow was repainting them. My mind hardly took in the rows of assorted giant buildings boxed together. If you had asked me then whether I knew that my very, very perfect life was about to change—I would have shaken my head 'No.' Change emerges incrementally. Most people only realize an alteration in the broad trend of their lives long after it's in place. Catch a cold and one day you wake up well. But you can never pinpoint the turning point, the exact moment you got better. The financial markets had taught me that life's winners always spot them early on, but even Ms. Money had no idea of what was coming.

I went into Hanlon's office, where he was eating pizza, and helped myself to a slice. The view of the Hudson was darkening seriously and fast.

"I know, I know—the snow is on the way," he said looking up at me.

"So let's really get the hell out of here."

He sensed my mood and meaning immediately. "Where do you want to go—California?"

I knew he meant the Lodge at Pebble Beach. It was the venture capitalists' biggest hangout. But we wouldn't have any peace there at all. I imagined a league of badgering PR paparazzi hawking stories about the latest and greatest dot-com thing. But then I looked out over the City's quickly whitening roofs, and asked "What about St Barts?"

"The French again," he complained. I had forgotten. The nudity embarrassed him. But he had an idea—"What about Parrot Cay?"

"Only if we leave right now—we can buy anything we need down there."

We made the last plane out of JFK. The blizzard of 1996 struck on January 6th—one of the worst to ever hit the eastern states. New York City was buried, Philadelphia recorded a record 30.7 inches of snow, and in Washington, DC the federal government closed for days.

But getting to the Bahamas wasn't easy. Instead of heading straight south to Miami, we were forced to fly west to Chicago. We missed the storm barreling up the East Coast, but the three-hour trip from JFK to MIA turned into a nine-hour ordeal. I had the feeling we would run out of jet fuel and somehow never make it. We got as far as San Juan in Puerto Rico, only to find that our connecting flight had long since left. Left without us. And if we wanted any further progress we would have to camp out in the Admirals Club lounge for what was left of the night.

To kill time, I decided on an airport shopping spree. Wrinkles had attacked my Italian, black jersey, travel dress. I had been wearing it since changing at the office. I needed clean clothes. But my plan failed because 24/7 shopping had yet to be invented at the run-down Luis Munoz Marin terminal. I stood disappointed in front of a tightly gated boutique. Then another woman traveler attacked the store. I watched as she rattled the gate and made a gesture of disgust with the closed shop. Despite a huge pair of sunglasses, I recognized her immediately. *Who wouldn't!* The perfectly styled hair and gleaming face were familiar from the covers of *Vogue, W, People, Elle, Cosmopolitan,* and *Allure.* It was Giustina Parker! Ms. Money and the model had crossed paths before in New York's media hive. She was one of the first super models whose face stared out at a less-than-beautiful reality from the covers of hundreds of high-fashion magazines.

The glamorous dark-brunette was the first to complain. "We were supposed to go to Parrot Cay. But now we're stuck here over some papers. Something about the charter. Oh! I know you—you're Ms. Money. I met you in New York?"

"It's Maggie," I told her. "I'm not on business." I was happy with the recognition. "I guess we're what they call 'birds of a feather'— we're headed for the same place. We tried to beat the storm. But our luck ran out. We can't get a plane out of here until tomorrow."

"Call me Gia," the model told her. "Come with me. I've got an idea. Maybe we can put some more feathers on the bird!" Then the taller woman practically pulled me back to the Admirals Club. "It's the only decent lounge in this dump. And wait 'til you see who I'm flying with. You probably know I'm between marriages."

But as she re-entered the Club, I saw that BJ Hanlon was already having a drink with Gia's surprise.

Gia marched up to the two men, and speaking for both of us, laughed out, "We're birds without feathers! And we're all going to Parrot Cay together if we ever get out of here."

"I'm working on it," said her companion. Seeing me, he quickly added, "What's Ms. Money doing here?"

I was totally shocked. I had heard the voice before—on TV. It was baritone but shading into base. My body pivoted and my muscles tensed into an involuntary pose. The man who knew Ms. Money was no stranger to me. Gia was traveling with billionaire Melrose Traub! The founder of a prominent nationwide U.S. brokerage firm—he was famous for his 'Tell Mel' TV ads. I had met him briefly at a number of business parties. Now he seemed taller, more powerful, like a filled-out version of Tom Hanks as Forrest Gump. But his hair was different— wavy light brown hair. His neck was strong, but it grew out of sharply sloping shoulders. Not as pretty a face, but pretty men don't usually amount to much. *Ms. Money would rather go to bed with a rich man over a good looking guy any day. Pretty boys are always hell on women—and as you know—that's because of women.*

I knew he was worth billions. He was rich enough to get himself listed in the *Forbes* 400, and nowhere near the bottom of the list. Traub's eyes were large and glowing with an amber tint. They challenged me immediately, but not with a sexual sweep. They didn't say what they were looking for. But I felt it was something deep. Then I knew! His eyes were looking for my secrets and measuring just how well I kept them guarded.

"BJ and I were running from the storm. I needed a break from the markets."

"But we got stuck here," Hanlon's voice interrupted. And then he told me, "Here's the good news. Mel's offered to give us a ride. His private jet wasn't cleared for international. He's chartering a small plane that can take us straight to Parrot Cay. We won't have to fly to Grand Turk and take the boat."

Gia applauded. I added a heartfelt, "Thank god," and stretched to kiss Traub on the cheek.

"We're just waiting for the paperwork to come through," the billionaire told us. "We only have to fly for an hour, but it's international. How long were you going for?"

"Just until things clear up in New York. Mayor Giuliani said to 'stay home.' So we left." I answered.

"Well fly with us. I don't care as long as I'm back before the Super Bowl. The Cowboys are going to hogtie the Steelers."

"Beach, beach, beach," Gia chanted.

She was cut off by a uniformed man, saying, "All set with the charter Mr Traub. We're ready to fly."

"I've just added two guests," he reported.

"No problem if they have U.S. passports."

And when Hanlon and I surrendered our blue books, the pilot led us all out to the field, where I saw a Gulfstream waiting.

The flight to Parrot Cay was short. Gia fell into the first available seat and slept right through it. Soon Hanlon was out cold against a window. I was overtired and awake. Traub was in the aisle seat across from me. He gave me a look, I read his mind, shook my head 'yes,' and he signaled the male steward who returned quickly with two Martini's.

I saw his eyes widen, when my drink arrived. I looked at him saying, "I like olives—the more the merrier."

"Well I'm green with envy," he laughed. I felt he wanted to relax me. But he still radiated power—more than a billion dollars' worth. Then he asked the expected question, "So while you're still in your Ms. Money outfit—tell me where this market's going."

I knew Traub Securities had captured the vast majority of 'self-directed investors' who made their own investment decisions and used the web to buy stocks. I had my answer ready, "Far enough for me to get out of these clothes and into the water. Dow 10,000 is still my call."

"Seriously?"

"The trend is still a friend. But you ought to know that. Your investors are part of what keeps it going." It was true. Trading volume had risen enormously as stock buyers rejected high-fee brokerage houses. Investors acting independently were still sending stocks higher. I knew I had scored a point.

"Thank you," he answered. "I'm glad you think that's why more buying power will keep the Bull charging." I heard the pride in his voice. "But I'm really interested in the long view. I don't want to make a mistake—I made one once."

"What was that?" My tone said I was impatient. He was getting somewhere, but I was just too tired.

"I sold to America First Bank. They were complete assholes." Then he bragged, "I walked away with half a billion."

"But you bought it back!" Ms. Money remembered.

"Damn right," he concurred. "Their investment goal was total mediocrity. My clients laughed and left. They treated employees like they were in kindergarten. Everyone deserted."

"That sounds a lot like Gotham—when they bought Bronson Bell. And they're still way too paternal. We insisted on complete autonomy."

"I heard you were instrumental in that deal. You had to be to get Fabricant to pay up."

She smiled back at him. "You could say I just pulled it off."

He smiled. "Look—here's the point. I learned something really important from selling and buying my own company. You've heard that famous quote, 'A man's reach should exceed his grasp'? Try harder, okay. I think it's bullshit! What you have to know is what you're worth. Then you know who you are. That's why I bought my company back. Because it was me, and I knew I was worth more."

He's really Mr. Money! That's what he means. I sipped my drink and then returned service, "All I know is that people need to understand what the risk they're taking really is—and why they're taking it. That's why you've got to know who you are."

"Precisely. I sold too early for too little. But no matter what the price was—making the re-acquisition was the right choice. It paid off in billions. Now I want to buy only what I want to buy."

I heard it in his voice at the same time that I saw it in his eyes. He wanted me. But he wanted something more than just me. Something he wasn't saying. *Do I have to sleep with him to find out? He wasn't just telling me he was worth it. Something else was on his mind. Was he thinking about buying Gotham? I would be very, very rich if he did. Ms. Money would be a billionaire!*

34

I awoke in a luxurious villa, only to find that I had almost slept on my pillow treat. An engraved gift card said it was a square of $500 a pound DeLafée Swiss chocolate made with flakes of edible 24-karat gold. I popped it into my mouth—so delicious! *Can you really eat gold?*

It was very early. Hanlon was still dreaming away, but the sun was so bright and there was the slightest sea breeze. I felt like I was back in paradise—what winter had taken away was somehow given back to me. I put on a luxurious terry robe hanging by the bath and slipped out to explore. Our villa was on a talcum powder beach ending in crystal electric blue water. I ran down to the sand, dipped my feet, and immediately threw off the robe. The nightmare escape had to be washed off. The water was absolutely perfect and there was no resisting its appeal. I could see the bottom with perfect clarity as I swam out, attracting a school of small silvery pompano and then a glittering neon needle fish right in the top of the slight waves. I swam back to the beach, feeling washed by a bath of light from the sea and sand.

I took a path, hoping it would lead to the resort's spa. I entered a world of perfect color—everywhere gleaming white walls and arches were smothered in masses of bougainvillea that spilled over them. Cascades of flowers burst from green leaves. They were set on fire by the brilliant sun— deep purple, bright fuchsia, gleaming yellow, white, beige, pink, magenta, red, orange—all sprinkled with white centers. I stared hard into the flowers because their radiance had a message for me. Each was perfectly and completely just what it was. They were utterly beautiful and totally unafraid. *Traub? What, me worry!*

I found the spa, and made a meal of a fresh-baked croissant and a just ready-to-eat juicy pink grapefruit, accompanied by some truly delicious coffee. After the tiny breakfast, I was massaged on an outdoor table by a woman whose perfect touch drove all thought from my brain. Then I was cleansed with a Shambala wash, oiled, and again rubbed into mindlessness by the woman's hands.

I ended the morning in a sauna that reminded me of the exclusive spa just around the corner from my San Remo apartment. A petite, very tan woman was sitting with her feet up at the end of a tile tier. Her hair was wrapped in a towel, but the rest of her was naked. I was glad I had waxed. The woman waved a greeting to me, "Just get here? It's the quietest spot on earth."

"We beat the storm and got in last night. Horribly late. But it's so beautiful. I think it's all about the light. Everything reflects everything—the beach is pure white. I mean the sand. And the water is crystal, and the flowers are color crazy!"

"My husband used to say swimming here was like floating in Bombay Sapphire. I'm Karen Koren. I used to be a Chicago girl. Now I'm total New York."

"I know—the designer. Right. Vera Wang told me about your line. She's a friend. I hear it's fantastic stuff. I'm Maggie Worth."

"Oh! Am I pleased to meet you! Ms. Money—wow! The Japanese just bought my company. I'm down here trying to figure out what to do next—maybe sell my villa. It cost $6 million."

BJ will be interested. But I asked a more pressing question, "I hope I can buy some clothes here—we left with practically nothing to wear."

"I can lend you anything you need—but you're tall. I made my first dress when I was seven. My mother sewed bras. Can you imagine? Now all the department stores want my label. But I'm leaning towards jewelry. I just love Paloma Picasso. If I could do something like that—with a Tiffany exclusive? It's all about money!"

"One of my favorite phrases," said a new female voice. It was Gia. Both Karen and I looked up at the fantastic towel-wrapped model who entered the sauna. For the first time, I realized just how beautiful she was. Her face was perfect. Every feature was finely shaped, and there was a tiny beauty spot just above her smile. "And I'll prove it to you," the model said. She turned her fanny towards us and dancing like a jerky puppet, she slowly unwrapped her towel.

I held my breath. Her body was exquisite. Envy was impossible. It was too good. Then I saw the tattoo on her delicate behind. 'More Than $10G' was inscribed in blue.

Karen Koren laughed loudly. "I get it" she cried out. "It's Linda Evangelista."

I realized the tattoo was a shorter version of one of the most famous quotes of the decade, when the famous Canadian model told

Vogue's Jonathan van Meter—"I don't get out of bed for less than $10,000 a day."

"Mel calls it my fine print," Gia laughed with them.

"Yes—your disclosure statement!" I joked back. But seeing Gia in the nude, my mind slipped back to the nights I stripped at The Box. I was older—my body had changed after Jason.

Then Koren interrupted, "Did either of you ever read *Bonjour Tristesse*? You know by Françoise Sagan? There's a really great line in it. It inspired me as a designer. Cécile—she's only 17—but a real jet set playgirl. She says, 'A dress is no good unless it makes men want to take it off of you.' Isn't that great?"

"Truly." I was enjoying being one of the girls. So much of my life was men, men, men. "Right now I love Candace Bushnell—she's writing a column called 'Sex and the City,' in the *New York Observer*. It's really hot."

"A lot of the runway girls read it," said Gia. "And I lived it," she went on. "My first husband was an actor. Sex with him was like identity theft. You know—he wanted to fuck me and be me at the same time."

"I'm in the process of dumping mine," Koren revealed. "That's really why I'm here. I had them fumigate the place as soon as I arrived. My husband's ladies stink." She held her nose.

All three of us burst out laughing. Then I burst out boldly, "Officially I'm Mrs Stringfellow of Greenwich, but I live with BJ Hanlon in New York—in the San Remo. We have adjoining apartments. He's here with me now."

"That is so Italian," Gia told her. "You have a husband for home and a lover for your apartment."

"What about Traub?" I asked.

"You're with 'Tell Mel' Traub?" Koren interrupted.

"I'm not going to kiss and *tell*." Gia said laughing again. There was a pause as a wave of heat swept down into the sauna. "But it really *is* better with Mel," she burst out giggling. He's between marriages. And looking right at me, she went on, "I bet you know how the money guys are. They never got any in high school. They were too short or fatties or nerds you couldn't be seen with. So now that they can have it—they really want it. But they remember when girls wouldn't even look at them. That makes them thankful. I like it when men thank me, the more the better, and preferably with diamonds. Years ago I made $2,000 for one night in Bungalow Eight. I was just seventeen. Now my fanny rules—she slapped her behind."

"Where?" Karen Koren asked.

"I know," I answered for Gia. "You were at a 'Predator's Ball.' The Beverly Hills Hotel. I can't believe it!"

"This Drexel guy recruited us. We were all fashion model wannabes—and actresses looking for their first picture. We needed money for portfolios and try-outs. You should have seen who was there! They were all takeover types. All the Coke you wanted—and I don't mean Diet. But I learned one thing. Make a lot of noise—it makes them feel they're so great!"

This time all three of us laughed at once. But my mind was almost angry. I remembered my conversation with Traub. *Women do have to try harder. Men know nothing about it.*

At least I learned what an LBO means," Gia continued, looking right at me.

"It's a leveraged buyout," I responded.

But Karen Koren immediately cut in—"In the rag trade it stands for 'Lick their Balls Off.'" Her hoarse words echoed in the sauna and set them all laughing even harder.

"You're very turned out," Gia told the designer.

"Who isn't," Koren answered. "I never wanted to play house. I'll show you." The tiny blonde stood and turned to face Gia.

Good boobs, I thought as she placed her feet together, and keeping her heels locked, she pivoted, twisting each foot to the outside. "How's that for first position," she said referring to the ballet stance. "You know in street talk—pimp slang—being 'turned out' means when a girl is ready to make money with her pussy."

"I learned that dancing topless!" I told them, getting a shocked look.

Then Gia interjected, "In France, when I was very young, the dancers were mostly poor girls brought up to be the mistress of a rich man. You can see it in the ballet paintings by Degas. The girl in the tutu belongs to the man in the tux. And now I own a Degas—so I guess I *turned out* well." She took a bow in the steam room.

"Believe me you earned it," Karen Koren replied.

"We all did," I said.

"So I'm throwing a party for us!" Gia concluded. Come to our villa tonight—very dressy—bring BJ. You come too," she invited Koren. "His number two guy is coming in today. We can be six—you know two single people, and then one single and one married, and two married people not married to each other. Just like New York!" After they finished laughing, she added, "Come at eight. Now I'm going to the pool."

"Be careful," said Koren. "I saw Keith Richards—he loves this place. He was at the swim-up bar yesterday. He's got more kids than god."

"I need a new bathing suit," I said. "I'll catch up later." *The Rolling Stones,* I thought. *What next?*

35

By dinner time, my skin was hot, and Hanlon's high forehead was burned beet red. We had gone swimming and snorkeling all day. There were a thousand fish to see in a million colors. I had coated myself with 50-spf blocker, but now my skin was giving back the sun's heat. And Hanlon had been hot too. He held me to him in the crystal water, his hands inside my new tiny bikini, pulling me tight on him, and he kissed me hard. It was just perfect as the ocean swirled around us. I forgot about New York, the markets and even the funny meeting in the sauna with Gia and Karen Koren. We made love again by the villa's small private pool just as the sun neared the horizon.

After we dressed, I told him I thought Traub could be after Gotham.

"You really think so?" he asked. By now I had earned his respect for my professional judgment.

"I can't be sure—but I think he's teasing me with it."

"We have to find out. I mean he did invite us. Even if it was through her?"

"I don't think he just wants to go skinny dipping. It's more than that."

"But he wants you," said Hanlon. "That's part of it?"

"So?"

"Me too!"

"But he can pay a lot more!" I said and laughed.

"We're talking billions."

The prospect of big money excited both of us. If Traub bought Gotham we would make a ton. I slid against him. I could feel he wanted to make love again. But it was time to leave. "No—you'll ruin my dress."

Luckily I had found a Halston 'shark' gown in the resort boutique for only $750. Thank god it was a seven, and they could let it down. When I stepped into it, fastening the side zipper, the off-the-shoulder neckline fit perfectly. A triangular keyhole exposed my back, with the cut out pointing to a cascading center-back ruffle, which gave the gown its name. It was 100% silk and pure black and I knew at once it was perfect for Traub's dinner party.

Karen Koren was there ahead of us, showing a lot of island tan that contrasted with the vivid coral matte shade of her strapless jersey gown and heavy coral choker. The dress clung to her tightly thanks to a ruched side panel bordered by a brilliant beaded seam that ended in a very high slit. I thought it was more sex than glam. Seeing my appraising look, she spoke loudly, "It's by my friend Ronnie Mandel. She started DryCleaners right at the beginning of the 90s, when I launched Karen Country."

"You both have fabulous taste," Gia interrupted. "But don't forget to try these conch fritters—they're super with champagne." Two servers provided by the resort were circulating with champagne and hors d'oeuvre. Then Gia leaned into the two of us and whispered, "I hope you know about 'conk' and men? It's supposed to be an aphrodisiac!" All three of us giggled.

Of course Gia had out-dressed both of us. She was wearing a straight-from-Paris Suzanne Ermann retro chic royal blue and gold Empire gown with a bustier cut low and an open back—truly beautiful. *It belongs on her. She's his Princess. The pearls around her neck must have cost $100,000.* Seeing the dress, I decided to tell my clothing stylist to aim higher. I could afford it now.

BJ was already talking with Traub by one of the villa's glass walls, which glowed deep pink as the last traces of sunset colored the magnificent cloud-streaked Caribbean sky. A man I hadn't met crossed the room obviously intending to introduce himself, but he was cut off by a server with a new tray of champagne-filled glasses. He paused, but Gia took charge immediately, saying, "This is Eric Vanderman—he's Mel's number two."

"Actually I'm co-CEO," he was quick to correct her. "Now what are you ladies whispering about?"

I didn't like him. He reminded me of the Three Stooges—maybe the worst one. His hair was red, and his pale grey eyes stared out from under bushy orange eyebrows. They were beady, set deep in a blocky face whose features were all too large—bulbous nose, full lips, sagging jaw. He was squat and hairy and wearing crumpled bright green twill golf pants and a pullover. He was one of those men who walk forward by swinging their legs sideways. *Not mister nice guy,* I thought.

"But Mel owns the company," Gia interjected.

"Of course—he and his trusts are the majority shareholders." Vanderman quickly agreed.

I saw his lips tighten, but I was glad Gia had put him in his place.

Seeing Vanderman in person only confirmed rampant rumors about his serial marriages and wife abuse. I'd met one female financial anchor Vanderman had tried to bed. She told me a popular joke, which said he had gone to a shrink because he couldn't find a wife. The psychologist tells him to try art to relax, 'Paint a tree.' Vanderman says 'I'll try it.' At his next session the psychologist asks how the art therapy worked. Vanderman pulls out a poorly painted canvas showing a nude model. 'But I said paint a tree,' the shrink screams. 'It is a tree,' Vanderman tells him. 'I'm just not into realism!' "He's ultra-boring," the woman concluded. "You know boooring," she drew out the word. "Women are only objects to acquire."

But Ms. Money knew that by rolling up acquisitions Vanderman had helped Traub Inc rocket from upstart to nation-wide financial presence. I could feel his overbearing personality already. He was restless to strut his stuff. *Had Traub summoned him for a purpose? That would be perfect.*

Traub and BJ crossed over to reunite the party just as the resort's private chef appeared and signaled dinner was ready. We ate outdoors on a deck illuminated by tiki torches whose light wavered in a slight breeze. The sea was calm and the full moon painted the water with a white glimmering path. The resort kitchen had cooked up a superb island meal—gazpacho followed by grilled wahoo in a mango sauce and accompanied by a chilled silvery-white Chablis.

Conversation resumed as we waited for a Grand Marnier souf-flé. "I'd like to know from Ms. Money here just where the market's headed to," said Traub. "Is 5000 the top for the Dow?" *Was it me or money he wanted?*

"Ninety-five couldn't have been better," I answered. "The volume just keeps coming in. What's amazing is there are now more mutual funds than stocks listed on the NYSE. I bet your average daily trades are way up. But since you asked, with Greenspan calling the shots there's no telling where this will all end."

"But what's next?" Traub pressed me. He looked hard at me. *Was it some kind of test?* As the night progressed his eyes had monopolized me.

"I plan to get a tattoo when the Dow crosses 10,000!" I replied. Seeing Gia's fanny in the spa had given me the idea. The model gave a loud giggle, and I got a flash of a smile from Traub.

"And I wonder just where you'll get it," Hanlon cut in.

"Well if it's small enough you'll have to kiss her ass to read it," Koren interjected.

Everyone laughed at that.

But Hanlon wanted to push Traub. "Some things are slowing down— tech M&A is high on hype and low on value. I like plain vanilla. We made a pile of money on the Castle Rock Drinks deal. Just soda, but I mean national brands, and after we sold off the snacks and did the IPO we netted almost half a billion."

"But you had to fight Gotham all the way. They just don't get it," I added a complaint, and sent a direct private message into Hanlon's eyes. It said *I see where you're going.*

Then Traub spoke, mimicking a finance textbook. "You can make a lot of money with very little as long as the internal rate of return on the whole deal including the exit money exceeds the weighted average interest rate on the acquisition debt. That's what the book says. But all it means is money talks! Is Gotham listening?"

"They have wax in their ears most of the time. That makes doing a deal hard. I have to pry the capital out of them," Hanlon answered.

"They grudge us our autonomy," I added and paused as the individual soufflés were served. "They're sitting on a ton of cash that's not being put to work." *Hint, hint, hint.*

I could almost see the calculation take place in Traub's mind. *Bingo!*

Vanderman put his spoon down. He hadn't missed the point. Gotham's cash hoard could easily fund a buyout. They were stupid to carry it on the books. Now it was his turn to send a message, "What's important is your own stock price. TRB shares are making new highs daily. They can pay for anything we want."

I felt that the conversation was taking place on two levels at once. My eyes immediately sought Hanlon's. *Had Vanderman said what I think he said?* I could read BJ's mind. It had happened before. At some point in a pitch both of us would suddenly and simultaneously know when a client was going to say yes. But this was different. *Don't push too hard.*

But Hanlon started to really sell. "Your self-directed investors have made a pile—they're going to need a trust bank soon. Maybe you could migrate them to a higher level where they would appreciate the family wealth approach," he spoke to Traub.

But it was Vanderman who answered. It was his job to take the bait. "Look our stock is at $60 a share—we've got to buy something. We can't keep growing on trades. Money management is where the business is going. We need to lever up—now—before the party ends and the Fed closes the bar."

36

I was looking right at BJ. His eyes were gleaming. But it was Karen Koren—clearly tipsy—who broke in. "Who said the party's over? What about your lever?" she screamed raucously at Vanderman. "You better keep your lever up."

Gia quickly entered the conversation by chanting to a Jimmy Cliff rhythm, "Lever up—lever up—keep your lever up mistah!"

"Please—let's leave the pecker-dillos to President Clinton," Traub intervened. I sensed he wanted to slow things down.

But Vanderman snapped back, "You mean just like keeping your tits up!"

"My mother used to sew brassieres—you don't know anything about boobs."

"Or women," said Gia.

"I'll show you," Vanderman said, jumping up. He practically pulled Karen Koren from the table to the rail, where she leaned back against it. Gia and I immediately rose and stood next to her.

"Now you're a company called Hot Babes, Inc," Vanderman lectured the group. "I'm the acquirer."

"No," Gia cried out. "We're Mermaids Incorporated. I'm the pearl," she said pulling on her necklace. "And Karen's coral—and Maggie's wearing a shark gown."

I pirouetted in the light of the tiki torches to show off my back ruffle. *And I'm after a big fish—a giant tuna.*

"I'll buy the whole company right now," said Traub, getting into the game.

"Two buyers already," said Hanlon. "I'll be the banker."

"See," said Vanderman, "the ducks are already quacking on Wall Street. That means they want to be fed. They'll finance anything for a fee. Am I right Ms. Money?"

"Hey—I'm a shark—remember," I answered back. "So how much are we worth?"

"Okay! You're the target!" Vanderman answered. He took a swig from the martini he was drinking, and then he turned to Hanlon, saying, "You're the banker—how much will you give me?"

Hanlon laughed. "I'll let you have $75 million."

"Not enough!" All three women objected at once.

"No," said Vanderman. "They're worth $100 million, easy. You're only offering me a lousy 75%. I'm bidding $100 million. I'll get another bank."

"I'm worth it!" Karen screamed. "Wait—you'll see!"

"Aren't you forgetting me," said Traub. "I'm the White Knight. I'll buy them for $150 million!"

"Love those knights!" Gia cried out.

"With what?" Hanlon asked.

"I'm putting up $10 million in hard cash, and you're lending me $115 million. That's $125 million. These mermaids have assets—I can leverage them for another $25 mill."

"Kiss my assets!" Koren yelled.

"That will cost you near to $10 million a year for interest. Is the cash flow there to service the debt?"

"Don't worry—you'll get it," Traub answered.

"Service who?" Gia laughed.

"Hard cash," Koren cried out. "Make sure it's hard!"

"I raise my bid. It's better." Vanderman cried out. "I'm offering $175 million. I'm going to strip out some assets to pay down debt in advance." He pointed to Koren. "How much will you give me for her dress?"

"A million," Hanlon answered.

"How about five?" Vanderman almost sneered back.

"You got it," said Hanlon.

"Yes, yes, yes," said the designer. "Just make sure his money is real! I'm not stripping for junk!" She unzipped the side of her tight gown which peeled off her, revealing only a hot pink bra and tiny panties in the same pink hue. I helped her step out of the long dress. Koren twirled in the moonlight. A sense of *dejá vue* made me feel like I was back at The Box.

"$200 million for the entire deal," Traub yelled at Hanlon. And I'll sell you her dress for $5 million," he said pointing to Gia.

"Merger, merger, merger—lever up Mistah merger." the model cried out.

"Do you have the urge to merge?" Koren and I chanted musical backup.

We helped Gia out of her gown. The model was absolutely stunning. Her shape was perfection and her skin tone radiant. She stood free in a gossamer sky-blue bra and panties that had to be by Aubade. There was a sudden hush—as everyone studied her incredible figure.

Koren broke the silence, saying loudly to Vanderman, "I know we're in the tropics—but that better be a banana in your pocket." His sexual tension was evident, and he passed a hand over his forehead.

"Okay," said Traub. "And I've got an outside buyer for the entire subsidiary." He pointed to Vanderman. "She's yours for $35 million," he stood up and dragged Koren over to his partner.

"Done," Vanderman countered.

"I love it," said the designer. She threw her arms around him, screaming, "I wanna be on your balance sheet!"

"Not so fast," said Traub. "I want to see the shark! Give me another five mill for her dress too," he said to Hanlon, draining a Manhattan.

"Don't choke on the cherry!" Gia called to him.

Vanderman broke in saying, "The one's I like are from France—they're drenched in Grand Marnier. They cost a 100 bucks a bottle, but they go down real easy."

"Do you?" Gia snapped back, making everyone laugh.

"We need some music," I interrupted and quickly popped into and out of the villa. Suddenly the night resonated with 'Where Does My Heart Beat Now' from Celine Dion's first English language album, *Unison*.

"When I take my clothes off," I said, looking hard at Traub. "I like to dance for my man." And I proceeded to slither rhythmically out of my silk gown—revealing a black mini bra and micro panties.

Gia applauded the striptease.

"Remember I still own you—and this deal isn't over." Traub spoke over the music. "Okay! I got 15 mill for the clothes and 35 for Karen Corp."

"But you owe him $140 million," I said. "Don't I still belong to BJ?"

"You're missing the whole point!" Vanderman cut in. Karen was wound around him and kissing him excitedly on the neck. "That's only chump change. Believe it! Mel owns you—he's taking you public."

"I want to do a line," Koren called out.

"This is better," I cut her off.

"What's your next move?" Hanlon asked.

"I bet you want to know" Traub answered. He was smiling. "We're going to raise $200 million for these two Mermaids. I'm selling ten million shares for twenty bucks each—that's the subscriber price. Do you want a piece of this IPO?" He leered and asked Hanlon.

"You better grab some!" Gia cried out as she joined me in a dance.

We were both excited. "Or you'll be," and we both mouthed Dion's 'The Last to Know.'

"I'll take three million shares," said Hanlon.

"Tough," Traub countered. "No advance sale. I didn't syndicate the deal. I'm the only issuer period. You'll just have to bid directly for the new issue. It just went public. Wow! They're already at $25."

"Thirty," Hanlon said.

"No luck," Traub shook his head. "Buy orders ahead of you."

"Okay fifty," said Hanlon.

"Done," said Traub. "And I got $100 million for what I sold before you got in on the offering."

"Wow!" I was impressed. "You're walking away with $100 million dollars." The thought of the huge profit was enough to sober me up.

"But now I'm holding 3 million shares—so they're mine," Hanlon snapped.

"No such luck!" Vanderman yelled back at him. "Mel still owns them both. He retained a controlling interest of four million shares."

"So I still belong to him," I said, moving into Traub's grasp. "But maybe I can buy myself back."

"You can have me," Gia cried out, and ran over to Hanlon, jumping on him with her hands around his neck and legs wrapped around his waist. "So let's go skinny dipping! Get this shirt off Mister BJ," she yelled at him. "I want to see you just BA—you know what that means."

"She's your carried interest," Traub called out laughing.

I was shocked for a second. But then I relaxed. Traub was sharing the buyout profit, and I knew why. Let Hanlon have her. Gia wasn't out to hurt—she was doing what Traub wanted. What he wanted was me all for himself. That was the important thing. He wanted me because he wanted something more too. And I would get what I wanted from him—a ton of money. I looked at Hanlon, and blew him a kiss. He gave me one of his special crinkly smiles. It was a private look he only shared with me in bed. I knew he understood. Nothing matters more than money.

37

The warm tropical night was glowing with the soft light of moon beams reflected from the iridescent beach. I ran off the deck, casting my bra and panties onto sand shimmering with pale silver. Further down the beach I saw Vanderman carrying Karen Koren away in the direction of the designer's villa. Where were Hanlon and Gia? As if to answer my question, a spotlight flared behind me. Gia had led him back around the wing of the villa by Traub's private pool. *They're in the Jacuzzi for sure.* Then I heard someone running behind me. It had to be Traub. My long legs had given me a slight edge, but he was narrowing the gap quickly. I went straight into the water, into the path of light leading to the moon. There was no shock. The ocean was like a warm bath. I swam out toward a distant line of bobbing white floats. I felt the limpid water's silken lotion coating my skin. But splashing noise nearby told me a strong swimmer was close.

I felt a hand on my side, as Traub's voice called out, "I see you know how to swim with the sharks."

"I am a shark!"

"What kind?"

"A mako—what about you?" He was holding me now. Our skin slid together in the water. I felt a tightening in my breasts and kissed him. *Yes—I wanted him.*

"Guess!"

"A big fish!" I said. "I have to see how big you are." I let my hand slide onto him. "Now I know. A great white—they're the most dangerous of all."

"They eat people—so we better swim back in."

"But then you'll be a fish out of water," I giggled. But he was already pulling me back into the sandy shallows. Time had arranged itself for what I wanted.

We rolled together at the edge of the gentle sea. His chest was pressed hard against my nipples. He was now very hard. There was no stopping him. He went fully into me as the water lapped on my body. I couldn't stop myself. My entire body wanted him— wanted him immediately—then and there. I grabbed his face and kissed him, arching against him, pulling him deeper into me. I was surprised by the electricity. He kept finding exactly where I wanted him to strike, where my tissue was sensitive and clustered for him. His steady thrusts were short, but they kept finding me. I wanted him to throb right on the hottest spot of all. But he still held back, and then bone against bone—bang, bang. I went spasmodic in a way that had never happened. I bit his tongue, and then with one final thrust he went deep into my internal pool and it overflowed as I tremored with pleasure and relief.

"Wow!" I gasped.

"You're terrific—you know it!" He kissed me—tasting me again. "It's like in a deal, if you do it right it gives you an advantage, you can find out something that's worth it."

"I'll tell you what I want to know. Were you already thinking about buying Gotham—from the start I mean? Before we met?"

"Vanderman wants an acquisition—but I decide what to buy. I wanted to buy you—Ms. Money is perfect for Traub Inc. You belong with us."

There it was. Traub was buying Gotham because of me. He wanted Ms. Money. I had become Ms. Money, and I knew what she knew. He knew it too—because he was Mr. Money. Women are money. Their value is as good as gold—because no man can devalue them ever. Hanlon was in love with Maggie Worth. But Traub wanted Ms. Money. And she wanted him. I pulled him further onto the sand, forcing him on his back and quickly excited him again. I went on top and rode him to a new climax. I wanted it. Because I wanted something from him that went beyond money. I got the merger and acquisition both!

Hanlon and I spent two more days and nights as guests at Traub's ultra-private villa. We were all drunk on visions of the buyout money we were going to make. The sex was torrid. We swam and sunned naked on the villa's private beach. I slept with Traub and with Hanlon. Gia marched around in heels and a diamond choker Traub had given her, with nothing more on than what she called 'French knickers,' which she pronounced 'knee-cares.' We did foursomes in bed. Hanlon and Traub both slept with her. And so did I, once when we managed to escape to the sauna. I have never been so absolutely free sexually. Ms. Money was not bi-sexual—she was all sexual. Having sex couldn't change me, couldn't change what I was worth. I could fuck anyone without fear. No one could call me a 'whore.' My body could do anything it wanted, and I would be the richer for it.

The only time we dressed was for dinner. We pretended it was a high social function. BJ managed to find a formal that fit. Traub looked like Bogart in a white dinner jacket. I borrowed an Ypsy outfit from Gia—sleeveless with a high but square neckline and bodice of overlapping lavender satin bands with a diamond clasp. She wore a Raoul strapless Forget Me Not gown of silk-blend satin in deep purple-toned grey. The top was embellished with white and silver crystal beads growing the flower design between her breasts. We drank and ate like royalty. But our conversation was not about estates and titles. Instead we planned Traub's takeover of Gotham Trust. The discussions continued in Traub's private jet on the way back to New York. Ms. Money would soon have more money than she ever dreamed of. My salary was huge, my stocks were making new highs, the buyout of Ledbetter had made me rich, and Traub's takeover of Gotham would make me a lot richer. It made me remember a one-liner I heard in Vegas. BJ told me it was originally by Mae West. "Too much of a good thing can be wonderful."

38

I met Gia for lunch at Le Bilboquet. Naturally when I got there she had already been granted the best seat in one of New York's snobbiest boites. She must have just arrived because her gloves were still on. The weather had turned chill with a snap of a breeze, so I wore a lovely forest green, cable knit, three-quarter sleeve sweater dress, a Fendi bargain. It was a special lunch because we had agreed we needed to exchange secrets. But, as you may have guessed, there was another reason for the dress, and my secret was already jamming the knit. Plus I was carrying another dead giveaway, a shopping bag with embossed balloons from Jacadi—a baby store just around the corner on Madison Avenue. Gia jumped up and screamed in Italian, "*Mia migliore amica é incinta,*" while pointing right at my belly. I saw the maître d' look up. Then Gia burst out laughing, gave me her million-dollar smile, and leaned over to hug me, concluding with. "How soon?—the baby?"

But I had already noticed her secret, and instead of answering, I asked back, "Why are you keeping your gloves on?"

With a flourish she pulled off her Bottega Veneta lamb skin gloves—exposing what had to be a ten-carat diamond solitaire engagement ring. "I liked it so much I was going to marry Harry Winston instead," she smiled.

It was just what I'd hoped for, and we kissed again. I knew the ring meant Gia was engaged to Jim Reckford, one of Wall Street's leading attorneys. BJ and I had introduced them at a private dinner party. Reckford had worked on the financial arrangements that ended the Iranian hostage crisis. Now a federal prosecutor, he had just charged Rittenhouse Bank with covert multi-million dollar money laundering. The bankers had been caught carrying out transactions for the Syrian rulership. Rashid al Assad had attempted to pull thirty million dollars out of the U.S. and hide it in the Caymans without disclosure. The money came from huge profits on U.S. defense contractor stocks, made with insider information. Syria was buying tanks, jets and artillery, and when the news hit the Street defense stocks soared. Rittenhouse was fined $10 million by federal and state regulators. They had defended themselves with the ridiculous claim that Rashid's wife needed the money to buy Louboutin shoes for her high-fashion wardrobe. *'Global greed rises with stocks,' said the papers. Personally I prefer Manolo's.*

We went on to chat over a lunch consisting of a pricey, miniscule, but delicious endive salad for me and a sliver of smoked salmon for Gia.

"Do you know the sex?"

"She's a girl." I smiled my answer back. Then I pulled a box out of my shopping bag and showed her a pale pink baby's body suit with a scalloped neck. I loved it.

She gave me another look, and I read the question on her face. This time I just nodded. And then I added, "I'm calling her Melanie."

She laughed and said, "I always said you were secretly European."

I couldn't remember being so distended with my first child. My belly just kept getting rounder and rounder and bigger and bigger. But at last, Melanie Eileen Stringfellow was born on October 1, 1996. As soon as she babbled, the baby began to refer to herself as 'me-me'—so very quickly she became 'Mimi' to all of us. I was ecstatic to give birth to a girl! And such a beauty—with her own jet black hair and fair skin and the brightest amber eyes. Gia was the only one who knew where they came from. She attended the christening as godmother. Her godfather, BJ, never guessed. Stringfellow never asked a question. Brian Connelly and our nanny, Moira, fell in love with Mimi at first sight. I sent a Tiffany engraved birth announcement to Traub.

Traub Securities (TRB) purchased Gotham Trust for $3.15 billion. I watched as the actual announcement crossed the screen of my Palm Pilot, one of the first made, which Hanlon had given me as a gift. Traub bid $50 a share for Gotham, to be paid with TRB shares, which were at a record high of $65. The takeover was friendly—the buy price being higher than anything Gotham's largest shareholders had ever expected. The market loved the merger, which Wall Street was quick to describe as a marriage made in heaven. Translation—everyone made a ton of money on the deal. Traub shares were firm and undiluted. More important, Gotham shares added $19 dollars to their current market price of $31. The Bull market did the rest. Money was easy, and the urge to merge was ever powerful. It was not long before the ExxonMobil union created the largest company in the world.

Along with Stringfellow and Hanlon, and our several overseas trusts benefitting Jason and Melanie, I exercised a hoard of options on Gotham stock. We held options priced as far back as the takeover of Ledbetter, options earned as salary incentives, options from annual bonus packages plus the options we purchased in the open market when it was safe to do so. The result was a huge stock-pile of Gotham shares acquired at an average cost of $18—that we sold for close to $50! Our profit was about $30 a share, times 100,000 shares equals $3 million, times a million shares equals $30 million, and times ten million equals $300 million! BJ, Stringfellow and I each banked a fortune. Traub pocketed even more than we did—on shares acquired and then quietly transferred long before the required SEC registration of his actual bid

Traub flew east. He had a permanent box for the U.S. Tennis Open, which he rarely missed. He invited me to the games, and we smiled all the way to Forest Hills. Traub was rooting for Californian Lindsay Davenport in the women's matches, and he cheered when she slaughtered Magüi Serna. But then she was wiped out by Martina Hignis, who went on to defeat Venus Williams for the championship.

"I'm putting Eric in charge here in New York. He's a house cleaner."

"And Ms. Money?"

"I'm reorganizing you. From now on you work for Traub Securities. You report directly to me. BJ too." Riding back in the car, I kissed him, sending a message that I wanted him for the night. BJ was in Pebble Beach. I was entitled to my private relationship with Traub. He remained unmarried. We were exceptionally discreet, avoided the media, but I didn't hide it from myself. I now had enough money to do whatever I wanted. Was I wrong? I didn't think so. I was Ms. Money. And Traub was Mr. Money. Things being equal to the same things are equal to each other. Traub and I were one in the same. That was what I believed. And he gave as good as he got. Our union was a mutual entitlement. I could enjoy him and owe him nothing. *So I thought.*

Ms. Money and her core staff were relocated to Traub's central branch in New York. My annual salary rose to two million dollars plus bonus. BJ Hanlon was appointed Traub Senior Executive Vice President for Mergers and Acquisitions, with offices in New York and LA. Eric Vanderman was appointed Gotham's new President and CEO. Peter Ray Tarturo, another long-time Traub Executive VP, became Gotham's Chief Investment Officer. The bank's independent board was retired. Vanderman would represent Gotham on Traub's own board. Gotham chairman Bostwick Maurer and CEO Fabricant were granted golden parachutes.

My daughter entered the world when a gain of 41 points lifted the Dow to a first close over the 6000 mark. She fulfilled the prediction I made on *Smarter Than The Street,* when as a joke I said, "The market is pregnant with possibility!" And as soon as Ms. Money returned to work she told investors stocks were going to 10,000! My forecast was writ large in a *Wall Street Journal* advertisement under my new title, Chief Investment Strategist for Traub Securities. 'Ms. Money Loves Working For Mel.' The ad's banner proclaimed above my full-page photo.

But Paul Stringfellow had plans of his own. The two of us took Jason ice skating in Greenwich, on a perfect winter morning, cold, clear, and no wind. The sun was so bright it almost made up for the season. Moira came with Mimi. Connelly took charge, when Stringfellow and I went for a private lunch at Delamar in the ice bound marina. Typically he arranged a private talk whenever Jason was the subject. I wondered if he wanted to sell their Crosby catboat, which was in winter storage at the marina, and buy something bigger. But Stringfellow surprised me with what was a big speech for him "You have to know, I'm not going to Traub Inc. I want to do something on my own. So I'm buying a big chunk of CVC, and I need your backing. It's a controlling interest."

"What's CVC?"

"It's Channel Vista Capital. I want to buy something. This is the right time for us. We need to buy equity—ownership. BJ knows how I feel. He's helping out too."

I knew that Channel Vista Capital (CVC), had earned recognition as a boutique research and investment banking firm focused exclusively on the Internet. They had racked up a track record of money-making dot.com IPOs. Typical of Internet merger mania, Planters Group, a high-tech industry consulting firm, acquired Opticom Securities to sharpen its financial focus. Then it raised capital through a merger with cash-rich Gulf Passage Capital, in a $300 million all-stock deal. The end result of that series of M&A hook-ups was Channel Vista.

Stringfellow was taking control of CVC for $120 million. "I ponied up $50 million of my own," he told me as we ate. "BJ went for $35 million. I want you to put in $35 million. It's your stake. We'll be in it together. We can take home a piece of every deal that goes down. Then I'll buy you both out—the Internet's not going away."

I had no hesitation. I leaned across the table and kissed him. "You deserve it, Paul!" *Isn't money wonderful!*

"The focus is right—it will pay off big!"

"Go for it!" I told him. I owed him big time. He was not only the perfect father, the man Jason loved and Mimi called 'Daddy'—he was my child too. And there was no way I could lose. A total of nearly 300 Internet-related IPOs would raise a mammoth $25 billion in the coming year. *A cut of that would be huge.*

"Plus it's right here in Greenwich. I can bike to work."

39

It only took 85 days for the Dow to go from 6000 to 7000. That was in spite of Fed Chairman Alan Greenspan, who suddenly reversed himself, raising investor doubts. The Fed chief was always frightened that the media would label him gloomy. So year after year, he told investors exactly what they wanted to hear. Ms. Money traveled to Washington to hear his speech at the American Enterprise Institute. He gave investors the good news first, "Sustained low inflation implies less uncertainty about the future, and lower risk premiums imply higher prices of stocks and other earning assets." *Rock on Alan baby!* But then the ever optimistic central banker asked his audience, "But how do we know when irrational exuberance has unduly escalated asset values, which then become subject to unexpected and prolonged contractions?" Was 'the Maestro' suddenly worried that the music would stop?

Ms. Money pounced on Greenspan's question, calling it "rhetorical." In the context of his push for "lower risk premiums," the question was typical meaningless Greenspan "double speak." When questioned by the financial media, I said the only "contractions" I knew about were birth pains. Soaring bank balances everywhere proved that investors were completely "rational" and Ms. Money declared exuberantly that "Dow 10,000 is coming!" And it was.

Jason was a beautiful child—bright, inquisitive and with an easy sweetness. I loved him so much I was almost sad to send him to school. But Stringfellow and I enrolled him in the Brunswick School, where his teacher just adored him. As a reward, Connelly and Stringfellow took him and a school pal to see the first *Star Wars* prequel, called *The Phantom Menace.* He came back from the movie and ran about the house chanting, "The Force—the Force—the Force is with me." And soon enough Ms. Money went on TV saying "The Force is with the Market."

The 'Force' sent dot.com stocks first to the moon and then to the stars. By the end of the decade Cisco was the most valuable company in the world, with a market capitalization of more than $500 billion. That was enough capital to focus dot.com eyes on old-line targets. Soon, America Online announced an agreement to buy media giant Time Warner for a huge $162 billion. Investors reaped the reward. Hanlon practically lived in San Jose just to keep up with the deals.

I interviewed Henry Blodget, the celebrity Internet research analyst, on *Smarter Than The Street.* Merrill Lynch was paying him a million-plus, and he was a media darling. Blodget was famous for his prediction that Amazon.com's stock price would hit a pre-split high of $400. Only a month later, after the stock gained 128%, his call came true. I danced with him at a private party at Tunnel—the madhouse disco. The music was in decibels. People stood on chairs and rocked—others danced naked on the tabletops. Later, he told me he had personally invested more than five million dollars in tech stocks. *Why not? I was fully invested myself for millions more.*

Long Term Capital Management collapsed, but the stock market stepped right over its corpse. The hedge fund was founded in 1994 by John W. Meriwether, former head of bond trading at Salomon Brothers. Noble Prize-winning economists Myron S. Scholes and Robert C. Merton were on its Board. LTCM made 21% in its first year, and double that a year later.

"So what went wrong?"

Stringfellow explained, "LTCM was all about bond arbitrage. The return is guaranteed—but it's earned in very small amounts. They're called "golden crumbs" on the Street. So LTCM had to take bigger and bigger positions to make money. That meant using more and more leverage. "Their leverage went from 25-to-1 to over 250-to-1. Then they got hit by a black swan—an unpredictable event. Something that could never happen did happen—the Russian Ruble crisis made Treasuries rocket way above their trading range. They ended up owing over $100 billion."

"But the Fed stepped in," I objected.

"Exactly. Greenspan organized a multi-billion dollar bailout. The big banks had to pony up. They didn't want the party to end. Easy Fed money is making them rich. Risk doesn't matter when money is free."

"In a month, nobody will remember what the initials stood for," said Hanlon when he called from LA.

Ms. Money's net worth was sky high. She proclaimed that Newton's Law had been repealed on Wall Street. Without gravity, the only direction for stocks was higher. Everything I forecast in client meetings and across every media outlet day and night came true. And then warp speed was achieved: On March 29, 1999 the

Dow broke through the 10,000 barrier! I was ecstatic. The media couldn't get enough of me. Traub sent me a ten-carat pink diamond with a one-word note: "Tattoo!"

To celebrate the milestone, I threw a private party in my San Remo suite in the form of a charity function commemorating my appointment to the Board of the New Hope for the Needy foundation. The event made the society columns. I looked great in the celebrity photos. My personal trainer, Kristin, had helped me erase the ravages of my second pregnancy. My skin was smooth and shining, my body fit and energetic. I wore my first Alexander McQueen gown by Givenchy. Its billowing layers of ice-mint silk-chiffon just swept the floor. It cost $10,000. Gia and her husband came direct from watching the Metropolitan Opera's new production of *La bohème*. Her face was tear stained. "Angela Gheorghiu opened her mouth and my eyes just overflowed. It was so sad." We went into my private room to fix her face, and Gia insisted on giving her goddaughter a night kiss. "Puccini is so sad," she told me and squeezed the child. "*Che gelida manina*—your tiny hand is frozen. Thank god my Mimi has enough money," she whispered.

No tragedy could stop the market—not even all the flowers piled high for Princess Di's death. Stocks rocketed higher in spite of mass murder in a Columbine, Colorado school. The Dow rose even when the U.S. House voted to impeach President Clinton for an illicit sexual relationship with 22-year-old White House intern, Monica Lewinsky. But Ms. Money understood! *How could anything stop the market when the President of the United States is completely oblivious to risk!*

Thirty-eight stocks gained 1000% each in 1999! A ten-dollar share doubled to $20. Then it doubled again to $40. It split in two, but investors bought more—so now you had two shares worth $25 each. When they doubled, your ten-dollar investment was worth

$100, ten times the starting price. Now multiply that by a thousand! You just had to live it. One day I made $50,000 before lunch. But even I gasped when, only 24 days after it notched 10,000, on May 3, 1999, the Dow rose 226 points to close above 11,000 for the first time! One thousand points in under a month! Ms. Money was worth more than her wildest dreams. Everything I touched turned to gold!

40

Please heed the warning. 'Danger Men At Work!' Feminists say this sign is sexist. But like most women, I think it should be taken literally. I mean it's definitely true isn't it? So don't say I didn't warn you. Further progress is highly risky. Every single shred of Wall Street advertising bears a similar disclaimer: 'Past performance is no guarantee of future results.' I don't have to tell you that because you are already thinking what I haven't said. You know what comes next! But don't be so sure. Don't forget that long ago I majored in Holy Orders at Divine Sepulcher of Maryland. That's where I read Christian philosopher Teilhard de Chardin, who was the first to say, "Everything that rises must converge." And back when I was a Pommie, I had already read a short story by Flannery O'Connor with the same title. If what goes up must come down, ask yourself where does it go after that?

The new decade couldn't have begun on a more ominous note. The death of Charles M Schulz, on February 12, 2000, stopped *Peanuts* forever. After some fifty years—no more Charlie Brown, no more Snoopy, no more Linus, no more Lucy. I worried how I would get to the office without the comic strip. Connelly always listened to the racing news when he drove me downtown. I read the comics.

After work, I would take the paper home and show the cartoon to Jason and Melanie. I should have paid more attention to the omen. The time for laughter had ended. As if on signal, the Bull market went into mourning. Worse, the Bear awoke from long hibernation. Even worse than that, I kept repeating my Bullish forecast, trying to make it real. *Bad error.*

Ms. Money told Traub clients that the market slowdown was only temporary. "Throttling back," I called it. "What mathematicians call 'a reversion to the mean' can hardly be called a Bear Market." I was not alone. No one on Wall Street had the foresight to realize that the Dow had peaked in January and the NASDAQ composite (COMP), an index of riskier mostly-tech stocks, would do so in March. But that was no excuse. The year 2000 came to a bad end. The Dow dropped almost a thousand points to 10,788. The COMP fell brutally from a peak of 5050 to only 2500. But on *Smarter Than The Street* Ms. Money continued to call the reversal, "A correction needed to let the economy catch up with a market that was ahead of itself. Stocks will soon resume their journey higher." But stocks went even lower, as the Bear dragged them down.

I missed BJ Hanlon more and more. I never dreamed he would have to stay in LA forever. We shared a bad joke about the Eagles' and their song, 'Hotel California.' It seemed like he could 'never leave.' But every time he called the news was bad. One by one, the dot.coms were blowing up—right in my face. I had bet on profitless Internet companies with on-paper-only business plans. Economic downturn wasn't helping. Disappearing acts were more and more frequent. Dog food supplier Pets.com, which I had bought for my own portfolio, sunk to zero in 2000—only a year after its IPO. The Pixelon story was more of the same. The video-streaming startup led by Michael

Fenne raised $35 million in venture capital, and spent $12 million on its Las Vegas launch party. But Fenne turned out to be fugitive embezzler David Stanley, who was arrested in April 2000. The Dow Jones Internet index, which consisted of 40 companies in March 2000—saw only 10 survive. Big holes developed in my bank account.

Gia told me about Chris Dawes, the founder of the software favorite Micromuse. "I heard it from the runway," she began as usual. "A girl I know told me about another model he kept like a prisoner." Dawes spent his IPO payout on a $4 million English mansion—with a dungeon. He was awaiting trial on possession of cocaine and for drugging and raping a model he held there. High on crack, he killed himself at 39, when his $2 million Formula One-style McClaren crashed. *Ouch!—Debit my account.*

Things turned worse in 2001. I wish to god that year had never begun. Hanlon, during a brief trip back to New York, had to reach over one night when I awoke screaming. In my bad dream, I was drowning. I was a passenger—just like Kate Winslet—on the *Titanic,* and I couldn't find a lifeboat. You would think I would have learned the financial talking head's first rule—if you have to forecast do it often enough to keep up with the market. No! Instead I clung to a Bullish call like a life preserver. I was insistent. The Internet was a "ground-breaking development—a once-in-a-lifetime opportunity for investors." That includes me. There were just too many solid net firms, and they would survive "a brief shakeout among the phonies." But the dot.com heavy COMP lost another 21%, falling to a low of 1950. Internet stocks went down and down and down. I couldn't look at my quotrons. Ms. Money learned what it is, in Wall Street wisdom, 'to confuse brains with a Bull market.' Yahoo, almost the largest Internet stock and another of my recommended holdings, imploded. It paid nearly $3.6 billion for GeoCities, a family of community Web sites that was entirely wiped out. Excite@ Home, Exodus Communications, Lycos, MP3.com and eToys vaporized, leaving me deeper in the red.

Fewer and fewer Internet stocks and even less investors willing to trade them dragged down Traub Inc revenues. As trading dried up, profits shrunk, Traub shares dropped from a high of $65 to under ten bucks a piece. That's a loss of almost $60 a share, and my personal pot of gold held a ton of Traub shares and even more options based on them. Now the gold had turned back to lead—helping my money sink. The consequence was even worse, much more worse. The dominoes just kept on falling. *And then disaster struck.*

The dot.com dump ruined Channel Vista Capital. As investors fled the web, NASDAQ capitalization, meaning total share value in dollars, fell by an immense two-thirds—from $5.4 trillion to $1.8 trillion. Stringfellow had to struggle just to keep the research boutique afloat. Everything soured at once. Institutional sales disappeared, and trading, in both over the counter and listed stocks, disappeared, and then market making operations died. Nobody wanted dot.coms—especially the big institutions that made up CVC's clients. IPO fees completely disappeared and profits shriveled. Institutional investors no longer wanted to pay for the firm's impeccable research. Costs quickly outstripped revenues.

Making matters worse, Congress passed Sarbanes-Oxley, aka Sarbox, or the Company Accounting Reform and Investor Protection Act. The law specified measures to restore investor confidence in securities analysts, by requiring them to disclose all knowable conflicts of interest. On Wall Street, Sarbox was seen as a deal-killer that would likely tie up CVC in one insider trading law suit after another. CVC shares plummeted—and my $35 million personal investment turned to zero.

I felt like the little Morton salt girl, famous for the mantra, 'When it rains it pours.' But I still had my umbrella. I was making money on Enron—Ms. Money's top recommendation. The energy giant had become the country's largest natural gas retailer, and the biggest position in my private investment account. I told investors Enron was different. I had been there and seen its traders buying and selling natural gas contracts. Ms. Money met Enron chairman Ken Lay at a private Bush fund raiser. I knew he was one of America's highest-paid corporate chiefs, earning close to $50 million a year. And he was smooth—smooth enough to invite me to tour Enron's gas operations and then divert my attention during the visit. He gave Ms. Money a personal tour. *Unfortunately, most of it was in my hotel room.*

Wall Street threw its arms around Enron, and Ms. Money embraced the company for more than ten million. *Fortune's* 'Most Admired Companies' survey listed Enron as 'the most innovative large company in America.' Enron stock gained a giant-step 87% in 2000, the only bright spot in my portfolio. Throwing caution to the winds, I doubled my stake. By December 31, 2000, Enron shares hit a record high over $80 per share. The stock market said the company was worth $60 billion. So I made an even bigger mistake. When Enron dived from $90 a share to $10, I doubled down all along the way. Counting on a rebound, as the stock fell, I bought more and more, cheaper and cheaper shares to reduce my average cost. Even worse, I bought even more shares on margin.

And then the Enron balloon burst!—turning a rainstorm into a torrential deluge. Ms. Money was ruined. On take-every-risk Wall Street, no one bothered to add up the accounting loopholes, special purpose entities, bad financial reporting and other high-risk accounting practices that allowed Enron management—the infamous Lay and Jeff Skillings and Andy Fastow—to hide billions in debt from failed gas trading. The storm blew away the little salt girl's umbrella, leaving Ms. Money soaked to the skin. Then it even ripped off my clothes. I was more than dead broke! More—because when Enron went to zero, leverage backfired on me. I had to cover my margin loan. Greed that drove me to use leverage, along with throwing good money after bad, and exposing myself to immense risk from options trading combined to make me more than a three-time loser. I was ruined. Ms. Money had learned the first of the aptly named golden rules of life. There was never a piggy bank that wasn't made to be broken.

41

How could I be Ms. Money when I had no money? I was a deadbeat. In that sense I truly was 'dead,' and the 'beat' component says that I was responsible. Literally, I had beaten myself. Foolishly, I thought I had nothing more to lose. My stocks went down, my Traub shares plunged, CVC cost me a fortune, and Enron was the ultimate in self-betrayal. But Dylan was wrong about having nothing left to lose. The phrase 'last but not least' says it all. All too often what comes last isn't least at all—it's an unimaginable, unmitigated disaster. Yes, it no longer mattered to me that market measures slid, fell further, and then collapsed. But not a single brain on Wall Street, not even Ms. Money, ever imagined that 'the street of dreams' would itself become a target for catastrophe.

The morning of September 11 dawned crisp and totally clear, with a brilliant blue sky that I would never forget. The colors of the city of metal and glass and concrete were brilliant as I stared at them from my limo. Connelly was driving both BJ and I to our office from a weekend spent in Greenwich. I was praying for a market rebound. "Sell in May and go away—don't come back 'til Labor Day," I quoted the long time trader rhyme to Hanlon, hoping that investors would begin buying again soon.

"So we should get a rally—right?"

"Maybe a Thanksgiving rally," I answered cautiously.

"Don't bet on it." They were the last words he ever spoke to me.

Right after the 8:30am research meeting, I was in my office about to pick up the phone, when a loud voice screamed out, "Plane crashes into World Trade Center!" My eyes jumped to my streaming news monitor and picked out the same quote. Trading hadn't begun for the day, but another monitor hanging overhead told me that stock futures had suddenly dropped sharply. *Not again.* Then I heard Robin, my Personal Assistant, scream back, "I know—it's on TV."

I got up from my desk. Looking through the glass wall of my office, I saw people clustering around TV screens. My first thought was that a small plane had gone down near the World Trade Center. But this was different! TV after TV glared with an image of one of the Twin Towers. Black smoke was billowing up. And suddenly the entire building I was in shook with a roar as a huge low-flying jet passed overhead. *That was strange. We're not on a flight path.* Then I screamed, "Where's BJ?" My mind flashed with a thought. *No, no, no—not him!*

"He's at Cantor—with Georgiana. He's meeting your friend Bill Meehan. Oh! My god! It hit Cantor. That's what they just said."

Before I could react, another voice yelled a new headline, "Second plane strikes towers."

"New plane strikes Pentagon," someone else cried out.

At that moment almost every man and woman in New York's financial markets froze. A second went by on every clock. Tick. I felt a strange but total pause that meant almost half a million people couldn't believe what was happening. The world had gone mad. I stood paralyzed. Then my heart beat again, but it beat too fast. I wished it had stopped. Because my heart knew that BJ Hanlon was dead. I just knew.

I grabbed my cell and frantically pressed the keys for BJ's private number. But the call went over to voice mail—and even worse his voice mailbox was full. Others had already called. I could guess what that meant. I wobbled and grabbed onto a desk and went back into my office. My body started to shake. So I grabbed a diet coke from my private mini-fridge, snapped it open and gulped. My three screens were all displaying TV now—all showing terror at the Twin Towers with weirdly distorted camera angles. Smoke and people spilled out of the World Trade Center. One camera caught a man and woman. Unbelievable! They were jumping from what had to be ninety floors up. I watched in total shock. I wanted to throw up. They were holding hands. Was it BJ?

All I knew was that I wanted to be with Jason and Melanie. I wanted to go home. But I was afraid to go there—because Hanlon wasn't coming back. *I just knew it.* All I could do was sit limply, ignoring my flashing phone, while staring blankly at the screens full of death and destruction. It was Connelly who rescued me. He had heard the news while driving back to Connecticut and immediately turned back, returning to the City. He helped me leave the office. We went back to Greenwich, but not before I had seen the cloud of smoke and dust rising from lower Manhattan and smelled the new odor many New Yorkers will never forget— the smell of charred resins mixed with ash and human bodies burned.

The exchanges were evacuated. The opening of the New York Stock Exchange was first delayed, and then all trading stopped— just stopped without a pronouncement from the governors. All quotrons dead! And one by one the global financial markets came to a halt. Trading in United States Treasuries ceased, with the leading government bond trader, Cantor Fitzgerald, blown to smithereens. NASDAQ canceled over-the-counter trading. Followed by the New York Mercantile Exchange, which shut down the commodities markets. Then the London Stock Exchange closed.

How many lives are destroyed when 3,000 people are killed in a matter of minutes? The answer came from an almost hysterical Georgie Dyer who called later in the sleepless night. After joining Hanlon at an early meeting at Brown Brothers Harriman, the mega-rich investment bank, she had gone shopping just before the first plane struck. She was in Century 21, the designer department store right across from the Towers. Pandemonium broke out. She had finally escaped, and then a horde of refugees fleeing Wall Street had forced her to walk across the Brooklyn Bridge. Her feet were bleeding and blistered. It was hours before she reached home and a land-line phone that worked.

Georgiana told me that BJ Hanlon had left Brown Brothers with her, and gone to an appointment at Cantor Fitzgerald on the 104th floor of the North Tower. He was scheduled to meet with investment strategist Bill Meehan. Ms. Money had lunched with Meehan only two weeks earlier. I remembered his trademark floral Hawaiian sport shirt. Meehan was so funny. I had told Hanlon about him. *Stupid, stupid, stupid.* BJ wanted to meet him. He picked the wrong morning. The worst morning ever. Because Meehan died along with another 658 Cantor employees. BJ Hanlon was dead. Everyone died. Everyone lost—husbands and wives lost, sons and daughters lost. Because Wall Street is such a close-knit community everyone lost someone. It was as if a cloud of despair arose downtown and spread across Manhattan. And I believed I had died. I just couldn't breathe without Hanlon. But there was no future in which he would be mine.

The Federal Reserve added $100 billion a day in liquidity to the markets, during the three days following the attack. The money was intended to help avert a financial crisis. But the human crisis was only beginning. *He's gone. Gone forever. And ever. Never. Lost forever— going, going, gone.* Months later I got his wallet back. It had been found inside the rubble, it was empty. Me too.

42

*T*he sky is falling. My nightmare always begins with a quo-tron screen glowing in the dark. It looks like an evil jack-o'-lantern. I watch the screen fixedly as the Dow plung-es—dropping to one new low after another. But then I'm the one who is falling. I'm cold and I'm falling faster and faster. My breath comes in gasps. I'm screaming. I want Hanlon to wake me up. Please BJ give me a shake. But he can't because now he's in the dream too. He's holding my hand tightly. His grip is tighter and tighter. He will never let go because we are falling, falling from the top of the Twin Towers of the World Trade Center. Down, down to our death. *They call it 9/11 to hide the pain, but on Wall Street it was the Day of the Dead.*

Night after night I fall with him. And day after day the markets fell too. The Dow didn't reach its lowest low until October 9, 2002, when it closed at 7286. The NASDAQ Composite index hit bottom a day later, recording a low of 1109. The loss was enormous. Investors took a combined total hit bigger than $9 trillion. Many went broke. They lost it all. I was forced to empty my overseas trusts to pay off my debts. But there was always the worst loss of all—I could never get BJ Hanlon back again. He was gone forever.

My reputation as a financial strategist and anchor was also at bottom. The Wall Street press threw Ms. Money's Bullish forecasts back in her face. 'Ms. Money Misses Big'—read one headline. Another Bearish critic jibed, 'Pretty Face But Returns Are Ugly.' I was haunted by the ghost of celebrity Internet analyst Henry Blodget. First, his personal investments backfired big time. Then Merrill Lynch bought him out of the firm. Finally, in 2002, the government discovered e-mails showing that Blodget's private assessments about the dot.coms conflicted with what he published for small investors—a major Sarbox violation. He was discredited, banned from the industry, charged with civil securities fraud by the SEC, fined $2 million and billed for another $2 million for reimbursement to clients. *Could it happen to me? Where would I find the money?*

I begged off Traub's invitation to Super Bowl XXXVI. He wanted me to join him in his skybox at the Superdome in New Orleans. But I pleaded my grief over Hanlon. I missed one of the biggest upsets in Super Bowl history, when the underdog New England Patriots defeated the St Louis Rams by 20 to 17. But Ms. Money didn't believe in a comeback.

Instead I let Stringfellow convince me to attend the 2002 Winter Olympics in Salt Lake City. We skied together as a family. Stringfellow had taught Jason, and we brought Moira along as nanny for Melanie. Connelly said it was too cold for him and went off to Florida. We rented an entire chalet high up in Sundance, on the slopes of Mount Timpanogos, which Utah locals call 'Mt Timp.' The view was breath-taking. There were two hot tubs and a game room that almost kept Jason from going skiing even though the powder was perfect that winter. *I paid with plastic.*

At the Olympic opening ceremony, we heard the Mormon Tabernacle choir sing the official theme, 'Faster, Higher, Stronger.' *But not any longer,* I thought, as I listened. And I cried when an honor guard of New York City police and firemen displayed the flag that had flown at Ground Zero while a NYPD officer sang 'God Bless America.' *Ground Zero was all that was left of Wall Street! One hundred thousand people died in Hiroshima. Three thousand was enough for me.*

Stringfellow arranged for a trip to the Olympic downhill site via one of Sundance's private Snow-Cats. Jason was thrilled to ride in the giant-size, glass-domed, tracked van. We watched Sam Bode Miller take two silvers. My eyes were fixed on his performance in the giant slalom. I grabbed Stringfellow's binoculars and followed Miller as he sped downhill in a high-speed zig-zag that curved and switched back from gate to gate, spraying the slope with bursts of powder. But on his third run he went after gold. I saw him fall! He went down in a blast of white. I read his performance as an omen. *That's it—I'll never get back.* It was the same when I made a special trip to the Delta rink to see my favorite star figure-skater, Michelle Kwan. Smooth as ever, but then I gasped. Suddenly skating backwards, Kwan swerved low and her hand dragged on the ice for support. She took bronze not gold. *That's what happens when you slip up big time!*

We went as a family with 9,000 other attendees to the Canada-USA hockey final. A call to Traub got us access to his private box. Eric Vanderman and a woman companion were there ahead of us. I recognized her. She was short and in her fifties and smiled back beautifully, but I couldn't remember her name. Vanderman introduced her as Bonnie Branch. Now I knew. She was the youngest daughter of Byron Branch, the famous West Coast financier who had helped bankroll Traub when he was starting out. The heir to a fortune, she married a famous Hollywood producer, but left him for a star actor. Now her star was rumored to prefer a gay lover. But I understood why Vanderman was happy with her company—Bonnie Branch was on Traub's board of directors.

The box was roomy, and the woman immediately lifted a bundled up Melanie onto her lap, telling me, "I've heard about her."

"She's just six."

"You're so lucky."

"Why don't both of you come for dinner at the chalet?" I asked. The invitation just popped out, even though Stringfellow jerked on my parka sleeve as I offered it. But to my surprise, Vanderman, who I expected to shake his head with a 'No,' said 'Yes' almost immediately.

"We'll come for sure—won't we Bonnie!"

Her answer was cut off by wild cheering as Canada tied the score at 2-2. Then the Canadians scored three furious goals in a row, to win 5-2, skating to their first Olympic gold medal in 50 years. The crowd went wild on both sides. The win was seen by more than 20 million TV viewers, earning a Nielsen 10.7. I knew the rating was huge because my own had fallen to no more than a third of that level.

The chalet staff had no trouble with an intimate dinner party for four. Standing with my back to one of the stone fireplaces, I surveyed the guests, from the heights of my Onorina platforms with 5-inch hand carved rosewood heels. I was casual in Prada black jeans with a blouse I had just bought in Bergdorf's—a Reed Krakoff man-tailored silk chiffon in the palest beige with a leather collar that gave it the riding outfit look I wanted. *At least my body hasn't deserted me.* I could tell from the leer Vanderman gave me as I joined the party.

He was lecturing on the hockey match. "Our team was just too old," he said. "Too old for gold."

What about me? I wondered.

"Well they beat Russia," said Stringfellow. "That's what really matters!"

I loved him at that moment. But he had cost me thirty-five million on CVC.

Then I was shocked to hear Vanderman say, "Mel's the same. He doesn't have it any more—you know—sex appeal. Traub has lost its big attraction." *He wants to be Number One.*

"The word you want is *mojo*," said Branch. She put her hand on Vanderman's very broad shoulder, saying, "Now you're 'a contender' for real."

"It's not so easy these days on the Street." I interrupted, before she crowned him 'Rocky.'

"Yeah—a lot of people are going to be fired," Traub's burly co-CEO answered back. "I hope Mel has the guts to clean house. Life is about surviving—sometimes you have to do things that aren't any fun. Mel's forgotten that. I've worked with him for twenty years. But he's not trying to win anymore. Maybe he has lost his mojo."

He was looking right at me when he gave the speech. I read his 'evil genius' message. He wants to end run Traub. Bonnie Branch holds a huge pile of shares. No wonder he's with her. *He's going to fire me. I'll get severance—but I'll lose my $2 million a year plus bonus. Shit!*

"It's really about share price," Bonnie Branch cut in. "I can't even look at Traub stock these days. It just makes me sick. And I'm on the Board." *Didn't I tell you?*

"Yeah, if it gets too low we may have to fight off a takeover," said Vanderman. "What we really need is an acquisition—something to give us lift off."

Just then the chalet's door chimes sounded. I was surprised. But my mind latched tightly onto Vanderman's last words. I told myself to remember them.

43

Stringfellow greeted the callers, and quickly escorted them into the lodge. It was Robert Redford! *I didn't believe what I was seeing! Wow!*

The star was in the habit of visiting guests who rented the most expensive of his Sundance chalets. Stringfellow had taken his call and agreed to a surprise visit. Redford immediately introduced the woman with him as Sibylle Szaggars, the German artist. I knew from Gia that she was now his companion. She was dark, as tall as Redford, with an asymmetric brown-red haircut. She had to be twenty years younger than the 65-year-old actor. But as much as Redford filled the room, the woman wasn't diminished, even wearing just a blue jean jacket over a floor-length beige tank-top dress. She had real aura. Redford was in jeans and a luxurious sweater—a heavy knit of alpaca and lamb's wool. I could almost feel how soft it was.

Stringfellow introduced Bonnie Branch and Vanderman and myself. We stood before a giant window overlooking a beautifully lit, snow-clad slope bordered by gladed trees and the jagged rocky outline of Mt Timp. When nature gets it right it's truly breathtaking.

"I bet you were hoping for Mel Traub," I remarked. I couldn't imagine the famous actor dropping in for a drink with just me and Stringfellow.

"No—it was you I was hoping to run into in this pack of Traubsters," Redford addressed himself to me. "I'm a Ms. Money fan. You're great on *Smarter Than The Street*. I came for your private forecast because I have a lot of money at Traub." Then he smiled at me, and the face that had attracted millions of women had its typical filmdom effect. I blushed. I couldn't believe he still had faith in Ms. Money's market forecast.

"The market's no different from a giant slalom—but you absolutely have to remember that's a downhill event." I had saved the thought from watching Bode Miller earlier.

"What does that mean?" Redford pushed back.

"You've got to ski the slope—time the turns perfectly. A rally in a Bear market can last a few weeks or months and then turn against you. If you don't get out at just the right time—you lose it all and end up back where you started." *I had finally learned to parrot the Wall Street consensus.* Strategist Elaine Garzarelli had spelled it out on *Smarter Than The Street.*

I saw that Vanderman was paying close attention. "Fantastic," said Redford, clearly impressed. Then he asked, "I heard you saw Bode win the Silver?"

But Vanderman couldn't resist. He looked like a fat lumberjack in his resort wear—as the contrast with the star made very clear. "Silver ain't gold," he told Redford. "The Norsemen are slaughtering us. Aamodt took Bode."

Redford gave him a hard look, saying "They're all World Class. But Bode will be back. That's what makes a true champion—the ability to stage a comeback."

"Yes. We saw it from the Snow-Cat. It was fantastic." I jumped in. Mentally my fingers were crossed. *Could Ms. Money do it too? Redford had no doubts.*

"I don't think so," Vanderman challenged. "He's a speed freak. He could have had an easy third silver. He wouldn't have lost it if he hadn't tried for gold. He had a big lead. Then he fell and missed a gate—he blew it."

I was ashamed of my sudden hope. *There's no way back for Ms. Money. I should have been satisfied with the little silver I had left.* But Redford's words were working on me. He was just like BJ Hanlon. Ms. Money *could* still stage a professional comeback. First I needed a new market strategy—a forecast that would restore my Wall Street credibility. But I also needed something that would be much harder to get. *The real trouble was that Ms. Money needed money to be who she was.*

"I love your movies," Bonnie Branch said to Redford—who had suddenly stiffened. Changing the subject diplomatically, she went on, "You can make me 'an indecent proposal' anytime." We all laughed at her joke. I knew it was a reference to his film—the one where he is billionaire John Gage and literally buys Demi Moore after she and her husband go broke in Las Vegas.

But Sibylle Szaggars quickly intervened and steered me away from the group for a private talk. "I was hoping to see you if we got back in time. You must call me Sibby. Gia wanted me to meet you."

"I love her. We met at Parrot Cay—years ago."

"I met her before that. She was only sixteen—in Europe. So beautiful. I painted her—you know? I painted her as the Virgin. How do you say? In the Adoration."

"With the three kings and the gifts." *Frankincense, myrrh, and gold. How nice—especially the last.*

"It's in a museum now. But only my friends know it was her. There's another face too. A boy I loved who was killed. The painting saved me. Now I know from her about you. She told me."

Told what? *my mind immediately asked. She couldn't mean BJ. Gia would never talk about what 9/11 cost me. Her own husband had barely escaped.*

"She told me that Traub is your friend. That's good, but it's not easy, yes? I met him with Robert. These men are born to be kings. People think I am not strong enough to be with Robert—I see it. They think I am too young."

I was surprised by her frankness, and I told her what I knew. "It's about power. They can have anything. We have to show them a woman belongs only to herself. We aren't afraid to live alone."

"You see it—we make them understand us. Kings must have Queens."

"Absolutely."

"*Perfektionieren.* You must see my paintings. I have new ones from Morocco. The desert is incredible. Come to my show in San Francisco—please."

"I'll come," I told her, and then kissed her lightly. We were friends. *Some women just know.*

We rejoined the group by the window. Redford was telling Vanderman, "I just finished making *Spy Game* with Brad Pitt—but I wanted to get back for the Olympics." Then he turned to me, "If you have any inside information I'm interested—strictly as an undercover agent that is."

"I'm coming out with a new report," I told him. *Under the covers all right!*

"I'm sure John Gage will love to read it," he answered, again referring to his billionaire movie role. I remembered that Demi had lost her bank roll in the casino. *She was wiped out.*

But Szaggars was at the door. "We have to unpack," she told them all. "Please enjoy the dinner."

"Compliments of Sundance," were Redford's parting words.

"They say he's getting a lifetime achievement award at the Oscars," said Bonnie Branch after the door had shut.

"I'm telling you who's going to win," Vanderman blurted out. "It's *Black Hawk Down*—you know about the warlord." It was the film about the U.S. raid to capture the Somali terrorist chief.

"Don't try to impress us," Bonnie Branch interrupted. "It's not even nominated for Best Film."

Stringfellow jumped in, "I'm backing *A Beautiful Mind!*"

"Never heard of it," said Vanderman.

"What do guys know about movies?" Branch asked. "*In the Bedroom* will clean up. You can't beat Tom Wilkinson, Sissy Spacek, and Marisa Tomei."

"I'll put a thousand on it," said Vanderman. "Since you're so sure."

"You're both covered," said Stringfellow. "*A Beautiful Mind* for a thousand." *Ouch! No more thousand dollar bets—please.*

"You're on," said Vanderman. "A thousand says it won't win. That's my bet." He banged his glass down on a table.

All I could think of was just how much he looked like Shrek—the big, green, oafish ogre played by Mike Myers. I had seen the video with Jason and Stringfellow. Mimi even sat still for it. Then I remembered another family movie. "There was one picture I really liked last year. *Harry Potter and the Philosopher's Stone*—did any of you go?"

Vanderman just laughed, but then he added, "Life's not a kiddie game. All that stuff about magic wands and wizards and werewolves is a joke."

"Well maybe what we need is a wizard to get stocks going again," said Bonnie Branch, staring at me. "I'm anxious to see what you have to say about the market—in your new report."

Later, my almost-asleep thoughts went back to the Harry Potter movie. There was something I was trying to remember—something about my favorite character, Hermione, the smart, pretty, girl wizard. Then I remembered. Rita Skeeter, the lying newspaper columnist, had written something nasty about her. She said Hermione had bribed Harry Potter—and she used love potions to "satisfy her taste for celebrity wizards." I was angry because it was all gossip.

But as I fell asleep, Harry Potter became Paul Stringfellow, and I was Hermione. We were in the movie, but it wasn't Hogwarts Academy. We were in a casino. I was losing big time. Eddie Murphy was the croupier and kept raking in my chips. Every time I lost he went, "Hee-Haw." I needed more money. Then Stringfellow turned into Robert Redford. But I didn't have the right love potion to seduce him with. Just then Shrek drags in a big trunk. I know the potion is inside it. So I sing 'I'm a Believer.' I have to use my wand to protect myself from an attack of flying keys. I strike one down, and give it to Redford who uses it to open the chest. Big surprise. Vanderman is inside. Then lightning strikes and Vanderman points his wand at me and I turn into a green ogre too, a lady Shrek. I look terrible. Redford runs away with Hermione. I run away from Shrek. I'm in a maze of tunnels. Shrek is after me. I scream because he has no head. There is no way out. Shrek attacks me. I wave my wand, and a cloud of smoke fills the tunnel. The next thing I know is that I'm in bed with Eddie Murphy.

44

I woke up knowing what I had to do. And once I started to believe in myself, I knew I could do what I needed to do. You already know that I believe women are a lot tougher than men. But they need to overcome their initial handicap, the lie that says they're the weaker sex. Men may have a physical edge in the battle of the sexes, but they're little boys compared to a determined woman. Whenever in doubt, always remember that Albert Einstein married twice and at the same time maintained a long-term extra-marital affair.

Seeing Redford had helped more than I knew. Once I climbed out of gloom and doom—the answer was staring me in the face. My dream only confirmed it. If Vanderman wanted an acquisition, I would give him one. He was President of Gotham Trust—all I had to do was get him to buy Channel Vista Capital. What he said about Traub losing his drive would help, and Vanderman was always keen when it came to acquisitions. Making it even easier or more difficult, depending on your taste, and I do mean taste, he was hot to trot after yours truly. A little pillow talk would pay off big time. Stringfellow would net more than enough money to pay me back my stake. Once I had money, I could work on restoring Ms. Money's Wall Street credibility. But as things turned out, the message came before the money.

Stringfellow and I ended our stay with lunch at Bearclaw, the tiny restaurant perched on the ridge at the very top of Sundance. We rode the ski lift, climbing more than 8,000 feet above the valley, and were rewarded with a spectacular 360-degree view of the Wasatch Mountains. But the view from the top was less important than what I had to say.

"I'm putting Greenwich on the market. We need the money. I need it. We're all moving into the San Remo starting when we get back." Luckily, before 9/11, I had bought Hanlon's adjoining suite out of the trust for his wife. "The kids can go to school in New York."

"I'm sorry the way CVC turned out—it looked really good at the time." He was his usual sheepish self.

"Leave that to me." I answered. "Just make sure you keep what's left running. Glitz it as best you can."

"But nobody will buy it."

"Don't be so sure!"

After lunch we talked about the trip. "It was great seeing Redford, but Vanderman is something else. He sure doesn't know about movies."

"I call him Shrek—but remember he can help us."

"Well, as long as he's good for it. I'm going to make a grand off him on my Oscar bet. You'll see, I'll take you to the movie. *A Beautiful Mind*—it's a sure winner."

"Tell me about it."

Stringfellow explained that the film was a bio-pic based on the life of the brilliant mathematician John Nash. Russell Crowe plays the numbers genius who turns into a schizophrenic after wartime code breaking for the Pentagon. But despite his delusions, Nash wins the Nobel Prize for his research on game theory. "Crowe was great. It will win, believe it," Stringfellow assured me.

"How does game theory get into it? Can it explain what's going on in the market? My strategy deck is way out of date."

"Game theory is about decision making—it can definitely apply to the market. What's happening now is all about what Nash called 'trembling hand perfection.'"

"I haven't got a clue."

"Nash proved that the equilibrium of a perturbed game is 'perfect' when the probability goes to zero. If each player has chosen a strategy and no player can benefit by changing strategies while the other players keep theirs unchanged, then the current set of choices constitutes a Nash equilibrium."

"Paul, I don't understand a word of what you just said. You've got to give me something I can use—please."

"Well I'm trying. Look at it this way," he began to explain once more. The longer an investor follows a trend, the longer it is likely to persist. That's because the longer it lasts, the longer we expect it to last. "But stability is what leads to instability. At a certain point the expectation that the trend will last forever is what introduces the instability that brings it to an end."

"The Bull market's been going on since 1980. That's a real long trend. It's persisted and persisted." I began to understand.

"It's like building a house of cards—it gets higher and higher and riskier and riskier. So if your hand shakes when you add a card, if it trembles, then it all could collapse."

"So the house of cards is the market?"

"And market risk increases with overconfidence. It's the most confident investor of all who will take the biggest risk. They forget about the possibility of a turning point. But if suddenly they stop to think about it—if they doubt for even a second—then probability re-enters the picture. The next thing you know you're in a Bear market."

"You mean they get surer and surer nothing will go wrong—so they don't see that risk is increasing."

"Exactly—they miss the clues! And because nobody is worried about risk, the risk correlations for different assets come together. So people are less and less diversified—just when they think they're more diversified."

"I get it—it's because every single thing is going straight up! Stocks, bonds, real estate are all rising at once. A vertical trend-line is a red flag. When the Dow goes straight up danger is over-due." I stood up and kissed him. The pieces of my puzzle were falling in place. He had given me the investment theme I desper-ately needed.

All the way down, I snuggled tight against him in the crisp cold sunlight. *What would I do without him?* He truly was the boy with the beautiful mind. And I gave him what he could never have without me, my son, Jason.

ℒ

Our collective move to New York went well. Jason was enrolled in Ethical Culture just down the street from the San Remo and was already bringing friends home from school. He was majoring in mathematics—influenced by Stringfellow's genius. *Maybe my own math genes had helped—at least a little.* And father and son, my two boys, big and small, had all of Central Park to explore, along with the Museum of Natural History and the Planetarium.

But I ran into trouble because I wanted Melanie to go to kindergarten at the 92nd Street Y—across the park and uptown. I confronted the admissions woman, and was told places were booked for years in advance.

"But I wasn't here then," I argued.

"Sorry."

"Money is not a problem."

"Yes it is," said the woman. "Too much money—and too few places!"

I called Gia—and found out why.

"I don't think so. The deck is stacked against you. You'll never get Mimi in there now. Not after what happened with the Gerber twins. Don't you read the rest of the paper? I mean after the financial section?"

The *New York Observer* had just broken a story exposing one of the highest paid analysts on Wall Street, Rupert 'The Gimme' Gerber. Reportedly, he had raised his certified research rating on a stock from 'sell' to 'buy' as a favor to his investment bank bosses. They were after a buyout deal, but a potential buyer wouldn't even look at a target that Gerber had stuck a sell on. After he changed the rating, the bank then pledged a million dollar donation to the 92Y. That was the 'gimme.' It put the Gerber twins on the pre-school admission list. But another parent blew the whistle on the quid pro quo arrangement. The media was calling it 'Kindergate'—and the name stuck.

"You know New York," said Gia. There were calls for an SEC investigation on the grounds that Gerber had committed a 'Sarbox' violation. Denials followed. The investment bank's CEO Ranford Weller defended the donation as typical philanthropy. A video emphasizing that the big bank ran four child-care centers for employee children, with testimony from thrilled parents, suddenly appeared on New York local TV, to provide cover-up PR.

"I guess that's what an analyst opinion is worth now!" I complained.

"Forget about it," said Gia. "They're biting the hand that feeds them. It's so stupid. Let them eat cake if they want."

A week later, I enrolled Melanie in Spence. Connelly was happy to drive her to school daily.

45

I took an unexpected call from Rudy Kaiser. He wanted me to co-anchor a new, up-to-the-minute financial news show on cable. I couldn't believe it. *He should be in a nursing home.* I stalled, telling him I would have to call Traub first. The next thing I knew, the network called with a counter offer. They wanted Ms. Money to take Kaiser's old job—I'd be Dean of *Smarter Than The Street* permanently. *I must have been hotter than I thought in TV land.*

I quickly called Sue McCann for an explanation. She told me that Kaiser was in huge trouble with the network after rebelling against plans to replace him with a younger host. While I was at Sundance, he had aired a kamikaze performance of *Smarter Than The Street*—actually going so far as telling viewers to get ready for a new show he was going to create on cable! He was fired immediately.

"Can you imagine? He wanted me to work with him," I told her. "And then the network called. I'll call Mel. But I don't want it. Just being one of the Profs is the best I can do."

"I'm filling in as Dean on a temporary basis only," McCann told me. "So you can be my first guest. I'll schedule Ms. Money for my debut—the format's longer so I hope you're ready."

"Perfect." It was just the opportunity I needed to showcase Ms. Money's new investment strategy. *But to complete my comeback, I still needed cash in the bank. How could I be Ms. Money without money?*

$\mathcal{Q}$

With McCann now in the role of Kaiser, Ms. Money faced the cameras. A clip of the falling Towers ran, riveting viewers inside and outside the studio. A graph showing the market downturn was superimposed over the collapsing buildings. "Make no mistake," I emphasized. "These events are linked, and game theory is what connects them."

"Let's look at 9/11," I went on. "Was it predictable? Were there no clues that it was coming?" I asked and then projected a list:

1993—World Trade Center bomb try almost works
1994—Jumbo jet strikes Capitol in Clancy's *Debt of Honor*
1999—Muslim terrorists train on jumbo jets in U.S.
2000—Al Qaeda threat of Jihad against U.S. broadcast
2001—Four planes diverted at once with no reaction

"Why did we fail to connect the dots?" I asked. "The answer is that the entire U.S. intelligence apparatus had no expectation of risk—absolutely none."

"It was no different with the end of the Bull market," I went on. "Investors were blindsided by accountants who were deliberately led astray and by paid-to-sleep regulators and even by wrong-headed strategists. Yes, that includes Ms. Money. Why? Because the markets had absolutely no expectation of risk." And again I showed a slide listing the early warning signals.

1987—Market crashes despite portfolio insurance
1990—Michael Milken jailed for junk bond abuse
1998—Long Term Capital Management failure
1999—Dot.com bubble bursts
2001—Enron Scandal

Then I asked, "What does game theory teach us?"

- When the short term becomes the long term—
- When performance is endlessly extrapolated—
- When contrarian investors are extinct—
- When the Bear has gone into permanent hibernation—
- When risk aversion has disappeared—

THE DANGER IS GREATEST!

Then I put up a chart showing the Bull Market's last years—when the Dow's climb was straight up. A house of cards was superimposed over it. Animating the slide, I showed a shaky hand drop one more card—bringing the house down!

"What makes the hand tremble?" Ms. Money asked and answered. "The reason is probability. We can never forget about probability—about doubt—about risk. Probability is why there is no such thing as a risk-free investment. Perpetual motion doesn't exist. Systems break down. It's called entropy—all things come to an end." Risk is real because:

ENTROPY ENDS EQUILIBRIUM

Shifting my focus, I asked the audience, "Where do we go from here?" I put up a chart showing that stocks rose for close to twenty years in the Fifties and Sixties and after a dip were flat through the

Seventies. They took off again in the Eighties and Nineties only to run into a wall as 2000 got underway. "Ms. Money expects a long-term flat trend for the 'Zero Decade.'"

WHAT SHOULD INVESTORS DO?

- Buy safest long-term bonds paying highest interest
- Buy blue-chip stocks with biggest dividends
- Buy gold and oil because commodities will rally

I emphasized that in order to stimulate the economy, the Fed will be forced to drop interest rates to new lows for longer time periods. "Lower for longer rates mean gold will glitter, dividends will be the best source of return, and AAA bonds will gain." So said Ms. Money. My rough count audience of 9 million beat *Star Trek*, but I lost out to *Ally McBeal,* which scored 12.5 million viewers. *Brilliant even if I say it myself.*

The flowers had already started to pour in by the time I got to the office. Traub called almost immediately. I accepted his congratulations, but I guessed something was up with him. He didn't have to call me from Los Angeles where it was 5:30am.

"You won't believe this," I told him. "Rudy Kaiser wants me to co-anchor with him on cable. You heard they threw him off the program? And then the network called and asked me to replace him."

Traub's temper flared. "I don't give a damn about Kaiser. Tell him no! I'm not losing you. And I'll beat whatever the network offers. I know it's been hard. BJ was a prince. Take time off if you want. But Ms. Money works for Traub."

Then he told me I now had a lifetime contract. He was raising my pay by another $500,000 and adding even more options on Traub shares. Ms. Money would continue with a base in New York and dedicated research staff in Los Angeles.

"You're not letting me negotiate," I laughed back.

"Of course not. You don't know how much I'll need you now. This is it. I'm getting out altogether. Eric can run the company his way. He's always wanted to. It's best. I need to do what I want to do."

I pinched myself. No. I wasn't dreaming. Traub was stepping down. That was the reason for the extra early phone call. *He can't be telling me this. But he was, even though I couldn't believe what I was hearing. With him out of the way I can do what I want with Vanderman.*

"What will you do?"

"My mojo's thinking about politics. I'm tired of the money racket. That's where I need to be—in government—the governorship. I don't know if Davis will win another term. What do you think?"

"Vanderman can run the store. He's ready for it."

"Do you think he can do it? Times are tough."

"It won't be fun for you anymore—and you're bigger than that. Let him have it. Vanderman is ready." *So am I!*

"You have to be my eyes and ears. Who else can I trust? Right?" *Perfect. I couldn't have scripted it better.*

"Always," I answered. *He was out of the way. And I was free to deal with Shrek.*

46

A month later, I read the terse press release: 'The Board of Traub Securities announces the appointment of Eric P Vanderman as sole CEO commencing Friday, April 26, 2002. His career in financial services includes twenty-one years at the company. From 1995 to the present, Mr Vanderman shared the CEO title with company founder, Melrose B Traub.'

But Vanderman was more scared than thrilled. "We're adrift," he told me during our first private meeting. "Traub has been a lax leader for too long."

"You've fixed his problems before." *Clearly, he needed me.*

"This time it's different. I don't even know if I should thank you. I know he would never have let go if it weren't for you. I heard you pushed for me. Some people would have stabbed me in the back."

"Traub needs a leader—it's got to be you. I'll do what I can. You need to talk to the troops and the clients and the media." I followed with a challenge, "You can lead your way out of this—unless you're scared."

"What about Traub?"

"Let him play golf." *The more Vanderman relied on me, the better.*

I hammered out just the simple message he needed. 'Traub Ain't Changing.' The nation-wide broker would do what it needed to do, to maintain its commitment to self-directed investors. Client retention mattered most of all. It wasn't an easy sell. Stocks were still falling. Even worse, soon after Vanderman's appointment, the markets were jolted when telecommunications giant WorldCom filed for bankruptcy. The single biggest ever! When it came to stocks, investors switched from love to hate. Trading volume was down 40%, and new accounts were drying up. Competitors were slashing commissions to lure away Traub's active investors. Vanderman was forced to follow suit. Worst of all, Traub stock fell below $10 a share. I gritted my teeth. *I'm still losing money.*

But I owed it to my own net worth to try and stop the erosion. Working until my throat turned sore and I could hardly stand in my heels, I helped lift Traub shares back over $10. Vanderman was no help. Even worse, he was part of the problem. He was a micromanager who couldn't see the big picture. And he acted just like a frenzied boss, reaching out everywhere for control. Ms. Money joined him for a nationwide dog and pony show focusing on client retention. I was the pony pulling Traub shares back up—he was the dog who couldn't even jump through a hoop. I spent as much time keeping Traub clients on board as on repairing his bloopers. For every two accounts I kept in the corral, he would lose one. We were both exhausted, and Vanderman insisted on a break. He wanted to see the World Boxing championship match between heavyweight titleholder Lennox Lewis and challenger Mike Tyson. The contest for the match went to Memphis, which beat Las Vegas with a bid of

$12 million. Tickets were $2,500 each. I accepted his invitation. The time had come.

We stayed at the Peabody in separate suites. After weeks of 'Traub Ain't Changing' branch visits, town halls and client functions, it seemed strange to check in without handlers and advance staff. But then I saw the ducks in the lobby fountain. I ran over—they were real. I wished I had taken Melanie with me. We went to Rockabilly's for lunch, and I bought tee shirts for Stringfellow, Melanie and Jason. Vanderman insisted on taking me to Graceland, where he kept humming 'Heartbreak Hotel' off key. *At least it's not 'Love Me Tender,'* I thought. We returned to the hotel, and I took a nap before the fight. *I expected a long night.*

Heat lingered in River City. I wore a short, pink silk cocktail dress from Issa, finished with elegant pleats and cappy sleeves. A pleated insert at the neckline sparkled with tiny diamond baguettes. *Very sexy.* My hair was up in a French twist that I hoped would outlast the humidity. I was sure Vanderman would be near ringside, and I wouldn't escape the TV camera. As it turned out, we were seated in the fourth row of the 20,000-seat Pyramid. I was sitting right next to Tania Keesha, who had just won the Best Songster award for 'No Permanent Wave.' She was with Halle Berry, and I congratulated the star on her recent Oscar. Berry invited me to go out with the Hollywood crowd after the fight.

"Who you bettin' on?" Keesha asked me. "I mean you're Ms. Money. I want to dog your bet!"

"I've never been to a fight before," I told the singer.

But Vanderman, looked at her, and said, "You have to bet the champ. I'm down for ten thousand."

He got a dirty look for his advice. "Tyson always gets a bad rap," the Black singer answered back.

Then Vanderman stood up to wave to Donald Trump—making signals that said they should meet later.

Black stars were everywhere. Denzel Washington was sitting nearby. I saw Morgan Freeman, Ruby Dee, Sidney Poitier and Cicely Tyson in the audience.

The bell rang for the first round, and the crowd literally roared. The noise was deafening, drowning out everything. The heat in the arena was thick, only pierced by shafts of incredibly bright light. I was close enough to see the hard expressions on the fighters' faces. They were ugly. Soon the men were sweaty and spitting, their huge muscles gleamed wet as they danced in front of me. I was stunned. It was a male version of The Box. But this time I wasn't on stage pretending to sell myself. It was violent and physical and real. The crowd yelled when Tyson connected with a smashing left hook to Lewis' jaw, catching him off-guard. I was stunned by the raw power of the blow. The taller fighter stumbled, then recovered, clinching Tyson and pushing him back into the ropes while landing a quick jab. Then the bell brought an end to the first round. I was amazed how fast things were happening.

"It looks like Tyson's got him," Vanderman yelled at me. The only thing I knew was that the boxer had gone to prison for rape. "He's an animal! You know he bit a piece off Holyfield's ear—five years ago. I saw him spit it out in the ring."

I looked at the woman sitting next to me. Our eyes met in shared revulsion, but the bell rang even before I could register my "Ugh!" The struggle was fascinating—like gladiators battling for life or death. It was brute versus brute, totally Neanderthal. *Why does physical violence have to be part of male conquest? The boxers were killing each other—the match was a death struggle.* Women are a thousand times more subtle. A smart woman knows how to twist brute desire back upon itself. The place to hurt people is in the heart. The scars are deeper. I watched as Tyson went on to head butt Lewis before connecting with a left hook. But then Lewis drew blood with a punch that painted Tyson's face red, and the crowd screamed for more. Vanderman was standing and crying out hoarsely. *I would have no trouble getting what I wanted from him.*

"Don't you love watching two men beat the shit out of each other," Keesha remarked loudly.

"It's just like in the market. You know, Bull versus Bear. The Bull tries to swing its horns up and gore the Bear and the Bear tries to pull it down with its claws. It's primitive." Vanderman spoke loudly, overcoming the constant roar in the arena. *He wasn't kidding!*

"It's all about power," I realized. *But women know there's more power in sacrifice than in conquest.*

Another round passed. Then Lewis landed two strong jabs followed by a powerhouse right. Tyson went down. Pandemonium filled the arena. But the Referee ruled that Tyson had slipped. Vanderman stood up and screamed, "You're a blind prick!"

I said nothing. If anyone was blind he was. Then the fighters were back at it, jabbing, striking, as they danced about the ring. I saw their faces going to pieces. Tyson was swollen and cut over both eyes and Lewis's left eye was closing. Bang, bang, bang—the gloves punished their bodies. Until Lewis landed a crushing right hook, and I saw Tyson stagger. Then Lewis hit him with a heavy right cross, knocking him to the canvas. The referee counted him out. The audience echoed every number. Tyson just lay there. *Slaughtered. How could I live without BJ?*

"Shit for him—but good for Traub," Vanderman screamed at me as he jumped to his feet and applauded furiously.

"Why?"

"Because Lewis is smart. He's invested with us."

"That is smart! Get an endorsement. We can pay. It's got to be worth something. Get your picture taken with him."

"That's tremendous. I'll make sure it happens. Not all our investors are golfers and tennis players."

I knew it was a dig at Traub.

47

We went in a big group to Beale Street. A fleet of limos took the celebrity party to BB King's, where it reassembled in the private third floor club called Itta Bena, after the musician's Mississippi hometown. The June night was sultry—and made more so by the on-stage soul singer's version of Bessie Smith's famous 'Nobody Knows You When You're Down & Out.' *Maybe down—but not out—I hope.*

I was alone. Vanderman was across the smoky dark room—a shadowy blob anchored to his pal Trump. The tall real estate mogul was in front of a pyramid-shaped heap of shrimp and crab.

"What's Ms. Money doing here?" a wiry man with spiky grey hair asked me in a hoarse voice. I'm always surprised to be recognized. But it was worse because Berry had mentioned the man's name, and I couldn't remember it. All I knew was he was someone in the movies.

"She likes the music," I said smiling because the singer had just started Smith's famous 'Empty Bed Blues.' *Another reminder. But I didn't expect my bed would remain solo for long.*

"Did you ever hear of Albert Collins—the guitar guy? He had the song for you all right. It's called 'If Trouble Was Money.'"

"Tell me."

"If trouble was money, babe, I'd swear I'd be a millionaire / If worries was dollar bills—I'd buy the whole world and have money to spare," he croaked out hoarsely.

"I'll have to do it on *Smarter Than The Street*," I told him. Even in the dark his face was red—like my dad's. "Thanks—it's perfect for a Bear market."

"Do you like boxing? You were at the fight?"

"I don't really get it," I told him. "Tonight was brutal."

"What about women boxers—have you ever seen a female fight?"

"Not in the ring," I laughed back. *Women boxing?* Then I joked, "As far as I'm concerned—sex is the only women's indoor sport."

The red faced man smiled at my remark, but then I excused myself. "I'm getting a drink." I needed to find Vanderman. *The ring was ready.*

It was only later that I realized I was talking with Clint Eastwood—whose *Million Dollar Baby* with Hilary Swank playing a female boxer took the Oscars two years later.

I told Vanderman I was leaving. "I'm going back to the Peabody for a nightcap."

"I'm waiting for Lewis," he answered. "I heard this fight was the biggest money maker ever. It took in over $100 million just from pay-per-view. We can use his endorsement. I'll meet you later."

"Don't keep me waiting. I like to go to bed early." His eyes widened. *Bingo. But I had another surprise planned for Shrek. Just wait until Ms. Money turns green!"*

I decided to walk back to the hotel. From around the corner, I could see its marquee lights only two streets away. A shopping plaza stretched right to it. A border of magnolia trees added heavy fragrance to the darkness. But my heels told my feet to stroll slowly. I stopped just a block from the Peabody, to give my ankles a rest. What happened next was like a video going into fast forward. Without warning, a man bolted from an alley and tried to snatch my silvery Miadora clutch. I was totally surprised. Stunned. *How stupid—just let it go.*

But my immediate reaction was to yank the bag back. I screamed. There were people nearby. But the thief came at me again. He was big, with a mane of dreadlocks— his hand was stretched out at me. I threw the bag at him, hoping to keep him away. It bounced off his shoulder and fell onto the sidewalk. He tried to scoop it up, but I screamed again. There was a loud screeching noise. I heard someone yell. The mugger turned and ran off without the handbag. A big black car was right up on the sidewalk. Vanderman jumped out and scooped up my clutch. I was gasping for breath and crying hysterically. He lifted me into the limo. I wouldn't let go of him. Back at the hotel he had to take me right to my suite. I kissed him hard. He pulled down my dress and lifted me into the bedroom.

We spent all night and the next day in the suite. He just couldn't get enough of me. We both called our assistants and freed up enough time to delay our return. His sexual appetite was voracious. But he was no great lover. He pounded me with his husky body, but his climax was weak. I made him shower with me, and managed to excite him to the point of no return. But there was no teaching him what I needed.

We flew back to New York in the company jet. Vanderman was so proud about his pilot's license that he requested the Captain to let him take the controls for an hour. I sat behind him in the cockpit as an observer only. Back in New York, we continued our torrid affair. *I was gaining altitude fast!*

48

Gia asked me to host a private business dinner for Carly Fiorina, the new CEO of computer giant Hewlett Packard (HP). She had known Fiorina for years. They met in Italy where, just after college, Fiorina had taught English. She was older, nearer to fifty, but her face was still beautiful with bright blue eyes shining from under her honey-blonde thinned-out and tossed page boy. I called Vanderman and insisted he fly in from Los Angeles, telling him he could attend the function and spend the night with me at the San Remo. *You know it's the perfect opportunity because it happens just when you want it to.*

Fiorina wanted Wall Street's support for the proposed HP merger with computer rival Compaq. So I rounded up a list of guests with big positions in HP stock. She told them that the old guard at HP, especially Board member Walter Hewlett, were fighting the hook-up. Fiorina wanted the support of major shareholders. But she was looking for even greater fire power. She wanted brokerage firms with client-owned HP shares that were held in house to vote them for the merger.

"We can recommend our clients go with the deal," Vanderman told her. "We're obligated to forward any proxy material. But they'll have to vote for it themselves."

"Merging with Compaq will make us the biggest PC-maker in the world," Fiorina told them. "Then I'll slash and burn. We need more focus at HP. Leaner and meaner is the way to go." Then she added, looking at me, "I want to go on *Smarter Than The Street* and make the case. What do you think Ms. Money?"

"I'll have to talk to the network," I delayed. From an investment standpoint I wasn't in love with the idea.

"Well I'll tell just you two my secret. I'm going to win. Definitely. Count on it. I'm absolutely certain. I have an ace up my sleeve," she insisted. *And you'll be a loser if you're not on my side, I completed her pitch.*

❧

That night in my bedroom, Vanderman's weight tilted the king-size mattress so that I ended up right against him. My hand was on his thigh. It was easy to tell his mind was pre-occupied. "How did it go with Lewis?" I wanted him to think back to fight night.

"Great, I got the endorsement. PR can take it from there. It was a super fight—just like the market. Bull against Bear and the best man wins!"

"The market is different," I contradicted him. But I slid my hand onto his tummy.

"What do you mean? The best man always wins." His hand now covered mine.

"Ask yourself, what makes him the best? It's because he wins! So if you know who's best, you know who the winner is. Right?"

"But you don't know who the best is. You're thinking backwards."

"If you're smart enough you do. Because someone is always better, always the best, especially with sports. The expert handicappers always know. But in the market you can't know—not even with all the research in the world. There are just too many inputs, millions of them. The only way to beat the market consistently is with insider information." *BJ had thought it out long before. He was rooting for me.*

I could hear the gears grinding. He must have liked the part about insider info. He slid closer.

"Okay—you're right. I see the logic. That's the trouble with Fiorina. She's wants to own it all—right down to the last penny. Compaq shares were way cheap. They nearly doubled when she announced her takeover plan. I'll bet she stashed away a pile of them before the word got out. If she wanted something from us she could have tipped the deal way before. I heard she made out like a bandit on the Lucent IPO."

"She has a ton of shares too." It was no secret that Fiorina's sign-on package included $65 million in restricted HP stock to compensate her for the Lucent shares and options she left behind. Add that to a $3 million signing bonus, a $1 million annual salary (with a guaranteed annual bonus of $1.25 million that could go as high as $3.75 million)—and you might think she was ungrateful. *Go for it girl!*

His tone was almost angry, but the idea of making money was stimulating him. He pulled my hand lower—I was touching him. He lowered his head and kissed the breast that had escaped my pale blue Italian silk nightie. I turned my face on the pillow and spoke into his ear. "If you want a merger that can make you money. I'm totally sure you can find it."

"That's just what I want."

"I'll tell you, if you let me in on it."

"Only if Ms. Money is a good girl."

"Like this," I said and started to rub him erect. Then I told him, "Traub Inc needs to focus on the institutions. We need the infrastructure to handle trading for big pension funds and endowments. We can make a lot of money if we have the kind of research big institutions want. You know, capital R. What you want is a shop like CVC—Channel Vista Capital. It's cheap right now. But they're already picking up momentum." *Then my head went under the covers, and I played my own hidden ace!*

Carly Fiorina won the HP war, but it was only after her victory that Wall Street learned that the card up her sleeve was Deutsche Bank (DB). To facilitate the Compaq takeover, way back in January, HP had retained the big bank's investment unit. HP under Fiorina agreed to pay DB a guaranteed fee of $1 million and another $1 million if the deal went through. In return, the bank voted its clients' proxies for the merger, allowing Fiorina to win by the narrowest of margins. It wasn't until a year later that the SEC got around to charging DB with failing to disclose a material conflict of interest and imposed a civil penalty of $750,000. In typical Wall Street style, Deutsche Bank consented and paid the fine without admitting or denying the findings. *But it still ended up over a million dollars ahead.*

I was more than thankful on Thanksgiving—a lot more! Stringfellow, Jason and Melanie, and Connelly were all at my table. The meal was catered by Abigail Kirsch. If we had said grace, it would have taken the form of the Traub Inc press release publicizing the broker's latest acquisition:

November 13—Los Angeles: Traub Securities (TRB) announces $375 million acquisition of Channel Vista Capital (CVC). CEO Eric Vanderman says buy strengthens Traub in capital markets and adds new focus on institutional investors. CVC equity research will support consultants to pension funds and endowments. Traub paid $17.50 per CVC share, a 70 percent premium over CVC's closing price of $10.25 on Friday.

Stringfellow exercised his huge stake of unrestricted CVC options before they expired and then resigned as Chairman and Executive Managing Director with a golden parachute. He paid me back the $35 million I was due plus a fifty percent split on his net profit. That was millions more. No longer a big loser—Ms. Money was now a very big winner. I felt like Elizabeth Taylor dressed for the title role in *Cleopatra*—when she was all in gold. I put on Patti Smith's *Horses* album, to hear the rocker sing "Free Money" and alone in my bedroom I danced a routine from long ago at The Box, repeating the title, "Free money, free money, free money, free money, free money, free money, free money."

By Christmas I was all smiles when I went to lunch at New York's fashionable Jojo with Gia.

"How was Thanksgiving?" my oldest girlfriend asked.

"I ate the turkey," I told her with a smile.

"But you got paid for it," Gia laughed back. "Let me tell you something. You know the best line I ever heard on Broadway was in *Mame*, when she says 'Life is a banquet and most poor sons of bitches are starving to death.'"

"You couldn't have seen Rosalind Russell on stage," I challenged.

"No—I saw the movie rerun on Turner Classics." And then after her teaspoon meal. "So what's next?"

"Now I have to get rid of the bones."

49

The market downturn entered its third year, turning the 'Street of Dreams' into 'Nightmare Avenue.' Not only were investment gains hard to come by, the Bear market was exposing fraud and crime across the financial world. Warren Buffett, the country's most popular money man, told investors that "when the tide goes out you can see who's swimming naked." And not long after, in March of 2003, the FBI raided HealthSouth headquarters. CEO Richard M Scrushy had sold $75 million worth of the insurer's shares just before it posted a huge unexpected loss. The million dollars Scrushy spent on his corporate 'James Bond' car, a jet black BMW750 Protection Edition, didn't help. After Scrushy was fired, Ms. Money watched Jill Clamor interview HealthSouth's new CEO. He told her the car had been put on the block to help raise cash.

Clamor was another Californian who broke into financial broadcasting in LA. Thanks to an introduction from Sue McCann, I had grown close to her. We shared stories about our career hurdles. I laughed with her over my first experience on Rudy Kaiser's *Smarter Than The Street*. Clamor told me that CBS had referred to the widely publicized search for *The Early Show* co-anchor as 'Operation Glass Slipper.' "But it wasn't really about your foot fitting the shoe. Oh no! You know men! The only thing they want us to wear with heels is panties."

I had also seen, and who hadn't, Clamor's interview with Martha Stewart. One of many, it may have been the first-ever streamed clip to go viral. The famous TV homemaker had received a Wells notice from the SEC charging her with insider trading. After receiving an illegal tip from her much younger, very handsome Merrill Lynch broker, Stewart sold ImClone stock ahead of bad news to avoid a loss of $45,000. She was furiously chopping lettuce on TV, when Clamor pressed her about the trade. She shrieked, "I just want to focus on my salad." Caught red-handed, Stewart did four months in prison! Plus, she had to pay almost half a million dollars in fines, fees and restitution. But as the market tide continued to ebb, Scrushy and Stewart were not the last CEOs to receive a Wells notice.

Vanderman's ego was so pumped up that he soon convinced himself buying CVC was his own idea entirely. He quickly forgot that my pillow talk had sparked the deal. *So much for Eve.* Admittedly Ms. Money had gulled him into buying the boutique investment banker at an astronomical price. But if handled properly the acquisition could still have helped Traub Inc turn a profit. The trouble was he just didn't know how to integrate the institutional focus. Without even consulting me, he brought in a new CEO whose only business experience came from owning a baseball franchise. To save on payroll, the new, minor-league boss replaced senior analysts with juniors. CVC's top researchers, heavy with industry contacts, took a walk—crippling its reputation in the institutional market. After-tax profit margin fell to under 10%.

The Street soon lost all confidence in Vanderman's management ability. I saw less and less of him as he holed up in his West Coast office. When I tried to help, he routed my direct line calls to an underling. Stupid. The trouble with Vanderman was that years as Traub's number two had turned him jealous of competing executives. He never let anyone come near his corporate throne. Now he was ignoring his management team, including me. I could feel he was envious of the media attention Ms. Money received. One analyst told the *Financial Times*, Vanderman was 'like a child banging on a clock with a spoon'—and the line stuck.

Traub was nowhere in evidence. The growth fund BJ Hanlon used to run dropped from over a billion in assets to less than $50 million, flushing management fees down the toilet. Traub shares once again started to test lower levels. Bonnie Branch called me with the news that Vanderman had hired a woman marketing executive from Bolt bank. No wonder my attentions weren't missed. She was supposed to create new services for Traub investors, in marketing lingo, to increase the firm's share of the client's wallet. But her experience was in life insurance, and she convinced Vanderman to raise trading fees. I had my PA, Robin, send him an urgent priority e-mail objecting to the move as a colossal blunder. But he spammed it. The price increase put him in direct conflict with Traub's self-directed investors. They believed safety was in low commissions that reduced risk because they allowed you to back out of a bad trade cheaply. Client defections rose sharply.

I made an emergency trip to Los Angeles to meet with Vanderman's hire. She was a short, chubby blonde in her thirties—just Vanderman's type. I lectured her on the state of the market, but she just didn't have the necessary experience. I didn't doubt it when Bonnie Branch told me the woman and Vanderman were already an item. To top it off, just before Traub's third-quarter numbers were released, the two of them left for Hawaii. Hoping to duck the bad news, they took Traub's jet to the big island, where Vanderman owned a private club condo. Traub Inc's quarterly numbers were a disaster. The big broker posted a first-time-ever loss. 'Eric in the Red!' screamed a *Financial Times* headline. The news took $3 off Traub shares. Ms. Money cobbled together a press release blaming it on the market. *If he wants me gone he can buy back my lifetime contract—for plenty.*

If bad management and red ink weren't enough to do Vanderman in—what happened next was. It started with a call from Jill Clamor, asking about a rumor she had sniffed out. Was Traub Inc for sale? I was shocked, and told her I knew nothing about it. But at one in the morning my time, I got a call from Bonnie Branch with the same question. I told her about Clamor's call. But there was nothing I could do until morning. I told her to get through to Traub any way she could. That was call number two. My nerves were sending adrenaline signals. I took half an Ambien, but at six in the morning, Gia called up. She was still in bed, but her husband had just called from his office. I should call him right away. ASAP. "I hope you're not fooling around with my guy!" she said, making me laugh. All she knew was it had something to do with Traub Inc. That was call number three. I put the phone down, but it immediately rang. Something was up. I ignored call number four, but by then the message light was blinking permanently.

I put a call through to Gia's husband. He immediately switched my call to another line—then told me he had been contacted privately by a friend at Oak Marsh Finance saying that the investment bank was looking for an independent legal advisor to join an M&A team targeting Traub Inc. That was all he knew, but, "Please keep me in the loop." No doubt Gia's accumulated hoard of TRB shares was on his mind.

You must have heard the expression 'Money talks!' My experience has been that it can't keep its mouth shut. The story broke that morning on *StreetWalker*, the influential finance website, and made the afternoon edition of the *New York Press*. The source was Oak Marsh. Vanderman wanted full control and intended to get it via a hostile takeover that would oust Traub! He had consulted with the bankers, but when Oak Marsh presented their funding package, he rejected it. According to *StreetWalker*, he complained that their fees were too high, and screamed that he wasn't going to be ripped off. They paid him back by leaking the deal. Trying to do everything himself, Vanderman hadn't paid up to seal their lips. Once alerted, Traub's board was furious. They met that morning in Los Angeles. Bonnie Branch had reached Traub, and received a proxy over his shares. Apparently at Traub's request, I was conference called into the meeting. But there was no discussion. The Board voted immediately. Vanderman was sacked.

He was escorted out of Traub headquarters, but the SEC was waiting for him with a Wells notice in hand. He was accused of an insider trading violation linked to the Channel Vista acquisition. I got the news via Bonnie Branch. Vanderman had bought over a million CVC shares through a Panama-based trust controlled by him only a week before the takeover. He sold them immediately after the news hit the Street—for a profit of over ten million. He must have counted on a crony to disguise the bookkeeping. That's the only way I can explain it. The trouble was that over the years his rash behavior had made him a lot of enemies at Traub Inc. One of them with a long-standing grudge must have blown the whistle on him. I was aghast. Just how stupid and greedy was he?

The answer to my question was much uglier than I thought. I remembered a cartoon whose voice was that of Lily Tomlin. It might have been Miss Fizzle, who said, "Things are going to get a lot worse before they get worse." They did. According to Bonnie Branch who trailed along to watch Vanderman leave. He was so angry that he crumpled up the Wells notice and threw it in the face of the SEC agent who had served him. Then he stormed into the street-level parking garage, and was last seen roaring off in his Porsche Cayman GTS.

Enraged, he charged onto Olympic Boulevard and connected with the 405 Freeway, heading fast for Santa Monica. He had bragged about his pilot's license in Memphis, and, on my last trip to Los Angeles, I had ducked out of his invitation to fly alone with him in his four-seater Cessna 350. That would have given me the chills. Later I learned his toy cost half a million. It was in an executive hanger at Santa Monica Airport. Apparently, he filed a flight plan for Napa. He was a regular at the French Laundry in Yountville, impressing his dates by flying them to dinner. But he cut the trip short this time. According to the tower, he took the plane up to 8,000 feet and then put it into a steep dive. His airspeed was close to 300 miles per hour when he crashed into the runway and exploded. *Don't blame me!*

50

Clang! Ms. Money rang the famous opening bell at the New York Stock Exchange. Under TV lights and extended sound booms, I announced that Traub was back. "Traub is Traub!" I told the cameras and cheering floor brokers—launching a new campaign. Standing next to me, all smiles, Traub waved down at the jammed exchange floor.

"I'm back for good," the returning leader told the media. The message to Wall Street was that Traub Inc was no acquisition target. Rumors to the contrary were dead wrong. He promised to waste no time putting his house in order, and he was as good as his word. First he slashed the workforce by 2,000 employees, to help cut annual costs by $500 million. The money went into a huge stock buyback, which bolstered the balance sheet by half a billion dollars. His next bold move was to unwind Channel Vista. "There wasn't enough synergy between our core businesses and the capital markets arena," he told investors. CVC was sold to a Dutch global financial giant for $265 million in cash. Traub didn't flinch at the loss of almost $100 million.

Next came the sale of Gotham Trust. Traub 'put lipstick on the pig' in the form of new management. Then he convinced American

Global Bank (AGB) to buy the glitzed-up subsidiary. Louis 'No Motor' Collier, president of AGB, was widely thought of as one of the most ridiculous bankers in the business. He wanted to make AGB one of the banking 'Big Four,' along with Bolt and Citi and JP Morgan Chase. Under Collier, AGB had acquired a string of bad banks with assets that always died on arrival. His idea of testing a potential acquisition was simply to kick the tires without looking under the hood to see if the engine was there—hence his nickname. AGB agreed to buy Gotham for $3.5 billion in hard cash. News of the deal put over $10 on Traub shares. "We're traders not bankers," Traub told the media.

Finally, Ms. Money and Traub toured a dozen cities, telling clients Traub was sticking with its basic strategic focus on self-directed investors, retirees with managed accounts, and independent financial advisors. We concentrated on the money towns—Palo Alto, Scottsdale, Salt Lake City, Dallas, Naples, Palm Beach, Nashville, Arlington, Boston and New York. Our PR entourage took up entire floors of major hotels. Traub and I beat the drum at private client seminars for the rich and town hall meetings for the middle class. 'Traub is Traub.' We were interviewed on radio, TV and the Internet. A guest appearance by Traub on *Smarter Than The Street* topped the campaign. With Ms. Money standing alongside him, he announced a 45% commission cut intended to restore the broker's leadership in the discount marketplace.

We ended the tour in New York so Traub could attend his sports favorite—the U.S. Open at Forest Hills. From his center-court VIP box, we watched Justine Henin-Hardenne win her 7th title of 2003. She was a superb player, who blasted her way through her first five matches. Traub and I watched the single greatest contest of the entire Open—the most incredible match I'd ever seen. In an over-three-hour struggle that lasted till midnight, Henin defeated Jennifer Capriati.

"My God—she's going to lose it," Traub screamed when Henin almost blew the second set. But she went on to demolish Capriati with a series of 120 mile-an-hour serves.

"She's the comeback kid," I argued. *Me too! Ms. Money has made her money back! Everything's the same. So why didn't I feel that way?*

The match turned into a cliff-hanger. Henin was as close as two points from a loss eleven times. Talk about living dangerously. But she still won. "That's victory if I ever saw it," said Traub. "She's tough for twenty. That's what makes a real winner. You have to spring back just when it looks like you'll fail. The important thing is never thinking you're going to lose—even if you're down. What you have to overcome isn't the pressure. It's the idea of defeat. Most people are too afraid to win—that's why they lose. Look at Vanderman!"

"Yeah." But I kept my thoughts to myself. Something was wrong. And Vanderman had rebuked me. When I dodged a ride in his private plane, my final excuse was my father's death. *Had I given him the idea?* At the time he had said he was sorry. But killing himself the way he did was a slap in my face. I was sure of it. *Did he blame me for the CVC deal? His suicide was aimed right at me.*

I felt safer expressing my dissatisfaction back in bed at the San Remo. "Your pal Vanderman was no comeback kid. I can't imagine how you could trust him with your company." My anger was driven by a sense of guilt. Vanderman was stupid. But he should never have killed himself.

"When he came on board, I promised him a chance. He was a dynamo. I owed it to him even though I had my doubts."

"They were calling you the Emperor without clothes."

Traub laughed back, "But you like me that way—don't you."

"But you wandered off to play philosopher king." *And left me to do the dirty work.*

"Golf too."

"I just don't see why? You knew he couldn't fill your shoes! They would never fit him. He just wasn't you at all." I dug for a deeper motive—not sure I wanted to know it.

"I owed it to him—okay?" Traub became defensive. "Yes, I made a big mistake. He looked a lot better back then. I should never have pledged the job to him. I even put it in his contract. I had to give him total control. I couldn't take it back. Believe me I wanted to."

"So all you did was give him enough rope to hang himself with?" *All they buried was scraps. The crash debris filled a 1,000 yard circle around the smoking plane.*

"It worked—didn't it? So don't complain. Look—I told you I made a ton of money when I sold the company. But it took a pile to buy it back. Eric helped with money, dirty money that had to be casino cleaned. There's things you don't know about, but he knew."

"It was a close call—way too risky." *So you killed him, and you tricked me into helping.*

"Hey! You made out like a bandit. He bought Channel Vista—didn't he? Don't you think I know why?"

"What do you mean?" I pushed away from him. *Had Traub seen through me? Very bad news.*

"Need I say your husband held a majority stake?"

"Okay—I made Eric do it. But he didn't have to. It could have helped if he knew what to do with it."

"You got your money back—right? That's what matters. If I took it to the Board they would have laughed in my face."

"He convinced them!"

"Because I wasn't there to say 'No.' I bet you smiled all the way to the bank." *I'd forgotten how well he could use a knife.*

"Then you're an absolute bastard—I had to sleep with him."

"Did it matter? I bet not."

"No it didn't—the only one he was fucking was himself." I gave him a safe answer, but all I wanted was to get out of bed, run to the bathroom and throw up. *I knew enough to tell him what he wanted to hear. But I hated myself for doing it.*

"That's true of a lot of men."

"That doesn't mean I feel good about it."

"Look—you're worth it—every penny of it. You're worth even more. Okay. But I can't make up the difference. I can't give you what you deserve—what you're truly worth. Not me. I can't share it. It's just not possible." *Mr. Money was cursed with the Midas touch. In the end it was a deadly scourge. Suddenly I hated Traub!*

"I don't understand," I dodged once more. *But I had. We could never really be together. The only thing he truly loved was money. Money not me.* "Fuck you," I cursed.

"Yes." *He took it as a joke.*

I laughed and gave him what he wanted. But my mind was screaming with anger. Traub had used me—badly. He had paid for my services— bought them— bought me. True my fortune had been restored. But at a price that just wasn't worth it. Ms. Money had made a comeback. But I didn't want to be her! Free money isn't the same as money free. The only word that can free us is love. I was back to being me.

The next day we watched Henin beat top seed Kim Clijsters in straight sets. She had been treated for muscle cramps and dehydration overnight but returned to win. She was one tough lady—and I was ready to prove just how hard hitting I could be.

PART IV:
MATT SHEPHERD

(2004—2010)

51

The year began badly, when all seven Columbia astronauts were killed during reentry. It ended even worse. Tragedy totally overwhelmed me. Jason could have died. That would have killed me for sure. But Stringfellow saved him. He died doing it. I was back in the world where there are only two sides on the coin. Heads you live, tails you lose it all. No matter how many times you toss it, even though the odds are always the same, nobody can flip heads forever. In the end my proxy husband proved he was worth even more than my proxy lover BJ—and both were more loyal than Traub could ever be. The only men I had left were Connelly and Jason. *If only Shepherd would grow up!*

On October 15, 2003, a private school holiday, Stringfellow and Jason decided to visit the Statue of Liberty. But crowds and bad weather kept them from a direct trip to Liberty Island. It was Stringfellow's idea to take the Staten Island ferry, to get a full view of the monument. But in the grip of rough water and strong currents, as it tried to dock, the huge ferry they were on slammed at full speed into a giant concrete piling—killing eleven people. As the massive abutment sliced into the ferry, panic struck. More than 1,500 passengers surged sideways to avoid being crushed to death.

Jason said people were screaming, and he was being pushed over-board. Stringfellow grabbed him and pulled him back toward a stanchion. The crowd swept over the boy, as he squeezed into the space between the metal post and the gunwale. But the human tidal wave carried Stringfellow with it. Jason returned safely, but Stringfellow was thrown into the icy water and drowned. My only consolation was that this time I had a body to grieve over. *I'm a zombie mother.*

Jason became my highest priority. After recuperating at home, he was back in school before Thanksgiving. But I could see he was changed. Stringfellow was 'Dad'—the father he loved. But much worse was what he had seen. People struggling to save themselves at all and everyone else's cost. He was alone and frightened be-cause he had experienced what the survival of the fittest means—way too early. I worked with the school's professional support staff. But I was worried. It was Connelly who came to my rescue. He spent every second of his time with my thirteen-year-old. Finally, he arranged for Jason to join his closest school pal and his family on a Christmas holiday tour of China. "It'll keep his mind off it," he told me.

Seven-year-old Melanie and Moira recuperated in Gstadt with Gia, who wanted me to join them. I said, "No."

"It's just the two of us," I told Connelly at Christmas. Then I started to cry. But no matter how much he tried to comfort me, Stringfellow's death resurrected waves of depression as terrible as those I felt after BJ died in 9/11. *The man I loved was dead, and the man I married had drowned, and now I knew Traub was incapable of lov-ing me. Matt Shepherd be damned.*

My career in politics began with a call from Traub right after New Year's. We hadn't met since Stringfellow's funeral. His message surprised me. "I want more early warning about politics—about what's going on in DC," he ordered. "We need to be better plugged in. I have a seat on a Commission—it's about financial education. I'm appointing you as my delegate." Almost without me knowing it, I left Wall Street for Washington.

"What about the markets?"

"Take some time off."

"Good." I was happy for the change of venue. Ms. Money's credibility was suffering once again. She had swung too far to the Bearish side. I was ready for a break from Wall Street, where, as the saying goes, you're only as good as your last trade.

But I was sure Traub had another motive. I quickly learned that, as usual, he was after more than political insider information. For all his money, California politics were a madhouse, especially when it came to the governorship. A home state post was going to be hard as hell to win. He was thinking Washington once more. He had made an attempt at a Cabinet post when Paul O'Neill was chosen as short-lived Treasury Secretary. John Snow had beaten him out as O'Neill's replacement. But Traub was convinced that if Bush Jr was reelected he would dump Snow—leaving Traub as the logical choice to replace him at Treasury. "Look," he went on, "the important thing is you have to supervise my new PAC. It's an election year. I want to make an impact." Translation—be my bag lady and buy me a cabinet seat.

I accepted without hesitation because I needed out of New York, where Stringfellow's ghost roamed and phantoms of 9/11 would dwell forever. Even better, there would be less day-to-day contact with Traub. My staff booked me into a fully furnished luxury apartment at the Embassy Suites, where I stayed three nights a week. I'd be back in New York from Thursday night to Monday morning. With Moira's help, Connelly could handle everything in my absence.

☙

The Financial Literacy and Education Commission (FLEC) was established in 2003 under the Fair and Accurate Credit Transactions Act (FACT). They love acronyms in Washington because they help disguise the truth that most legislative titles mean exactly the reverse of their formal name. Such is 'Big Government' policy. If you want an example take a look at the so-called CAN SPAM Act passed by Congress. Its full name is the "Controlling the Assault of Non-Solicited Pornography and Marketing Act of 2003." You might think this allows you to spam junk e-mails, but what it actually does is protect junk mail sent by your local politician from being spammed.

FLEC's stated goal was improving the financial literacy and education of U.S. citizens. *Just what I've been doing for almost 30 years.* But the government was far behind the private sector when it came to keeping citizens informed about financial developments. The Federal Reserve was still giving out economic comic books to high schoolers with four-gig laptops. Traub's own investor training seminars were state of the art and totally interactive. I was shocked by the waste of tax payer money. Expensive untested projects designed by academic educational consultants were truly stupid. Even worse, I could see that politics were steering the government's efforts. It looked to me that driving people deeper into debt was the real mission of big government.

On May 18, 2004, Alan Greenspan was nominated to serve for an unprecedented fifth term as chairman of the Federal Reserve.

Privately, on Wall Street, he was thought of as the most powerful 'empty suit' in Washington. His real job was preserving his job—and he was good at it. He had held onto it from one President to another by satisfying the politicians and the people with mouthfuls of economic gibberish and by lowering and/or raising interest rates only in baby-step quarter-point moves whose effects were self-defeating. Greenspan, originally a saxophone major at the Julliard School of Performing Arts in New York before becoming an economist, serenaded government with its favorite 1919 lyric—"I'm forever blowing bubbles." He kept the castles he was building in the air from tumbling into rubble with lower interest rates for longer and longer stretches. Soon after his swift repeated confirmation, Greenspan, hosted a speaking luncheon with FLEC.

Ms. Money had met him briefly a number of times. But now I found myself sitting next to him. The arrangement was deliberate. *What did Greenspan want from Ms. Money? The obvious answer—he wants to be on Smarter Than The Street.* Greenspan's currying favor with the media was legendary—his relationships with one prominent television anchor after another were well known. After an early divorce, he partnered with Barbara Walters in the 70s, and then MacNeil-Lehrer producer Susan Mills in the 80s. I couldn't imagine how news correspondent Andrea Mitchell—his 90s date—could marry him. She was 20 years his junior. Greenspan was over seventy when they were wed. He was a better match for the woman who conducted the ceremony, 64-year-old Supreme Court Justice Ruth Bader Ginsburg. Traub told me Greenspan's earliest lover was conservative author Ayn Rand—whom he jokingly called his 'laissez-faire lassie fair.' *Which only shows you how little* noblesse oblige *meant to him.*

Greenspan's lunch time remarks were a rehash of his recent media comments—always designed to appear profound but proving stupid when you thought about them. This time he added a new twist: "I hope you teach Americans how to take advantage of the new mortgage products," he told FLEC. "Because not long ago more-marginal applicants would simply have been denied credit, but now lenders are able to quite efficiently judge the risk posed by individual applicants and to price that risk appropriately. These improvements have led to rapid growth in subprime mortgage lending, which I hope this Commission tells the public about." In other words—show them how to buy a house for nothing down.

My god! I looked down at my plate to hide my expression. I was aghast. Greenspan was telling non-qualified homebuyers to take out no-pain, subprime adjustable-rate mortgages (ARMs). He was throwing gasoline on the fire whose hot air was swelling the housing bubble. The Fed's own funds rate was at an all-time-low of 1%, to help homeowners refinance and spend and boost the economy. But the rock bottom rate had another purpose as well. Banks could borrow nearly free money from the Fed. But to make a profit they needed to lend it out—first to homeowners too poor to buy a house in the first place, then to McMansion buyers with dried up credit lines, and then to real estate speculator flip-buyers. All you needed to get a sub-prime mortgage was to prove you were alive. And borrowers using the names of the dead were not unheard of. I was frightened because I knew that when the last real estate balloon burst it was followed by the Great Depression.

I applauded with the rest of the audience. Greenspan nodded his thanks and then quickly sat down, making sure he brushed against me—while I was still clapping. His arm grazed more than my side. "You're brilliant," I said, smiling at him. *This man is the true Mr. Money! He's the king-pin of the global drug cartel supplying a world of free money addicts.*

Greenspan turned towards me, but his face, with its permanent 24-hour shadow, twisted smile and perpetual leer, was no fun to look at. I felt his eyes staring down the neckline of my Max Mara business suit, hunting for a trace of bosom. "Tell me more about your job," he asked. "I'm very sure they don't call you Ms. Money for nothing."

"It's *nothing* compared to the Fed—I'm sure." I applied another dose of hero worship.

"Did you find what I said something of interest for investors."

"I understand you perfectly," I told Greenspan, and just to provoke him, I let my knee touch his trousers. "It's okay for government to protect us. But people need housing—shelter is a basic human want."

He stared back at me hard, and I pulled my leg away. His mind was working on a sound-bite that could be quoted. "Yes, the Garden of Eden was probably the only place where affordable housing wasn't an issue." His smile was horrible.

I knew Greenspan was taking the biggest risk possible by dropping interest rates and allowing home prices to soar. But I wasn't going to get on the wrong side of the Maestro's baton. "People just ran around with nothing on." I thought the image would distract him, but I was surprised by what he said.

"They must have been loaded with germs! I mean the primitive world is filthy."

I went back on topic. "Since the mortgage lenders are good at their jobs, the economy has nothing to fear from affordable housing." *That had to be just what he wanted to hear.*

But he was off on his own trajectory. "You can't imagine! I swim in the Congressional pool. Half the people there don't use the footbath. You know before they go into the pool. It's disgusting."

Suddenly Greenspan interrupted himself by picking up his coffee cup and holding it to the light. "I think this is cracked—there's a lipstick stain on it too," he almost shouted. His personal assistant reached from behind and instantly removed the cup. A waiter immediately came with a replacement.

"I'm sorry," he apologized. "For some reason these luncheons are always in the dirtiest dining rooms. There are germs all over. They need more health inspectors." His aide passed him a container of handy-wipes.

"I can't afford to catch a cold," I smiled back. "I just don't have any time."

"Any infection can be serious," he told me. "They should follow the health code. You can't be too careful." Then he got to his real interest. "I've seen you on *Smarter Than The Street.*"

"I've been filling in whenever the network needed." *He's a health freak. Who would have guessed it? Doesn't he know he's creating a financial plague by pandering to the banks?*

"I don't know if it would be appropriate to appear. Perhaps we could have lunch and discuss it." *His eyes had that look.*

"I'll have to get back to you. In your case the network will make the decision. Of course, I'll do what I can. Is the Fed thinking higher interest rates are needed?"

"I don't think I could talk about that," he said as he stood up to leave. But it was not long before Greenspan began to raise interest rates—even while he was still pushing subprime lending. It would take two more years before rate increases effectively let the air out of the housing bubble, triggering the worst crash since 1929.

52

Ms. Money morphed into 'Graft Gal.' Helping dole out Traub's million dollar campaign contributions. I met almost daily with the executive director of his PAC. It was called To Reelect the Best, or TRB for short, and designed to match the symbol for Traub stock. I became a lobbyist, seen frequently in the offices of the California delegation along with those of key Cabinet members and the Republican National Committee.

Soon I was drawn into the Presidential campaign. I was pro-Bush, whom I thought of as victimized and vilified. Criticism from the Left was outrageous and far beyond the boundaries of civility. I mean—he was The President. Smearing him so rudely insulted not only the people who had voted for him, but our Country itself. With the help of Traub's PAC, I earmarked a $100,000 personal contribution to the Presidential race.

I couldn't imagine a woman who would vote for either Kerry or Edwards. I read *A Change of Heart,* and was fascinated by Julia Thorne's bitter comments on politics—bad—and politicians—even worse. I was certain that Kerry had gotten his marriage to her annulled just to wed billionaire heiress Teresa Heinz, leaving Thorne to die of cancer. And Edwards was no better—he too was unfaithful to another cancer-stricken spouse. Everyone in New York knew about him and the model Rielle Hunter. Gia gave me a copy of Jay McInerney's *The Story of My Life*, the super novel that chronicles the model's coming of age in the boom years. You become totally engrossed in her life. The dope, the men and the money. I put it down one night, and fell asleep on memories tinged with remarks remembered from my meeting with Greenspan.

I dreamed I was in the Garden of Eden. It's absolutely wonderful because I'm totally free. I can glide through a lush green world without a care. There's even a heated, salt-water, horizon pool for bathing. I'm naked and beautiful and happy and free. I'm not worried about anything because I don't know what it means to worry. I'm Eve, a woman, the woman! When it comes to men, Adam is just a good friend. I keep him company when I want to. He looks a little like Paul Stringfellow. God is another story. He sort of resembles Traub. I'm not sure about him. He's never told me why he made me—and whether he wants me or not. A typical male.

The only problem is the dietary restriction. We get an incredible lift from the fruit of the Tree of Eternal Life. It's a cross between mango and pomegranate, and better than any haut-cuisine dessert I've ever eaten, including the $100-a-bite cherry-pistachio chocolate financier with bourbon sauce at Maxim's. But God laid down the law to us. There's one tree whose fruit we're not supposed to eat. It's in the middle of the garden. God called it the Tree of the Knowledge of Good and Evil. I don't understand what good and evil are. I mean we're innocent in Eden. Perpetually innocent. For all I know it could be poison sumac. I can understand God not wanting us running around naked with a rash.

But the fruit on the Tree of Knowledge was very attractive. It was gold-colored and shiny—really quite tempting. You can see yourself in their mirror polish. I have one of these great perpetual perms.

Not too kinky, and my hair is very long and parted in the center. My face is a perfect oval with flawless features. I look like Eve in the Hans Memling painting I saw long ago in the Museum in Brooklyn when my mother and I met Alice Powers. I'm more Low-Country than Italian.

Oh, yeah. There's one other creature in Eden, a long, slimy serpent with a face that for sure is just like Alan Greenspan's. He hangs around the Tree of Knowledge a lot. At first I thought he was a guard. But he says God doesn't like him anymore. He makes me laugh a lot—mostly with jokes about Adam. He seems to have known him from before I came on the Eden scene, and calls him 'lily white,' which he thinks is funny. He asked me how Adam introduced himself. Of course all I remember is waking up and he was already there. "Didn't he say, 'Madam I'm Adam'?"—the serpent asked me, laughing at his own joke. When he explained it, I thought it was cute since it says the same thing from either end. But later on I found out he got it from Cole Porter.

Then he told me why God doesn't want us to eat the fruit of the Tree of Knowledge. First of all it's because the fruit is made of gold—something God doesn't want us to know about. It's connected to another thing called money. Of course none of this made any sense to me since everything in Eden is free. As far as I was concerned he was speaking babble. But then he told me that if we ate the fruit we would become godly. That was a bit more interesting. It's because to be god you have to know what the difference between Good and Evil is. "Look," he said "God is like Good, and Evil is very close to your name Eve. It means something that you're not Fred and Alice. It's a clear case of what Chomsky would call explanatory adequacy. You'll just be fulfilling your destiny." The idea of becoming godly convinced me. I'd be on the same level as the boss. That's the executive suite. I took a bite, and of course the snake watched me chew until I swallowed. Men again—what is this thing with swallowing? If you're interested, it tasted like a mojito.

I immediately conferenced Adam into the dialogue. He was close by and popped over for a bite. He must have liked the taste because he smiled as it went down. But that was his last joy. God flew down with a roar and fireworks and a belching smoke machine. He went right to the edge of the stage and pointed his finger at Adam and me where we had started to boogie in the mosh pit. We were evicted. Out! Vamoose hombre. We couldn't go around naked. But God gave us clothes. A fur coat mind you. Frankly I liked it. I could see Adam's eyes light up when I put it on.

God said we could never go back, and never again eat the fruit of the Tree of Eternal Life. That means we have to die. Death is the end of life, something new at least, but I wasn't sure I liked the idea. But God gave me a real blue-light special. I get to have babies. It's supposed to be very painful. I'm also going to be subject to menstruation, which has something to do with the moon, not with men. I don't think I'm going to like it. But my children get to live on after me. And there's one interesting thing that just might make it work. Adam and I get to have sex. Sex is how you make babies, and it's hot. Sex could be worth it because Adam is already turning onto me. And to seal the expulsion God threw in a low-rent affordable housing project apartment. It was a deal-maker all right!

I returned to New York, to host a private, million-dollar-a-seat, fund raiser for Bush. Traub flew in for the dinner, which was catered in my San Remo suite, and where I acted as his unofficial campaign manager. He couldn't have been more pleased with the opportunity to show off his merits as a potential Secretary of the Treasury. We ruled out personal contact, and he agreed to spend the night in a suite at the Waldorf. Bush thanked me personally for the $20 million I raised. As he was leaving, he asked, "What does Ms. Money think about housing?"

"It feels like the dot.com bubble all over again." I told him that my meeting with Greenspan had made me even more worried about the housing market, and I repeated Ms. Money's warnings to Traub investors. Housing prices were flashing red as their trend line approached vertical. "Whenever investors forget about risk—that's a danger signal for sure."

After my guests had left, Connelly surprised me with two-dozen gorgeous red roses. They were for Valentine's Day. I took one look at them and cried. They were just too beautiful. I would never get the flowers I needed again. I kissed him, and he held me as I sobbed. "I miss your mother," he told me. His tone of voice said it all. I squeezed him harder.

The event and my personal campaign donation gave a surprise lift to my political career. The President must have heard my fears. Not long after his second inauguration, I received a letter bearing the gold seal of the White House. I had been appointed to the President's Advisory GSE Review Panel—charged with drafting the Administration's future policy proposal on mortgage market giants Fannie Mae and Freddie Mac.

I called Traub and offered to turn Bush down. But he insisted I accept. "Snow's got to go," he told her. "I need you in DC now. Get as close as you can to Andy Card. He's still in as Chief of Staff." *I was happy to be 'farther removed,' as they say.*

My appointment letter was followed by a thick briefing study, which made very clear that Bush the younger was worried about a repeat of the Savings and Loan crisis. He had argued for regulatory overhaul of the housing finance industry back in 2003, but the Democrats opposed his plan, claiming that tighter regulation would cut off financing for low-income high-risk home buyers. But the Government Sponsored Enterprises (GSEs for short), meaning Fannie Mae and Freddie Mac, were taking huge risks. The mortgage giants had lowered their underwriting standards to grab a huge share of the ballooning market. The GSE watchdog, the Office of Federal Housing Enterprise Oversight (OFHEO) was worried about widespread accounting errors at Fannie Mae and Freddie Mac, and the President wanted to make sure the GSE balance sheets were risk free.

Meanwhile, hammers were pounding everywhere—building the biggest housing glut ever. Homebuilder stocks were soaring. Housing developer Horton's stock went from $3 per share in early 1997 to an all-time high of $43 in July 2005. The last time I met Gia for lunch, she had casually mentioned that her husband was buying a condo near Yale. It was for his daughter by his first marriage to live in during college. "It's cheaper than a dorm room—and he's going to flip it when she graduates. He'll make money for sure!"

53

On February 17, 2005, ex-Senator Matt Shepherd, Chairman of the GSE Advisory Panel, delivered the President's charge from the stage of the Marriott Wardman Park in DC. The Panel was responsible for recommending legislation that the President could support, meaning a broad policy that recognized the importance of homeownership in America and at the same time protected the mortgage market from excessive risk. *A lot easier said than done!*

Congress had already jumped the gun. In the Senate, Chuck Hagel, the Nebraska Republican, had just introduced S-190—the Federal Housing Enterprise Regulatory Reform Act of 2005. Shepherd made them laugh by calling Hagel a 'Nervous Nellie from Nebraska.' And soon enough the House got into the act by proposing HR-1461, the Federal Housing Finance Reform Act of 2005, which was also contrary to what the President wanted.

I opened my laptop and quickly Googled ex-Senator Shepherd. He was born in Philadelphia, and was eight years older than I was. After his mother's first marriage ended in divorce, she resettled in Alabama. Shepherd made a fortune developing retirement community real estate, and had served as an outside director on the board of Lehman Brothers. He was also a horseman, who owned a stud farm and raced thoroughbreds. He went into politics, first as a member of the Alabama delegation to the House of Representatives and then in the U.S. Senate. In his Senate race, he won every county in the state. His career was distinguished by laws on workfare, public housing reform and environmental protection. Rumors were that he had given up his seat to plan a Presidential campaign.

Shepherd's personal electricity was way brighter than the TV lights. He was one of the most beautiful men I had ever seen. *Gorgeous.* His good looks were understated owing to his perfect poise, and his rich baritone voice kept me from missing a word. He immediately fascinated me. I sat mesmerized. He could have been Peter O'Toole in *The Lion in Winter*—tall and slim in a perfectly cut, very expensive, deep grey suit. His hair was a glossy mixture of black and grey, cut short and combed forward. His beautifully proportioned head sat perfectly on a long neck that turned his Energizer blue eyes right at me. They were perfectly spaced and for a second seemed to look right into me. His long, lean nose pointed to a million-dollar mouth of gleaming white teeth. His lips were so perfectly shaped I couldn't stop myself from imagining what they would be like if they pressed against mine. *Elegant wasn't the word for Matt Shepherd,* I thought in a rush. The perfect patrician, he was a man on horseback, whose bearing said he held the reins and commanded at will. He was married, and I wanted him as soon as I saw him.

Holding public meetings twice a month, the Presidential GSE Panel crisscrossed the country, hearing testimony from local government, community groups representing home buyers, and from builders, bankers, real estate brokers, and mortgage lenders. Everyone wanted to fix the GSEs, but Washington political interests totally disagreed about how to do it. The HUD attorneys on the Panel leaned left—while the President's people, myself included, leaned right.

There was standing room only at our hearing at the Westin Hotel in Charlotte, North Carolina. We met at the San Francisco Mint, just before it closed after being sold to the city for a dollar by the Federal government. Asked to comment, Ms. Money joked, saying it was the best real estate deal ever!

In Chicago, with the headquarters of the National Association of Realtors (NAR) close by on North Michigan Avenue, we heard David Lereah, NAR chief economist. Quoting his own TV-broadcast 'Anti-Bubble Reports,' he told the Panel, "There is virtually no risk of a national housing price bubble based on the fundamental demand for housing and predictable economic factors." But I knew the numbers told a different story. Reports from my Traub research group and the Panel's staff clearly pointed to a dream-house bubble in the making. Home prices were accelerating rapidly. In some metro areas they were jumping over ten percent a year—versus a long-term average annual increase of only about one percent! *Bubble, bubble, I thought, and soon comes trouble.*

The Panel heard from politicians as well. The Democrat's housing point man, Rep Barney Frank, was the most vocal when it came to advocating greater GSE risk. Frank had already testified, "I do not want the same kind of focus on safety and soundness in the regulation of Fannie Mae and Freddie Mac that we have in the Office of Thrift Supervision. I want to roll the dice a little bit more in this situation towards subsidized housing." Ms. Money was appalled. *Doesn't he realize we're in a housing mania?* Hearing Frank gush about 'affordable housing,' I understood why the President was worried about the Democrats giving away the store by creating a new home ownership entitlement, just to improve their voting edge.

The more I saw of Shepherd, the more I liked. So don't be surprised when I say that it wasn't long before I saw all of him. On the second night of the Panel's two-day meeting at the Mission Bay Hyatt in San Diego, we met privately. Shepherd's practice was to sound out individual members in one-on-one sessions, and I lured him with a plan to use Traub's superior research to corroborate data supplied by the GSEs. We met for a private dinner in my penthouse suite, with giant-size views of the bay and the Pacific opposite. I ordered a private working meal for the meeting, and dismissed room service as soon as it came. I was still in my forties, hurting, and I sensed that Shepherd knew it. Our attraction was planetary in its magnetism.

I put on an absolutely perfect Helmut Lang pearl-grey long-sleeve jacket over a silvery draped neck top with a shirttail hem flapping over the tightest glossy-silk skinny jeans. The outfit stopped him cold at the door. I could see he was excited, and brought him a drink while he took in the room's spectacular views. I asked him to help me out of the jacket so we could get down to work. In a second I was in his arms. His face, the face I wanted, was against mine. Shepherd was so beautiful I couldn't stop kissing him. And I couldn't help myself—it was spontaneous ignition. All the electricity between us sparked and then exploded. I had seduced men before, but never quite like this. I was crying within a minute. He put a finger to the tear slowly falling down my cheek, and then tasted it. Then he kissed me, and I could feel my own tears on his lips. He smelled of sandalwood. I was right to play no games with him. His hands slid up under my top, gently lifting my breasts. Then he pulled down my jeans—and my tiny thong. We were on the sofa, and then he was inside me and I couldn't stop coming. I had never been like this with a man. I felt my hot balm wetting him as he rode me deep and throbbing, and then he climaxed. Immediately he started on me again, and I arched into him. Then I twisted myself on top of him and sliding over him. I rode faster and faster, and then I let my body give him its own message.

Later, we sat up to have drinks. I knew he wanted to talk. But I was feeling light headed and giggled.

"What's so funny?" he asked.

"I never did it before the salad," I smiled.

"Just as long as you know what this is about." He was frightened by the explosive union. But I didn't worry.

"I'm fine with it," I said. "It was something that had to happen, you know? It doesn't change our job."

"I was going to show you this," he said, and then handed me an internal memo stamped SECRET. It was addressed to Richard F Syron, the CEO of Freddie Mac, from David Andrukonis, the lender's former chief risk officer. The mid-2004 memo warned that rules disallowing high-risk loans from counting toward affordable housing goals were being completely ignored. The mortgage GSE was buying shaky loans that threatened its financial stability and 'posed an enormous threat.'

"I'm not surprised. You know what this is really about—money. The President wants tighter lending rules so he won't have to pay out, and the Dems want to give people free money to buy homes with."

"Spoken like a woman who knows her politics," he said. "You know why Freddie and Fanny were cheating?" he asked and answered. "They cooked the books to fill their pockets. Even worse, they used some of the take to bribe Congressmen who could keep the regulators off their back."

"The problem is we're reaching crisis levels in the housing market. Anyone can get a mortgage—alive or dead. But I'm more worried about something else."

"What?"

"If the GSEs lend loose, when the bubble breaks the contagion could be very dangerous. If even one GSE fails—it could be a lot worse than the S&L crisis. I don't think anyone realizes how bad this could get."

"Well at least I know how bad you can be," he said sliding against me.

"I could be even worse than that—wait and see." And then once again I owned him.

54

Treasury Department spokesman, Bradley Lufkin, announced that after eight months of hearings, ex-Senator Shepherd would present the GSE panel's final report in New Orleans on November 1, 2005. And to whet media appetites, following Lufkin's announcement, Shepherd added, "The President knows that his call for a substantial overhaul of Fannie and Freddie has widespread support. We've had a lot of leeway to make recommendations."

But Matt, as I now called him, had told me privately he had another reason for publicly delivering the Panel's final report in the still-ravaged post-Katrina city. His Presidential ambitions were hoping for a future Southern primary sweep. Going to New Orleans would show concern for the voters of his neighboring state. So shortly after arriving, the Panel, led by Shepherd, made a show of touring the hardest hit areas of the city. The wreckage was appalling. The hurricane had rammed the broad delta region. The levee system of dykes failed catastrophically, flooding almost the entire city. Only the central district had really escaped the worst of Katrina's stronger than 150 mph winds. Katrina killed more than 1,800 people, and total property damage was estimated at a huge

$81 billion tab. My photo, I was in boots and rain gear, appeared in the *Picayune* the next day.

The Panel assembled forty floors up in the Riverview ballroom of the New Orleans Marriott. A crowd limited to 200 had assembled to hear Shepherd preview our final recommendations. After months of working together closely, I had drafted most of his executive summary myself. The room was thick with reporters and TV camera crews. As an Alabama neighbor, Shepherd began by thanking the people of New Orleans for agreeing to host the presentation in the aftermath of Katrina's destruction. Then he followed the outline Ms. Money had helped him write.

He began with the typical blessing: Fannie Mae and Freddie Mac had striven always to improve home ownership for low and middle income families. To further that goal, the Bush administration had established a new agency to oversee Fannie Mae and Freddie Mac to make sure the GSEs had properly hedged their $1.5 trillion risk. The Panel's report showed that regulation had protected "the ordinary homebuyer's right to obtain a 30-year fixed-rate mortgage with a low down payment and the continuous availability of mortgage credit under a wide range of economic conditions." That was Gospel—but I knew it was also total bullshit. Reading between the lines, the report said that risk control was more important than affordability. The GSEs had to be restrained from uncontrolled lending—once and for all. Ms. Money knew that was what Bush really wanted, and I had been responsible for much of the report.

Shepherd concluded by emphasizing that the Panel's recommendations were intended first and foremost to avoid a repeat of the government bank bailout that followed the 1980s S&L crisis. Preventing a GSE meltdown came first. He didn't say the real trouble was that the regulators had fallen asleep at the switch or been paid to. The sticking point was that the GSEs were now hugely over-extended—the housing bubble had stuffed them with more than $3 trillion of worthless debt. But Fannie and Freddie would now be forced to shore up their underwriting standards—to protect home affordability! *You didn't expect anything else from the President's Panel did you?*

During the Q&A that followed, Shepherd finessed the media by directing attention away from the GSEs and onto special housing aid for Katrina victims. As a past Senator, he would press the President for even greater housing aid in the wake of the hurricane. Bush Jr had told him face-to-face that FEMA would expedite spending $2.7 billion on 145,000 trailers and mobile homes intended to house newly-homeless storm victims. Both as a native of the Camellia State, and Chairman of the President's Advisory GSE Reform Panel, he wanted to assure all 'delta folk' that foreclosure was not an option for those who were driven out of their homes. "Nobody's going to be evicted," he told the reporters. That wasn't in the script as I wrote it, and it was a promise he should never have made.

Ms. Money was spotted by a New York correspondent, who put a mike and a cameraman on me. I emphasized that a GSE failure would certainly devastate not only real estate, but the larger financial markets as well. "We are in the midst of a housing bubble," I added. "I know Alan Greenspan told the public only a month or so ago that 'at a minimum, there's a little froth' in the U.S. housing market. So I want to remind you that froth is made up of a lot of bubbles." My remarks brought a laugh from those nearby—and were subsequently aired on evening TV.

Matt Shepherd and I decided to end the presentation with a casual private celebration of our own. I didn't know where things were going.

We had been in each other's arms since our first night together in San Diego months before. I was crazy about him. But he was going to run for President. Our job was done, but that night we both refused to think about the future. The November evening was perfect, and Bourbon Street was still mostly intact owing to its high ground location in the French Quarter. I let my hair down, and we both wore jeans. Even so, we were recognized at Nola, where Chef Emeril Lagasse insisted on opening a bottle of Billecart-Salmon brut rosé champagne for us. He greeted the Senator warmly, but then surprised me with a hug. He kissed me on each cheek, and called me 'Mlle Monnaie.' I knew him from New York, when he worked just around the corner from the San Remo at one of my favorites, Taladega, the Cajun-inspired restaurant.

I was happy for the attention—seeing that Shepherd was impressed. Lagasse made a special dinner just for us. It was a totally erotic meal with foie gras and shrimp remoulade with green tomatoes. He blended Creole and Vietnamese cooking, for the main course, crispy smoked duck and mushroom boudin balls and tomato-bacon jam. The assortment of tastes was fantastic. Shepherd just ate and ate. We ended up with Lagasse's famous warm 'Ooey Gooey' chocolate cake. I kept smiling at the giant-sized chef because his menu suggested he knew we were headed for bed.

"I'm stuffed," I told Shepherd as we strolled past Galatoire's.

"I just don't want things to end," he said and kissed me. His body told me we were going back to his room.

Then I heard music blasting out of Cat's Meow. A crowd of young drinkers swarming into Razoo surprised me. It seemed Katrina had done nothing to make Bourbon Street less lively. At the upper end of the Quarter, near Canal Street, we looked into Babe's, the strip club. It was late, but suddenly I dragged him inside.

I was back in The Box. I would show Shepherd what it meant to be loved by me. Now I would be the temptress. I was worth millions, but all I wanted was for Matt Shepherd to say he couldn't live without me. The music was loud and the room smoky and full of girls wearing anything from micro-panties to glittering gowns. Madonna was blaring at them, singing 'Justify My Love.' The 1990 single's super sexy video, banned by MTV, was on a huge floor-to-ceiling screen.

I flagged down a bare breasted waitress who brought us an overpriced bottle of bad champagne. After the sleek girl with blonde hair down to her waist poured our drinks, I grabbed her, shoved money into her shimmering blue skirt and pushed her onto Shepherd's lap. Under her silk-strand hair, the girl's large breasts were bare, and I put his hands on them. She threw her arms around him and started kissing his neck and squirming over him. The music changed to 'Slashed' from Bent Razor's *Tie Me Up*—slow and totally slinky. The lyrics wailed, "You let me violate you / You let me vandalize you." The girl boogied bumps and grinds to the intense keyboards and distorted guitar that increased the sexual tension. I gave her a tip and pulled her off Shepherd. Then I stood up and started to dance. I climbed onto Shepherd, and said, "A hundred for a lap dance!"

He was stiff already, and asked, "How much for a kiss only?"

"We never kiss the clients," I answered.

"But I'm in the band," he objected. "I was a drummer when I went to Auburn."

"Then I'll make an exception."

My arms went around him and their message was I will never let you go. "I want to do very nasty things to you." I said.

We left the club and took a cab back to the hotel. "Just to you," I whispered to him.

55

By Christmas I was back in New York, hoping to hear from Shepherd. Instead, I heard about him. *Not Good!* His name appeared front-screen on the popular financial blog called *StreetWalker.* The story quickly became a banner headline 'Shepherd or Scrooge?' blaring its way across the front page of Louisiana's leading tabloid. *Very Not Good!* A blown-up photo showed him touring Katrina destruction along with the GSE Panel. I was somewhere in the pack. Next to it, a contrasting picture showed him leading a thoroughbred into a horse van. The caption screamed: 'Horse Vans for House Trailers?'

The story was even worse. 'Ex-Alabama Senator promises to bail underwater Katrina homeowners—but washes them out instead!' shrieked the paper. And as the news went viral the headlines were uglier, 'Presidential Hopeful Forecloses!' shouted the *Picayune.* Sources claimed that Shepherd had sold a controlling interest in MIN Mortgage LLC, which had risen to prominence atop the housing bubble, to billionaire investment bankers Silverstein Roth. MIN was a big seller of subprime loans to mobile-home owners with poor credit histories. It was acquired by Battlement Financial, an unregulated off-balance sheet subsidiary of Silverstein, called a SIV for short, or Structured Investment Vehicle. Battlement, owing to the reduced capital requirements for SIVs, could employ greater leverage than its public parent. It had gobbled up subprime mortgages. But Hurricane Katrina had frightened Wall Street. The SIV started foreclosing on the homes of storm victims. The article quoted a Black woman with nowhere to live. Following a foreclosure, she had moved her family into a barn. Asked about Shepherd's claim that government would prevent foreclosure, she said, "Tell him sleepin' in a manger ain't what it's supposed to be."

I didn't have to guess that Shepherd must be furious. The stories spattered his Presidential ambitions with mud. But no matter how hard I tried there was no getting through to him. He refused to take my calls. I was frantic. I used lines of communication reserved solely for the GSE panel. A skeleton staff was still on board to supervise printing and distribution of the final report. But all I was told was that he would be spending January with his family. Finally, a message sourced through Traub's Birmingham office, was sent directly to my PA Robin in New York. It was worse than I feared, Shepherd blamed me for leaking the story. It had to come from Wall Street—so it must have come from me. I was just being "a jealous bitch because he wouldn't leave his wife." He didn't want to see me again—ever! *I was stunned. I wanted him. I wasn't giving him up. As soon as I told him the truth, he would change his mind.*

Ms. Money's rising political status got me invited to the swearing in ceremony for Benjamin Bernanke as Chairman of the Federal Reserve on February 1, 2006. I had met him briefly when, as head of the President's Council of Economic Advisers, he had testified before the GSE Panel. Of course, and more important, I was hoping to run into Shepherd. After two months, I wanted to confront him. But he wasn't in sight. I saw Bernanke chatting with a man I recognized as Bradley Masterson also a Fed higher-up, and already rumored to be Bernanke's 'Mr Fixit.' But a second after I grabbed a white wine from a passing waiter, Bernanke himself caught my eye and made a beeline for me.

"I've seen you on TV. Please don't call me 'helicopter Ben' on your show," he introduced himself. I knew the nickname was a joking reminder that he had once said monetary stimulus could be accomplished by air-dropping money onto the streets from a helicopter.

"I'm back with Traub. The GSE Commission has presented its recommendations," I said. I wondered if Greenspan had trained him to cozy up to the media. He was the Maestro's protégé. Still, the Greenspan days were over, and nothing could bring them back.

"Shepherd did a good job. We don't want too much refinancing cash speculating wherever it can."

"There's too much money in the real estate market already. Investors need to be very careful."

But then Masterson joined us. "No need for alarm," he interrupted. "The markets are sound. Chicken Little can stop fretting." He stared hard at me, but his brown eyes weren't warm. He must have known my Wall Street critics had been calling me by the nursery rhyme name.

"Our Traub strategy is very risk averse," I told them. But then I changed the subject with an appeal to Bernanke, "My son's thinking about Princeton. He wants to be a math major." I knew he had gone from the faculty to the Fed.

His round fringed head leaned in, and he whispered in my ear, "Just send me a note."

"Thank you," I said with a smile. "He's very good with numbers. But I'm the one who has to deal with the tuition. I'll probably have to sell my condo to pay for it."

"Now's the time," said Masterson.

"Maybe I can get more if I wait," I replied, and then parted as both men laughed.

But soon enough all political hell broke out in the housing finance sector. The story was front page in the *Wall Street Journal*. The SEC charged six Fannie Mae and Freddie Mac executives with securities fraud. The stock watchdog called public statements that the GSEs had only minimal exposure to high-risk loans 'deliberately misleading.' The crackdown spread when U.S. regulators filed over one hundred financial mismanagement charges against Fannie Mae's chief executive, Franklin Raines and other highest-level executives. The *Wall Street Journal* reported that Raines also had received loans below market rate from mortgage giant Countrywide Financial. The government demanded more than $115 million in bonus over-payments and almost $100 million in fines—no small change!

The investigation heated up and quickly spread from the GSEs to the mortgage lenders. Countrywide's CEO, Angelo Mozillo, had funded a 'Friends of Angelo' VIP loan program for a large group of Fannie and Freddie executives. And Congressmen who super-vised the GSEs turned up among the same 'Friends.' Conde Nast's *Portfolio* reported that banking committee chair Christopher Dodd and Senate budget committee chairman Kent Conrad were among the 'Friends' too.

Then came an even bigger bombshell. Freddie Mac was accused of illegally hosting almost a hundred fundraisers for selected Congressmen at a cost of more than a million bucks. *That's not rhinestones!* I saw the story on the front page of the *Financial Times*. Even worse, it said investigators had found that Fannie and Freddie had made huge illegal campaign contributions to Congressmen serving on the committees that supervised GSE regulators. The biggest recipients pocketed more than $100,000 each, including, Spencer Bachus ($103,300), Christopher Dodd ($116,900), John Kerry ($109,000), and Barack Obama ($120,350). Then my eyes widened. I couldn't believe it. When in office, Matt Shepherd had pulled down $106,000. I was furious. The GSE Panel was nothing but a smokescreen. *He must have known it all along. He can't blame me for that!*

56

One morning, Connelly looked up from breakfast and told me Shepherd was running a horse in the Belmont. The famous million-dollar last leg of racing's Triple Crown was scheduled for its 138th running at Aqueduct in New York.

"We're going," I told him. I had to meet Shepherd. This was my chance. I would bet on it.

But Connelly complained that it wasn't worth it. Kentucky Derby winner Barbaro had broken his leg in the Preakness. "There's just no possibility of a Triple Crown winner."

"We're going," I repeated. I hadn't seen Shepherd since New Orleans. I had to talk to him—a year was a long time to set the record straight. The worsening media attacks and smears were no fault of mine. I was determined to confront him. In spite of my anger and hurt, I was worried about him. His Presidential plans were in the shredder. *Angry or not, I just knew he needed me!*

The racetrack was on Long Island, but close to the City. June 10, 2006 was a perfect day for the event—not too hot and with high-definition clarity. But I had to hold down my big floppy hat after a stronger puff of breeze. I had chosen it to be noticed—a large, bright red, broad-brim ascot straw with white feathers and ribbons. I bought it at Barney's for a small fortune. It was a Swanepoel, and I loved it when I saw it. It matched my Adam Lippes designed shell, pure silk in scarlet red dappled with white. In the mirror it was just the effect I wanted. After all, I was a woman scorned. *Vivien Leigh would conquer Rhett Butler once and for all.*

Shepherd just had to be there. He was a part-owner of Jazil, the Number Eight horse, with his partner, Saudi Sheikh Hamdan. But there was no sign of the tall ex-Senator or the Saudi royal at the Paddock parade of twelve horses. I stared at the sleek thoroughbreds as they pranced by, shining and combed and totally beautiful. I could see why Shepherd was into horses. Jazil was a deep mahogany, polished, with muscles like a dancer's. He was guided by a jockey in sky blue silks. One by one, the horses filed into the crowded gate. Their energy had yet to be released, but I felt its power in the sudden silence. Then a bell rang loudly, and the gate jolted open. The crowd shouted, and I saw a huge mass of horses lunge forward. I watched—amazed by the explosion of animal power—the horses, the dust, the noise, the jockeys flailing with ferocious intensity.

The favorite, Bob and John, identified by Connelly, took the lead. My bet, a horse called High Finance, dropped back and stalked the pack along the rail. Even though the contest would be over in two minutes—the horses, the jockey's, and the crowd wanted to win, wanted the trophy, wanted the prize money. The track resounded with their roaring desire.

"He's tiring," said Connelly, handing me his binoculars. I saw Bob and John dropping back. But Jazil, who was at the back of the pack, after a poor start, had started to hit his best stride. I saw the sky blue colors and the blazoned Number Eight begin to gain—passing horse after horse. The jockey struck with his whip and the horse went even faster. The finish line was in sight, and Jazil powered through to win!

Connelly's bet, Bluegrass Cat, finished second and he went off to collect, saying, "Please. Don't do anything I wouldn't do. I don't want to come back and find you a mess."

Left alone, having used my influence to get a pass for the winner's circle, I slipped through a madhouse of photographers jammed up against a crowd of Arabs in kufiyahs and sunglasses. I watched as the green winner's blanket studded with giant white carnations, a Belmont tradition, was draped over a still steaming Jazil. Then the huge Tiffany-designed silver Belmont trophy was passed to a man in a blue blazer, who posed for photographers with the winning jockey, Fernando Jara, still wearing his spattered sky-blue colors. The crowd applauded. I was close enough to hear the jockey call out to a reporter in an exhausted voice, "I thought I had the race won after a mile. I moved at the right time. It's amazing. I got clear, he got way, and we win."

The man in the blazer answered back loudly, "I could see he believed you. That's what matters. You fit him to a tee." It was Matt Shepherd.

The breeze flapped my hat, and the horse danced. The jockey gave me a look, and Shepherd turned almost right into me.

"What are you doing here?" he asked harshly. Surprise didn't keep the anger from his voice. He was bitter, "You know what you did to me!" *It wasn't a question.*

"I didn't do anything—you're wrong! That story didn't come from me."

"That's not what I heard." He was almost screaming at me.

"You have to believe me! I didn't know a thing about your money." I was yelling and people were starting to look at us.

"You wanted me out of the way—to clear the track for Traub."

I flushed with anger, "That's not true! Mel has nothing to do with us."

"It doesn't matter—damn it! You and your TV pals were wrong anyway. Most of my money is with Lehman—not Battlement."

"Matt," I cried out, putting a hand on his sleeve. "What are you doing? I would never hurt you. Just believe me. Please."

"You don't have enough money anyway. I heard you lost a barrel full."

"You're all wrong! Matt—don't destroy us."

"I'm still going to run for President—and don't think I'm going to let you set me up again with your whorehouse tricks! You know what we're doing with this horse? He's going to our stallion barn in Lexington. That's where you belong, Missy Money—on a stud farm!"

My reaction was immediate. I slapped him hard in the face. Then, regardless of my heels, I clomped quickly out of the circle without a backwards glance. I was furious.

On the ride back, Connelly told me, "Your horse came in tenth."

I threw my crushed ticket out the window. "How much did you win?

"Forty bucks." Then he asked, "You know what the old jockey said?"

"Please don't tell me."

"Never look back," he answered anyway.

I leaned over and kissed him. *My mother knew how to pick 'em.*

Then it happened. What was never going to happen finally happened. Big surprise! Housing prices stopped rising! Real estate cheerleaders dropped their megaphones. Finally, Greenspan's baby-step increments stopped the long-running free-money MTV housing video. Over the course of two years ending in June 2006, he had raised interest rates 17 tiny times. Finally, get-rich-quick break-dancing home buyer speculators ran out of cash. The party that seemed like it would never end finally did. At last, Ms. Money was 'spot on.'

National Association of Realtors mouthpiece Bill Lereah was forced to sugar coat the pill, telling mortgage buyers only that he expected "home prices to come down five percent nationally. A few cities in Florida and California might experience hard landings." Ms. Money rebuked him on *Smarter Than The Street,* insisting the future was bleak. Lereah swiped back, "Ms. Money can stop wailing! The expected housing price correction marks a slowing in the rate of increase—not a precipitous decline. This will not spark a chain reaction that will devastate homeowners, builders and communities. Chicken Little, the sky is not falling." *What can you expect from a realtor who thought housing at any price was guaranteed by the Bill of Rights?*

But Lereah was too little too late. Ms. Money invited conservative economist Nouriel Roubini to speak at a special pod cast for Traub's wealthiest clients. Another voice who had long been crying in the wilderness, he called his talk, 'Housing Perma-Bull Spin-Doctors and the Reality of the Coming Ugliest Housing Bust Ever.' Suddenly, Maria Bartiromo, the CNBC financial anchor, switched to worrying that a housing recession was on the way. And the *New York Times'* paid-economic-cheerleader Paul Krugman revealed a new vision, writing, "A significant decline in prices is coming. We're going to see major retrenchment in hot markets that could fall 50% from their peaks." Finally, with every housing indicator now in free fall, the man behind the housing bubble, the Maestro of free money, got another headline when he finally admitted to the financial news media, "I didn't get it."

57

Yoko Ono invited me to be a guest in her personal party for the New York debut performance of former Beatle Paul McCartney's choral oratorio. We were friends and neighbors. Yoko lives in the Dakota, only a block south of the San Remo. After a falling out with McCartney, she had reconciled with him, and asked me to come. Carnegie Hall was sold out for the November première. Gia told me her tickets had cost over a thousand.

I wore black because the hymn was a celebration of the tragic death of McCartney's beloved American wife, Linda Eastman. I was prepared for tears. But the event had an even more powerful emotional impact on me—far beyond what I expected. When Sir Paul took the stage to translate the Latin title, *Ecce Cor Meum*, as 'Behold My Heart,' my emotions unsealed my own grief. Everyone knew that he had loved Eastman deeply. She was his wife of 29 years, and the mother of three children by him. He was devastated when she died of cancer in 1998, surrounded by all her family and whispering to him in their final embrace. McCartney told us that "the beautiful thing about our marriage was we were just a boyfriend and girlfriend having babies." That was purity. Crying wet my face, as much as I tried to contain my sobs. But many in the audience were weeping openly as he spoke of his love.

The event wasn't intended to be so somber. McCartney joked that he was finally 64 after writing 'When I'm Sixty-Four' at age 16, and the audience laughed. But then he made a special point of saying he wanted to apologize for a mistake Linda had told him he made once. "I'm sorry I ever said 'Money Can't Buy Me Love' should have been 'Money Can Buy Me Love.' That was wrong. I know better now!" The words went straight into my heart. I was stunned. *Was he talking to me? Telling me the truth!*

Then the deep moving music of the oratorio took over. I was totally open to it. The high notes of the boys' choir reached into me, drawing forth new tears. BJ, Stringfellow, even Vanderman. I gripped my seat tightly when the soprano's voice entered with an aria. The spirituality surrounded me. I heard Sister Tina singing to me. I wanted the truly human love that I felt in the music. The hymn was about more than worship. It was about purity. That was what Eastman had meant—still meant—what love gives us. I sat there knowing I needed Shepherd. I hadn't seen him since that awful moment at the race track six months ago. *Did he understand— could he love me? Or was it love that turned Shepherd against me? One thing only mattered, he was the man I needed.*

On *Smarter Than The Street*, Ms. Money's new watchword was 'contagion.' I warned investors that the exploding housing bubble could destroy Wall Street. Three powerful factors would help it spread like the Black Plague: Environmental Change, Viral Mutation, and Diminished Immunity. They became my mantra.

The critical change in the financial environment was fast becoming obvious to all but the diehards. The housing bubble had stopped inflating. The Case-Shiller home price index, after peaking at 190, had failed to make a new high. By year-end 2008, it would sink by over 40 points. As home prices tanked, foreclosure rates soared. By August 2008, almost ten percent of all U.S. mortgages outstanding were either delinquent or in foreclosure. Housing winter had arrived.

Virulent mutations speed up the plague's spread from rats to fleas to humans. Similarly, Wall Street had Frankensteined the risky subprime Mortgage Backed Security, or MBS, into the highly toxic Collateralized Debt Obligation or CDO. The CDO was far more deadly because it multiplied the players linked to even a single high-risk mortgage. CDO issuance grew from an estimated $20 billion starting in 2004 to a peak of over $180 billion by the start of 2007. When asked what a CDO was, Ms. Money repeated Warren Buffett's definition, 'a financial weapon of mass destruction.' By slicing, dicing and then mixing various MBS issues, a CDO turns lead into gold, meaning a higher rate of return at the price of greater risk. And to take risk and reward up another notch, the Wall Street alchemist can stir in synthetics—hybrid securities whose performance is determined by a home price index or even a purely hypothetical measure.

Wall Street pseudoscience turned billions of dollars' worth of high-risk subprime mortgages into trillions of dollars of hazardous debt. And for worried investors suffering from paranoia, brokers created a mutant form of CDO insurance called the Credit Default Swap (CDS), which guaranteed third-party repayment from an insurer. But the insurer of last resort turned out to be an unregulated SIV, which reinvested its fees in more CDOs. That meant there was no last resort! If you want to know what went wrong—it all boils down to that. The last resort couldn't possibly cover debt that was immense beyond belief. *Beyond belief. Think about it. Not just unbelievable, but impossible to believe in.*

With housing prices falling, the multiplying mutant CDO virus searched for what epidemiologists call diminished immunity—meaning a host organism with high exposure and low tolerance. The task of creating just such a being fell to Wall Street's credit raters—Standard & Poor's and Moody's and the like. Synthetic CDOs were too complicated for the rating agencies to judge. So they simply took the issuer's word for it. Self-deluded issuers led crippled credit raters who relied on them blindly. Plague-infected securities were sold with a clean bill of health.

Ms. Money dragged famous bond guru Bill Gross on *Smarter Than The Street,* where he blamed the rating agencies for slapping triple-A ratings on subprime MBS. The lean, wild-haired manager of the world's largest bond fund criticized the credit raters sarcastically: "AAA? You were wooed, Mr Moody's and Mr Poor's, by the makeup, those six-inch hooker heels, and a just-above-the-butt tramp-stamp tattoo. Many of these good-looking girls are not high-class assets worth 100 cents on the dollar." The network almost cut him off. But Ms. Money thought calling CDOs 'hookers' was the absolutely perfect risk assessment!

I summed it up for my viewers this way: Harry and Jane Poorfolk just have to have a million dollar McMansion that they can't afford. They go to a bank for a traditional mortgage but are turned down. So they obtain a subprime mortgage from Countrywide Financial, which grants them a loan over the phone without their signature and on their word only about their credit history. There's no down payment and no interest for five years. Except in the fine print, which says if 10-year U.S.

Treasury bonds rise above five percent, the Poorfolks will have to pay as much as thirty percent on their mortgage. Countrywide then discounts the risky-as-all-hell subprime loan and sells it to Freddie Mac who packages it into an MBS which it sells to Bear Stearns, who mixes and slices and dices the bond-like MBS turning it into a CDO, often retaining the best loan component for itself. Over-leverage becomes quantum leverage. Then Bear advertises the up-front high-yield CDO to attract investors.

The CDO gets sold to an institutional investor who then hedges it by buying a CDS from an American International Group (AIG) offshore SIV, which earns increased fee revenue. When an interest rate increase triggers the clause in the subprime mortgage agreement that requires Harry and Jane to make huge monthly payments with money they don't have—they default. Countrywide eventually forecloses, but by then the Poorfolks, who had no down payment to lose, have skipped and mailed back the keys. All along they were betting that ever rising home prices would make them rich if they sold before rates went up. Then they could have started the cycle over again with a new mortgage on an even bigger house. But their speculative dreams didn't come true. The MBS is now worthless and the CDO worse than worthless. But when the investor with the CDS demands repayment from the SIV owned by AIG—it turns out that the SIV reinvested its cashflow back into another high-yield CDO—issued by Merrill Lynch—which also defaulted. The SIV is bankrupt! AIG is in deep do-do. Wall Street has accomplished the impossible—it has screwed itself—and everybody else with it. "Nobody knows what happens next," Ms. Money warned. But Wall Street was about to find out.

58

*P*lease *Take Notice:* You are now back at the beginning. This is where you came in on the story of my life. I began, as your English teacher probably once told you, *in medias res,* meaning 'in the middle of things.' In literature starting off like that goes back as far as Homer. Usually writers like to start, and I'm trusting my editor on this, just before the moment of crisis that tests the hero. The hero is shown just as the door opens on the struggle to come. He is challenged—will he measure up? Victory is in doubt. The author then flashes back to the hero's humble beginning. We learn how our champion developed the mental and physical energy needed to overcome and triumph. Is the hero strong enough, tough enough, we worry? Check out those biceps. Then we return to the present and the final battle begins. But we know the hero will triumph because he is dedicated. There will be frightening setbacks. But he is devoted and therefore cannot lose. The screaming heroine must be rescued. That's how men have told the story for years. *Is it time for a change?*

When you first met Ms. Money, she was flying to New York, for a critical meeting of the Presidential financial crisis committee, chaired by Treasury Secretary Paulson. She stood by as the ritual murder of investment banker Bear Stearns was carried out. She kept her plans to herself. But she was cool-headed under pressure, and poised to do battle with the coming financial disaster.

Now you've seen how I became Ms. Money, a highly paid financial strategist and TV stock market commentator with a bank account to die for. I took off my clothes, so to speak, and bared it all. I have two children who are worth more to me than anything in the world. Even more important you now know that the hero of my story is a woman. She is neither slave girl, nor princess, as central casting would have it. She knows that women can be heroes not heroines. And she knows what she has to do to become one. What I am is a woman who understands the heroism of being a woman. I'm ready now for grueling arduous conflict. But please pay careful attention because my struggle is a woman's. Fire-breathing dragons have been extinct for centuries.

Near the end of August, I heard rumors that Goldman Sachs' fund managers were cutting short their Hamptons vacations and leaving their rented summer palaces to return early to the City. The death of Bear Stearns had convinced me that *'yersinia pestis,'* aka the Black Plague, was already virulent among the rats of Wall Street. That made it easier to undergo the goring I got from the financial media's Bulls. Ms. Money continued to tell investors to 'Get off the Street'—by selling the money center banks, brokers and investment firms. Big surprise. Nobody listened. But pandemic was about to break out.

Then, on Labor Day, the Plague mutated from bubonic to pneumonic. Once it was airborne a cough in your face could kill you. Wall Street was hit with a cash panic. The mammoth financial-center banks pulled $200 billion out of their money market accounts. Suddenly frightened by the possibility of huge CDO write downs, they struggled to raise cash. To stop the bleeding, they dumped tons of Fannie and Freddie stock, whose share prices cratered drastically. It happened so fast there was no time for PFEAC to meet. Instead Paulson's staff arranged for an emergency conference call. Paulson told the Committee that the two GSEs were 'too big to fail.' Fannie had over $500 billion in toxic securities on its books. Freddie, with almost $400 billion of super-high-risk subprime and Alt-A exposure, was a close second. Most of the debt-paper was worthless—almost a trillion phantom dollars. There would be no vote on their fate. The next day, FHFA director James Lockhart, with Paulson standing alongside him, announced that Fannie Mae and Freddie Mac had been put into Federal conservatorship. Calling "the action one of the most sweeping government interventions in private financial markets in decades," the Treasury injected $100 billion into the GSEs. It was only a stopgap!

My mobile chimed just as I was having an introductory meeting with Mimi's new fourth grade teacher. Paulson wanted a PFEAC crisis meeting on Friday, September 5th. Briefing papers sent by messenger told me that Merrill Lynch had gone into septic shock. Blue-black plague sores were visible. Death was imminent! As much as I had forecast catastrophic collapse—even I found it hard to believe.

To be sure it had a steady supply of MBS in hand, Merrill acquired Franklin Financial, one of the country's largest subprime lenders. Then, in order to turn MBS into synthetic CDOs in its own offshore hydroponic tanks, Merrill hired Christopher Ricciardi and his high-power CDO team away from Credit Suisse First Boston. Soon it was bragging about its ability to maximize leverage any way a buyer wanted. By 2007 it was the "number one global underwriter of CDOs," with exposure of near to $200 billion. Just repeat the number—$200 billion. 'That ain't hay,' but when housing prices hit bottom, it turned into nothing more than a worthless pile of straw.

Merrill's chief, E. Stanley O'Neal, a loner given to playing solo golf, went into denial. His staff hid the seriousness of the situation from him because of his reputation for brutal retribution. When O'Neal finally grasped the truth, he stupidly thought Merrill could simply refuse to sell the plummeting CDOs. Then Merrill announced it would write-down $8.4 billion in losses. That was worse than too little too late. It was a lot too little and way too late! O'Neal went behind his Board's back and approached Wachovia bank about a merger, but the news leaked out. On *Smarter Than The Street*, Ms. Money told investors Merrill was a dying AIDS patient trying to buy a blood transfusion from a known HIV carrier. O'Neal was fired. Then, just before the PFEAC meeting, Goldman delivered the *coup d'grâce* by downgrading Merrill's stock to 'Conviction Sell.'

I sat with seven others around the conference table in Geithner's office at the NY Fed. The eighth attendee was the black plastic polycom in the center of the mahogany table. Ex-New York Stock Exchange chief, John Thain had been appointed Merrill's new CEO. He was about to hear his company's death sentence via conference call. Paulson called the meeting to order, sliding the polycom to Masterson. Beth Rooney sitting next to me, leaned over to whisper, "It's all done. They had a private dinner last night."

"Who?"

"Don't you know where Thain worked before NYSE? These boys are in the loop—always."

Then Carol Carson nudged me. Masterson was glaring at us. Rooney slid her pad in front of me. There was a single word on it—'Goldman.' *Of course.* At one time Thain had been co-COO of Goldman.

Paulson looked at Masterson, saying, "See if he's off the commode."

Both Dimon and Masterson burst out laughing, even I smiled. Everyone on Wall Street knew that Thain had spent over a million to redecorate his new office at Merrill, which traders were calling 'the golden fleece.' That's because the redo included $35,000 for a gold-plated commode on legs. It was a bad omen, when a sucking noise could already be heard.

Then Thain's voice crackled from the polycom. "I'm here Hank."

"Thanks John," Paulson replied. He was cool.

"We all know you tried hard," Masterson took the lead. This time he was conciliatory.

"It was a no go," said Thain. "Every time I managed to borrow ten million, I found I needed a hundred million more. They sure dug some hole for themselves. It's a bottomless pit! The deeper down you go, the further you are from the bottom. It just keeps sinking." We all heard the stress in his voice.

Masterson switched off the speaker phone, looked around the room, and said, "O'Neal wanted to turn Merrill into Goldman. What a joke, they even sold CDOs on the mortgage for Uncle Tom's cabin!"

There was an almost audible gasp. Ms. Money saw Paulson's eyes roll. Ex-Merrill boss O'Neal was the highest-placed Black on Wall Street. Masterson was blaming him for single handedly destroying his company. *He was right.*

"Please," said Pimco bond manager El-Erian. Ms. Money gave him a mental point for courtesy. I felt that I shared his outsider, private-sector status.

Geithner motioned at Masterson, who switched the speaker phone back on.

"We all know you tried hard with Temasek," said the IMF's Zuger.

My briefing paper explained that Thain had found a white knight in the form of the Singapore sovereign investment group, Temasek Holdings, which put up over $6 billion for a stake in the broker. But only two weeks later, to keep Merrill afloat, it had to increase its investment by another $3.4 billion. But even $10 billion wasn't enough. Merrill's leverage was malignant. *Yes, a bottomless pit.*

Masterson again switched off the phone and huddled with Geithner. Then he turned the phone back on saying, "The Fed will help make Temasek whole." I saw shock wash over banking chief Carol Carson's face.

"A billion here a billion there just wasn't enough," said the polycom. "I got Lone Star to buy a garbage can full of CDOs for almost $2 billion in cash and a $5 billion loan. Everyone else just turned their back on me."

"Yeah," said Paulson. "The trouble was you were losing over billion a week."

I stared at the numbers in the briefing paper. Merrill was close to $100 billion in the red. *Billion not million!* And Merrill's remaining backers had completely lost their confidence, destroying its ability to refinance even short-term debt.

"So what's next?" Thain asked over the polycom. "Does the Fed's cup runneth over?"

"Like I told you—no equity. This is not a bail out." Paulson answered, maintaining his stance.

"Not a chance," said Masterson at once. "We're not pulling you out of the briar patch. We're marrying you off."

I saw El-Erian frown beneath his dark, bushy brows. All ears cocked for the speaker phone, but it was silent.

"I've convinced Ken Lewis," Paulson took charge. "Bank of America is buying you. That's the deal on the table—the only deal." There was an eerie silence in the room. Ken Lewis was widely thought of as an idiot after he acquired Countrywide Financial, the biggest-of-all subprime mortgage lender, right at the peak of the housing bubble. Selling Merrill to folksy Bank of America was the kiss of death—like putting a high school coach in charge of a big league team. We all knew it.

"Take it or leave it." Paulson ordered.

"How much am I getting?" Thain asked.

"They're ponying up $50 billion in stock. That's it." Masterson answered.

"Sounds like a marriage made in Washington," Thain snapped.

Paulson followed, saying, "Exactly—so don't turn it down."

"Better take it," said Masterson. You can't expect a big dowry with a face a mother would only love on pay day!" The joke made everyone laugh.

After a pause, the polycom blurted out, "I'll take it Hank. Thanks."

As the others left, I got busy on my HP calculator. It looked like B of A was paying about $30 a share for Merrill. At the top the stock was worth almost $80 a share, but at the bottom $5 was closer to its actual value. When asked about the deal on TV, the next morning, Ms. Money remarked, "They were lucky to get thirty dollars a share. Secretary Paulson arranged a bazooka wedding. With a shotgun marriage the dowry would only have been five bucks a share!"

59

The weekend of September 12th, was a madhouse of crisis meetings. Bankruptcy bred bedlam. Wall Street looked like an insane asylum run by the patients. Paulson ordered PFEAC into continuous executive session at Fed headquarters. But not before I ran down to a deli on the corner of Water and Wall for a quick salad. I needed to escape for a second of fresh air, but I had to cut through a crowd of shocked, suddenly laid-off workers streaming out of one tower after another, with stunned looks on their faces and cartons in their arms. Finally I was able to scoop some greens and grab a seat, only to be surprised when Masterson, Bernanke's man, jumped into the place next to me.

He was the youngest of the players, but I sensed he understood the politics of what was happening better than the rest. He wasn't Bernanke's fixer for nothing. Only the Fed could stop the craziness on Wall Street, and I was sure Masterson knew who would get the meds and who would have to wear a straight jacket. There was a kind of Southern stoicism about him that reminded me of Matt Shepherd. He was smaller in build than Paulson, but not short and wiry like Geithner. His eyes were dark brown beneath the sandy hair spilling over his brow. I loved his smile.

He had a mouthful of ultra-white teeth that were now chewing through a tuna sandwich. But his eyes were studying me. He wanted something from me. But sex wasn't part of it. What he wanted, I guessed, was to be sure I understood what he was going to tell me. Bernanke's tough-talking messenger wasn't going to say anything to me unless he was sure I knew what it meant.

"Did you know what was coming?" he asked between bites.

"You were the one who called me Chicken Little," I told him what was on my mind. But then I softened the criticism. "I was worried about contagion, but nothing as bad as this. The leverage is immense—way beyond anything, way, way beyond. There's just no limit to it."

"The Fed doesn't pay a lot of attention to the brokers. We're closer to the bankers. I'm sorry we were on Zoloft like them. But one thing you can be sure of now—there will be damn few winners when this is finished. I want to be sure you understand that. You won't be able to save any firm or any person."

"Why?" *Did I suddenly see where this was going?*

"Because only the best players will survive. The deadwood has to be pruned. You've heard the term 'creative destruction.' Investment banking needs to contract. We think we're headed into a long period of slow growth."

"Who's we?" I demanded. *I wondered if he would tell me!*

"Did you ever see *Revenge of the Nerds?*" he asked instead of answering. "It's my favorite movie. You remind me of Betty—she was cool."

"You mean the one who goes over to the Nerds at the end? It was Julia Montgomery—I think." *Stringfellow loved the movie.*

"Look, the point is that Wall Street always messes up. They ought to call it the 'Street of Greed'—not 'Dreams.' But somebody has to keep the economy on track. That's the Fed's job."

"You've been a very harsh critic." I said. It was more of a question than a rebuke.

"The Chief wants to be sure Wall Street feels the heat. We can't afford to be politically correct when it comes to providing a lifeline. This time they've screwed up big time. Real big time. Look, the Fed is just like the Nerds. They weren't good looking, and we're not out to win a media-driven popularity contest. But the Nerds were more than just tech savvy, and we're a very big-brain team too."

"So?"

"We can't be wasting time patching holes in a leaky dike. The economy is slow moving. It's hard to shift gears rapidly. That's why the Fed needs to stay ahead—we need to know in advance what's going to happen next. Only the best people can play on our team. They've got to be loyal."

I was getting it now. There would be both winners and losers on Wall Street, and the Fed was going to decide who won the prize. They had killed off Bear Stearns and Merrill Lynch—'creative destruction' Masterson had called it. He wanted to know if I would get in the way? I wasn't going to protect Traub. No problem there. But I was worried about Shepherd taking a hit on his Lehman holdings. I was sure Masterson didn't know about me and Shepherd. "I don't see what you're worried about? The Nerds win—don't they?"

"Yes. But when they graduate they go into the public sector and sacrifice their pay checks. At some point they will need to go into the private sector—you know, for a house, tuition, retirement." His face was very close to mine. "They'll need a high-paying job, and it has to be waiting for them at the right place and time." *I was on to it now. The Fed would decide who survived on Wall Street to make sure the revolving door between the Treasury and the Fed and Goldman kept turning.*

"It's only fair that altruism is rewarded. Public service has to be compensated. You can be sure I believe that—because it makes sense. I have no personal allegiance to Traub Securities." *Passed with highest honors.*

He put down the remains of his sandwich to swig on a Snapple. "Sorry to eat and run. It's time I got back—Lehman Brothers is the next basket case. I need to call Washington first. Fuld's a wild bull too—what the Spanish call a *toro bravo*. You'll see."

"I'm on record that Lehman's not 'too big to fail.' Traub clients are not big holders." *That's what he wanted to know for sure.*

"Glad to hear it." He finished off his bottle of Diet Peach. "You probably don't remember, but I met you when your committee on Fannie and Freddie heard testimony in Washington. Matt Shepherd was the chair. Shame about him—isn't it? He's supposed to have a ton of bucks at Lehman—and you're right they're not TBTF."

"I haven't seen him in ages." *He knew a lot more than I thought he did—a lot more!*

I rushed back to the Fed after my break. Maiden Lane was completely full of black cars. Not a single government service Ford. A fleet of big luxury limos had the Fed surrounded. It was time for the main event. I paused to cover my ears to shut out the loud drum beat of a helicopter headed for the landing behind Goldman headquarters. But one thought continued to ring in my head even after I passed through the metal detectors. *They were taking Lehman down and Shepherd would sink with it. There was no way I could protect him, whether he liked it or not. Just don't blame me Matt!*

Inside the meeting room, I found they had let the bull into the ring early. He was a mean-looking 1,200 pounds of stamping, snorting anger with horns over a foot long—in the form of Lehman Brothers Chairman, Richard S 'Dick' Fuld, wearing a $10,000 black, custom-tailored, Italian suit. Labeled 'belligerent and unrepentant' by the press, the Lehman chief was known on Wall Street as 'The Cannibal.' He got the name because he once told the firm's brokers, "When it comes to short sellers, what I really want to do is reach in, rip out their heart and eat it before they die." I suddenly thought of the violent boxing match I had seen in Memphis. Vanderman said Tyson had bitten off a piece of another fighter's ear!

My imagination transformed Dimon, Geithner, Cox and Masterson, into a grim-faced *cuadrilla*, each of the team of toreros wearing brightly colored and richly embroidered bull-fighting garb and a *montera* black hat that didn't seem funny at all. Paulson was the matador, glaring back at the Lehman chief. I scanned the courtroom, looking for Fuld's well-known loyal defenders, but CEO Joe Gregory and CFO Erin Callan had lost their jobs and shields. I had met Callan before. She was strikingly beautiful, and wore provocative designs from Chanel and Chloé. *Why not? Can't a woman wear what she can afford—what she's earned?* Rumors about Callan's recent divorce increased my sympathy for her. So did the gossip about Ros

Stephenson, Lehman's top female corporate finance honcho, who was said to have told Fuld that Callan wasn't qualified for the CFO post. *Women stabbing women—just when they ought to help each other.* I wondered if the rumors were true that Fuld had actually put Callan in place just to send her over the 'glass cliff.' Two of Wall Street's top women executives who managed to break through the 'glass ceiling' had recently hit the skids. Zoe Cruz was pushed out of Morgan Stanley in 2007, and Sallie Krawcheck had just been turned out of Citigroup. *If Ms. Money had learned anything it was never to play by men's rules—until Traub had tricked me.*

My attention returned to Fuld, just as the defense attorney rose, and after hemming and hawing, told PFEAC that Lehman needed at least a $10 billion dollar credit line—preferably from the Fed. *Here we go again.* I saw Paulson react with a grimace. But before he spoke, Fuld jumped up. He was furious, and his demand was defiant. He literally bellowed, "We need a capital injection. Nothing less than $100 billion— or we'll take down everyone else with us. The Street will burn." *He meant it!*

Paulson stared at him, and then replied coldly, just like a father to an unruly child. "Dick—don't you remember what I told you after Bear went down?" Then he slowly enunciated, one word at a time, "I told you to get closer to home." It was a brilliant tactic, patient while belittling. He followed with another question, "Didn't you understand me? Where it's safer. You had to dig in and put up the fences, start raising capital fast and look for a buyer at any price. That was good advice." *From a father determined to disarm an angry child.*

But the Lehman boss was all scorn. He lowered his horns and charged. "I need $100 billion. You know we've been looking for a Buffett! Where would Goldman be without him?" Fuld was loud and bitter. It was a close pass. I stared across the table at Beth

Rooney and Carol Carson. Their faces said they had seen it too. The bull had almost gored Paulson. Then Fuld screamed right at him, "We're willing to sell preferred stock to the government. We'll give up equity. We ARE too big to fail—you know it—everyone knows it!"

I have to hand it to Paulson. The Matador just shook his cape at Fuld. "No equity," he said flatly. "No taxpayer bailout period." I recognized his 'you're talking to the Secretary of the Treasury' tone.

I got the point immediately. It was a Star Chamber trial whose outcome had been decided in advance. But Fuld still hadn't grasped that Lehman's demise was written on the wall. Then the picador on horseback rode in, driving his lance deep into the bull's back, even as his horse dodged a goring. I was shocked by the blood. "Don't expect us to throw good taxpayer money after bad. You're leveraged almost 50-to-1. There will be no equity, no Fed money period. That's final." Masterson replied harshly.

Then, to my surprise, the IMF's Zuger cut in, jabbing a verbal *banderilla* into Fuld's hide. *A woman torero.* "I know you talked with the Chinese and the Koreans, Monsieur Fuld." She pronounced his name like 'fool,' and I wondered if the sarcasm was intentional. "You know they have spoken with me. The IMF cannot do a thing. They told me you wanted to sell them a controlling interest— but you wouldn't give up control. They asked me if you are crazy, Monsieur. And now the Japanese, Mitsubishi, are buying a big piece of Morgan Stanley. They are safe. But you were a fool, a very *stupide* one, Monsieur. You had a chance—and it is wasted."

The French woman's speech must have hit home. The Lehman chief switched to arguing with the Matador. "You pumped up

Fannie and Freddie with billions," he insisted shrilly. "We're just as important—way bigger. We deserve just as much as they got!"

"You're expendable." Masterson jumped in with another *banderilla* that struck Fuld, drawing blood once more. "There isn't enough money left in the pot to save your ass! And nobody's going up the Hill to ask Congress for more money to rescue Wall Street."

I thought the Bull would have a heart attack. Fuld was astounded. People just didn't speak to him like that. But he was not above begging for his life, "So find us a partner. You took care of Merrill. We're worth even more."

"Nobody wants to go to bed with a hooker with AIDS," Masterson countered. Again he brought on a hush, before continuing, "We know what you did. Instead of eating it when you could, you doubled down. That's the stupidest mistake an investor can make. You *raised* your exposure in CDO toilet paper to over $400 billion."

"Hank," Fuld screamed right at Paulson. "You sold us Abacus. Doesn't that count for something?"

I knew it was a reference to another super-high-risk CDO peddled by Goldman. The papers said it was originally designed as a short. But Goldman sold it as a long to investors seeking sky-high yield. Then it turned around and shorted Abacus for its own account—and gave big clients, including two Congressmen, a chance to get in on the short side, which was the right side when the reckoning came due!

"Have you forgotten what I said?" Paulson blared back. "Remember—I told you to get closer to home."

Fuld was speechless. Then he turned to Dimon. "What about Morgan?" His tone was that of a man begging a friend for a last chance.

"We're busy with Bear." The answer was noncommittal.

"Nice deal, you got over a billion in real estate for a third of the price." Fuld retorted angrily.

"We're not the ones sitting on a trillion-dollar debt bomb," the banker countered. "We know what it means to hedge."

It was too much for Fuld. El toro was covered with blood, and splattered with mud and slime. "You're just another Goldman. Always playing both sides. They sold us crap, and then they bet against it," he bellowed at Dimon. Everyone knew he was right. But no one would admit it. He was cornered, and now he knew it. But he wanted to take Goldman down with him. I saw Paulson turn white. Masterson was looking at me. I kept my hand down and my mouth shut. *A death sentence for Lehman would leave Shepherd without a dime. Would he ever believe me again?*

I watched as Paulson, raised his deep red *muleta,* signaling that the *tercio de muerte,* the 'time to kill,' had begun. But instead of exposing a steel sword, he was holding a bazooka. His finger tightened on the trigger. Then he fired and blew the bull away. He couldn't miss at that range. "Look, Dick—you can't bluff your way out of this one. You're not TBTF—just not big enough. You're going down." *Boom! My eyes tracked the missile's trail right into the Bull. Kaboom! There wasn't even an ear left to award the matador.*

Fuld knew he was finished. He turned on his heel and stalked out of the chamber. In the intervening silence, Paulson stood up, saying, "Excuse me," and left the room. He didn't look well. He had complained publicly that the tension was giving him the dry heaves. A minute or so later, I stepped out of the meeting into the massive marble hallway. On my way to the Ladies Room, I passed Paulson, half-hidden behind a polished travertine column, his head bent over, with a cell phone to his ear. I saw a smile on his face.

60

Paulson began the final meeting of PFEAC with a shout: "There's an avalanche of bad MBS out there!" Continuing to speak loudly, he gave his charge to the Committee, "We need more money—a lot more—a ton more! The banks are hurting. Congress has to pony up. I want a 'Sense of the Committee' motion to support what we're going to call TARP. That's for Troubled Assets Relief Program. After that Treasury will carry the ball."

But then Beth Rooney, the Bolt Bank boss, stood up and glared at him. There was no mistaking her anger. "Screw TARP! Tell me about WAMU. I want to know who carried that ball?"

I didn't understand why she was so angry. I knew that Lehman's demise had triggered a run that had forced the country's largest savings and loan, Washington Mutual (WAMU) into bankruptcy. But then Carol Carson grabbed her microphone before Paulson could answer. "Washington Mutual was handled through the existing bank failure procedure. You have nothing to complain about."

"You didn't even give us a chance to bid on the branches before you gave them away to Mr Dimon here," Rooney screamed at her.

Then she turned on the Morgan Chase CEO. "What did you pay for them? I'll tell you—chicken shit."

"I'm not going to be a party to this," Dimon said haughtily, as he stood up and left the room.

"Don't forget your party favor," Rooney cried out at his retreating back. "You paid a measly $2 billion for $20 billion worth of branches. That's some deal all right."

"I'm sorry," Carson interrupted once again, speaking shrilly, "Office of Thrift Supervision (OTS) seized the bank and accepted it in receivership. Our job was to protect the depositors. We sold the branches free and clear to JPM Chase. End of story."

Paulson raised his gavel, but he didn't have to use it. Rooney stormed out of the meeting.

Our paths crossed in the Ladies Room. She was still very burned up. "They got those WAMU branches on the cheap. We would have paid twice as much for them—maybe even three times. We never had a chance."

"You couldn't win for love or money."

"You're right. I should know better than to fight with little Miss Carson. She's never done anything she wasn't told to do. She's always in the loop. OTS reports to Treasury—and Treasury is Paulson—and Paulson is Goldman—and Goldman is Morgan's best buddy! I should have kept my mouth shut."

"Morgan got the Bear deal too," I said, thinking aloud.

"You don't know the worst of it. Goldman's going to get a very big share of TARP—huge! That's why they're doing it. Paulson's already picked one of his juniors to run it. Goldman's going to convert from an investment bank to a bank holding company. That will allow them to qualify for funds. I bet they get $10 billion from TARP and they'll still be able to borrow from the Fed."

"Why am I not surprised?" *Of course—Goldman had eliminated its three biggest investment banking competitors, shored up its balance sheet, pumped up its friend JP Morgan Chase and left Citibank out in the cold. 'Creative destruction,' Masterson had called it.*

"Because you're smart. Listen—they have their eyes on you."

"Who?"

"I'm sure you know," she ended the conversation.

To get back in, I had to squeeze past a crowd of angry men spilling out of a meeting in the main auditorium. Things were worsening. There wasn't enough money to go around—talk about life boats on the Titanic! I squeezed back into the PFEAC meeting just as Paulson rose to complain, "American International Group—AIG—was supposed to be the insurer of last resort. It's about to fail. This nightmare isn't over yet." He was clearly upset. Panic plus epidemic equals pandemic. Bodies were falling everywhere on Wall Street. You couldn't buy immunity if you tried."

"We have to do equity," Geithner told them. "This is it—if we don't take a stand here it's all over." He was tense. I heard real fear in his voice.

AIG was the biggest reinsurer of all, meaning the insurer who insured other insurers. Now AIG was broke. Everyone wanted every cent of its remaining assets. Beth Rooney told me the state insurance commissioners wanted to protect mom and pop policyholders if AIG went under. But the big securities brokers wanted to be first in line. AIG owed them $100 million in cash. Screw the little people. If that wasn't bad enough, through an off-the-books, London-based SIV, the giant insurer had sold coverage for almost $450 billion worth of CDOs. That's $450 thousand millions! No wonder Paulson was shaken. As the soaring numbers slowed to the point where they could be read, the very existence of Wall Street was now in doubt.

"You want the government to buy in?" Paulson cut him off. "I'm against any kind of equity deal." He stuck with his habitual argument.

"I don't understand you," Carol Carson complained. "If a bank goes belly up the FDIC would step in. Isn't that what we're here for?" she asked.

"No, you don't understand," Paulson snapped back. "These guys are crooks. I don't think they had any intention of ever paying off on the Credit Default Swaps that were supposed to insure bad CDOs. Their CDS paper was bullshit from day one." His justification was interrupted by a call on his emergency line. He canted his head, pressed his hand over his ear bud, then said, "Excuse me, I have to step out for just a second."

It must be very, very important for him to take it.

A minute later Paulson stepped back into the meeting room, and Geithner jumped up arguing again for a Fed loan. "Look this is very bad. AIG has just been downgraded by S&P and Moody's. They're going to have to deliver $10 billion to their counterparties on Monday."

"Money they don't have," added SEC head Cox.

Dimon then cut in forcefully. "Hank is right! Their guy Cassano, the one who ran their London SIV, made millions—big money. His townhouse in London cost a fortune. It's right by Harrods. He sold CDS by the bushel full. He had to know they were over exposed—way over."

But Paulson suddenly crumpled and switched sides. "Look this is just too big. Tim may be right. We may have to go the way of Fannie and Freddie."

Dimon rubbed his jaw, covering his expression. Clearly, something had made Paulson change his mind.

Then Masterson took charge. "I've got Ben Bernanke's plan. He's asked me to spell it out." He looked slowly around the room, then spoke directly to Paulson. "The Fed has authorized an $85 billion immediate credit line for AIG." Eighty-five-billion! The number was met with a collective silence.

"What's the collateral?" Paulson asked.

"Eighty percent of the company," Masterson answered. "In exchange for the credit facility, the U.S. government gets warrants for an 80 percent equity stake in AIG and the right to suspend both preferred and common dividends."

There was an audible gasp. I saw Dimon roll his eyes. This was the biggest ownership stake the government had ever taken in a private company in U.S. history. Everyone in the room knew it. AIG was saved by being nationalized.

"And Bob Willumstad has to leave," Masterson went on, ousting the reinsurer's most recent CEO. "The Fed is appointing Ed Liddy to run AIG. He will resign from Goldman's board immediately."

Paulson blurted out, "It's a done deal!" Then he stood and immediately left the room. He must have guessed what everyone was thinking. *Goldman uber alles.*

Geithner grabbed the polycom and relayed the news to AIG's lawyers. They accepted the government's terms at once.

Hunger drove me back to my favorite deli. Why wasn't I surprised to find Masterson already there? Somehow I knew he'd be waiting for me.

"You did good in there," he told me.

"See no evil," I answered.

"The important part is the 'speak no evil.' I told you Wall Street was due for some creative destruction." He looked at me.

"So you engineered a cut back?" *This time I got it. Down-sizing the Street was the game plan all along.*

"Like I said—someone has to keep the train on the right track."

"Yes—but you had to tie Mr Secretary to the rails. Or is he just a bad actor?"

"People do forget their lines."

"And sometimes they stay in the part for too long."

"That's very perceptive of you. Sticking with no bailout would have cost Goldman a ton. That's really why I'm here. To make sure everyone follows the script."

"I wondered." But just then I saw ex-Attorney General Eric Holder at the cashier and asked my thoughts aloud, "What's Holder doing here? Isn't he working for a Swiss bank—UBS?"

"He's Barack's political fixer. He's slotted to return as AG, Attorney General. He's already trying to tell Paulson what Obama wants. Obama's sure for the Presidency. He's going to walk right into the aftermath of the biggest financial crisis in years. We need him to understand. You remember what Holder did for Bill Clinton?"

"The Rich pardon?" I had talked about it with Traub. Clinton pardoned the billionaire fugitive financier in the final hours of his very last day in the White House. The clock was only minutes from midnight. The Democrats got a million from Rich's wife, the Clinton Library took in another $500K and Hillary got an extra $100K for her Senate campaign. "That was just *too rich* to believe." I smiled at him as I spoke.

"Holder was the key political player. He drove it through Justice while we were asleep. Sometimes we can stop deals like that. Evil shit goes on all the time. That's the reason we have to protect the economy. We need to keep the pols and the stooges and the crooks and idiot investors out of it. Don't you agree?"

"I bet Holder is here about TARP. Does Obama want a piece of the action?"

"Why do you think Paulson wants it over and done before the election? We can't let the bureaucrats handle that—it's way too important."

"We?"

"The people in the loop. You know, the people who matter. We're the ones who keep the economy running. Who else can you trust? The politicians are all hopelessly corrupt. We have to remind them constantly that their job isn't just a winning lottery ticket. They're the ones who demolished Fannie and Freddie."

"You're not telling me anything new. I watched Barney Frank in action."

"It doesn't stop there. Greenspan went paranoid on us. He was a scarecrow who began to think he had a brain. We finally got him out, but it was too late. Believe me. We didn't want this to happen."

"He fell asleep at the switch and started dreaming impossible dreams."

"You can't trust the hedgies either. They're all trying to make a billion on insider trading. The speed freak arbitragers are into high-frequency trading and very dark pools. Who do you think is going to keep them honest?"

"Wall Street has bought into a culture of risk. That's very bad for the economy."

"Spot on. And the investing public is getting dumber by the minute because that's the way the media wants them. We're very sure you know about that!"

"Credibility matters. Educated investors are very risk averse."

"Exactly—we want them that way. So we do need you."

I was nervous. I tried to distract him. "What about Traub for Treasury?"

"No. Geithner has a lock on it. That's another reason Holder's here. Traub should focus on California. Tell him the Senate needs fixing."

"Ms. Money?"

"We're not fighting the woman thing. It's about credibility and communications. Ben Bernanke wants more of both. We need to broaden our input. Look, we know about you. We want you in the loop—now that we're sure you understand how things work." *Lehman was a test case!*

"My son just got early admission to Princeton," I told him. "He's going in January." *I switched signals to let him know the answer was 'yes.'*

"Yes Mam!" He smiled. "That's what I mean. You mentioned it to Dr Bernanke. He knows how to listen."

"You mean 'Ms.' don't you." *Because Ms. Money had told them what they wanted to know. She was in the loop, but she is a woman named Maggie Worth. That's who I am, and I'm going to find Matt Shepherd and make him listen to me.*

61

Jason taught Connelly how to download the *Daily Racing Form*. He read it on a laptop every morning—early. When he saw me coming at that hour, he didn't have to ask. One look at my face told him what I wanted.

"He's probably gone over for the Saint Leger."

"In France?"

"No," he laughed, "in England. It's in the north, at Doncaster. I'll find out for you. But only if you *don't* tell me why you want to know."

"I've got to see him."

"You shouldn't be doing this. Look what happened at Aqueduct!"

"I think I do."

"As long as you promise not to call me an 'I told you so.'"

He called me later in the morning. "Sorry! You missed him. The Saint Leger was on the thirteenth—he was there. They were trying to outbid a Japanese group that was after Frozen Fire, the Irish Derby winner." *He was at the track hoping for a winner—just as I expected. He still didn't know what he had lost.*

"But he's got a horse in the Miami Mile—in October."

"At Hialeah?"

Connelly snorted. "They haven't run there since 2001. It's a National Park now! He'll be at Calder. His syndicate has put up Fair Weather Stan in the Miami Mile Handicap in October. The purse is $150K. But I don't think he'd be living in Miami Gardens. It's totally Cuban country."

"I remember him saying something about Gulfstream. Is there a Gulfstream Village?"

"It's by Hallandale. I'm going with you."

"Not this time. I'll let you know when I get there. It's okay." *I would always be his surrogate daughter. But this time his worries about me were wrong. I knew what I was doing was right because it was what Maggie Worth wanted.*

I flew to Miami, rented a car and took the Interstate north. It was easy. I just entered Shepherd on the keyboard and the GPS in my heart did it all. *Did you ever know a man who could ask for directions?*

Hallandale was between North Miami and Hollywood, less than fifty miles from the airport. Finding former Senator Matt Shepherd was no hard matter. He was in a low-rise in the Golden Isles condos between the Gulfstream Park and the beach. It was listed under his wife's name, Amelia.

I was nervous and drove too fast and got there too early. It was eleven in the morning, and his wife was probably still home. I had thrown together an excuse about needing to contact him on government business. I was wearing a business suit with my hair tied back. I sat in the car. *There was still time to turn around.* But after waiting impatiently, I got out, walked past a swimming pool, and confronted the stucco villa with its heavy Spanish doors. The door to his unit was half open, but I pressed the button and heard chimes. Noises were coming from somewhere—upstairs. A woman was shouting, banging on a door, calling out, "Matt stop! Stop!"

The downstairs was a wreck. Booze bottles were everywhere mixed with beer cans and white containers smelly with leftover Chinese food—more than a day old by their odor. Here and there a pizza box littered the furniture. A big palmetto bug was crawling out of an open one. Ugh. The ashtrays were full of cigarette butts that had spilled onto a glass-topped table. Dirty paper napkins littered the rug. A 'Man of La Mancha' reproduction was askew on one wall. I turned my back on the clutter and quickly climbed the carpeted stairs towards the noise.

The woman was standing outside a bathroom door near to a bedroom. She was in her thirties, thin on top but wide below. Definitely not his wife. Her big hair was a total mess. She was wearing a cheap housecoat, pink with horizontal stripes of white and aqua that must have come from Walmart. It was food-stained. Her eyes were ringed with runny mascara. The cigarette sticking out of her mouth shifted as she challenged me, "Who the hell are you?"

"Just get out of here," I snapped.

"Who says?"

"This," I answered. I reached into my tan Coach tote, found my wallet, snapped it open and pulled out a fifty. I put it up to the woman's face.

"Not enough. I got a job in the casino at the track. I've been here for a week. He took me home."

I pulled out another fifty.

"He's just an old piece of shit. Drinks all the time. Did some coke when he had the cash. You heard his wife left him." The woman grabbed the money out of my hand.

"Look—just get your clothes and get out. I'll take care of him."

"You better—says he's going to kill himself in the tub. He lost a ton at the crap table the other night. He's just another deadbeat trying to get back. I don't know why I even came here," she said, attempting to restore her lost dignity. "You got another one of those fifties, just to help me out, you know." I complied, and the woman went past me into the bedroom. A minute later she was gone.

I turned my attention to the bathroom door. I put my ear against it. No sound was coming from inside. Then I leaned against it. Much to my surprise, the lock clicked and it opened.

Shepherd was passed out in the tub, one arm hanging over the side, his hand dragging on the floor. He had dropped a cigarette that was still smoking on the tile. There was a plastic prescription bottle too. I grabbed it and read the label—it was Ambien. But the container was almost full. He couldn't have taken enough to kill himself. His head was thrown back against the tile at the end of the tub. He needed a shave, and his once patrician salt and pepper hair was matted. I looked in his eyes and saw only pinpoint pupils. A scratch on his nose signaled that he had fallen on something. He was naked, but still in a pair of golf shoes. They were beneath the water level, which was up to his bent knees.

I stared at him. He had everything—now he was reduced to this. That's the trouble with most men. They can't admit a mistake. So they can't bounce back from it. They end up beaten. Women are a lot smarter. I had lost a fortune and made it back. *So why was I here?* Part of me wanted to go back downstairs. I would clean up the mess—straighten out the duplex. Leave. Shepherd would eventually come to. But another mental directive told me to wake him up. *There's still a chance.* The important point was to get him somewhere. Somewhere we could be together. Somewhere safe. I had my own reputation to consider—and his too. The hooker I had paid off might say something. I shook him, but he was out cold.

I turned on the shower—the cold shower. His body jolted. He moaned. I saw his eyes recognize me. I turned off the tap, and half-dragged him into what looked like the master bedroom, where he collapsed on the bed. It was a mess of dirty sheets and underwear. His head almost fell on a whiskey bottle. I knocked it away, but some left over-brown fluid ran out onto the already stained sheets.

I pulled off his sodden golf shoes, jerking his body, making his penis flop at me. I smiled at the thought of our past lovemaking. What I wanted was something he could travel in. We could buy anything else we needed. After rubbing him dry with a towel, I sorted through the walk-in dressing closet. Finally, I got some casual clothes and runners. His heavy breathing said he had fallen asleep again. But I still needed one other thing. Where was his wallet? I went through the hanging clothes. Nothing. There was an expensive suit stuffed into a shopping bag. An Armani. The woman must have been planning on selling it. I pulled it out—his wallet was still inside, but there was no money in it. No credit cards either. It didn't matter. I had enough money for us both. Thank god his driver's license was there. From the corner of the bed, while he slept, I called my office and then I left a message for Traub on his direct line.

Shepherd was still woozy as we drove back to Miami. The crew of the small charter seaplane I hired helped me get him on board. Then we were in the air—on our way to Parrot Cay. By then he was awake. He turned towards me and asked, "Why are you doing this?" There was more dismay in his voice than anger.

"Because I can."

"What happened to Tina?"

"I paid her off."

"Can I have a drink?"

"No!" I knew he wasn't asking for bottled water.

He said nothing more.

Our arrival was expected. Traub's personal staff had already alerted the resort that guests would be occupying his villa, and the COMO resort group had done the rest—including a temporary immigration card. There were no obstacles. Owning a $10 million villa is a big help in the Turks and Caicos. I smiled thinking that no one asked about our lack of luggage.

Shepherd wasted no time getting back into bed. I ordered a dinner for myself and then slept on a big wicker chair in his room. I was happy. The fact that it had all worked out only proved I had done the right thing.

My dream was strange. My unconscious went back to my last time in Traub's private villa, when BJ had auctioned me off. Only this time he sold me to Vanderman. But I turned into a fish—a very strange fish. Vanderman tried to sell me in a fish market. I had to lay on ice in a case. I was frozen stiff. But the ice became glass, and I turned into a goldfish in a bowl. I knew I was beautiful. My fins were long and delicate. Men came and fed me. I was given to a princess, but an evil servant emptied the bowl into a toilet. I was flushed out to sea. I swam to the bottom of the ocean—very far down. There was something glittering. It was gold, gold coins, pirate treasure. And a mermaid with long blonde hair helped me put the gold into a sack. And I swam upwards, but the sack kept pulling me down. I had to swim harder and harder. The money bag was too heavy. I was struggling to get to the top. I had to let the bag go. Now I was a girl, and we were fishing, trolling for tuna. And I hooked a fish and pulled and pulled on the fishing rod. It was stiff. But I caught the fish. It was shiny with blue and silver and the mate cut it open and it was full of gold.

62

I wasn't sure if I was still dreaming. But the beach-white sunlight streaming into the villa reminded me where I was. I heard water running in the bathroom, and my mind said it was Matt Shepherd taking a shower. He must have found a blue denim shirt that fit over a pair of tan twill shorts. Soon he sat on the deck with me. He ate a huge breakfast. I had some fresh pineapple with yogurt. The brilliant Caribbean morning was blooming with fuchsia and gold bougainvillea and the hummingbirds poking into the hibiscus greeted us.

"Where are we?"

"Parrot Cay."

"Whose place?"

"Traub's."

"I see."

"Do you? Because that's what I want. I want you to see."

He wasn't ready for my challenge. "I need to walk—and swim. I'm full of poison. Too much booze and pills. You heard of the Shepherd Diet?"

"Jacuzzi—pool—or beach?" I ignored the bad joke.

"On the sand."

So we spent the morning walking on the hard packed beach just at the edge of the incredibly crystal blue water. He took my hand— but after a second I let go. We were only on tentative emotional ground. Clouds moved in. It was hurricane season.

"Why the hell didn't you just listen to me? All you had to do was pick up the phone?"

"You were just an easy target. It wasn't you. I know that now. I wouldn't be here."

"You sure know how to make a girl feel real good. Just refuse to speak to her, and when she won't be ignored, you insult her."

"It was all manipulation. They used you to get at me. I went along with it like a fool. All they had to do was tell me your boss was aiming for the Presidency and let my jealousy do the rest. That's why I thought the Katrina story came from you. I should have known better. They lied to me. It was sabotage. My own party screwed me over."

"All Traub wants is Secretary of the Treasury—he's failed to get it four times running."

"It was like waving a red flag in front of a bull. As soon as they made me suspicious, I got angry. That made it very easy for them to set me up. They put out the Katrina story and said you were the source. And of course I fell for it. They didn't want me to run. Said the ticket would be better off. Romney had ideas. Rove had ideas. I had five maybe six states I could have taken in a sweep, but I never even made it to the starting gate. Instead, I found out what my Washington friends were worth. They're great when it comes to stabbing a guy in the back."

"You should have listened to me. I called and called."

"Look—I was stupid. I wanted back in. My own party ruined my chances. They fed me lies, and I fell for it. I don't know which is worse. I'm sorry. It was too easy to blame you. They even stuck my name on the Spitzer client list. How's that for a political smear?"

"You didn't trust me when it came to Fanny and Freddie? The head of the GSE Panel bags more than one hundred grand. You must have thought I was pretty stupid."

"That was before I ever met you. I was still in Congress. And I paid it back. Every cent—as soon as I found out. You have to believe that. That's what my great friends in the media forgot to mention. I wrote a check and fired the staff man. At least that's one thing they can't hang on me. Now I'm going for a swim."

He pulled off his shorts and long shirt and ran into the waves. At first I just sat down on the beach. I was thinking about him. He had turned against me once. And he was still bitter. But the water was perfect. I pulled off my clothes and followed him. But we didn't come together.

Later we lay on the sand. But the skies were dark, and soon a squall chased us back to the house, where I ordered lunch. Our conversation continued over a bottle of chilled white wine and a gourmet meal.

"Okay—I was jealous too. What is it with you and Traub?" he asked.

"I have a lifetime contract—not a wedding ring!"

"I'm not twelve. He loves you. Right?"

"No you're not. But you're a Southern boy all right. I mean boy! The only thing Traub loves is money. I helped make him very, very rich, and he made me rich. That was our arrangement—it was all about money. Even on a personal basis. The thing is he didn't need to own me. That's very important. He means something to me because of that."

"Everything?"

"No! But I don't need to play pure when I want a man. It's over now. He used me. He didn't trust me. I got burned—badly. I'm through with him in bed. And I'm leaving Traub Inc."

"What will you do?"

"I'm through pimping the markets. Ms. Money is retiring. I'll see what happens next."

She wanted Shepherd to know one more thing. "A long time ago I was a topless dancer."

He laughed, "I think I knew that after Bourbon Street."

"Did you know I was almost a nun?"

This time he didn't laugh. He must have heard the seriousness in my voice. "You mean in a convent? Did you go to a church school?"

"I was in Holy Orders at College—at Divine Sepulcher of Maryland. But I couldn't make my vow."

"What stopped you?"

"I was in love with a Sister. It was a desperate crush, girl on girl. It meant everything to me. And after I started dancing—I saw it was the same. The virgin and the whore thing exists because men use it as a way to control women. A girl can be only safe or sexy—a plaster saint or a Barbie doll. According to men, those are the only choices. They marry the Virgins and have kids and go out and buy the Eve's for fun. Jesus made Mary Magdalene his earthly lover to show us the truth. If men grew up—they wouldn't be afraid of women who are women. They're too afraid to love the real thing."

"I don't see it?"

"How typical!"

"My wife's gone for good. She cost plenty."

"You want to know about me and Traub—ask yourself what money is. The books all say money is a medium of exchange. But I learned that sex is the ultimate medium of exchange. Sex and money are the same. It's a natural exchange between people."

"You are more natural than any woman I've ever known."

"Just ask yourself what happens when two people trade with each other. What each of you gets has to be worth what you pay. Otherwise you wouldn't make an exchange."

"Okay. I can't pay with bad goods or counterfeit money. That's bad. Buyers and sellers have to give each other the real thing."

"Yes. Fake watches, glass diamonds, underwater land, a clipped coin, lead painted to look like gold, worthless paper money when prices are inflated—it's a very long list. It all comes down to trusting the person on the other side of the trade. Sex is men and women trusting each other. Women know that counterfeit sex is worthless!"

"It sounds like you met my latest consort—in Florida?"

"You're lucky I got rid of her before she walked off with the Armani suit that was rolled up in her shopping bag. I bet she was going to sell it at a thrift shop."

"Okay—I see. You have to trust the people you love."

"You have to trust people to be able to love. You know what it says on a dollar bill!"

63

S hepherd crashed after lunch. I went swimming by myself. I remembered a rip farther out and somewhere to the right along the beach. I swam out to it, and let the current take me. My skin came alive in the ocean. The water was like lotion—utterly silky and just the perfect temperature. The sensation was incredible. But the current petered out around the point, and I swam in. As I walked back, I saw Shepherd looking for me. He was at water's edge, a hand screening his eyes. I couldn't pass up the chance. I ran quietly behind him, scooped up a pile of sand in my hands and dumped it on his back.

He jumped, turned around and threw a rain of talcum powder sand all over me. I laughed, and we fought a sand war until we were both coated. He tried to catch me, but I dodged and ran quickly into the water. He followed me into deeper water and held me against him, skin on skin, and he kissed me the way he had when we were in San Diego. Kissed me just the way I wanted to be kissed. A new first kiss. We floated back onto the wet sand, and I curled over and sat on his lap in the slowly swirling water, put my arms around his neck and my lips on his ear—just letting him feel my body. He turned and took my face in his hands and kissed me. But I had one thing left to confess.

"They finished off Lehman. *Hasta la vista,* baby." I didn't say I had done nothing to stop Paulson's crusade.

"I heard you were there, and I don't blame you. Fuld had no idea of the risk. He thought he was all powerful—beyond mega!"

"It was unreal. He thought he was living in a world that was completely in his control. There could be no risk. But there's no such thing—unless you're god."

"I bet a lot of people just couldn't imagine Lehman Brothers going under. I should have pulled my money out. You were telling people to dump the stock."

"I lost it all once," I admitted. "Big time. Right after Enron. I was a financial wreck."

"Well, I'm certainly out—out of a reputation, a career, a trophy wife, and I'm broke. I'm glad you saved my Armani suit. It's probably all I've got."

"People say they don't want any risk, but secretly they're tempted. And they give in—always. I wish you had met BJ. He was the guy I fell in love with first. But he was trapped in the past. He just couldn't escape."

"Sorry—I mean it."

"He died in 9/11. He used to say 'Not losing is winning' was the only investment rule that mattered. Most people never understood him. He wasn't just saying don't lose—it was deeper. He meant the words literally. It was rhetorical. Not losing *is* winning!"

"Look—I want to tell you a story. It's from when I was twenty-five. I was a junior trainer for Catawba Stables. We ran mostly at Calder—in Miami. You know it's a Latino track. I mean it's a launching pad for jockeys coming from South America. They're small with tremendous strength in their wrists. You wouldn't know the names, but the Castellano brothers from Venezuela started there—and Prado from Peru and Rodriguez from Cuba and Cruz from Brazil. Lots of guys. They're great riders."

"There was this kid—almost the same age as me. Nickie Navarro, from Panama. It was just after the second race. He had come in ninth on a sixty-to-one long shot called Noble Mischief. I still remember. But he was good. He ranked third among the jockeys. He weighed in after the race and was going back for a rest. I had a horse in the fourth race—a mare called Bank Run. He was supposed to ride her. So he stepped off the scales and headed back to the clubhouse with the rest of them. But I wanted to talk with him about the race, and he saw me coming and stopped. I wish I had never been there. He put his hand up to wave to me. Right then—right then! He was struck by lightning. Dead. Blast! Boom! You wouldn't believe it. It felt like a shotgun went off right next to my head. I felt the electricity in the ground. So did the others. There was an electric smell. My legs went numb. I saw him on the ground. He was dead. They cancelled the rest of the races. It was in the papers. He was dead—really dead. It was just four days after Christmas and he was dead."

"Seeing him die like that said something to me. It said—don't die! Because when you're dead you really are dead. So when I tried to swallow a bottle of pills I couldn't do it—right."

"I don't get it. What's wrong with being alive?"

"Because now I want to be dead!"

"What's wrong with you—are you just being stupid? Or has your self-pity gone ballistic?"

"I'll never be a winner ever again."

"Let me tell you something Mr Big Deal, Mr Winner Take All." I spoke harshly right into his face. "You saw some kid die and that made you want to win. You think winning means you don't die. But all you're doing is racing against a clock you can't beat. You know what it really did? It made you scared shit of dying. But life isn't about winning. It's about not losing. Not missing all the good things. It's hard because you always lose in the end. That's what death is—the end. You can fight for an edge, but when you get it you still have to give it up in the end. You need to learn how to give even when you're losing. That's what the real winners know. I learned it the hard way."

Then I kissed him and pushed him back on the wet sand at the ocean's edge. I went on top of him. We were sticky with the powder white sand. But my love making was forceful. I was in charge of the passion and I drew it out, riding his peaks but not bringing him to an end. I bent to kiss him, sliding my sandy hands on his nipples. My breasts caressed his chest. Ripples wet his feet as I brought him through wave after wave of inner heat. Then I set him off just when I wanted to, meeting his throb with my own. I showed him what I wanted him to know.

A soft rain wet us as we lay on the sand.

"You shouldn't swim so far out here. I was worried."

"How worried do you think I was about you? Do you know what you really wanted?"

"Tell me," he answered.

"I want to hear you say it."

"Okay—it was the risk. I realize it now. I lost big time because deep down it was the risk I really wanted. I was living on it—like a drug. Not something to put you out—more like heroin to make everything perfect."

"That's why I hate free money—money for nothing. It makes people crazy. They'll take any and every risk. It's because they think free money means they can be anything—anything they want to be. It's not true. You are what you are. Period."

"I made myself lose you. It wasn't about the smear campaign, or about Traub—it was you. You can be very scary. I knew I'd have to trust you."

"That's the real reason I hate risks. It's so hard not to take them. Trust me."

We spent three more days in Traub's villa. I ordered a double private massage on our deck. We swam before the daily afternoon squall. We only drank grand cru wine. The meals were four-star. And the sex five-star. Our last conversation on Parrot Cay was the shortest.

"I'm trusting." Shepherd said as we left the villa.

"That's an easy one," I told him. I knew what he wanted to know. And I had a surprise ready. "Ms. Money will keep working, but only until Traub Inc's year-end numbers are in. I'll do the earnings release—then I'm outta there." *If Masterson delivered, I would ask Shepherd about it. But I had already thought about another plan. Connelly would love it.*

"And Traub?"

"He doesn't need me. He doesn't need anyone."

"And me?"

"We're partners in a new stable—a real joint venture—starting from scratch. Ms. Money wants her pony. And you better teach me to ride!"

"I promise you a horse!"

"Just make sure it's a winner," I laughed.

64

Three weeks after I returned from Parrot Cay, Traub called me on my direct line. He was nervous about rumors that the SEC was about to bring charges, which would unleash a major market scandal. The market had dived in October, and the Dow's grip on five digits suddenly looked shaky.

"It came up from one of the RIAs, you know, from a Registered Investment Adviser. But he's not the only one. The blogsters are scared, and trading has fallen off a cliff. Somebody who's supposed to have a ton of other people's money hasn't got a cent."

"It's real," I told him. "I just got a call about it from Sue McCann. It's the biggest scam ever. But we're out of it."

"Who's the guy?"

"Bernie Madoff. He runs money in New York."

"Bernie, he was Chairman of Nasdaq. It can't be."

"It is! They say it could be as much as $50 billion."

"Holy shit! What about our clients?"

"None of ours—unless they did it independently. We never fed his funds. It's the biggest Ponzi of them all. Lehman took him down with them." *It's always about risk. Somebody's always taking a chance. Betting on the future is easier than living in the present.*

On December 11, 2008, Bernard Madoff was arrested and charged with securities fraud. He was, in his own words, "one big lie." The mastermind of the largest financial fraud in U.S. history, Madoff cost investors close to $30 billion in losses! His profits on the decades-long Ponzi scheme exceeded one billion dollars. After Judge Denny Chin revoked his bail, Madoff was sentenced to 150 years imprisonment and forfeiture of $17 billion. Subsequently, it was revealed that the SEC had conducted repeated prior investigations of Madoff, but failed to uncover the massive fraud. *What a joke!*

A month after Madoff was arrested, I flew to Los Angeles for the release of Traub Inc's fourth-quarter and full-year results. Traub threw a luxurious party at the Four Seasons to celebrate the earnings announcement. Close to 1,000 were invited to fill tables in the Burton Ballroom. The event was streamed live over the Internet to additional parties at Traub branches across the country. I turned up in a $2,000 Alexander McQueen black velvet tuxedo jacket with gold-toned notched silk lapels, matching gold silk-covered buttons and gold piping and heavy silk trousers with a wide gold stripe. My black silk pumps sported gold bow-tie buckles.

Following Traub's introduction, I read the earnings report from the center stage. The *Financial Times* recapped the details the next day: "Margaret M Worth, aka Ms. Money, Chief Investment Strategist for Traub Securities, announced fourth-quarter 2008 results of $1.5

billion in revenue and $268 million of net income—owing to what she labeled 'accelerated business from a risk averse investment model.' Due to the company's relatively low exposure to mortgage backed securities, Traub was able to escape the turmoil of the 2008 financial crisis. Full-year revenues were $5.6 billion with net income of $1.4 billion. Future earnings guidance was for full-year revenues of $6.8 billion with net income of $2.0 billion."

"The news is good," I concluded with a scream of delight that my wireless mike transmitted. The applause was literally deafening. The audience was well aware that the earnings report could send TRB shares back over $20. That was money in the bank. "And now I've got one more surprise for you," I told the audience when it had calmed down. "Ms. Money is retiring! So it's goodbye time." The band struck up an *auld lang syne* theme, and I blew farewell kisses with both hands.

But shocked silence greeted my announcement and the music. They just didn't know it was coming! Then Traub stepped closer and wrapped his arms around me with a bear hug. It was a signal that he both knew and was in agreement with my decision. "So thank you all," I said, wiping tears from my eyes. "I love you!" I thought the burst of applause would never stop. *It's over.*

Traub saved me the trouble of answering questions, and spoke from the stage with his arm around me. "So now we have two good reasons to party tonight. We've made a lot of money, and Ms. Money, the woman who helped us make it, is taking a much needed rest. So let's get back to partying. I'm not saying anymore." His words were greeted with a fanfare from the band and another massive burst of applause. *He was jealous, and I knew it!*

Much later, after what seemed like hours of personal goodbyes, I met Gia at the very private after-party at the hotel's top floor, with its sweeping views of the city. Large windows glowed with the deep-blue night and glittering lights of Los Angeles. Taking time away from the modeling agency she had founded, Gia came on my personal invitation, and we were sharing the Presidential suite. Seeing my tall, still very beautiful friend, I thought back to our first meeting. We had been together since the great snowstorm back in 1996, when I first met Traub. Traub and Gia were the only actual attendees who knew the secret of my future. But the best news of all was that Gia's husband had been offered a key Treasury post in the new Administration. Thank god we would still be close.

I felt like I was standing in the departure gate to a new life with Shepherd. That was why I hadn't wanted him at the goodbye party. He accepted my decision, understanding just where it came from. I wanted to put the world of Ms. Money behind me. That was something I had to do alone. But Shepherd was the third who knew where I was going. The others would learn very soon. I felt so lucky. *Maybe Shepherd should have come? No. I wanted him free of my past—of an identity I no longer believed in.*

I broke through the circle of Gia's admirers, and gave her a teary hug. The former model was splendiferous in a floor-length deep blue gown with long sleeves, whose fabric was a leafy patchwork of crepe and velvet. One of the roving photographers called out, "Is that McQueen?"

Gia laughed. We had both deliberately chosen to wear the young British designer's clothes. "Ms. Money is my King for tonight—so I had to wear it," she answered the camera lady.

"I asked my best friends to wear McQueen, but that's insider information—so you can't report it. Just say Ms. Money wore McQueen's pants!" The group of admirers laughed, and then I took the lead and danced Gia off into a quiet corner. "I'm so glad you're here. I can't wait 'til this is over."

Gia gave me a new hug, and immediately whispered a question. "Do they know yet?"

"Only that I'm leaving. Ms. Money is through with Traub. They'll find out the rest tomorrow."

"So I have a secret too—guess who I just signed?" And when I quickly shook my head, Gia went on. "Remember the name Ashley Alexandra Dupré? I watched the Diane Sawyer interview, and I wanted her for my list."

"What can she model?" I asked. "Isn't she too short?" I had missed the Good Morning America anchor's talk with the famous ex-call girl about the emotional effects of the Spitzer scandal. But then Gia answered my question.

"La Perla!"

We both giggled. But months later Gia fedexed me a copy of *Playboy,* showing Dupré in the nude. The model-cum-hooker reportedly turned down an offer of $1 million from *Hustler.* I left the magazine out for Shepherd, who took one look and dropped it in the trash.

The Administration's press release announcing my new job came out the day after the party. President Barack Obama formally nominated me, along with Harvard University economics professor Walter Sidmouth, to the Federal Reserve Board. In a statement from Hawaii, where he was vacationing with his family, Obama praised both candidates for agreeing to serve in his administration at a critical moment for the U.S. economy. "Their distinguished backgrounds and experience coupled with their impressive knowledge of the financial markets and economic and monetary policy make them tremendously qualified to serve in these important roles," Obama told the news media. Later, after my speedy confirmation, an Administration spokesperson remarked that my appointment would give the Fed a 'markets guy,' replacing academic economist Randall S. Kroszner, who resigned in January.

I received hundreds of calls congratulating me after the nomination. But I had an even bigger reason to be happy. The new job meant I could sell my entire holding of Traub stock, plus my employee stock options, including the final special bonus grant awarded directly by Traub's board. Just as in Paulson's case, my capital gains taxes were waived.

I was jumping up and down, close to the rail and near the finish line. "Go girl—go!" I screamed. "Run—run for it. Go, go, go! Now!" Connelly didn't have to hold Mimi up. She was already tall enough to see. I was wearing my lucky big-brim red straw hat, and its white feathers were dancing. The Minox wide-field-of-view binoculars hanging from my neck bounced against my breasts. Then I screamed, "We won!—we won!" Shepherd was next to me. I turned to kiss and hug him.

"We better get to the Winner's Circle," he said. And we pushed our way through the VIP crowd.

Little more than a year and a half since I left Traub Inc, on Saturday, July 17, 2010, I watched my horse, Ms. Money, win the $250,000 Virginia Oaks at Colonial Downs. As the *Racing Form* put it: "Sired by Hard Cash on Dollar Dolly, the filly led the pack for the Grade III turf race with a time of 1.51.85. Though she lacked speed along the rail at the start, after breaking outward, she split her rivals at the three sixteenths pole to finish ahead by two lengths. Peruvian jockey Reynaldo Prado said, 'No tricks. She run real good. She could tell they wouldn't last long in front.' Ms. Money is owned by Margaret Worth and Matthew Shepherd, of The Foxhall, Massachusetts Ave, Washington, DC. She was trained at their newly built Worthmore Farms, in New Kent county, Talleysville, VA. The victory marks former Alabama senator Shepherd's return to the Winner's Circle of the thoroughbred industry."

ACKNOWLEDGMENTS

Special thanks to those who helped and believed: Eleanor, Betty, Tim, Waverley, Tom, Mark Kaufman, Elizabeth Bigelow, Mildred Rizzo and Howard Pease. Thanks to my former colleagues at Prudential Securities, Salomon Brothers, U.S. Trust, Charles Schwab, Bank of America and TD Ameritrade, whose help contributed. Special thanks to investment strategists Ralph Acampora, the late Peter Bernstein, Jimmy Chang, Mark Faber, Dave Fry, Stephanie Giroux, Tim Leach, Peter Martin, 9/11 victim Bill Meehan, Mark Pado, Brian Piskorowski, Richard Rippe, David Rosenberg, Gary Shilling, Greg Smith, and Liz Ann Sonders. I am in debt to many financial journalists including the late Alan Abelson, Maria Bartiromo, Jim Cramer, Vito Racanelli, Richard Rescigno, Michael Santoli, and the late and truly wonderful Larry Wachtel. Thanks to analysts and fund managers, Marcel Idiart, Boris Kazin, the late Jack Lafferty, John McDermott, Bruce Tavel, and Adrian Sancho. Authors Jennifer Belle, Tracy Gardner Beno, Sheridan Hay, Renee Lovins, Jon Michaud, and Peter Walker were inspirational. My reading group consists of the wonderful and talented: Jeff Cravens, Amy Lorowitz, Lindsay Potenza, Azra Qizilbash and Megan Youngblood. Books which contributed include: *On the Brink: Inside the Race to Stop the Collapse of the Global Financial System* by Henry M Paulson; *Too Big to Fail* by Andrew Sorkin, along with the HBO movie of the same; *Frozen Desire: The Meaning of Money* by James Buchan; *Ubiquity: Why Catastrophes Happen* by Mark Buchanan; *All the Devils Are Here: The Hidden History of the Financial Crisis* by Bethany McLean and Joe Nocera; *The Partnership: The Making of Goldman Sachs* by Charles Ellis; *The Big Short* by Michael Lewis, the first to portray Goldman in laughable colors; *Griftopia: A Story of Bankers, Politicians, and the Most Audacious Power Grab in American History* by Matt Taibbi, who early on saw through the Greenspan Maestro myth and is brilliant on the financial crisis; *And the Money Kept Rolling in (and Out)* by Paul Blustein of *The Washington Post*, who was years ahead of everyone and knew it would happen again; and the truly excellent; *The Predators' Ball* by Connie Bruck, a writer who understands why one billion equals more than 1,000 million. Erin Duffy's, *Bond Girl* and Martha McPhee's *Dear Money,* were fun to read. But the book I owe the most to is Candace Bushnell's, *Trading Up*. Special thanks to JC Chandor for *Margin Call,* the only movie that comes close. Lastly to Jay McInerney for his wonderful words in *Bright Lights, Big City,* "The guys who understand business are going to write the new literature. Wally Stevens said money is a kind of poetry, but he didn't follow his own advice."

Made in the USA
Middletown, DE
19 November 2016